Also by Molly McAdams

The Forgiving Lies Series

Forgiving Lies

Deceiving Lies

Changing Everything (novella)

The From Ashes Series

From Ashes

Needing Her (novella)

The Taking Chances Series

Taking Chances

Stealing Harper (novella)

Trusting Liam

Stand-Alone Novels

I See You

Lie to Me

Secrets in L.A. Novels Still to Come

Love

Fame

Passion

Molly McAdams

New York Times Bestselling Author

Published by Jester Creations, LLC.
First Edition

Molly McAdams
www.mollysmcadams.com
Cover Design by RBA Designs
Photo by © dmitri_gromov
Editing by Unicorn Editing

Print ISBN: 9781950048038
eBook ISBN: 9781950048021

For Leon

Prologue

ADAM

I stepped into the twenty-four-hour diner, stare glossing over the bright neon signs that boasted the name *Ampersand* and completed the hipster vibe of the place, before taking in the rest. The boards revealing their offered foods and the display case partially filled with pastries. The people standing behind the counter, not paying any attention to me as they gave directions to a group of people sitting in one of the booths.

That was fine.

I preferred it when people didn't notice me.

Slipping my phone out of my pocket, I opened a new note and quickly tapped out the order as I walked up to the counter.

The instant I held my phone out toward the man standing near the register, the air in the diner shifted. Grew thick.

The man tensed and slowly looked over at me before glancing down at the screen. All hesitation and blatant fear that I could feel amplified and reaching over to me from the booth overflowing with people.

The older woman behind the counter started stepping away. Reaching behind her with shaking hands just as the guy bent in half with a groan that bordered on a cry.

"Oh God," he said loudly. "Oh my God." Straightening, he held a hand to his chest and glared at me. "Jesus Christ, you scared the crap out of me. What is this?" He tossed the same hand toward my phone with his demand, but I just stood there, waiting for him to take my order.

The older woman stepped up beside him then, leaning closer and trying to glance at the screen. "What does it say?"

"I think it's an order," the guy said, voice accusing. "You couldn't have just said something?"

The woman hushed him. "Well, maybe he can't. Maybe he's deaf, Tucker." She looked at me then and yelled, "Is this what you want?"

I sucked in a slow, deep breath to calm my racing heart and scratched at my temple as old panic and uneasiness flared inside me.

I'd had to deal with this sort of thing more times than I cared to remember throughout my life. But it'd been a long damn time since anyone reacted to me this way.

"Can you read lips?" she yelled and waved a hand at me. "Do you want this?"

"You guys are being so rude!" one of the girls from the booth hissed as she came rushing up beside me. Gently touching my arm to get my attention and offering me a reassuring smile that slipped away when I looked at her.

No fucking way.

That night from years ago ripped through my mind, freezing me in place. Everything about it and her still so vivid even though it felt like a lifetime had passed.

Her full lips slowly parted, and those unforgettable,

mesmerizing, green eyes danced across my face, taking me in the way I was her. A little taken aback and a whole lot intrigued. Studying me as if I'd surprised her—and she was most definitely a surprise I hadn't been expecting.

Not ever again.

Especially not here.

And I couldn't help but linger on the soft curves of her face and the way it was so easy to get lost in those eyes. Lost in the current of electricity that hummed between us. Just as thick and tense and intoxicating as it had been then.

"It shouldn't feel like this," she'd whispered as we'd come down from the high of our night together, bodies slick with sweat and chests pitching with uneven breaths. Legs tangled together because any sort of distance from her felt wrong. "Nothing should feel like this."

If it had been anyone else, I would've ended the night there. But I'd been drawn back in, unable to resist another taste and then another. Unable to let go of the girl who'd captured my attention from that first moment and refused to let go as she'd slowly stripped away her inhibitions throughout the night.

Because it was like she'd said, we shouldn't have felt like that—all passion and consuming need. It shouldn't have felt like I'd been scraping through my life just so I could find her and finally breathe.

But it had.

And then she'd walked away from me in the morning.

"Do I . . ." she began, then gave a subtle shake of her head, a touch of pink staining her cheeks as she looked away. "I'm sorry. Um . . . um, okay. I can do this." Blowing out a quick breath, she focused on me again, a hint of worry taking over her expression—*oh shit, she's signing.*

I watched as her hands and fingers moved through the air

and tried to focus on the words she was mouthing . . . but her eyebrows drew close as though she was doing something wrong.

"I'm messing this up," she whispered and clenched her hands into fists.

I hurried to pull up a new note on my phone. Tapping quickly and turning the screen toward her.

I don't know what you're saying

"I haven't signed in years. I'm so sorry, I'm trying," she whispered as she continued signing, this time slower.

I shook my head and moved my fingers across the screen again before offering it to her.

I'm not deaf

Her eyes widened and filled with embarrassment. "Oh God. You're not . . . but . . ." Realization settled over her features, and a flash of pity and sorrow crossed her face before she could force them away. "I feel like an idiot. I just—" She sighed and dropped her face into her hands for a moment before glancing up at me with that hesitant smile that touched every ruined piece of my soul in a way nothing else ever had.

And then I noticed it.

That whisper of familiarity mixed with wonder in the way she was looking at me. Like she was looking at a stranger who triggered an obscure memory and nothing more.

She didn't know who I was . . .

But that current was buzzing stronger and stronger. Pulling tighter and begging me to inch closer.

"I'm sorry." She released a soft exhale, her smile shaky as she swayed back a step. "Please forgive me. And these two," she added on as an afterthought, waving toward the people watching us from behind the counter.

"Hey," the older woman said, hands raised as if she didn't want to be part of it, then headed toward a set of swinging doors. "I'll start on the order."

"He came in like Michael Myers," the guy said in exasperation. "All silent, psycho status." He pressed a hand to his chest. "I thought he was going to rob us if he didn't kill us first."

Jesus Christ . . .

The girl in front of me widened her eyes in mortification before quickly looking back at me as the air in the diner once again shifted.

And I hated it.

Hated the pity and discomfort pressing down on me as if no one knew how to even speak to each other anymore. Hated the curious stares I could feel from the rest of the people slowly piling out of the booth.

"Please don't listen to him," she whispered, head moving in subtle shakes as she reclaimed the step she'd just taken. "Some people are terrible human beings."

"I can hear you," the guy said.

"Then let me say it to your face," she hissed softly, looking at him. "You're rude and obnoxious."

I touched her arm, the simple action causing her to inhale

and bringing an assault of memories. Making me ache to move my hand and trace her curves. Pull her close. See if she tasted the way I remembered.

Instead, I forced my hand away, my head already shaking before her stare lifted to mine from where it had been focused on where I'd touched her.

Gesturing between the guy and myself, I waved my hand through the air, letting her know it was fine. Then hurried to tap another message to her as I forced my mind and my dick to remember exactly what happened last time. To remember that she had no idea who I was.

Let it go

She looked at me again, eyebrows pulling close as that wonder swirled in her eyes again before she shook off that out-of-reach night when one of the guys from her group stepped up beside her, already talking.

"Hollis, we should probably go."

The girl barely spared him a glance before her focus shifted back to me. Eyes pleading with me as if she wanted me to give her a reason to stay. As if she wanted me to make sense of that elusive memory.

Not that I would.

When the guy took a possessive step closer to her, I moved toward the counter and looked away dismissively even though everything about the girl made me want to get closer.

Made me want to look.

Touch.

Listen to her *speak*.

"Right, uh . . ." She laughed uncertainly, the sound soft and so damn pure and so unlike what I remembered from that night that I had to stop myself from turning to see if that hesitant smile followed. "Right, yeah. Let's go."

I drummed my fingers on the counter as I listened to the door open and the voices of her group get louder as they talked about wherever they were going next. My stare pulling over my shoulder despite knowing I needed to continue facing straight ahead.

And then she stopped in the doorway.

Wavering as one of her friends danced around her to leave and another stopped beside her before she turned and hurried back to where I stood.

Face set in determination as she reached for where my phone was in my hand so the worker could ring up my order. Cheeks filled with heat and mint-green eyes darting up to meet mine before falling again.

"Maybe you should find me," she said as she handed my phone back, the soft words sounding like an offer and a challenge.

@HollisD

I glanced up from the social media handle she'd typed in time to watch her back away before turning toward the door, the corner of her mouth lifted in that same smile that was doing cruel things to me.

Even still, years later. Across the fucking country. In a goddamn diner.

And she didn't remember me.

One

HOLLIS

Two Years Later

The rich scent of coffee filled the kitchen, and I took a deep breath in as I poured the dark liquid into two mugs. As if inhaling the sweet and smoky smell enough might kick-start the much-needed wakening process.

I didn't have to look to know one of my roommates was shuffling into the kitchen, looking like a zombie. I'd known it was only a matter of minutes once I'd started brewing the coffee.

Set an alarm clock for Stevie? It'll continue blaring until one of our other roommates turns it off.

Yell at her? You'll just exhaust yourself.

Hit her over the head with a pillow? She'll reach for it in her sleep so she can curl up with it.

Brew coffee in the house? She'll be awake and out of bed in no time.

"Ugh," she grunted, then flopped onto me so all her weight was on my back. "Coffee."

"I'm waiting on you," I said in a singsong voice as I

finished pouring creamer into the mugs, one I knew she hated hearing when she'd just woken.

There was a brief pause before she sighed and shoved away from me. "Cereal or cereal?"

"Tough one," I said as if I was actually deciding between two options while turning for the fridge to switch out the creamer for milk.

"I don't appreciate your perkiness on the mornings after you dream about Ampersand Guy."

"I didn't dream about him," I lied, a flash of heat raking over my body and mixing with my regret as the dreams faded away to that night in the diner two years ago.

The way he had so wholly captivated me, from his commanding and slightly terrifying presence to his eyes that told something else entirely and stirred up a sense of déjà vu.

"And if you aren't going to appreciate me, I could always stop making coffee for you." When Stevie didn't respond, I turned to find her cold glare on me as she shuffled back with a box in hand.

"I also don't need you for coffee," she mumbled as she messily poured the granola, getting chunks all over the counter.

A soft laugh rolled up my throat as I poured the milk in. "Never said you did, but we both know you'd sleep until our next show without me." I pressed a loud kiss to her cheek and then danced out of her reach to put the milk back.

Once we were settled in our spots on one of the couches, I set my bowl in my lap and brought my mug up to my lips just as one of our other roommates rushed toward the entryway.

"Hi, bye," she said breathlessly.

"Hi, Mia," I mumbled into my mug before taking a long sip.

"Bye, Mia," Stevie finished for me, waving her hand lazily without looking up from her bowl.

I paused from taking another sip of coffee and turned to look when the front door slammed shut. I gestured in that direction with the mug and spoke slowly as confusion filled me. "Is there usually a 'hi/bye' when we're eating breakfast?"

Stevie let some milk trickle from the corner of her mouth as she thought over my question, then quickly wiped at her face with the back of her hand as she glanced in the direction of the front door too.

"Huh," she finally said. "Yeah, isn't she usually gone?"

"Maybe she has an audition," I said hopefully. "Did you see what she was wearing?"

Stevie looked at me with a bland expression and chewed her next bite slowly, obnoxiously. "Yes. Clearly, I paid attention to her outfit when I'm not even sure what cereal I'm eating."

"You look like a cow when you eat like that."

"Moo, whore."

I rolled my eyes but had to bring my mug back up to hide the smile that tugged at my mouth.

As much as Stevie liked antagonizing people, I knew it was nothing more than a shield, and I'd come to find her attitude endearing. In her own proud words: she was a bitch, but she was a bitch who liked me. She didn't trust easily and had very few people she viewed as friends. I considered myself lucky to be one of the few.

The night I met her, she'd owned the stage at Raven. Her confidence as she'd danced had been what stopped me from leaving with the rest of my friends.

I'd wanted that confidence. I'd wanted the ability to look alluring and untouchable. I'd also been terrified of her brashness when I'd met her. But she'd seen something in me . . . and much to everyone's shock, had taken me under her wing when I'd gotten hired on at Raven.

She hadn't let me go since. Going so far as to move me in with her and her two roommates without so much as asking me. Not that I'd complained or had anywhere to live after leaving the dance company.

And this house? I'd lucked out with these girls. They were the only real family I'd ever had.

Mia was gone most of the time, either working or at an audition, and was the kind and reserved one of the four of us. She was also who we all went to when needing to vent or cry.

Ariana had been Stevie's best friend since Kindergarten and was a labor and delivery nurse. She was the mom of the house . . . you know, if a mom was always half-naked and really easygoing. But she kept us in line and was a good balance between mine and Stevie's crazy and Mia's quiet.

And then there was Stevie . . .

She rested her head on my shoulder once she finished her granola and cupped her mug in her hands as a slow sigh fell from her lips.

If I didn't know better, I would think something was wrong.

But I *did* know her. She was a cuddly person when she was tired, and whatever she was thinking would soon follow to reassure me that my best friend's cold, black heart hadn't suddenly warmed.

"If Jenny messes up that second routine one more time, I'm going to punch her perfect nose so she has to have surgery on it again. And you're breathing your coffee breath on me."

There she was . . .

"You're on my shoulder. If you don't want to smell it, move away."

She snuggled in closer. "You're comfortable."

I drained my mug then blew out a rough breath in her direction as I picked up my bowl.

"That was so sexy."

"I know," I said with a smirk that froze in place when she asked, "Was the dream about New York Guy then?"

I slowly chewed the bite I'd just taken, refusing to acknowledge the chills sweeping across my arms at just the thought of that night when I'd still been attending Julliard. The way he'd held me and worshiped me, all unrestrained passion and need. Chemistry unlike anything I'd ever experienced or could fathom even still.

It'd been unreal.

A fantasy, even though there were times I could still feel the memory of his lips on mine. Feel the way my heart had called out to his as if he'd claimed a piece of it from that very first kiss.

"They're the same person," I said as I moved the granola around in my bowl and prepared for her response.

"Ampersand Guy and New York Guy?" When I hummed in acknowledgment, Stevie sighed as if she was about to let me down even though we'd had this discussion too many times to count. "As fun as that would be, New York Guy lives three thousand miles away."

"Right," I murmured in acknowledgment and said what I knew she would remind me of next. "And looked different than Ampersand Guy."

She pushed away from me, twisting on the couch to better face me. "Also, Ampersand Guy is non-verbal." She lifted her mug in the air as if that proved her point and closed out her argument.

A sliver of doubt formed in my gut as it always did. "I know, but—"

"But there was something in his eyes, and you had this feeling," she said into her mug, already knowing what I was going to say.

"If you start making fun of me again . . ."

"I'm not awake enough to do that," she said matter-of-factly. "Give me a few more hours."

I rolled my eyes and went back to eating as that night in Ampersand teased me with what I'd so obviously missed.

I *knew* what it was like to be trapped in his gaze. I *knew* that charged connection. And yet, I'd been so overwhelmed with the night that had led me on a path to a new life and this enigma of a man with the ability to make me feel something so powerful, that I hadn't been able to fully grasp the elusive memories he triggered—grasp who *he* was—until the next day.

Until it had all been too late.

"So, this dream?" Stevie made a *go on* motion with her free hand as she took a long sip of her coffee.

"It was New York Guy," I said, finally indulging her. "But it wasn't in New York, it was at Ampersand . . . because they're the same person." The last was added on quickly before I took another bite.

"I get it," she said, trying to placate me. "You had this once-in-a-lifetime, Romeo-and-Juliet-style connection—minus the whole mortal enemies and death—and you're trying to find that connection again."

"I thought you needed a few more hours before you started making fun of me."

She lifted her free hand in mock surrender. "Babe, I do. As freaking epic and soulmate-as-hell as it would be to find New York Guy again that way, I'm just trying to bring you back to reality. They're two separate guys."

I worried my bottom lip even as those nights danced through my thoughts, the electricity between us something impossible to ignore.

Too incredible to be real.

"Nothing should feel like this."

The corner of my mouth lifted as the memory of his knuckles brushing down my cheek wove through my mind, teasing me with what I'd missed out on.

"Do you think the guys you've slept with know you're comparing them to these memories and dreams?"

I choked over the bite I'd just taken.

Stevie held out a hand as if she didn't know what my problem was.

"I'm fine, by the way," I rasped once I'd gotten the food down.

"Obviously," she said with a teasing grin.

"First, that's gross."

"Says who?" she argued.

"Second," I said loudly over her and then hesitated before answering because she was so right. "They absolutely do not."

Her grin came back and widened. "I knew it. New York Guy set a high bar."

"Or I'm just pathetic."

"*My* best friend?" she asked as if it personally offended her.

A soft laugh left me, and I patted around the couch when my cell phone began ringing.

"I'll bet you those Jimmy Choos I've been drooling over that it isn't your boyfriend."

"The boyfriend I don't have?" I asked dryly.

Stevie faked surprise. "Oh wow! Thanks, Hollis. Size eight, but you already knew—" All traces of humor left her when I finally pulled out my phone from between two cushions, and she caught a glimpse of the screen. "Hello, Mommy Dearest."

I sucked in a quick breath, tapped on the screen, and then tapped on it again to put it on speaker since Stevie would just try to listen to the conversation anyway. "Hel—"

"Goodness, Hollis, is it really necessary for you to wait until the last second to answer my call?" My mother sighed, and I could just imagine her pinching the bridge of her nose delicately as if I were giving her a headache.

"Actually, I couldn't fi—"

"The reason I'm calling . . ."

Her voice droned on as Stevie and I shared a look, and Stevie tried not to laugh as she mouthed, "She's my favorite."

It was rare that my mother let me finish an entire sentence, and if she did, it usually meant something was wrong.

" . . . we're in the area for the benefit tonight, we should probably get together for lunch tomorrow."

My stomach dropped, as did Stevie's face.

My parents left Connecticut often enough, usually for vacations or fundraisers. But in all the trips they'd made out to Los Angeles since I'd moved there, I'd only seen them four of those times. One of which had been after I'd decided to start living for myself and not for them.

They'd been too busy with their social lives to notice that my life no longer revolved around the prestigious dance company I'd left long before. Still, knowing they were here, so close to me and my life and easily able to find out things they couldn't know, made it hard to breathe.

"I'm sorry, did you say you're—"

"Yes, Hollis, please try to keep up. You're not dense, and I have an appointment at the spa I need to get to."

"So, tomorrow you—"

"We're having lunch early in the afternoon. I'll let you know of a place near the hotel we're at, and a time. Do not be late, and do not bring that roommate of yours. She looks like a prostitute."

"Listen, Mommy Dearest, I get paid for the show, not for the sex!" Stevie snapped, but the call had ended before she began.

No *goodbye* from my mother, no *I love you*, no nothing.

Though, to be fair, I'd only ever heard the word *love* from her when she was referencing décor, clothing, or accessories.

I sat there staring at the screen of my phone as the seconds ticked on, trying to calm and reassure myself that they wouldn't find out. That the lunch would go by smoothly, quietly, and then my parents would go back to Connecticut, and I wouldn't hear from them for another handful of months.

Stevie scoffed as she stood from the couch and pointed at my phone with her empty bowl. "Can you believe what that trick said?"

My eyebrows rose and my lips twitched as I tried to suppress my smile. "Okay, not even going to touch on the fact that you just called my mom a trick. You do realize that you take pride in dressing like a prostitute." I glanced at her body pointedly.

Stevie was still wearing what she'd slept in, which wasn't any different from what she normally slept in: The sexiest, most uncomfortable-looking lingerie.

Her reason? *If the house ever catches fire while I sleep, I won't wake up. Which means I'm going to need to be rescued. You can be sure I'm going to look like that fireman's favorite fantasy when he rescues me.*

The day I'd found that out had been one of those days I'd wondered how we were friends.

"Yeah, but that's so beside the point."

A short laugh burst from my chest. "How?"

She stared at me for a moment, mouth parted before she huffed irritably. "Well, that's something I'm going to have to figure out later. But if Mommy Dearest is going to call me a prostitute, then I at least want to be getting paid like one."

"This fake temper tantrum is really over that new pair of Jimmy Choos you want, isn't it?"

Stevie's mock anger immediately faded. "You know I love my shoes." She studied my narrowing eyes and guessed, "You're wondering why we're friends, aren't you?"

"Mind reader."

"Because you love me," she called over her shoulder as she turned toward the kitchen.

"I'm reconsidering that."

"No, you aren't." Once her dishes were in the dishwasher, she padded toward the long hall. "I'm going back to bed. Wake me up when it's time to go on stage."

I rolled my eyes even as the first stirrings of excitement filled my stomach for tonight's show.

I placed the jeweled mask over my eyes and pulled the thick ribbons from each side around the back of my head. Stevie took the satiny material from my fingers, and I forced myself not to bounce up and down on my toes as she expertly tied and pinned the ribbon into my wildly curled and teased blonde hair.

As soon as I felt the absence of her fingers, I turned to face one of the many mirrors lined up in our dressing room and paused as I glimpsed myself for the first time.

Our costume designer had been working on these up until the last minute tonight, so we hadn't been able to see ourselves in them until now. But this?

The open-swirled design of the masquerade mask showcased my green eyes but still gave that hint of mystery . . . still gave that extra alluring edge.

My attention traveled down the length of my body in the mirror as I took in every detail of the rest of the outfit. Years ago, I would have covered myself—or just not ended up in this outfit in the first place. Now? I felt empowered and beautiful and sexy, and like I could have walked down Sunset Boulevard dressed in nothing but that.

The same jewels that covered the mask were the only things to cover me. They strung across my body, cascading over the curves of my hips and breasts. A few strands were taped in place so nothing would slip out that wasn't meant to. It was by far the most revealing of all our costumes.

It also may have been my new favorite.

It looked like I was dripping with diamonds.

Stevie's face popped over my shoulder in my reflection, a

mischievous smile playing on her lips. "What would Mommy and Daddy Dearest say if they saw you?"

My lips twitched into a hint of a smile in response to hers. But that familiar pit of guilt and worry flared in my stomach at the thought of them—especially with them so close this weekend.

My parents had sent me to all the right schools, enrolled me in all the right ballet classes, and got me the best tutors and private instructors so I would *be* the best. Because anything less wasn't acceptable.

I'd hated every minute of it . . .

They hadn't even congratulated me when I'd gotten into Julliard or when I'd claimed the role of prima ballerina in a Los Angeles company because it had just been expected of me.

But it hadn't been my dream; it'd been my mother's. It had been the life my parents told me I needed to live to touch my trust fund. It had been the path I'd been forced to follow to help my father's political career.

Then one night, some other dancers and I had stumbled into the wrong club, not realizing what we were getting ourselves into, and I'd found another path laid out before me in the form of a burlesque club named Raven.

That night changed my life.

The next day, I'd quit the dance company—not that my parents knew or even noticed with my father having just been elected Senator—and hadn't once looked back.

I'd found a home I'd never had with my parents or the company I'd been a part of for three years. I'd found confidence I'd never known as a ballerina.

I'd found my passion . . .

I quickly stamped out any remaining guilt I felt over

thoughts of my parents as I stepped into my stilettos and did one last check in the mirror.

As it always did before I performed, nervousness flooded my veins. But as it had over the last couple of years, excitement mixed with it, building into something so great that my smile couldn't be contained as I turned to follow Stevie and the rest of the girls out to perform our new opener.

Two years in, and I still loved it just as much. Two years in, and each show gave me as much of a thrill as the first one had. Two years in, and I had never been so sure that I was where I belonged.

As I took the stage, my face transformed, morphed into the look that drove the audience wild. Lips at just enough of a smirk that it didn't take away from their natural pout. Eyes on fire, begging and challenging each and every one of them to take me home. Not that I would ever let any of them touch me.

Sliding down Stevie's leg, I rested my body lightly against hers and let that smirk tip up a fraction more just before the lights came up.

Showtime.

Two

HOLLIS

"Your friends are here," I hissed at Stevie during one of the few acts that one or both of us weren't on stage.

I quickly shimmied into my next bustier, then helped Stevie unzip from her previous outfit.

"Not my friends," she corrected, then turned around to finish zipping up what I couldn't on mine. "You don't fantasize about taking a rusted fork to your friends' balls."

"And yet, you sleep with one of them."

Stevie grinned like a schoolgirl rather than the twenty-five-year-old, black-hearted, heart breaker she was. "But Russell's adorable, he doesn't count."

After what was supposed to be a one-night stand turned into them never leaving her room for two solid nights, I'd only managed to drag Stevie from the house by bringing Russell to Raven with us.

Ever since, he'd been coming about once a week for the past year with his friends. Okay, fine, sure—he was like Stevie said: Adorable. But his friends were out of control and disgusting, and it made me hate whenever Russell showed.

Not to mention, whenever that group came, Stevie was always too distracted by Russell to ever notice what I was left to deal with afterward.

"Russell's friends think this is a strip club," I argued. "They're one night away from throwing dollar bills up on the stage."

She lifted the hand that wasn't grabbing her bustier and echoed, "Rusted forks, babe. Rusted forks. Fantasize about it, and they won't bother you anymore."

"As long as that one continues grabbing me after the shows, they're all going to bother me."

It wasn't until Stevie froze that I realized I'd said that out loud. And then I was mentally cursing myself when she asked in a low tone, "Come again?"

"Not a big deal," I said with a forced shrug. "You know I can handle myself."

"And I'm sure he'll enjoy the spiky end of my Manolo in his dick if he tries to touch you again. Which one?" she demanded.

"We're up next. You need to get dressed."

"I'm about to go do a whole new kind of show that will ultimately involve police if you don't tell me which one."

"I said I can handle it," I said firmly and held the same tone to cover my lie. "It's a butt graze, nothing more. I've got it under control. They all just piss me off."

Stevie stared me down for a few seconds before releasing me from her glare and wiggling into her bustier.

"Can I help you?" she snapped as she switched out her ruffle panties and stepped into different heels.

I looked up to see Jenny, one of the other dancers, staring at Stevie with an equally confused and irritated look. "I'm walking."

"No . . . no," Stevie huffed. "If you see me standing here, you don't walk this way. Find another way to wherever you have to be, or I'll punch you in the face."

Jenny just rolled her eyes and turned around. Her mumbled, "Bitch," still audible as she walked away.

My head shook as I checked my makeup in the mirror.

Stevie's hands lifted out to the sides as she watched Jenny leave, then she glanced over at me. "I was nice!"

"Nope."

"Well, I was nicer than I'd planned on being tonight."

I paused from fixing my smudged eyeliner and lifted an eyebrow.

"Okay, fine. Next time I'll try not to tell her how much I hate her."

"What a sacrifice that will be," I said sarcastically and laughed when she swatted at me.

Turning once I was ready, we quickly looked each other over to make sure everything was in place. But just as I stepped to the side to head toward the wings of the stage, Stevie stopped me.

Her blue eyes held mine, the look in them so severe, it stunned me. "Rusted forks, and it's like they're not even there. Do you hear me?"

It took me a few seconds for my shock to wear off enough to be able to answer. "I hear you."

"Why are you here, Hollis?"

"What?"

"Raven." She said the name of the club with reverence. "Tell me why you came here."

Stevie already knew this. She'd asked me the same question after I'd gotten hired. "To be free."

"Dirty jackasses make it hard to want to get back out

there and perform. But don't let them take that away from you. Don't let them make you hate this. *Rusted forks,* they disappear, and you're free again."

I nodded slowly at first, then faster before wrapping her up in a quick hug. "Thanks, Stevie."

"Got your back, babe."

I know.

Once we were out of the dressing rooms and waiting in the wings of the stage, I let my eyelids shut as I listened to the music still playing from the routine before ours. Embraced that feeling of nervous excitement I got before every show and routine as I forced away the disgusting calls and whistles from the tables up front.

As I forgot everything but *this.*

"Who let Jenny come with us?" Stevie hissed as she grabbed my arm and pulled me closer to Ampersand after our show that night.

I rolled my eyes and squeezed her hand. "You have to stop being so mean to her."

"She tripped me, Hollis."

"Not on purpose."

She held out the arm that wasn't linked with mine. "You don't know that, and I still fell."

"The lights had already gone down. No one saw you."

"I would really love to know whose side you're on," she said dryly. "But I'm starving, so I'm likely to kill you if you say the wrong answer."

A laugh bubbled free as we stepped into the diner that her dad owned. "I'm always on your side. I just don't know why you're so harsh with her." I dipped my head closer, a smile breaking across my face as I whispered, "I also think you're grumpier than normal because you didn't go home with Russell *and* he wasn't there for a few days before tonight."

She gasped and whipped her head to face me. "I don't give a shit if he shows or doesn't. He could never come back, and I wouldn't care."

I lifted a brow, and she deflated a little.

"Okay, but like . . . also stop judging me."

I gave a knowing hum and started turning for our usual booth, only to be yanked back by her.

"Hollis," she hissed at my side. "Hollis, ten o'clock. I need to bear his children."

A shock of a laugh touched my lips. "Wha—" I inhaled quickly when I followed her line of sight and saw the man who'd been dancing through my dreams for years now.

Tall body folded into a booth. Dark hair cropped close on the sides and longer strands in a state of chaos on top, as if he'd been running his hands through it, and matching the scruffy beard that made my fingers twitch. Broad shoulders and chest stretching an old Quiet Riot shirt. One of his long legs peeking out from beneath the table, Converse-covered foot tapping out a beat as his thumbs flew across the screen of his phone.

His face was hardened the same as it had been when I'd met him, matching the threatening energy rolling off him. But I knew if he glanced up from his phone, his eyes would tell a different story.

"Oh my God."

"Do you think it's too forward to propose marriage within the first minute of meeting him?" Stevie asked only to mutter, "Never mind. I already decided I don't care."

"That's him," I whispered, stopping her when she began strutting toward him—probably intending to do exactly that. "That's Ampersand Guy."

"What? No," she said just as softly, drawing out the last word as if I'd just crushed every one of her dreams. "I need to have his children."

"Who's that?" Krystle, one of the other girls, asked as she started getting into our booth, eyes narrowed on the guy like a predator watching prey.

"The love of my life who Hollis has already laid claim to," Stevie said as she untangled herself from me and dramatically fell onto the bench. "No big deal."

"Stevie," I hissed, cheeks heating since she'd made no attempt to keep her voice down.

"Is that a *no*?" Krystle asked as she pushed so she was fully standing. Repositioning her boobs inside her bra, she let a smirk shape her lips. "Then don't mind if I help myself."

"No," I said quickly, scrambling to step in front of her. "Not that one."

Stevie's laugh followed me when I started walking across the diner, but I didn't take my attention away from *him*.

There are moments in our lives that can change the course we're on. When I'd met this man in New York, it'd been easy to see he could change *everything*.

He was absurdly handsome, sure . . . but I'd grown up surrounded by gorgeous guys. Guys that came and went and couldn't hold my attention because their personalities never matched their looks.

But there'd been something that seemed to cling to his body, warning people not to get too close, all while his dark eyes had begged me to step closer. A soul-deep pain that made me want to push past his barriers to try to heal whatever his hurts were.

But I hadn't been ready to take that risk yet, so I'd walked away from that inexplicable bond.

And I'd regretted it every day since.

Then when a stranger appeared in front of me years later who had somehow felt so familiar—enticing me closer with all that charged energy . . . triggering memories and promising the kind of connection that shouldn't have belonged to him—I'd let my hesitation and uncertainty keep me from stepping fully onto that path.

Instead, I'd left a crumb, leaving the rest up to him.

Then I'd been met with another one of those *moments* later that night when I stumbled into Raven. Grabbing it tight had changed my life in the best possible way, but in taking it, I'd also made the decision to hide *Hollis Donahue*.

And I'd taken away his ability to find me.

Something I'd agonized over for two years.

Now when faced with those moments, I didn't shy from the unknown paths. The risks.

The excitement, the opportunity, the love . . .

And he was a path I refused to miss again.

Grasping every ounce of confidence I possessed, I sucked in a steeling breath and slid onto the bench across from him. Only for it to falter when those eyes shifted up and locked on me.

All buried pain that lit with recognition and wonder. Igniting a spark that danced between us, promising a wildfire if we crossed that distance. Pulling at something in me that I'd been afraid I would never feel again . . .

He straightened and pulled AirPods from his ears as he studied me unapologetically. The corner of his mouth tugging into a smirk that was pure sin as he pocketed them and lifted his hand in a half-wave.

Right.

Because I was just sitting there, staring at him.

"I didn't think I'd ever see you again." The words came out on a relieved sigh that immediately had heat rushing to my cheeks when his brows lifted with amusement. Shaking my head, I hurried to salvage this meeting I'd only dreamed about a hundred times, blurting out, "I mean, not that I was hoping to see you," I lied. "Not that I don't *not* want to see you either, I just didn't think I would. Oh my God, this is already a disaster. Can I start over?"

His hand clasped around my wrist when I pushed against the table to slip out of the booth. His smile bright and tortured eyes dancing as he held up his phone in request before setting it on the table and sliding one of his fingers across it with the hand that wasn't lingering on my wrist.

Searing me with a heat that went so far beyond his warmth. Reminding me of his touch from years ago that had felt like a promise and a claim and a brand. When one of his fingers slid down the side of my wrist as if on impulse, my entire being trembled.

His smile was softer by the time he turned his phone toward me, but the amusement in his eyes hadn't faded.

Hi

The breath I'd been holding as I waited to see what he would say left me on a rush as I read the simple word.

"Do you remember me?" I asked, the question pure hesitation as I waited for him to put my desperate thoughts to rest.

A few seconds passed before he leaned forward, studying me expectantly as if *he'd* been the one to ask. Without turning the phone, he tapped out a response upside down.

Kind of hard to forget the girl who tries to save you by signing to you

I let my head fall into my hand. The embarrassment burning deeper and mixing with a profound disappointment before my stomach dropped when he added another line.

And then ghosts you the next day

"I didn't—at least, it wasn't what it seemed." At the subtle doubt mixing with his amusement, I explained, "I fully deleted all my social media accounts the next morning, not even remembering until after it was done that I'd given you those handles."

Or who you were, I thought lamely as his response and Stevie's arguments caused all that doubt to swirl again.

Half of his face scrunched up in obvious disbelief, pulling a soft exhale from me.

"Yeah, I guess that does seem a little unbelievable."

He nodded, then took his phone back only to return it just as quickly.

. . .

You disappearing on me the next morning seems to be a theme with us Hollis

The air rushed from my lungs, and I could've sworn the earth rocked beneath my feet.

I read the words again and again, trying to convince myself I wasn't seeing them incorrectly before I met his expectant stare. "You're New York," I whispered, unable to speak any louder.

Just breathing life to my dreams was enough to shake my soul.

One of his dark brows ticked up in response.

Adam

"That's right." I'd struggled to remember the moment we'd been introduced for years now, and his name had always evaded me. "But you're—*how?*" I nearly begged. "How are you here?"

He gestured to me as if tossing my question back at me.

"I'm sorry, I just . . ." My head shook and I pressed my fingers to my temple. "I've been sure it was you, but it's still hard wrapping my head around the fact that you're here. That, somehow, we're both here."

A whisper of disbelief touched his face as he grabbed his phone. Thumbs quickly tapping on the screen before he set it on the table again.

. . .

You sure

Because when I first ran into you in here

You didn't seem to know who I was

"That isn't fair," I muttered, feeling the frustration in his words as I stared at the phone for a moment longer before meeting his gaze. "There was something familiar about you. I just couldn't figure out how I knew you until the next morning because you looked completely different."

He gestured to me, amusement bleeding from his lips.

"You didn't have a beard then," I argued. "When I met you in New York, you were wearing glasses and your hair was incredibly short, and that was when you took off your beanie. Not to mention, I didn't know you were non-verbal."

His brows lifted in surprise as if he was wondering how that could've slipped by me.

In all honesty, I was embarrassed that it had. But our friends had introduced us before we'd been pulled apart again and again, and that night had been more physical than anything. There hadn't been much talking on my part until I'd started leaving. And if I remembered correctly, I'd been irritated with him because he hadn't responded.

He scooped up his phone and tapped out a message before handing it to me, those dark eyes piercing me as he waited for me to take it.

You disappearing again

You struggling to remember me

None of that has anything to do with you panicking before bolting on me in New York

With you wanting me to forget you
That night
Everything

A shuddering breath ripped from me, my head moving in subtle shakes as my stare slowly lifted to his again. "You don't understand what happened that morning in New York."

A huff left him.

No I understood perfectly
I was a mistake you shouldn't have made
I was a world you shouldn't have stepped in

"You don't understand," I repeated, my voice twisting around the words. "And I don't expect you to."

Try me

My eyes widened as they bounced from the screen to his. "I can't." At the shake of his head, my brow furrowed as frustration and unease swirled through me. "My life . . . Adam, I can't."

His jaw twitched as he studied me. When I pressed my lips into a firm line, he nodded and let all his frustration bleed into his next words.

. . .

What is it you wanted exactly

Two years ago

Right now

Another night so you can have another morning to panic over your decisions and disappear

Or just another step into a world that puts your perfect one at risk

My breath came out on a rush, and I reared back at the bitterness of his words. My tongue darted out to wet my suddenly dry lips as I fumbled for an answer when I'd never felt so out of my element.

I'd thought of this man for years. I'd wondered how big of a mistake I'd made by not taking that path with him each time it was presented. But even through the screen of his phone, it wasn't hard to understand the coldness of his words. It wasn't hard to feel that the warning clinging to him, urging people not to get too close, was now radiating from him. Stretching across the table and reaching for me just as much as it was pushing me away.

But I was beginning to wonder if I'd romanticized a night that meant nothing to him.

Humiliation swirled, but I took a steadying breath and admitted, "For two years, I've wondered if you would've even tried to 'find me,' and I've hated that I couldn't know. For even longer, I've wanted this moment to happen. And now I'm wondering what I was waiting for."

Surprise and longing flashed through his eyes at my whispered confession, only to disappear when a bag of food was set on the table.

I looked up and offered one of the workers a weak smile. “Hi, Eileen.”

“Hollis,” she said warmly as she turned to go.

When my gaze pulled back to the man in front of me, he was looking at the table, stare vacant.

Before I could gather up the courage to say anything else, his eyes snapped up. All those old pains burning deep as he got out of the booth, rising to his full height and scooping up his phone.

Right.

I stilled from getting out of the booth when he turned his phone around for me to see as he grabbed the bag of food.

Nothing

You were waiting for nothing because we can’t do this
You don’t want to get mixed up with a guy like me

I stared at his words for a long time. Reading the pain in them . . . the subtle threat that so clearly matched the clashing energy now pulsing off him in waves.

Finally managing to slip out of the booth when he pocketed his phone, I offered a smile that felt as pained and confused as the rest of me and whispered, “Right, sorry. My mistake.”

I forced myself to turn for where the girls sat at our usual booth, telling myself I imagined the twitch of his jaw at my parting words. The way he subtly rocked toward me. The longing that flashed through his eyes and faded into frustration.

Telling myself I'd imagined those glimpses of his own pain and regret within his coldness.

Or that I was imagining that connection between us, calling out to me still. Begging me to stop and turn.

"Hey!" Stevie said when I made it to the edge of the booth, eyebrows lifting suggestively. "How'd it go with—*oh.*" Her gaze drifted to something behind me. And despite how hard I tried to keep my stare on my best friend and away from him, I looked at the reflection of the windowed wall behind her to watch him walk past me.

One of the other girls made a noise as if she knew it hadn't gone well.

Once he was outside and the door to Ampersand was shut behind him, I reached out to grab the table so I wouldn't crumple right there.

"Really, babe?" Stevie said sadly. When I didn't respond, she scoffed. "Well, his loss. Fuck him."

"Right," I said on a breath.

The girls were talking to each other and maybe to me, but I couldn't be sure anymore because, at that exact moment, he looked over his shoulder as if he couldn't help but search me out as he stepped into the parking lot.

All regret and indecision wrapped up in such a complicated man.

And something in that simple action gripped me. Those tortured eyes hidden beneath all that terrifying exterior forcing my heart to race in a way only he could make it.

Because nothing had ever felt like him.

Three

ADAM

I dropped my head back and scrubbed my hands over my face as I told myself so many things. To crank the engine. To drive away. Go back to the house. Forget that I'd ever shared a night with her.

But every one of those felt more impossible than the last.

Hollis had been someone who stumbled into my life and my bed before disappearing with a clear message that what happened between us was a *horrible* mistake.

Still, she'd consumed my mind for weeks. Her hypnotic eyes and hesitant smile had fueled dreams for months. The connection between us had been a taunting memory for years. Only for it all to roar back to life when I'd bumped into her in Los Angeles.

I'd told myself not to fall for it again—not to get trapped in her. I'd deleted the notes with her, but the handle she'd left me had burned into my mind the second I'd seen it. By the next afternoon, I'd given in and looked her up only for her to be gone just like all those years before.

Until tonight.

And my goddamn heart had just about thrashed out of my chest in an attempt to get to her when she'd sat in front of me.

Except my heart had never once decided to get involved before her, and I sure as shit couldn't let it now. Not only was it insane to want someone this way, but I couldn't want her at all.

Turning on my car, I huffed out a sigh and pulled away from the diner before I could do something dangerous . . . like go back inside just so I could be near her. So I could apologize when I *needed* her to want nothing to do with me.

By the time I'd made it back home, I was practically trembling with the strength it took not to turn my car back around.

"Adam?" my roommate called out when I was only a few feet into the house, worry wrapping around my name even though he had yet to see me.

So in tune with each other from years of living and working together that he already knew something was off by the way the door had shut behind me.

"What happened?" he demanded as he came stalking into the entryway.

I shook my head and continued deeper into the house, but he stopped me with a hand to my chest. Lethal eyes searching my face as he repeated the question.

"What happened? Everything good?"

I lifted the bag in response and pushed past him.

When I got into the kitchen, his girlfriend gasped excitedly and set down the book she was reading.

"Favorite!" Sarah cried out as she stood. "Did you get extra mozzarella sticks?"

I nodded, slipping my phone out of my pocket as I set the bag of food on the island.

Where do you put all this food

She swatted at my arm, a soft laugh tumbling free as she reached into the bag and pulled out one of the mozzarella sticks. “Don’t be rude.”

Leo slanted a menacing glare at me as he pulled her against his chest, even though I knew he teased her about it just as often because the girl didn’t have an ounce of fat on her. His natural look was just threatening and scary as shit.

She did a little dance, holding a mozzarella stick in each hand, looking deliriously happy as she allowed Leo to take a bite. Nurturing and kind and bubbly . . . Sarah was everything we weren’t. How she put up with us, I still didn’t know.

“Thanks for the food,” she said on a sigh as she fell deeper into Leo’s hold.

A smile tugged at my mouth as I slid my phone toward her.

Anytime

Sarah made a humming noise before pointing half a mozzarella stick at me. “Leo’s right—why do you look so angry?”

Leo gestured to me as if to say he wasn't the only one who could see it.

My brows raised and I pressed a hand to my chest before gesturing to Leo, the perpetually angry one.

"No," she said around the bite she'd just taken. "No, you definitely look angry."

I slashed a hand through the air, head slowly shaking.

"Adam, I know you," Leo stressed. "What's going on?"

I released a sigh and grabbed my phone.

Fucking hell

Nothing

"Fine, whatever," Leo muttered, dismissing it. But from the way his hardened stare flashed my way, I knew he had no intention of dropping it.

Sarah gave me a look as if she wasn't as sure as Leo. But after finishing off the mozzarella sticks in her hands, she wiggled excitedly, glanced up at him, and asked, "Can we tell him?"

My head slanted as I looked between them, attention catching on the way Leo was holding himself.

As if he wasn't breathing.

But he was all smiles for her as he nodded.

She squealed softly and looked back at me, pressing her hands together in front of her as she bounced in Leo's hold. Her smile impossibly wide as the silence stretched on and grew thick with anticipation.

"We're going to have a baby!" she finally said. "I'm pregnant!"

Oh fuck.

I struggled to keep my expression from falling and then forced a smile. Hoping like hell my excitement didn't look as faked as it felt as I rounded the island and pulled her in for a hug. Looking into Leo's grave stare for a long moment before releasing her and then hugging him for good measure.

For her.

Always for Sarah.

Grabbing my phone once I was back on the other side of the island, I slid a finger across the screen before handing it to them.

Holy shit

Congratulations

"Thank you," Sarah said, still wiggling with excitement. "We can't believe it. We're so excited. Shocked," she added, glancing back at Leo with wide eyes and laughing softly. "Obviously weren't planning this. But excited."

I nodded and hurried to tap out my excuses when she handed my phone back. Needing to get away before I ruined all that happiness.

I'll let you celebrate

I need to get to work

. . .

I grabbed my food from the bag, nodding at them as I turned to leave. My expression falling as soon as I did. My own struggles nearly forgotten with the bomb she'd just dropped.

Using my free hand, I started tapping on my phone, already knowing he would follow me.

Not ten seconds after I got in my room, he shut the door, and I tossed the phone at him.

What the fuck

He threw it back, his eyes the same dark warning they'd always been even though he looked like he might get sick. "I love her."

I lifted my hand. Gesturing as if I hadn't already known that.

What were you thinking

Pregnant

Fucking pregnant Leo

"You think I meant for this to happen?" he bit out from where he'd moved to stand beside me so he could watch as I typed. "But it happened. Can't exactly take it back now."

I stared him down for long moments before sliding my finger across the screen.

You better know what you're doing

. . .

"Yeah," he muttered. "I know."

He scrubbed his hands over his face and released a heavy breath before focusing on me. "Were you able to get it?"

Couldn't

But I'll take care of it

"Is that what's wrong?" he asked, refusing to let it go.

My head slowly shook even though, one look at Hollis, and I'd forgotten my whole purpose for being in that diner.

I'd forgotten everything but her.

And then my entire focus had been on putting a stop to my wants and needs and making sure she wanted nothing to do with me.

"Then what happened tonight?" he demanded.

But, even more so after his and Sarah's announcement, I couldn't let Leo know what was really going on with me.

That a pair of green eyes had nearly knocked me to my knees all those years ago and still had the ability to. That a hesitant smile made me want *more* for the first time in my life. That everything about her had been wholly unexpected and had called to me from that very first night.

And that I was so fucking screwed because I knew I would do anything to see her again. To get wrapped up in that energy that pulsed between us—get wrapped up in her.

Sliding my finger across the screen, I held up my phone and waited for Leo's infuriated glare, knowing it was coming.

. . .

Absolutely nothing

As soon as his dark eyes met mine, I gave him a challenging smirk and walked to my door, opening it meaningfully.

"This isn't done," he said softly, voice a menacing rumble. "You're hiding something, and we don't do that shit. We *can't*."

I nodded and just waited for him to leave, mind already back in the diner and on a girl who could change everything.

Four

ADAM

I glanced at the door of the coffee shop when it opened a couple days later, my body going still when I saw the people walking in. It was instant . . . the way seeing her made my heart do that thing. As if just the sight of her forced it to beat harder. Trying to find a new rhythm amidst the frenzy she'd always created inside me when it had settled into a dull, darkened beat when I was a kid.

I wanted to embrace it as much as I knew I needed to run from it.

Using my phone as a buffer, I kept my stare on her and the girl she was with as they went up to the counter to order. Watching every move Hollis made and trying so damn hard not to get lost in the lithe way she moved. The easy way she held herself. So different than when I'd first met her.

But there was something else about her that had me openly studying her and forgetting about pretenses.

Something in the way her shoulders seemed weighed down. Matching the sadness in her eyes and the way her full lips looked like they were pulling into a frown, even when she was smiling.

"Adam?"

My attention snapped forward to where the barista was pushing a drink toward the edge of the counter.

"There you go, man," he said, giving me a half-wave as he went back to the espresso machines.

I nodded my thanks and grabbed the drink, catching Hollis's shocked expression from where she stood on the opposite side of the shop when I turned.

I let myself linger for a moment. Let myself take her in even though I knew I shouldn't. Then I pushed back the need to pull her into my arms and feel her pressed against me again . . .

To kiss that shock right off her face.

To hear her moan—*fuck*.

I shook my head and forced myself to focus again.

But when I started walking toward her, all I saw was New York and everything I wanted with her again and again and again.

"Can I bear your children?" the girl with her asked when I neared them, tearing my attention away.

"Stevie!" one of the workers whispered before coughing out a laugh.

"Oh my God," Hollis muttered, eyelids fluttering shut. "You did not just ask him that."

The girl didn't take her stare off me even as she lazily patted Hollis's face. "I'm sorry . . . I would like to have your children."

Hollis finally opened her eyes, looking all kinds of embarrassed. "Forgive my roommate, she has no filter. She also has a boyfriend."

Stevie gasped in horror and moved away from Hollis. "How dare you say such vile things!"

The corner of my mouth twitched with amusement as I tapped on my phone and held it out for Hollis to read.

Two days

This is progress

Her eyes darted over the words before she looked at me in suspicion. "What are you doing here?" When my eyebrows lifted, she hurried to add, "Like you said, it's been two days after we went two years without bumping into each other."

"I see no problem with this," her roommate said before winking at me. "I'm fine with seeing you every day."

"Stevie," Hollis hissed.

My smirk widened into a smile in response to the exasperation and horror that crossed her face.

If I'm not mistaken I'm here for the same reason you are

Coffee

And you're about to be disappointed if you're insinuating I'm following you

I come here almost every day

Not sure I'll be back though

Just realized the customers are sort of rude and extremely paranoid

. . .

Hollis's mouth dropped open as she scrambled to defend herself, irritation briefly flitting across her face when she looked up and saw the smile I was fighting. "You're joking," she realized, sounding wholly frustrated with herself that she was slipping right back into that place that I already had.

Getting trapped in that energy.

Getting lost in that pull.

Forgetting how bad of an idea it was to let myself want her.

With a sigh, she took a step away when she realized how close we'd gotten and asked, "What do you want, Adam?"

And there it was again.

That weight on her shoulders and that frown pulling at her lips. The sadness in her eyes that screamed accusation as if I'd crushed her.

God damn.

I swallowed down the apology knotting in my throat and tapped on my screen. Nodding toward the front doors of the shop as I held out the phone to her.

I'm sorry

Can we talk outside

Tension built and wove through the charged space between us, thick and weighted in the seconds that posed as an eternity until she dipped her head in a nod.

Stevie threw her hand in front of Hollis and pinned me with a glare. "Try anything funny with her, I will rip you apart —starting with your favorite appendages."

My eyes widened as horror and something close to respect

moved through me. Lifting a hand in surrender, I turned to follow Hollis outside.

She walked down the side of the building, then turned on me. Face pinched with frustration and hurt and head shaking. "Look, I don't know why you apologized, but you don't owe me an apology—you don't owe me anything." A shaky smile teased her lips as she took another step away. "Because I'm the girl who left and then unintentionally ghosted you again, and you've made it very clear that I also greatly misinterpreted that night in New York because it obviously meant nothing to you."

My brows lifted. Lips parting and taunting me as if I might actually be able to utter the denial furiously clawing up my throat and getting stuck there.

A soft breath tumbled free when she continued. "If you want an apology . . . I'm sorry. You have no idea how sorry I am for leaving the way I did that morning—for leaving at all. It's one of the biggest mistakes of my life. But I was absolutely terrified."

A tic started in my jaw as my fingers flew across the screen.

Never said that Hollis
And I didn't want an apology
I wanted to know what you wanted

Her chest shook with a ragged exhale as she read the words again and again before looking up at me, looking at once pleading and wounded and defeated. "You knew what I wanted. You just didn't want the same."

I should've left it there. I should've *left*.

Let things end between us this way and go back to what I was supposed to be doing. But this was Hollis, and I'd never been able to think clearly when it came to her.

Besides, you know what they say about good intentions . . .

And I was pretty sure I was already going to Hell anyway.

I angrily tapped on the screen and then shoved my phone in her hand when she wouldn't look away from my eyes.

You think I don't want you

Hollis do you have any idea how much I've hated that you ONCE AGAIN disappeared from me the next day without a fucking care

"I told you what happened," she ground out. "I know how it sounds, but I didn't lie to you. It had absolutely nothing to do with you."

I shook my head and tapped on the phone so she would continue reading, then stepped closer, watching every reaction.

The flare of her eyes as they darted across the screen of my phone.

Her soft inhale.

The slight blush rising to her cheeks.

Like each time you showed up in my life didn't completely ruin me because you were all I could think about for months

So yeah I've been a little pissed about that

But aside from that I need to keep my distance from you because it's best for you

But I hate pretending for even a minute that everything about you hasn't called out to me from that FIRST night

Her stare slowly drifted up to meet mine, her face creased with emotion as she handed my phone back. Body straight and tense in a way I hadn't seen in six years.

There was the girl I'd first met.

The one who hadn't belonged in that world. The one who'd first destroyed me.

I took another step forward until I was so close that she had to arch her neck to meet my stare.

All her confusion and pain reaching out to me and mixing with that need that always hummed between us. And I embraced it. Took it and let it fuel my own selfish desires.

Nothing should feel like this

Her body shuddered and her eyes begged so many things. "But you don't want me."

My head shook roughly as I hurried to correct her.

I've never wanted anyone the way I want you

But I need to keep you away because it's best for you

. . .

A hint of fear slipped through her growing confusion as she read the words. "What . . . what do you mean by that?"

When I just continued watching her, she glanced away. Her tongue darting out to wet her lips and her spine straightening. "Right," she murmured and let out a long sigh. "Then why did you stop me from leaving the other night, and why come up to me today? Why not just let me go or ignore me? Why are we standing here?"

Because I was an idiot who was willing to destroy everything for the girl in front of me.

My fingers moved slowly across the screen before I handed her my phone, the confession leaving me and crossing a line I couldn't come back from.

Because I crave you

She slowly looked up at me, her cheeks darkening as one of those hesitant smiles teased the corner of her mouth.

And fuck me if it wasn't like a punch to the chest every time.

Gripping at my cold, useless heart and forcing it to beat harder. Urging me closer. Making me want to lean in and taste and touch and ask for something I couldn't let myself have.

Maybe because there was something about the way she held herself that let me know there was nothing hesitant about the girl, and yet, that smile was as genuine as they come.

It wasn't a game she played.

It wasn't a lure just meant to be intriguing . . . but goddamn had I always been intrigued.

Her head bobbed in a subtle nod as she tapped something onto my phone, talking as she did. "I don't know what's going on in your life, but I know what it's like to feel trapped—to feel like someone else is controlling your life. I know what it's like to feel like you might crawl out of your skin if you don't escape . . ." She gave me a meaningful look as she handed my phone back to me, and I knew from her tone and that look what she was implying.

What she was trying to explain.

New York.

Her leaving . . .

"I don't waste second chances, and you and I are somehow here. Together. And despite what you've thought about me all these years, I wasn't lying the other day when I said I've wanted this moment to happen." A breathless laugh left her, her expression all disbelief. "But I refuse to be repeatedly pulled closer and pushed away by you. So . . ." She lifted a shoulder and started stepping away, movements slow as her stare swept over me. "I guess I'll wait to see if you want that second chance too."

I watched as she turned and headed back into the coffee shop, forcing myself not to move. Not to stop her.

Telling myself I had to let her go.

Everything about it feeling so similar and yet entirely different from that morning in New York.

Once the door had shut behind her, I stepped back to start for my car and glanced down at my phone. At the number she'd left with the message: *This won't disappear tomorrow.*

I held my thumb over the icon to delete the entire note.

My heart pounding out an unsteady beat and hand fucking trembling—rebelling what I was about to do even though I knew it needed to be done. With a harsh exhale, I tapped the icon and stalked off to my car.

My frustration growing and growing until I was slamming the door behind me and throwing my phone into the seat beside me. Raking my hands through my hair and wishing more than anything that the yell building in my chest would break free.

But it was for the best.

For her, it had to be . . .

With a shuddering exhale, I pulled the phone I'd slipped from Hollis's back pocket out of my own and set it on my center console. Leaning over, I grabbed mine from where I'd thrown it and opened it up to send a message.

Me: *Done.*

Leo: *Good. Were you able to get it this time?*

Taking a picture of her phone, I sent it to Leo. My chest tight and heavy from the secrets I'd been keeping from him.

Me: *Yep. Coming back to clone it.*

Leo: *Who's taking it back when you're done?*

Leo: *1 2 3 not it.*

Me: *What the fuck?*

Me: *What are you? Six?*

Leo: *By the way, Sarah wants mozzarella sticks.*

Me: *I get her food, or I take back the phone. Your call.*

Leo: *. . .*
Leo: *Sarah wants mozzarella sticks . . .*
Me: *Then you're taking the phone back. Be home soon WITH food.*

I cranked the engine and dropped my phone into the cupholder. Just as I was about to pull out of the parking space, I grabbed it again and went to the recently deleted notes. Recovering the one from today and saving Hollis's number to my phone like the bastard I was.

Five

HOLLIS

"Brunch!" Mia called out as she rounded the corner into the living room that weekend, her expression brightening when she saw me passing the end of the long hall that led out to the kitchen. "Hey there, stranger." She held up a large pastry bag and drink carrier, boasting the Asterisk logo. "Saturday usual?"

The corner of my mouth lifted in response to the delicate smile playing on her lips. "Please and thank you. How was your shift?"

She did a little side-to-side head bob as if she was considering my question and how to answer it as she walked over to the breakfast bar. "Pretty uneventful. But it was only my first shift of the day," she teased as if something truly outrageous might happen. All in that Mia way—soft and wholly sweet. The girl was good to her core and an absolute knockout on top of it.

Not that she noticed or cared. She didn't have time in her life to even consider the idea of dating.

"And what about you? How was your workout?"

My smile faltered before I could fix it in place. “It was fine,” I answered after a delay and grabbed the pastry bag to start sorting everything out, but Mia just studied me.

“I know it bothers you, I just don’t understand why,” she said so her words wouldn’t carry.

“It just isn’t something I really want to talk about,” I whispered, hoping she would drop it.

A handful of months after I’d left the dance company for Raven, I’d realized something was missing from my life. But whenever my gaze would stray to the boxes of my ballet shoes, I would force the thought away.

After a month or so of desperately trying to avoid looking at the boxes, I’d found myself sitting on the floor, holding my pointe shoes. Shoes I’d spent so much time tailoring and perfecting. All while silently cursing the dances I’d had to do in them, for no reason other than I’d hated every second of my life.

And I’d missed it.

Not my life or the company . . . but something in it, I’d missed.

It wasn’t until I’d taken my shoes to Raven a few weeks later that I realized the movements I’d hated for so long, I actually loved.

Maybe because it was no longer forced. Maybe because every dance and movement was of my own making. Maybe because my parents were no longer a part of it, I wasn’t sure.

But on the few mornings we didn’t have rehearsal, I continued stealing away to Raven.

No one in the audience.

Just me and the house lights and my pointe shoes.

Still, despite how freeing it was now, I was angry that it’d taken hiding from my parents and running from my life to realize how much ballet meant to me. There was almost a shame to my anger when I left Raven on these mornings. As if a part of me was still rebelling against letting myself enjoy what had been forced on me for so long.

And since only Stevie knew the extent of what my life had been like, it wasn't something I could just explain to Mia or anyone else.

"Well, if you *do* ever want to talk," Mia began, gently knocking her shoulder against mine, "you know where to find me." She gave me one of those gentle, teasing smiles. "You know . . . running out of the house or at one of my many jobs. Speaking of, I need to get going to the next one."

"Thanks, Mia," I said, sincerity weaving through the words. "See you tonight?"

She glanced to the side as if mentally going through her day. An odd, bothered look briefly touching her face before she smiled at me. "Maybe. You and Stevie have fun tonight. Don't break too many hearts."

"No promises." I winked, giving her my usual response. Grabbing Stevie's coffee, I gestured toward the ceiling. "Time to wake the monster."

Mia's soft laugh left her as she gathered up her own food and drink and darted for the front door again.

"Bye, Mia," Stevie said when the door shut.

"Hey!" I said, not bothering to hide my surprise as I held the coffee toward her. "You're already awake."

"Obviously." She made a face like it was normal for her to wake up without going to extreme measures.

Ariana came running up behind her and jumped on her back, a shit-eating grin on her face. "I waved a bag of coffee beans near her."

Stevie rolled her eyes and let Ariana's feet fall to the floor.

"Yeah, and it won't work again because asleep me now knows your evil trickery."

Amusement punched from Ariana as she looked at me. "She loves us."

"I know."

Stevie grabbed the cup from my outstretched hand, head shaking. "No, no. No love. Did you miss the part where you betrayed me?"

"You have coffee." Ariana waved a hand toward the cup in Stevie's hand. "Ta-da."

"Have you noticed she's much more dramatic in the mornings?" I asked as I walked back to the counter for my own drink.

"I'm still standing here," Stevie said irritably.

"That isn't a denial," Ariana muttered as she walked into the kitchen.

Stevie watched her, eyes wide, before she looked at me. "You know how you sometimes wonder how we're friends?" She gestured between the three of us. "Right now . . . that's me. Wondering."

"Because you love us," I said confidently.

"Nope," she said stubbornly before taking a sip of her coffee and climbing onto one of the barstools.

I slid a blueberry muffin toward her, and she pointedly glanced away from it for a second before grabbing it and moving it even closer. "I mean, it isn't a new pair of shoes, but I'll accept it as apology."

Ariana laughed as she gathered fruit to start cutting up.

The front door opened again, and just as we started looking that way, Stevie's dad called out, "Girls?"

Mr. Russo liked to pretend he was letting us know he was there so whoever was home would come chat with him. But it was really his way of warning us he was there so we had time to cover anything that shouldn't be exposed.

And, in Stevie's case, hide any men who may be naked in her room at the time.

"Hi," we called back just as he rounded the corner, smile warm and arms spread as if just seeing us made his day better, but the smile slipped when he walked farther in and saw Ariana.

"For Christ's sake, Ariana. I let you know I was here."

She held an arm out to the side, wearing nothing but a sports bra and women-style boxer briefs. "I'm covered."

I managed to hold back the laugh crawling up my throat, but Stevie shook her head in response as hers broke free.

Mr. Russo pinched the bridge of his nose and pointed at her before gesturing toward the ceiling. "Clothes. Now."

"I'm cutting up fruit," she argued.

When Mr. Russo just sighed, I said, "I'll handle the fruit," and moved into the kitchen to take her place.

"I'm covered," she mumbled, maintaining her argument.

"You're in underwear," I said in the same soft tone.

Her dark brows slowly lifted as she set the knife on the cutting board. "Yeah . . . covered." But one of her signature smirks pulled at her lips just as she passed me to wash her hands.

"I'm buying her clothes for Christmas," Mr. Russo said once she'd left.

"She has more clothes than I do," I informed him.

"It's true," Stevie said as she twisted in her chair to face her dad. "It's Ariana—you know how she is. So, what brings you?"

He released a sigh that had nothing to do with Ariana's dressing habits and looked at me as he went to stand against the bar. "Went to take care of the tips at Ampersand this morning, and Eileen asked to talk to me." He gave me a knowing look. "Wondering why I'm just now hearing about this."

Well, shit.

"About what?" Stevie asked, looking between us.

The realization that Stevie didn't know surprised him even more, but he just waited, giving me the chance to tell him.

"It wasn't a big deal," I finally said, voice soft and filled with a mixture of shame and anger even though I knew I had nothing to be ashamed of.

The guy was an asshole, and I'd done nothing wrong . . . other than keep it from my best friend.

"What wasn't a big deal?" Stevie demanded, having gone from zero-to-pissed that I'd kept something from her.

"I already saw the camera footage," Mr. Russo added.

Ariana came walking back in with a pair of low-hanging workout shorts on as she slipped a tank top over her head. "There," she said as if the clothes were already irritating her.

"No, *shh*," Stevie said quickly. "Hollis has explaining to do."

Amusement lit Ariana's eyes as she scooted back into her place and took the knife from me. "Someone's in trouble," she said under her breath, then louder, "Oh, is this why you've been moping?"

"I have not been moping."

"You have," she and Stevie said at the same time.

"Why do you think I've been making all your favorite foods this week?"

I thought back to the pasta we'd had last night and hesitantly asked, "Because you love me?"

She sent me a playful wink. “Always.”

“Hello,” Stevie cried out. “Can we go back to what wasn’t a big deal?”

With a sigh, I looked at Stevie. “That friend of Russell’s I told you about? He sort of showed up at Ampersand last week and got handsy. Again, not a big deal, I handled it,” I ended on a rush.

“The fuck he did and is still able to walk around,” she yelled, then pointed at me. “This was before you told me about him, wasn’t it? I can’t believe you didn’t tell me!”

“You *should* have told one of us,” Mr. Russo added, looking all kinds of enraged even though I knew his anger wasn’t directed at me. “If anything happens to you girls, you should feel comfortable enough to tell each other. If something happens in one of my stores . . .”

“I know, and I’m sorry. But I handled it.”

He dipped his head in acceptance. “And you did it well, but I don’t like that it happened at all. That’s why you girls stay in groups when you’re out that late.” He looked at Stevie. “Where were you?”

Stevie’s mouth parted, her stare shifting to the side to come up with an elaborate lie.

“I don’t want to know,” Mr. Russo said, lifting his hands as if he was trying to block out even the thought of where she might’ve been.

Ariana snorted, then asked, “You staying for brunch, Mr. R.?”

“Thank you, but I have to swing by Asterisk. Speaking of . . .” He pointed at the pastry bags and cups, then looked around. “Is Mia here?”

“She was only here for a couple minutes,” I answered. “She’s at work.”

"Asterisk?" he asked.

Ariana stayed silent, looking between Stevie and me.

"I don't know where she went," I said. "She just said she had more shifts today, but she didn't change."

"I only heard her leave," Stevie said with a shrug.

Mr. Russo hummed as he stepped away from the counter. "I was hoping to catch her here. She left a message, saying she needed to talk about her hours. Oh well, you girls be good," he said, but just as he began turning away, he stopped and pointed between the three of us. "Stay in groups at night. If something happens, tell each other or *call the police*, Hollis. If something happens in one of my stores, you tell me. Understood?"

"I understand," I said softly.

"I *can't* believe you kept this from me," Stevie scolded as soon as he left, and I sagged. "And bullshit about you handling it—if he's *been* doing it and if he still has reproductive appendages, then you aren't handling it."

"He's one of Russell's friends?" Ariana asked as she grabbed a platter for the fruit, continuing without waiting for me to confirm. "Does Russell know?"

"*I* don't even know which one it is," Stevie responded for me.

"I don't know his name either," I said defensively, then held my hand up high to show his height. "The tall one with the curly blond hair."

Her mouth dropped open wide. "*Chris?*" When I just lifted my hands to my sides helplessly, she pointed at me. "Rusted fucking forks."

"I know. I got it."

"First this, then you fail to mention how ungodly hot the love of my life and future ex-husband is *and* exactly how head over Louboutins you are over him." She scoffed. "Honestly, who are you?"

My stomach dipped as the encounters with Adam last week danced through my mind. "I'm pretty sure I did tell you," I said slowly. "Numerous times."

"Brunch," Ariana said pointedly. "Coffee getting cold. Argue at the table."

I grabbed mine and Ariana's pastries and coffees, stopping Stevie with a look when she opened her mouth. "I should've told you," I admitted when she forced her lips into a firm line. "I'm sorry."

She nodded in acceptance and moved past me to grab smaller plates for us.

Once we were all seated at the table, Ariana gestured between us with her fork but kept her eyes on me. "So, who's her supposed-future-baby-daddy that you're in love with?"

"I never—no—I'm not in love with him." I dropped my head into one of my hands and suppressed a groan. "The weekend was kind of a disaster, okay?" I rambled awkwardly.

"Um . . ." Stevie began, a coy smile crossing her face. "The last way I would describe dodging another lunch with your parents and finding Ampersand Guy is a *disaster*."

"Your parents were here?" Ariana asked, brows lifting as her shoulders shook with silent laughter.

"I don't know how that's funny," I said as I stabbed at a piece of melon. "I was trying not to panic for an entire twenty-four hours until I got the call from my mom that they had to fly back early."

"I'm sure you spent a lot of time panicking while obsessing over men who don't speak," Stevie goaded.

My chest ached with longing and a deep sadness that made no sense because I hardly knew Adam at all. "Except nothing's going to happen. So, let's just drop it," I begged softly.

"Yeah, see, you said that . . . but I still don't believe it." She waved a berry-covered fork at me and looked at Ariana. "You should've seen the way they looked at each other. You could *feel* their chemistry all throughout Asterisk."

Ariana's brows lifted with veiled interest before furrowing. "What did you mean when you said he doesn't speak?"

"He can't," I said slowly, trying to figure out her complex expression, as if she was figuring out a difficult problem. "He's non-verbal."

Her stare shifted from the table to me. "And you met him at Asterisk *when*?"

"No, no," Stevie said, practically bouncing in her seat even though I was horribly devastated over the entire thing. "She met him at *Ampersand* after our show on Saturday—well, technically, she met him there years ago." She waved a hand through the air as if that didn't matter. "Then we bumped into him again at Asterisk on Monday."

Ariana's head dipped slowly as she returned to her food, looking like she was fighting a smirk. "I didn't get to hear these stories. Tell me."

"There's no point—"

"Babe, chemistry," Stevie said adamantly. "Like, I got turned on watching the two of you looking at each other."

"You don't—" I hesitated, pressing my lips tightly together because I'd only told Stevie bits and pieces without actually revealing anything.

Not wanting to voice the confessions and vulnerabilities when we'd left everything so up in the air. Afraid if I did, I'd start getting my hopes up and would be devastated if he didn't reach out to me.

Turned out I was still devastated.

With a sigh, I dropped my fork and blurted out our entire conversations from Ampersand and Asterisk.

"One, holy shit. He really *is* New York Guy?" Stevie asked, making a spastic hand gesture as if she couldn't believe it. "That's Romeo-and-Juliet, soulmate type of shit."

"Not soulmates," I whispered as my stomach continued twisting uncomfortably.

She waved me off as if she didn't believe a word I said. "Two, I can't believe you've had sex with my future ex-husband. And three," she said, her voice lowering and dripping with curiosity as she leaned closer to me, "when he said he craves you, did you have an orgasm right—" She and Ariana broke into laughter when I shoved Stevie away. "It's an honest question. Have you seen him? He *craves you*, Hollis!"

My eyes rolled and I picked up my fork again, pushing the fruit around my plate. "I also haven't heard from him since, which is pretty telling."

Stevie's amusement faded immediately. "Wait, *what*?" She gave me a look like she was angry on my behalf—knowing Stevie, she was. "Nothing? Like . . . *at all*?"

I lifted my shoulders, a deep sigh leaving me.

"Moping," Ariana murmured. "Makes sense now."

A pathetic laugh tumbled past my lips. "It doesn't matter, right? Because I hardly know him."

"Babe," Stevie muttered as she leaned over to grab my hand. "Say the word, and I hate him. I know I've been the one trying to bring you back down to reality when it comes to him, but I was standing right there. I saw it. I felt it."

"I would've heard from him," I reminded her.

"I mean, maybe he has a busy job," she offered even

though she looked like she was struggling to find reasons for his silence.

"So, do I get to hear the Romeo and Juliet part of the story?" Ariana asked, leaning back in her chair with her pastry. "Or do I just get to guess at why we might hate him so much?"

"Oh, you totally need the story," Stevie said around a bite. "Both of them."

I started to object, but Ariana just gave me an expectant look. One of her slow smirks pulling at the corner of her mouth as she waited.

With a sigh, I thought back to New York. Wondering if everything would be different now if I'd never left that morning. "I was at a party I never should've been at, but he immediately caught my attention. He's contradictory in an incredibly intriguing way. . ."

Six

ADAM

"Adam!"

I looked up from where I was gripping my hair and forced a smile, trying to push aside the agitation and frustration I'd been drowning in the past week when I saw Ariana coming my way. Standing, I pulled her in for a quick hug as she said, "You actually showed."

I gave her a dry look and slipped my phone from my pocket to remind her of how she'd been hounding me for over an hour.

You've been texting me every few minutes to make sure I'd be here

She lifted her coffee and free hand as amusement tugged at her mouth, looking not at all apologetic. "It got you here, didn't it?"

. . .

You could've asked just once and I would've shown

Disbelief crossed her face. "Says the guy who's always holed up in his house because he lives like an old hermit. I never even see you anymore," she added. "It's been forever."

I rolled my eyes as I reclaimed my seat.

You and your sister are so dramatic

A soft laugh left her as she took the chair opposite me. "Well, considering I see Sarah and Leo at least once a week and it's been, what . . . *months* since I've seen you?" she asked even though her playful stare said she was already sure of her answer. "I'd say that's forever."

I shrugged.

Fair enough.

She took a sip of her drink, her expression lighting with excitement as she leaned closer. "Speaking of which—baby on the way. Crazy, right?"

I'd been working on maintaining my feigned excitement around Sarah all week, so it was nothing to continue smiling and nodding my head.

She cried last week because she wasn't sure if oranges wanted to be peeled

That should've been our first clue that she was pregnant

. . .

I gave her a dry look as she read and fought back a laugh when hers burst from her.

"Fair point," she said, trying to defend Sarah. "What if they *don't* want to be peeled?" She lifted her hands, palms out when I rolled my eyes. "Okay, okay, fine. But I'm excited for them. Then again,"—she gestured to herself—"babies are my specialty. And I'm obviously going to be the favorite."

You have an unfair advantage

"You become an L&D nurse and then try telling me that's unfair," she challenged, then mouthed, "Favorite." She smacked a hand close to me on the table and narrowed her eyes as if I'd been the one to get us off track. "But this is about you. What's up with you having history with my roommate and conveniently forgetting to tell me?"

Shit.

"Better question," she added quickly, leaning forward, "what are you doing leaving her hanging now?"

I exhaled roughly, my fingers twitching against my phone as my mind raced back six years to the night I'd met Hollis.

The girl who had so clearly not belonged in that place or at that party. The same one who'd said, *"Screw it,"* when offered a shot and about choked on the burning liquid. The one who'd danced around me all night as we'd been pulled in different directions. Hypnotic eyes finding me over and over before she'd marched right up to me and said, *"If I don't kiss you, I just might go out of my mind."*

And in the morning, the one who'd fucking *panicked*.

Hastily dressed while rambling, *"Oh my God. What did I do, what did I do? They're going to kill me if they find out—no one can find out,*" she'd claimed in one of the few moments she'd actually looked at me.

Maybe because each time she did look at me, she'd stop and waver as if she were going to take back everything she was saying and crawl into the bed beside me. Her sorrow practically bleeding from her and reaching out to me, mixing with that undeniable pull.

"I'm sorry, it's just that . . . well, I'm not this person, and I'm not someone who can do this." She'd gestured wildly around the room. *"Who can go to these kinds of parties and drink and have sex with people like you—not* like you, *that isn't what I meant. I just meant I'm not the kind of person who can have random sex with people I don't know. Oh my God,* what have I done?" Her voice had dropped to a hushed whisper on the last before she'd demanded, *"Aren't you going to say anything?"*

My throat had worked and constricted, straining as I'd lifted one of my arms helplessly. Looking around for my phone or a pen—anything—but she'd continued as she finished dressing.

"You know what? It doesn't matter. You clearly don't understand or care about the ramifications of what I've done, and I have to go." She'd hurried for the door, stopping once she reached it to look at me. Her worried and saddened eyes lingering on me for a while before she'd begged, *"Please forget last night. Forget you met me. Forget everything."*

And I'd just sat there, watching as she'd disappeared. Never once trying to stop her even though she'd plagued every thought for months after.

I blinked away the past and looked into Ariana's expectant gaze, struggling to remember her question before it came to me another moment later. But I was *leaving Hollis hanging* because I didn't have a choice. Because it was better if I wasn't directly *in* her life. And that wasn't something I could tell Ariana.

I couldn't tell Ariana anything at all because I wasn't even supposed to know who her roommate *was*.

Keeping my expression impassive, I hurried to respond and twisted the phone to show her the screen.

As much as I appreciate you coming at me like this
I don't know what the hell you're talking about

"That's nice, Adam," she muttered dryly. "If I'd known you had a line of women waiting for you, I would've told her not to waste her time with you."

A tic started in my jaw, but I kept up the pretenses.

Think you know me well enough to know that isn't true
I haven't slept with anyone since I moved here
So again
I don't know what the hell you're talking about

Her brows lifted as she took a long drink of her coffee, a mischievous glint to her eyes as she pulled out her own phone and began scrolling through it.

"And what if she isn't from L.A.?" she asked as she set her phone on the table, leaving a picture of her, Hollis, and Stevie on display.

My heart stuttered as I stared at the picture.

Looking at the girl who haunted my every thought.

The girl who was within my grasp and yet couldn't touch.

"Yeah, that," Ariana said, tapping just above Hollis on the screen. "Small fucking world, right? But I just found out about this a few hours ago, and I already want to hit you because my girl is seriously crazy about you, and you're just going to let her slip away."

I don't have a choice.

I picked up my phone, fingers flying across the screen before I tossed it onto the table and sat back in my chair. Rubbing my hands over my face and letting every ounce of my exhaustion and frustration with keeping myself from Hollis heave out in a sigh.

As much as I want to I can't let anything happen with her

I would destroy her without trying

She deserves someone so far from who I am

"Jesus, now who's the dramatic one?" she asked, offering me a wicked smirk as she picked up her iced coffee. "Sarah's peeled oranges have nothing on you today."

My head shook as I scooped up my phone and tapped out a response.

This is something you can't understand

But understand that it is best for Hollis if I'm not in her life

. . .

"Yeah, I call bullshit," she said, eyes narrowing in blatant challenge. "You're both miserable. You clearly have feelings for her that you're trying to bury. And in the years I've known Hollis, she's never really cared about a guy. But she cares about you."

My head continued shaking as I told myself I was doing the right thing. That I *needed* to forget her.

Because letting myself want Hollis? That was something I couldn't allow myself to do.

But with each chant, with each reminder of what I was doing, that voice got weaker and weaker as everything in me begged to go to the girl in the photo. To let her drive me crazy with that hesitant smile and her soft pleas.

Fuck.

I rubbed at my forehead and leaned forward to rest my elbow on the table as everything I knew and everything I wanted crashed together in a battle I was slowly breaking under.

"Well, if you're going to stick with this whole she-deserves-better thing, I guess I should tell Hollis she should move on."

I went still.

My stare snapped to the side when Ariana slid her phone from the table.

"Shouldn't be too hard for her. She's got guys lining up for her."

I slowly lifted my head, my jaw aching under the pressure I was putting on it.

She sent me a wry smirk as she settled deeper in her seat. "That's what I thought."

Seven

HOLLIS

I looked at the closed door of Ampersand for probably the thirtieth time in the ten minutes we'd been there and tried to ignore the disappointment swirling in my stomach.

Not that I'd expected Adam to show or that I would expect his wants to be different if he *did* since his silence was a very clear answer. Still, it was hard not to hope for him to appear while sitting in this place—I'd known telling Stevie about our conversations would get my hopes up.

I swallowed a sigh and looked at Stevie when she nudged me, chomping on a fry and staring at her phone as she spoke. "Ready to go?"

Glancing at the still-closed door again, that sigh slipped free. "Yeah, sure."

Stevie choked over a curse, her eyes widening as she hurried to put the phone on the table, face down.

"What—"

"I got an alert," she said, putting her lips close to my ear to keep her words soft.

"For me?"

When she nodded, worry clenched my stomach at the thought of whatever might've shown up.

Once I'd told Stevie about my parents and upbringing and life before Raven, she'd set it up to get alerts whenever my name crossed the internet. Thankfully, it wasn't often. And so far, nothing had ever had to do with Los Angeles or Raven, but I was sure the day would come.

"Raven?" I asked softly.

"No, but look . . ."

She slid her phone over to me, and I flipped it over. Holding it close so none of the other girls would see what we were looking at.

It was a Reddit thread with me as the subject.

Does anyone remember Senator Donahue's daughter????

I just remembered CT Senator Donahue had a daughter. I think her name was Holly? Maybe Hollis? She used to be in every picture with him and his wife and was in a relationship with some politician when she disappeared like years ago.

Strange. No?

—Maybe she got fat so they have to hide her from cameras.

——Or maybe she got older and told her stuffy parents she wasn't standing for photo ops anymore . . .

——No she FRFR was getting married to a NY senator or mayor or pope. But there was a major scandal around it. Or was that an actress? Shit I'm so high.

—I bet she's dead and it was sketchy so they covered it.

—Didn't she go to Julliard?

——Yup. Here's one of the articles about it.

———Pretty sure her parents got her in, but whatever. Privileged kids and all that.

————Someone's bitter.

———Then she's probably still there.

————That was years ago. Maybe there's a secret society at Julliard that's protecting her.

—————Yes . . . "secret society"

——————Codeword for dead.

———————I'm worried for the state of our world if this is our next generation . . .

It spiraled off into absurd conspiracy theories after that, and I breathed a sigh of relief as I handed Stevie's phone back to her.

"I'll watch it," she promised. "Ready to go?"

"Yeah," I muttered, feeling that well of disappointment grow.

"See you Monday, bitches," Stevie called out as we slid out of the booth, tossing a middle finger Jenny's way for good measure.

"Stevie," I murmured disapprovingly, pulling her away. "*Why* do you hate her so much?"

She made a face as if she had no idea what I was talking about, but still answered, "Because she sucks?"

"I know you, and I know how you react to people in all kinds of situations. You don't respond to people like this unless you feel threatened by them. Considering she isn't about to take your place on the stage, I have no idea what your deal is."

She snorted. "I am not threatened by that trash."

I stopped her just outside the door and lifted a brow when I heard the waver in her voice. "You're lying."

Stevie's stare darted to the side as if she was contemplating telling me or maintaining her story, and then fell to her phone when it chimed.

Just as she had before, her eyes widened and a curse fell from her lips as she pressed the phone to her stomach, looking as if she'd just seen something terrible.

"Is it another alert?"

"What?" Her head snapped to me, a crease forming between her brow. "No. Of course not."

"Then what's wrong?"

"Nothing," she murmured, stare drifting to the side as she began fidgeting with her phone.

"Stevie—"

"*Nothing.*"

"Okay, you're clearly lying. What was on your phone?"

She hesitated for a moment before admitting, "Russell," on a breath.

"Great," I said when she didn't elaborate. "It's been, what, over a week since you've seen him? That's long for the two of you."

"No, it isn't," she said quickly. "I wouldn't care if I saw him at all."

I gave her a knowing look. "You've been really defensive when it comes to how much you *don't* care about Russell lately."

"Because I don't," she said adamantly, but there was that waver in her voice again, the one that was her biggest tell. And from the way her shoulders sagged, she knew I heard it.

She glanced to the parking lot and then looked back at

me. "I said something last week, and I didn't mean to. It just came out."

"To Russell?" When Stevie just gave me a confirming look, I asked, "What'd you say?"

She sucked in a shaky breath, a look of panic flying across her face that told me all I needed to know.

"Oh my God, Stevie," I said softly. "You're in love with Russell?"

"I am not," she hissed. "I can't be because . . . because there's so much I want to do, and a guy would ruin that. So, *absolutely not*."

"Is that why he hasn't been around this week?" I asked cautiously. "Did saying that scare him?"

Her shoulders jerked up. "I told him to leave me alone. Besides, I doubt he cares either way. He'll probably just go back to Jenny," she mumbled, and my mouth popped open wide.

"*What?*"

Stevie's eyes rolled even though she looked more insecure at that moment than I'd ever seen her. "They dated, like, all throughout college or something. Whatever, it doesn't matter." She looked at me and lifted her hands. "It doesn't matter because I don't care about him. Right? Right. Let's go."

"Right," I mumbled and followed after her as she charged across the parking lot.

"Why are we even wasting our breath talking about boys who don't matter?" Stevie asked as we slid into her car. "Can we please talk about how you killed Krystle's number tonight? I'm pretty sure every person in the building fell in love with you." She huffed. "I think I fell in love with you."

I rolled my eyes even though performing that routine off

the cuff had given me such a high. "Well, it was only for one night, so . . ."

"Yeah, I doubt they'll give the number back to her after seeing you do it."

"It's Krystle's routine," I reminded her. "She came up with it."

"Yeah, and she randomly disappears for days at a time because she's found a new guy to sink her teeth into. And the days she is there, she's looking for the next," Stevie argued. "Losing that routine to you is the least of it—she's going to find herself without a job soon."

I think I hummed in agreement, but my mind had already gone back to the loop it'd been playing for the past week . . .

To that night we'd walked into Ampersand to find Adam there—more handsome than my dreams remembered. To the night two years before in the same place—stealing my breath and teasing me with memories of when I'd met him.

A night that never should've happened.

A party I never should've been at.

A guy I never should've looked twice at for so many reasons . . .

Some friends and I had been dragged to the party in a part of New York I'd never seen, and found ourselves surrounded in illicit substances and whispers of criminal dealings. Throughout trying not to hear things I was sure I shouldn't, struggling not to breathe in the tainted air, and desperately trying to avoid a panic attack, he'd continuously captured my attention.

Absurdly handsome and contradictory in the most captivating way with his thick-framed glasses and his absolutely terrifying demeanor.

Except he'd belonged there. It'd been clear in the dangerous energy pulsing from him.

And me? I'd belonged far, far away at a social dinner. With a fake smile for the cameras and trying to appease my indifferent parents. Continuing down the path they'd laid out for me long ago and doing everything to help my father's political career in way of securing my relationship to a young, ambitious, *insufferable* mayor of the *oh-so-charming* New York town I didn't give a shit about.

Instead, I'd given in to that energy pulsing between us, growing thicker with each passing minute. I'd done something for me for the first time in my life.

I'd drank a little and kissed the dangerous guy who made my heart beat all kinds of erratically. I'd been careless in my desperate need for him, unable to part from him for more than a few breaths as he'd taken me back to his place. And then I'd let him take me to bed, forgetting everything but him and the way he made me feel.

What we felt like together.

How the world fell away when he touched me.

Until the next morning when I'd been slammed with the reality of my life—of my place on my parents' path. How I'd risked so much by ignoring my responsibilities for the first time. How I could've thrown away what I'd worked tirelessly toward with one thoughtless night of passion.

"Hollis."

My head snapped to the side and then around to look out the car windows when I realized Stevie was standing outside it, holding onto the driver's door.

"I've only said your name a million times . . . you coming?"

"Yeah," I said, the word coming out weak as I forced away the encounters with Adam and got out of the car.

Lazily following behind as she rambled about how she didn't know why she'd even slept with Russell again after finding out he'd dated Jenny because she was no one's sloppy seconds and absolutely *not* into Russell anyway.

"Are you even listening?" she asked as we entered the house.

I hummed unconvincingly. "Yeah, you're in love with Russell."

"You slut," she said on a horrified gasp, then grabbed my arm, her feigned anger slipping away instantly. "Seriously, are you going to be okay?"

I mumbled some sort of agreement as we rounded the corner out of the entryway and into the living room—and my heart went absolutely wild.

Taking off in a sprint at the sight of him standing from where he'd been on one of the couches with Ariana. Apprehension rolling off him and mixing with that cautionary energy that always clung to him.

He roughed a hand through his black hair, the corner of his mouth falling into the barest hint of a frown as he studied me. His dark eyes locked on me even as he took his phone from Ariana and began sliding his finger across the screen.

"I know we're mad at him, but can you get pregnant from looking at someone?" Stevie asked a little breathless.

I didn't respond.

I was too focused on trying to decode the harsh set of his expression and how restless he seemed even when standing still.

When he lifted his phone, I released a sigh and hesitantly looked at it.

. . .

Can we talk

"Nice try, but no," Stevie said with a scoff. "I had high hopes for you, baby daddy, but you're looking at my girl like you're about to break her heart. So that makes me want to hurt you almost as badly as I want to climb you like a tree."

"Stevie," I muttered and lowered my head into my hand as Ariana choked over a laugh.

"Maybe you should let them talk," Ariana suggested.

"Then talk," Stevie shot back.

"Stevie." I lifted my head and shook it meaningfully at her before meeting Adam's stare.

All that old pain mixing with a worrying amount of unease.

Just as I was about to respond to Adam, my head jerked back and I looked between him and Ariana. "Wait, how are you here?"

"Right?" Ariana asked, amusement dancing across her face. "Small world, dude. Imagine my surprise when you started talking about Adam this morning. Adam,"—she clapped his shoulder—"who is Sarah's boyfriend's roommate."

"No shit," Stevie whispered.

My lips parted as shock swirled through me. The coincidence stunning me for a moment before Ariana went on.

"And he wants to talk to you."

"Right," I whispered, studying the way he was watching me. Waiting for what I would do. Releasing a sigh, I started stepping away, nodding toward the long hall. "So, let's talk."

After a few feet, I looked back at him and asked, "Is this the kind of talk where you'd like to have a quick getaway? Should we be outside for it?"

He worked his jaw for a moment before offering me a brief smile as his stare fell to his phone.

That really depends on you

I studied the words for a while before continuing away from him and through the house to where my room sat on the far side of the second floor. My stomach twisting and turning and my body begging me to look at him the entire way.

But I continued staring straight ahead until I was in my room and setting my bag down.

When I finally turned, Adam was right there. Filling the space of my room the way he'd filled every thought and dream for years.

So large and consuming with all that danger and mystery and pain.

Straightening my back, I tried desperately to hold onto some sense of indifference when I said, "Considering you never used my number, I have a feeling you're only here because Ariana confronted you, and I'm seriously regretting telling her anything now. And like Stevie said, you don't look like you're about to deliver good news . . . so, why are you here, Adam?"

His expression creased uncomfortably even though his eyes stayed locked on mine for a few tense moments before falling. Everything about him and the way he tapped out his next words was all hesitation and pain.

. . .

I needed to see you when I said this

When I glanced back at Adam, his throat bobbed from his forced swallow.

My lips parted but no words came out, so I just nodded for him to go on and wrapped my arms tightly around my waist as that twisting in my stomach grew more intense.

I studied the frustrated lines of his face as he typed. The way he worked his jaw. The way his movements would go from slow and cautious to quick and angry and back again.

And it all had me so afraid when he finally handed me his phone.

What you said

The pulling you closer and pushing you away

I can't stop that

Hollis I've spent my entire life pushing people away because caring about anyone was always a weakness I couldn't afford

And now my life just doesn't allow for it

But you

Fuck you terrify me because like you said I pull you close and I've never wanted to pull anyone closer in my life

And every time I tell myself to push you further I find myself doing the opposite

So I will continue pushing you away because that's who I am

Because I know I need to

But you're all I think about

You're all I want

My tongue darted out to wet my lips as my heart and mind raced.

One screaming that he was once again making me melt while pushing—that he was admitting he would continue doing the same. The other hushing every doubt and worry.

"Why doesn't your life allow it?" I finally asked when I looked up at him.

Something dark crept across his face when he took the phone back and offered a quick response.

It's complicated

Right.

I sighed as unease wound through me. "I remember what the people were like that night in New York. I remember the things they were doing and the things they were talking about. And I don't know what you're mixed up in, but I have a feeling whatever made you say all that isn't because of the people you surrounded yourself with. It's something deeper. I—"

I swallowed back the knot in my throat and let out a soft laugh because I was about to embarrass the hell out of myself. "Adam, I see it in your eyes. There's a deep pain there, and I feel like that pain has a lot to do with why you push people away."

For a long time, he just stood there watching me. Dark

eyes narrowed on me and completely unreadable until he dipped his head in the barest hint of a nod.

"Okay." The word fell from my lips on an exhale as I continued searching his hardened stare. The worry and pain mixing with a deep sense of longing and contradicting all that danger rolling from him.

Just as he had all those years ago, everything about him wholly captivated me. Made my heart beat erratically and had wings taking flight in my stomach. Made it hard to breathe.

And he was telling me what he wanted.

He was laying out his faults and asking if I could handle them . . .

But I'd been waiting for this moment for years, there was no question of if I wanted this chance with him. I'd take this chance with him again and again, so long as he wanted it too.

Reaching out, I took his phone and locked it. "Adam, if you don't kiss me, I just might—"

He crushed his mouth to mine, stealing my words and swallowing the soft whimper that climbed up my throat. One of his hands weaving into my hair as the other curled around my waist. The touch familiar and somehow new and making my body come alive as we poured these years and frustration and need into that kiss. All teasing tongues and torturous bites and demanding lips.

A stunned laugh broke free when we stumbled over my bag as he led me back, and then he was capturing my mouth for another brief kiss before pressing me to the wall. His powerful gaze shaking my soul and sending a tendril of heat through my core as he studied me.

With a sigh, he brought his hand down to where mine rested on his harshly moving chest, and then his brow furrowed as his stare fell to look there and then around for his phone . . . that I no longer had.

"Um, I think I dropped it. I'm sorry."

A soft smile flashed across his face, his fingers gripping my waist tighter before he released me to retrieve it from the floor.

And I just stood there, trying desperately to prepare myself for him to already start pushing me away. To tell myself that I had to be okay with it because he'd warned me, and I'd said I could handle it.

By the time he'd returned to me with his phone extended, I had my jaw clenched tight and a smile in place so I wouldn't ask him to stay. But before I could read what he'd written, he pulled the phone back to type something else and then held it out to me, finger pointing to the bottom.

Why do you look like this

I glanced up to find his eyebrows drawn together in confusion and worry as all that dark energy pulsed off him. "What?"

He straightened his spine and pulled his shoulders back to mimic my stance, then gestured to where I had my arms wrapped tightly around my waist.

"I'm just standing."

He made a sound that was clearly disbelief and quickly swiped his finger over the screen.

You're uncomfortable

. . .

"I—" A frustrated noise caught in my throat as I conceded. "I just wasn't expecting you to leave so soon and especially *then*. It just seemed to be going—it doesn't matter. You told me you're going to do this, and that's fine. I'm fine. I'm just standing."

Amusement slowly wove through all that dark warning. After a moment, he nodded and scrolled up on the screen so I could read what he'd originally written.

I can easily get lost in you

We already know that

But I'm not going to make the same mistake with you Hollis

I don't want to wake up tomorrow to you panicking and leaving

I'd like to get to know you

So how about we talk

"Oh," I breathed, my stare lingering on the words a little longer. My heart racing in a way that was becoming exceedingly familiar with Adam. "Technically, you're at my house. So, even if I left, I'd have to come back." The words were all a hesitant tease and earned a smile from him. "But I'd love to talk."

He captured my mouth for a slow kiss. Pressing me harder and harder against the wall and making my knees weak and head spin until he pulled away just enough to slant his eyes to the side to glance at his phone.

. . .

We need to leave this room

My chest shook with a hushed laugh. "Okay then."

He grabbed my hand when I slid out from between him and the wall to stop me, then released me to mimic typing on a keyboard.

"A computer?" When he nodded, I gestured over to my desk. "My laptop's over there."

He took a step that way and held up his phone, the look on his face all question in a way that screamed indifference even though nothing about Adam said *indifference*.

His stature gave the impression that he would only wreak havoc, destroying everything in his path. But each of his movements had a calm, terrifying sort of deliberation to them as if he was innately aware of the ripple effect our actions caused. All while that energy and those tortured eyes hinted at a darker past.

"I don't . . ." Confusion filled me, slowing my words. "You want my laptop?"

It's easier
Faster
But it doesn't matter either way

I glanced from the screen to him and then over to my laptop, taking far too long to understand *why*. "Oh, to talk?" I realized just as he waved a hand through the air, dismissing it. “Of course.” I hurried across the room to gather it up for him, feeling like an idiot as humiliation swept over me.

In a hollow attempt to move right past my embarrassing moment, I asked, “So, what’s Poison?” when I turned to face him.

His eyebrows drew close in confusion until I pointed at his shirt, and then he was looking at me in utter shock.

“Is it a brand or something?”

Adam made some kind of move that was so not deliberate or calm, showing just how badly I’d stunned him, and hurried to pull up his phone.

Sorry what

“Um . . . your shirt. It says ‘Poison’ . . .” I trailed off when he began typing again.

Right

What do you mean WHAT’S POISON

“I feel like there’s a wrong answer here.”

How do you not know Poison

. . .

An embarrassed laugh crawled up my throat, and I placed a hand over one of my burning cheeks. "I don't know, what is it?"

Not what Hollis
Who
Come on I'll educate you

The corner of his mouth twitched into an amused smirk, the sight of it making my heart take off in all that wild chaos as he slipped his free hand into mine and led me from my room.

Eight

ADAM

"Want something to drink?" Hollis asked as she placed the laptop on the long breakfast bar and slipped away from me, mint green eyes finding me over her shoulder as she waited for an answer.

When I shook my head, she continued deeper into the kitchen. Her spine straight and shoulders back as she went from the cupboards to the sink, but this wasn't the stiff, uncomfortable girl I'd met in New York.

Her movements were all easy grace. Light and free in a captivating mixture of the girl from six years ago and the one who'd been consuming my mind this past week.

My stare pulled down when she pressed the point of her shoe flat to the floor and started pushing up on the toes of her other foot before dropping back down when she turned off the water.

"You sure you don't want anything?" she asked as she started my way, faltering when she noted my expression. "What?"

. . .

You dance

Her eyes widened in surprise and mischief as she read the words and leaned a hip against the counter. "Ariana told you?"

I listed my head as I tapped out a response.

In New York, Hollis's perfect posture and the way it'd looked like she was trying to hold herself together had screamed her unease with the situation. But I'd been sure that stance had everything to do with the money she'd been dripping in—whatever her upbringing had been. I hadn't seen it for what it was until long after.

Just watching you

"Oh," she said softly, and I felt my heart go wild at the slant of her lips.

All hesitation.

The girl so fucking beautiful that it took every effort not to close the distance between us.

She glanced around, a whisper of wonder touching her face as if she wasn't sure what she'd done or what I might've seen, before a soft laugh slipped free. "Well, yes, I dance." She lifted a shoulder in a shrug as if it wasn't a big deal and grabbed her laptop. "And what is it you do?"

I gestured to her computer, and she made an apologetic face.

"Okay, sorry. I'll wait."

My chest pitched with a laugh, but I just let her lead the

way to the large, open-spaced living room, already getting a note ready for when she settled on one of the couches.

She took my phone when I offered it and let her face fall into her palm a few seconds later when she read what I'd written.

I was telling you what I do
Computers
Coding
That's the extent of my exciting life

I watched as she lifted her head, somehow already knowing her lips would be tilted in that same hesitant smile I'd dreamt of for years. "Oh my God, Adam—" She sucked in a soft gasp, her eyes widening and voice lowering. "Wait, are you a hacker?"

No it's all legit

In a way, I mentally added when I handed my phone back to her and slowly took her laptop, giving her the chance to stop me.

"Oh, sorry. I have a password on . . ."

I looked over at her in time to see her lips part in surprise as she stared at the unlocked screen of her computer.

She blinked slowly and then shook her head. "I thought you said you weren't a hacker."

I shrugged and sliced my hand through the air, letting her know I wasn't. Technically.

"Do I want to know what you're doing?" she asked carefully a moment later.

Taking my phone from her hand, I tapped out a quick response before giving it back to her.

I don't want to make you uncomfortable because I'm on your computer

So I'm getting on mine

"You're getting on . . . yeah, okay," she said softly. "I'm going to pretend I believe that you aren't a hacker."

I flashed her a smile before going back to getting through my firewalls.

Not that anyone else could get past them. I just left doors for myself in case I needed to access my system . . . like now.

Once I was in, I pulled up a note and typed out a response to her.

Not a hacker.

A stunned laugh tumbled past her lips and her eyes narrowed playfully. "So those nerdy glasses weren't just a look you were going for?"

My shoulders shook with a laugh.

. . .

Not remotely. I still wear them when I work.

"Really?" Her eyes brightened with excitement. "I liked them."

Is that right?

Blood rushed to her cheeks, and from the look in her eyes, her mind had gone back to New York the same as mine. "So, what is it you do?"

I already told you what I do.

Computers and codes.

"Right, except you aren't a hacker, and that doesn't actually tell me anything," she said with a deadpan expression as she settled deeper into the couch and closer to me.

And fuck if I didn't like her right there, pressed close.

Information security analyst.

Her brows lifted and her head moved in a slow nod before shaking. "Okay, well, I don't know what that is."

. . .

I set up network security for businesses and organizations and help protect their systems from cyberattacks.

"Really?" she asked, sounding impressed. "And how'd you get into all this?"

It'd been something that started off as a hobby when I was a teen to escape my home life. One thing had led to another, and before I knew it, I'd started edging into the illegal side of hacking until Leo found me and turned my life around.

But I couldn't tell Hollis that . . .

I was bored one day and decided to figure it out.

She watched me for a while as if waiting for me to tell her the truth, then her eyes widened. "Seriously?"

Seriously. How'd you learn to sign?

"That was embarrassing," she said on a groan and then released a sigh. "Nothing as cool as *figuring it out*. It was just a class I took growing up."

Disbelief built in my chest at the way she quickly tossed out the last part as if wanting to move past it, but she continued on.

"Can I ask something that might be offensive?"

A smile tugged at the corner of my mouth as I studied the

blush already steadily filling her cheeks at just the thought of whatever she wanted to ask.

You're not going to offend me.

"You don't know that," she whispered and then took a steadying breath. "Why didn't you learn to sign? Wouldn't it have been easier?"

Jesus, you sure know how to offend a guy.

She pressed closer to my side, gripping my arm as embarrassed heat filled her checks. "Oh my God, I'm—" Confusion and wonder filled her expression when she realized I was laughing, and after a moment, she sat back and smacked my shoulder. "Adam!"

I flashed her an apologetic grin even though the brief distraction had given me a second to think about what to say to her—what all I was *willing* to give her.

And finally offered her the smallest portion of the truth as I had with everything else.

Learning to sign wasn't an option given to me.

"Oh, Adam," she whispered. "I'm so sorry."

My head was already shaking and my fingers moving before she finished speaking.

Don't be. Besides, not everyone knows how to sign, but nearly everyone can read. And I got really fast at writing things out for people. When I got a smartphone? Holy shit. Game changer.

A soft laugh moved through her. The corner of her mouth lifting even though she still looked sad. "I can imagine it was."

I hated that look on her face because the last thing I wanted from anyone was for them to be sad for me. But I also wasn't ready to go deeper into that part of my life with her. To explain *why*.

So, I went into my music and turned on *Nothin' But A Good Time* by Poison to lead us into safer territory.

"What's this?" she asked as I switched back to the notes.

Poison

Her eyes widened in understanding before she sat back a little. "Wait, it's a band?"

One of the best classic rock bands, and there's no way you've never heard this song.

. . .

Her face scrunched up adorably as she listened for a moment, her head slowly shaking. "Yeah, I have no idea who this is. But I've never really listened to rock either."

We can't all be perfect.

Her chest pitched with a sharp laugh. "Wow, thanks. I'm glad my musical knowledge determines that."

I tried not to let it show how much I liked the way she fell back into my side as if the action was natural and comfortable. Just fought the smile tugging at my mouth and let my fingers drift over the keyboard.

You really haven't ever listened to rock?

A hum sounded in her throat. "No. I wasn't allowed to listen to anything other than classical music growing up," she said, the admission coming out soft and fast and shamed. "I just started branching out a couple years ago."

I kept my stare on her as I typed out the word 'Classical,' the curiosity practically pouring from me.

"Uh, yeah." She shifted uncomfortably, her shoulders pulling back. "My parents had a lot of control over my life—you know, it's kind of a thing I don't really get into."

Understood.

Then why don't you tell me why you deleted your social media?

She hesitated, face full of indecision for long moments before she released a sharp breath and moved away so she was facing me, legs tucked under her and eyes locked on mine. "An opportunity was presented to me the night I first ran into you here in L.A. Where I work now," she clarified, nodding a little as she did. "But in taking that job, I couldn't continue being the girl I'd been raised to be, and I couldn't let people connect my job *to* that girl." Her brow furrowed. "Does that make sense?"

As rushed and twisted as her ramble had been, it did.

More than she understood.

"And I could very easily be connected to so much—too much," she went on when I nodded. "And I just . . . I needed to disappear from all that."

I studied the weight that had settled on her shoulders and let a teasing grin tug at the corner of my mouth as my fingers moved across the keys.

Connected to too much . . . we talking Goodfellas or . . .

A stunned laugh left her, easing all that burden in an instant. Her eyes rolled and her mouth twitched with amusement. "No, not at all. Just . . . my parents," she said in way of explanation, then swallowed forcefully as if choking back whatever else she'd been about to say.

Her parents were clearly off-limits.

Then again, her life seemed to be one big thing she didn't want to talk about, not that I'd expected anything less. Not that I could exactly fault her for that. My life was something I couldn't talk about . . . ever.

People needed to have their secrets.

Still, there was so much about Hollis that I didn't know, and I wanted whatever she would give me.

Do you like your job if you have to hide who you are?

Her eyebrows drew close as if my question surprised her. "I, uh . . ." A sharp breath burst from her. "I don't think I've ever thought of it that way." Her stare fell to the side for a moment, gaze distant before she focused on me. "When there's a chance of someone finding me there, I worry over it. But I've honestly never felt freer than I have the last two years. Taking that job, finding Stevie and living in this house, saved me. I feel like I'm finally living for me instead of someone else."

She inhaled quickly, her eyes widening and cheeks staining red. "And that was really probably more than you wanted to know. Sorry, *yes*. That's the answer to your question. I love my job."

I reached out to touch the heat radiating from her cheek and searched her eyes as words gathered and choked me. That familiar fear and guilt and loathing racing through my veins until I shoved it all back and reached for the keys instead.

. . .

You don't have to tell me anything you don't want to. But I think we're long past giving veiled versions of the truth, don't you?

At her grateful smile, I went on.

So, what is your job?

"I—" Her smile faltered, and she made a face as if trying to remember something. "I thought we talked about this. I dance."

Even though I was already well aware of where she worked, 'I dance' could mean just as many things as 'computers and coding.' And I had to be careful with what I already knew of her—the ground beneath us wasn't as unsteady if I pretended not to know her at all.

Ballet?

"No." Her response was immediate and cold, but she recovered quickly. Excitement lighting in her eyes and that hesitant smile pulling at her lips when she said, "I'm actually a burlesque dancer."

Really?

. . .

"Yes, really. What?" she asked, a soft laugh tumbling free as her stare bounced all around my face, taking in my expression.

I just shrugged and fought a smile as I typed.

Trying to picture New York you dancing burlesque.

A humming sound rose in her throat. "Definitely wouldn't have ever happened."

Is this something I'll get to see someday?

Her smile slipped a little and then fixed into place, and I hurried to continue.

I'll take that look as a no.

"No, you can do whatever you want," she said quickly, head bobbing faintly. "If you want to go to a show, you should." I gave her a disbelieving look, and she relented with a sigh. "I just have this thing about guys who come to the club—I refuse to date them."

We're dating?

. . .

"No!" Her eyes widened with mortification and she scrambled to backtrack. "That isn't what I meant, I just—guys who come to the—I don't—*Adam,*" she said, all exasperation and accusation when she saw the smile I was fighting.

Jesus Christ, I liked the way she said my name, and it scared the shit out of me. Because it made me want all those things I'd been fighting.

Made me want to pull her closer and keep her there. Not just tonight. Not just physically.

I wanted her in my life. I wanted the way that hesitant smile did the craziest things to me. I wanted the way she forced my heart to beat in a way that was all kinds of unfamiliar and frenzied and addicting.

I wanted *her*.

But letting myself be with her, letting myself *have* her, would be the cruelest, most selfish thing I'd ever done.

I was sure of it.

"If you want to go, you should," she repeated with a feigned glare. "Just do me a favor and don't tell me if you decide to go."

And why's that?

Fuck, there it was.

All soft hesitation and sending my heart into a frenzy.

"I'm not sure I'd be able to focus on anything other than the fact that you were there."

Is that why you don't date guys who go there?

. . .

Her stare danced over my face before darting away. "No."

Just *no*.

But the blush darkening her cheeks again told me enough.

I like this . . .

The corner of her mouth lifted in curiosity as she read the words. "What?"

I waited until her attention pulled back to me before lifting my hand to brush my fingers across her cheek again. Eyes tracking the movement and taking in the heat still warming them.

She placed her hand on my forearm, the touch gentle yet claiming. Telling me in the soft way she clung to me just how much she liked *this*, how much she wanted me to *stay*.

"Keep saying the things you have been tonight, and I'm likely to forget that you want to push me away."

My head dipped in agreement.

We were in dangerous territory, no doubt.

"Okay, I didn't want to do this to you so early on," she began when I lowered my hand to her thigh, words full of warning. "I really don't want to scare you off or anything, but it's time I ask you something important." When I lifted an eyebrow in question, she blew out a slow breath and pinned me with a grave look. "How do you feel about pineapple on pizza?"

My chest pitched with a laugh, and I used my free hand to respond.

. . .

Oh God. That . . . that's really serious, Hollis. We barely know each other. I don't know if I'm ready for this kind of commitment.

She let her mouth tick up. "That depends on your definition of 'knowing' each other."

My fingers flexed on her thigh at the memory. At the energy that sparked back to life at the mention of that night.

Begging us to pick right back up where we'd left off. Begging me to touch and taste and hear the way she moaned—

Fuck.

I ignored the need coursing through my veins and let my left hand drift across the keyboard.

Definitely doesn't belong on pizza. I'm a pepperoni and black olive kind of guy.

"Okay, did Ariana already tell you that?" she asked dejectedly. When I gave her a confused look, she gestured to the screen but didn't take her stare from me. "They all hate olives, so I always get the pizza to myself."

She hadn't.

But you don't get them to yourself anymore.

. . .

Her eyebrows lifted in wonder and surprise, but she didn't comment on how my words had once again negated that deep-rooted need to keep her far away from me. Just leaned against the back of the couch as her fingers trailed down to weave through my own.

Since we're getting into the real heavy and deep stuff, I need to know if you know this song.

A breath of a giggle left her and ended on a cautious groan. "I feel like I'm losing major points with the music department, so can we go back to the fact that we like the same pizza?" she asked after listening for a moment.

My shoulders shook with amusement as I typed out a response.

It's blowing my mind that you've never heard these. It's Metal Health by Quiet Riot.

Her head started moving in a slow shake, her face scrunched up in apology before she gasped in excitement. "Oh! You were wearing a Quiet Riot shirt the other night at Ampersand."

Curiosity tugged at the corner of my mouth.

I had no idea how she knew that. Not that I doubted it—half my wardrobe consisted of old band and concert shirts—but I couldn't remember what I'd been wearing yesterday.

. . .

So, this thing with my shirts. Is it a fetish I need to be worried about or . . .

She buried her face in her hands as a silent laugh rocked through her body. "I'm going to crawl in a hole now," she mumbled when I squeezed her thigh teasingly.

Or you can tell me why you moved to California.

She blew out a deep sigh and sent me a mocking glare before letting her eyes shift to the screen. And I saw it—the way she stilled and the edges of her mouth pulled down in a whisper of a frown. The way it looked like she was searching for the right way to phrase it.

Lie about it.

Then offered me a smile and a portion of the truth the way I'd already done so many times tonight. "For a job." She lifted one of her shoulders. "Not the one I'm at, obviously. But it led me there, so I'm thankful for it." She curled her hand around mine again and asked, "And what about you? How did we both end up in a diner on Sunset Boulevard?"

Easy answer? Leo and I had just moved out here. We'd been working all day and were getting really fucking tired of fast food.

. . .

Her eyes flashed to mine, searching and searching for hidden truths there. "And the hard answer? How did you end up in L.A.?"

Years of tireless work and numerous cities flashed through my mind in broken pieces and blurs. All leading to this moment . . . with *her*.

I gave her the same forced smile as I tapped along the keys.

My job.

Nine

HOLLIS

I jolted awake when the space next to my head dipped and threw my hand out to catch myself when the abrupt shift made me think I was falling.

"Tell me *everything*."

I blinked quickly and looked around as I tried to orient myself because I wasn't in my room, Stevie was perky even though it was morning, and the scent of coffee was near me.

And Stevie was perky . . . in the *morning*.

"What is going on?" I asked, voice groggy from sleep as I rolled back and finally realized I was on the couch, and Stevie literally had a mug of coffee directly beneath my face.

"I made you this," she said with a wave of the mug for emphasis. "The least you could do is start talking."

I pushed at her arm and straightened to sitting as I gave her a look. "What happened to you, and where's the real Stevie?"

"Um . . . we so do not have time for body-snatcher questions when you're holding out on me." She handed me the coffee, carefully curling both my hands around it to make sure I wasn't going to drop it. "Ariana came bursting into my room this morning to let me know you and my baby daddy were asleep. Together. *Right here.*"

I sucked in a quick breath as everything from last night and this morning came rushing back. I wasn't sure when Adam and I had fallen asleep, only that I hadn't wanted that time to end.

Talking with him long after the sky had started turning gray and then purple outside. Our conversation that had easily moved between fun and harmless interrogations and deeper questions that'd left us both sidestepping pasts and offering as much of the truth as we were ready to share.

Clearly, I wasn't the only one with secrets.

But from the way he'd started holding onto me and then pulling me closer, from the way his stare had continuously danced over me, I'd known I hadn't imagined and romanticized the connection between us in New York. I wasn't the only one still wrapped up in the other.

I'd felt every bit of his adoration and longing and need intertwined in all that reluctance, and I'd embraced it. Sure that, whatever the root behind his pain, he'd tell me when he was ready, and we'd work through it.

And, God, that kiss . . .

Except, he was already gone.

I glanced around the living room, skipping over where my laptop sat on the coffee table, and asked, "Where is—*wait*." My attention snapped back to Stevie. "How exactly did Ariana wake you up without dumping a vat of coffee in your room?"

She held up a hand. "Honey, she said you and my baby daddy were asleep on the couch. Do you know how fast that pulled me from sleep?"

My expression deadpanned as I thought of the numerous attempts at waking her over the past two years. "So, how long do you think this whole 'baby daddy' thing is going to last?" I asked as I glanced around again, my mouth pulling into a frown when I only saw Ariana making breakfast in the kitchen.

"Oh, forever. No doubt. But do you see the way he looks at you?"

My stare shifted back to Stevie. "What do you mean?"

"Hollis . . . last night, it was like he didn't even notice us. It was just you." She made a dreamy look and sighed. "Like, *swoon*. Freaking Romeo and Juliet. Now, spill on everything that happened last night and how the two of you ended up all cozy and freaking adorable out here and not in your bed, and don't you dare leave a single detail out."

My mouth parted, but I didn't have a chance to play down our night before an unexpected voice said, "Oh, you're up!"

I glanced to the side and blinked in surprise when Ariana's sister came walking out of one of the halls. "Hi," I said on a delay.

"Sorry for ruining your morning," Sarah said, her face scrunching with apology. "I just wasn't expecting to see Adam when I stopped by, and I think I might've freaked him out."

"Well, you were crying," Ariana said, voice all amusement. "You imagine waking up to a crying woman standing over you."

"I have *no* control over my emotions right now," Sarah shot back defensively.

"Why are we crying?" Stevie asked, voice soft.

"Um . . ." My tongue darted out to wet my lips, my head

slowly shaking as I looked between Ariana and Sarah. "I don't know."

"I fully get it, and I'm here for you. Always," Ariana said as if she'd already said it once this morning. "But put yourself in his shoes. He woke up to some crazy person, standing over him and crying."

Sarah huffed in frustration, looking like she just might start crying again when she said, "*Zero* control. I just got really excited, okay." She looked at me, hands raised placatingly. "I'm sorry. Adam's never shown interest in anyone or even in the idea of dating. So, to find him here with you this morning was really exciting for me."

"See?" Stevie said, shoving at my shoulder.

My lips started pulling into a smile, but I reached forward, sucking in a sharp inhale when I saw a piece of paper sticking out of my laptop. I slipped it out, my heart kicking up in pace when I saw the masculine scrawl.

I'm not panicking and bolting, I just have to leave.

Pizza with olives tonight? Unless it's too soon to share a pizza.

I get it. That's an intimate experience. Not sharing food, just eating pizza. I mean, I would fight you for the last slice . . .

By the way, I pulled up another band for you to listen to.

I set down my coffee and hurried to wake up my laptop. Wondering again how he'd managed to get through my password in a matter of seconds and deciding it was probably best if I didn't know.

"I approve, I approve, I app—*no*," Stevie said just as my stare caught on my music app, where he had Foreigner ready to play. "He likes *olives*?"

I snatched the note away from her and held it close to my chest, not realizing until she was pointing at my face and smiling widely at me that my lips were stretched into an uncontrollable grin.

"You still owe me details."

"I would like breakfast first," I said as I closed the laptop and scooped up my mug as I stood from the couch.

"You know how impatient I am," she complained as she followed me to the kitchen . . . and right into a conversation I wished I hadn't heard.

". . . that isn't possible," Sarah said from where she was gathering plates for us.

Ariana scoffed, the sound all offense. "Okay, except Hollis told me how they met."

"Then she's lying. Adam never—" Sarah's expression fell when she turned and saw us standing there. "Hollis, hi." Her head shook quickly as she looked from Ariana back to me. "I'm so sorry, I didn't know you were there."

"Right." I cleared my throat, my head bobbing awkwardly. "No, it's uh . . . it's fine."

"Jesus, Sarah," Ariana muttered, then asked me, "Didn't you say you first met Adam in New York?"

"Ari," Sarah hissed, shooting her a look to drop it, but Ariana ignored her.

I looked between them before nodding, the action hesitant. "Yeah. Yeah, about six years ago."

"Crazy, right?" Stevie asked. "I've been trying to bring Hollis back to reality for years because there was no way the two guys she was telling me about were the same person. But

Hollis here apparently has soulmate-style history with that piece of yum."

"Not soulmates," I reminded her even though my entire being claimed otherwise.

"Okay, nega-Shakespeare. You're not the one telling the story," Stevie said, swatting at me before launching into my entire history with Adam as if she'd lived it all.

Considering how many times I'd told her about it, she basically had.

And I just stood there, listening while Ariana dished up breakfast. Never once taking my eyes off Sarah to watch her reactions.

Her surprise.

Her confusion.

Her doubt.

"Does he know?" she asked once Stevie finished.

"Does he know . . . about our night together?" When Sarah tilted her head in affirmation, a soft laugh left me. "Yeah, I actually didn't realize it was him at first because he looks so different with a beard and longer hair. But we've talked about it—he's pretty aware."

She studied me for a long while before taking the plates to the table.

"Um . . ." Ariana began with a hesitant laugh as she followed with a couple of the dishes. "Are you going to expand on that?"

Sarah released a heavy sigh and dropped into one of the chairs. "You said he took Hollis back to his place." Her questioning stare shifted from Stevie to me. "Is that right?"

"Yeah," I answered, my stomach shifting with unease.

"Adam's never lived in New York—Leo and Adam have

never lived there." She gave me an apologetic look as she explained, "They moved out here from Virginia."

"And Hollis is from Connecticut, and yet there she was," Stevie said as if it wasn't that crazy of an idea. "At Julliard. In New York. Where there happen to be other colleges."

"Which would be a reasonable explanation, except Adam never—"

"He never went to college," I whispered over Sarah, giving details of Adam's life that I'd just learned last night.

Her apologetic expression deepened, and I could tell she hated putting this doubt in my mind—that she was truly just trying to help me. Protect me from whatever she thought was happening.

Whatever *might* be happening.

Except I'd been there through it all.

I'd experienced that indescribable draw to him. I could still feel the current beneath my skin, humming along my veins from his touch. From his lips on my skin. Could acutely feel the searing ache in my chest when I'd walked away.

As if a night was enough for my soul to know I was making a grave mistake.

Shit, Stevie was right.

"I don't know what to tell you," I said, breaking the tension that had settled around us again. "Adam was there. He took me to an apartment that he had a key to and knew his way around. So, I'm hoping it was his, or that night will suddenly be very awkward."

"Okay," she said after a moment. "Okay."

"Okay," Ariana echoed, drawing out the word. "So, are we eating?"

I settled in my own chair and tried to ignore the worry

twisting in my stomach. Looking between the three of them, I forced a smile and said, "Yep."

"I'm sorry, did you say Adam was *funny*?" Sarah asked a couple of hours later since Stevie had refused to drop the whole Ariana-found-you-and-Adam-on-the-couch-thing until I'd spilled all about last night, shock taking over her expression. "Like, *Adam*, Adam. Leo's best friend, Adam."

"Yes," I said with a soft laugh. "Incredibly funny."

She looked at Ariana in question, but her sister just lifted her hands and said, "I think she might've dreamt part of last night."

"No, I'm serious."

"Adam is not a joking kind of person," Sarah said. "I'll admit he teases every now and then, but it's incredibly rare. He's always very serious and very, um . . ." Her head listed and her nose scrunched up, making her look so much like Ariana. "How do I put this nicely?"

"He's a broody bastard?" Ariana offered.

Sarah snapped her fingers and pointed at Ariana. "Yep. That."

"Really?" I asked even as the last week danced through my mind when he'd switched to that cold, angry person in an instant.

"Oh yeah," Sarah said. "More often than not, he answers by glaring at you before walking away."

"And that glare is terrifying," Ariana added.

"So terrifying," Sarah agreed as she lifted her glass to her mouth.

"Nothing on Leo's though."

Sarah choked on the water, her shoulders jerking with a laugh. "He wishes he was scary."

Ariana made a face that was all shock. "Have you *seen* your boyfriend lately? He is honestly the scariest person I've ever met."

Amusement teased Sarah's lips as she shrugged. "He's harmless."

"Hi, bye!" Mia yelled as she ran through the living room where we were all gathered.

Sarah pointed in the direction of the hidden entryway with her glass. "Didn't she just do that a few minutes ago?"

"Next job," we all answered at the same time.

"I'm trying to figure out how this,"—Stevie gestured to Sarah before doing the same to me—"and *this* somehow found themselves with these super-terrifying men." She sat up and did a dramatic hair flip. "I mean, *me*, obviously. It goes without saying I'd end up with some big, hulking, scary guy. But wholesome Sarah and the princess over here?"

"Excuse me?"

She lifted a brow at me, daring me to deny it.

"And what do you mean it goes without saying?" I continued. "Russell is the sweetest person on the planet and in no way scary, and you're exclusively sleeping with him."

Stevie stared at me as if I'd just said the most offensive thing in the world. "We are *not* exclusive. There is *no* exclusivity with Russell—how dare you!"

"You're just freaking out and getting all anxious over him because you told him you love him."

"You slut," she gasped, but I just blew her a kiss as Ariana and Sarah laughed beside us.

"To clarify," Sarah began, "Adam isn't a scary person. He just has this way of looking at you that is very scary.

"Like Leo," Ariana added and coughed out a laugh when Sarah smacked her arm. "You know I'm right."

"But I've never once been afraid of him, and you shouldn't either," Sarah said encouragingly even as her stare fell to the side, once again avoiding eye contact with me while talking about anything to do with Adam and me together.

"I'm not afraid of him," I assured her.

I was afraid of how badly I wanted him.

I was afraid of how fast I could feel myself falling for him.

I was afraid of why Sarah was so sure he'd never lived in New York.

Ten

ADAM

Leo came walking into the living room when I made it home, expression drawn tight in apprehension that immediately gave way to confusion when he saw me.

"The hell?" he hissed, straightening and looking around as if he couldn't figure out how I was walking through the front door. "You were gone?"

I lifted an arm and continued past him to the kitchen.

"You said Ari got you an 'in' at the Forest Knoll mansion. I thought you were going to take care of it and come home."

I shot him a glare and released a sigh as I pulled out my phone.

Jesus fucking Christ

Can you at least let me get to the coffee maker

. . .

His irritated huff sounded behind me as he followed, stopping to continue pouring the bowl of cereal he'd had out. "Did you get it done?" he asked once I had a mug in hand.

I caught my phone when he slid it across the island and tapped out something to placate him before sliding it back.

Ariana was having a party
Had to stay for a little bit
But I 'went to the bathroom' and found Hollis's computer
It's linked to mine now

"Good," he muttered as he lifted the bowl to his chest and took a bite. "Then, where've you been all night?"

I lifted my arms out in exasperation and once again caught my phone, then set my mug down as I hurried to think of something that would appease him. My stomach twisting as I wound myself deeper and deeper into this lie.

My head was demanding I come clean.

But my heart was so twisted up over Hollis, I wasn't sure that would ever be a possibility again.

The fuck
Did I miss curfew or something
Went to a bar
Met someone
We clearly didn't end up coming back here

. . .

His eyes rolled, but he moved past it. Launching into everything we hadn't been able to talk about these past few days that Sarah had been off work. Things we'd learned. Things that had popped up and needed to be looked into. Connections we'd made and others we were grasping at.

"I was following this—" His brow furrowed when he glanced at his phone, his head shifting back before his stare snapped to me and narrowed. "Why is Sarah asking if you've ever lived in New York?"

Fuck.

I forced my outward expression to remain neutral as I shrugged, feigning ignorance and pretending to think while I scrambled for any way to twist this.

"Adam," he seethed. "Why the hell—"

I smacked my hand on the counter and hurried to grab my phone.

Shit I think I said something to Ariana yesterday

She was talking about her roommates and said one of them was from the East coast

I might've said something without realizing

"What the fuck, Adam?" Leo bit out from where he'd moved closer to read as I typed. "How did you let that slip?"

I made a gesture for him to back off it, that it had clearly been an accident even though accidents weren't something we could afford.

Just tell Sarah I have family there that I visit

. . .

He mumbled curses and frustrations as he responded to her, head shaking when he said, "Get your story straight, or we're done."

I gave him a look, then swiped my finger across the phone.

Yeah tell me that again right after you finish texting your PREGNANT girlfriend

His jaw ticked as he stared me down. "Get your story straight," he repeated, this time slowly. "Your story has to be my story. Always. Making mistakes like that is how this falls apart. Understood?"

I just nodded and turned to leave the kitchen, my steps faltering when a text came through my phone.

Sarah: *I already thought it was weird when you said you didn't want Leo knowing where and how I found you this morning. Not that I'm agreeing to anything because I don't like the idea of keeping something from him . . .*

Sarah: *But now I'm wondering who exactly you're keeping things from.*

I swallowed past the barbed knot in my throat as I deleted her messages without responding.

I was so screwed.

Eleven

ADAM

I fucking hated people.

I forced myself to drag in slow breaths as the guy in front of me recounted for everyone in the coffee shop exactly how he'd thought I was going to kill him the first time he'd met me.

Two years before, in a diner.

How fucking small was L.A. anyway?

"Swear to God, with how silent and scary and still he was —exactly like how he's being right now—I was *sure* that was my night," he said loudly, smiling like he was enjoying his own story, then turned his attention on me. "And here you are, coming in like Michael Myers all over again."

"Tucker, I think that's enough," one of the other baristas said, looking nearly as uncomfortable as I felt.

"You weren't there," Tucker said, emphasizing each word, still smiling like he was so damn proud of himself.

He let out a loud sigh and finally started punching in my order, even though I'd been holding out my phone for a couple minutes.

I'd never regretted stopping for coffee more in my life.

But I'd gotten maybe two hours of sleep this morning when Hollis and I had passed out sometime in the middle of talking. And after the impromptu meeting with Leo and near blowup over Sarah's text, I'd thrown myself into work and hadn't stopped until about an hour before.

So I'd made the colossal mistake of stopping at Asterisk since it was on the way to the mansion, and I wished more than anything that I'd stayed home.

"So, is this some kind of artistic venture you're doing?" Tucker asked when I began reaching for my wallet. "Or are you actually a mute?"

"Tucker," the other barista snapped.

He lifted his hands in surrender. "Just wondering if he can't actually speak, or if he's, like, a monk and took a vow of silence."

I didn't bother with any form of response as a lifetime of uneasiness came flooding back. I just kept my stare locked on him as I pulled some cash out and tossed it onto the counter.

But by the time I got to the other side of the café, I was trembling.

My breaths coming fast and shallow as all that anxiety and anger built in my chest and got trapped in my throat.

"Hey."

My stare snapped up at the sound and caught on the other barista.

She lifted a hand before dropping it back to the drink she was making. "I'm sorry about Tucker. His uncle is the owner, so he thinks he can get away with everything. He's an asshole, and you didn't deserve any of that."

I dipped my head in thanks and felt my stomach drop when a familiar face came walking in from the back.

"Hey! Adam, right?" she asked as she finished tying on her apron, her expression all soft excitement.

The girl making my drink looked between Hollis's other roommate and me, who I'd officially met when she'd gotten in late last night. "You know Mia?"

"Yeah," Mia answered for me, then gave me a teasing grin. "He's, um . . . he's sort of *hanging out* with one of my roommates."

The barista's eyes widened as she turned to Mia. "Girl, then you need to know about the shitshow that just went down."

I quickly knocked on the counter to get her attention, head shaking gravely.

She gestured to Mia. "She's roommates with—"

One of my hands fisted when the urge to beg her to stop talking overwhelmed me, but she must have seen something on my face because she choked over her next words.

"Um . . ." The barista stared at the espresso machine for a second and then huffed out a laugh before looking at Mia again. "Some random guy just came in, professing his love to everyone in here."

Mia looked between us and then smiled unconvincingly. "Wow. That definitely sounds . . . crazy." She pointed to the registers. "I'm gonna see if Tucker needs any help."

Shit.

"Sorry, you're right," the barista began once Mia walked away. "That wasn't my business, and you didn't need that put out there again."

I waved off her words.

I just didn't need that shit getting back to Hollis. I didn't want the pity that followed.

And more than ever, I wished I'd stayed home. Forgotten

I'd told Hollis I'd see her tonight. Focused on what I was *supposed* to be doing.

Maybe this was punishment for once again lying to Leo, considering he thought I was going on a date with the girl from last night.

Not a complete lie. Still . . .

"Here you go," the barista said with a subdued smile as she slid the drink my way.

I returned the smile and grabbed the cup, lifting it in thanks as I turned to leave.

"Bye, Michael Myers!" Tucker called out just as I was nearing the door. "Try not to kill anyone."

The person at the end of the line looked at me and took a cautious step away, and I swallowed down all the rage and discomfort as my trembling hand reached out to open the door.

All of it burning deeper and hotter as I stalked to my car and slid into the driver's seat, the smell of the pizza barely fazing me as I forced myself to set down my coffee.

To turn over the engine.

To sit there and not do something I'd regret—like go back into the coffee shop . . .

I pulled my phone out of my pocket, my shaking fingers messing up the words over and over again as I furiously tapped on the screen.

Me: *I'm not coming tonight. I'll see you*

Fuck.

I tossed my phone across the car without sending the

message and tapped my fingers rapidly against the steering wheel before jerking the car into reverse and tearing out of the parking lot.

And instead of going home, I went to her. Because there was nowhere else I wanted to be. Listening to her laugh and making her blush and feeling the way my heart got all tripped up every damn time she smiled at me.

But then Ariana answered the door.

"What the hell happened?" she asked as she took the pizza boxes from me.

My eyebrows drew close in question as I followed her into the house, and then lifted at the sound of someone yelling.

"Mother fucking insensitive *asswipe*."

"I'm heading there now," a masculine voice responded. "I'm going to handle it."

I pointed to the door as they spoke and took a step back toward it, but Ariana just shook her head and gestured for me to follow her.

"Everyone's versions of *handling it* are not the same as mine and definitely not as good," the girl yelled. "If I handled things, they would be taken care of the first time."

"You'd also probably be in jail."

That was Hollis. Forcing my heart to beat and making my blood race.

"But I have no doubt what they're saying happened is what actually happened," she went on. "A couple years ago, I was at Ampersand with some people from my company. Tucker was working that night and was horrifically rude to Adam."

Shit.

"Right," Stevie said as we made our way deeper into the living room. "The night the whole *Ampersand Guy* thing came about." She saw us then and pointed at me. "Speak of the Devil."

Hollis turned, that pity I hated so much covering her face as she studied me.

"Who's this?" the man standing with them asked as he turned to see me.

"It's Adam, Dad," Stevie said. "Catch up."

He released a sigh that was full of frustration and embarrassment. "I've heard you were treated terribly at one of my stores."

I lifted my shoulders, head shaking subtly.

Ariana bumped me with her shoulder. "Mia called just before he showed up. There's really no getting out of this."

I just gave another slow shake of my head.

Stevie's dad slid his hands into his pockets and let out another sigh. "While I appreciate you not making this into a bigger deal than it very much is, what happened isn't tolerated, and you don't need to pretend that it *didn't* happen."

I pulled out my phone and opened up the notes to type out a message, then showed it to Ariana since we were still half a room away from the others.

"He said nothing happened," she said dryly before walking away to place the boxes down.

"Adam," Hollis whispered, and my attention snapped to her. Begging her to drop it.

"Oh my God," Stevie began, "that *is* a terrifying look."

"See?" Ariana said.

My head jerked back, confusion filling me and mixing with my unease.

"The dramatics of you girls never ceases to amaze me," the man said as he walked away from them to approach me, his voice lowering once he was in front of me. "We don't know each other, but I've heard a hell of a lot about you in the last fifteen minutes. I'm David Russo, but everyone calls me Mr. R. Now . . . like I said, I appreciate what you're trying to do. But since you're holding a cup to the store where Tucker's currently working, and since Mia is the one who called, I'm going to take a wild guess and say that it actually happened. However, I'm heading over there to do tips right now, so I'll see the video for myself."

I slid my thumb across the screen of my phone before turning it around for him to see.

I prefer to let these things go

He nodded for a long time before shrugging. "Doesn't change that they happened. Doesn't change that my employees can't act that way." He glanced back toward the kitchen and called out, "Girls," in parting before heading past me.

And then I was standing there under the weight of pity and unknown as the three girls looked uneasily at me.

Fucking hell.

"You good?" Ariana asked me, breaking the thick silence.

"That fucking jerk," Stevie snapped, turning around to look at the others. "He's always been an ass, even when we were kids. My dad never would've given him a job in the first place if he hadn't been trying to cling to my mom's family. *And*"—she looked back at me—"he's already had way more chances than other employees get."

"Isn't that the truth," Ariana murmured as she set out a stack of plates.

"My dad moved him to Asterisk after he'd had too many

issues at Ampersand with the other employees and refused to do certain parts of the job. Anyone else would've been fired. He better be fired after tonight."

I scratched at my temple. My body twitching anxiously as I thought of how quickly I could get to the front door.

To my car.

"Hey."

I looked into mint green eyes just as her fingers slipped into mine. Her expression all soft understanding and worry as she gently pulled me away from the spot I'd been rooted in.

Away from the door.

"Dinner?" Ariana asked when Hollis started leading me away from the kitchen.

"Save ours," Hollis called back, never taking her eyes from me until we were past the den and winding our way up the stairs and through the halls.

Keeping me close when she'd clearly known that I was about to leave.

"Stevie is . . ."—she listed her head, an adoring smile touching her face as she thought of how to word whatever she was saying—"vocal when she's passionate about something. And she's passionate about very few things and even fewer people. Because of that, there are times when she doesn't realize she needs to stop."

She shut her bedroom door behind us, never stopping as she took my coffee and set it on her dresser while pulling me toward her bed.

"Can I ask something?" she asked when she released me and sank onto the bed, turning to sit up against the headboard and chest pitching when I climbed on after her. Cheeks stained pink and eyes unfocused for a long moment after I was settled in beside her. "I don't think it's fair that you can make something like crawling onto a bed look that good."

My shoulders shook and a smile tugged at my lips.

"Anyway . . ." She cleared her throat and twisted so her body was pressed against mine the way it had been the night before. "What happened out there reminded me of that first night I saw you at Ampersand—also with Tucker." Her eyes rolled irritably. "You wanted me to drop it that night too. I'm just wondering what it is that you don't want? The focus on you? Or do you really not get bothered by these things?"

The last was said with doubt, but her expression never showed anything other than curiosity and understanding.

That earlier pity was all but gone, but I knew just how easily it could come back.

I knew what it felt like.

And it wasn't just her. It poured from people. Crawled from them and reached out to me. Making me more uncomfortable than I'd ever been.

Focus is part of it

I'd be fine if people never noticed me at all

"And the rest?" she asked softly.

Pity

She stared at the word for a long time before slowly lowering her chin in a nod. "I see."

. . .

So it's easier to let them go

To not make them into a situation

Because if I make them into something then other people make them into something bigger

I'd rather act like it never happened

"That's sad, Adam," she whispered. "No one should live like that for any reason."

I lifted a hand and let it fall because whether or not she thought it was sad, it was how I preferred it.

"You can leave if you want," she said after a while, the hesitation in her voice not at all like the hesitation that made my heart race.

When I looked over at her, her stare was fixed on where her knees were pressed to my side and she was nodding subtly.

"I saw the way you looked when Mr. R was talking to you. Like you were already mentally gone, you were just waiting to physically leave too." Her stare drifted to meet mine. "You look like that again. So, you should go," she said more resolutely, forcing a smile that did nothing to hide the disappointment in her eyes when she pushed away from me and started getting off the bed.

I grabbed her wrist when she placed a foot on the floor, curling my hand around her neck and crushing my mouth to hers as I pulled her back onto the bed.

Because she was absolutely fucking right, but I knew if I left, I would want to come right back.

To be near her.

To have my heart beat freely.

To feel like *this*.

A groan built in my chest when I rested against the headboard, and she effortlessly followed. Sliding one of her legs over my body so she was straddling me and trailing her fingers through my beard. Opening up for me and giving me the cruelest tease of her tongue before sitting back.

Stealing my breath with the way she was looking down at me.

Like she craved this time every bit as much as I did. Like she wanted to make sure it was *real*.

And so damn beautiful that my heart faltered.

I brought her mouth back to mine and drank down the whimper that tumbled past her lips. All that energy that always surrounded us building and building as the kiss shifted from soft and teasing to hard and unyielding.

Promising bites and tempting flicks of tongues and demanding kisses. Until she was my air, and I was hers. Until we'd stopped holding onto each other and began learning each other's bodies all over again.

Gripping her subtle curves and pressing her closer, and about losing my fucking mind when she rolled her hips. Her searching hands finding the hem of my shirt and dipping beneath. Teasing the hard planes of my stomach and sweeping down to the button of my pants.

And bringing me crashing back to reality . . .

I'd thought of her, of this, of having her again, more times than I could remember. But I couldn't let this happen.

I'd already crossed so many lines with her. And if she ever found out the truth, she'd hate me so much more if I let us go further than we already had.

Curling my hands around hers, I moved them until I had

them pinned behind her back and shifted my head to the side until she sat up. Her chest pitching as roughly as mine and her face full of confusion and alarm.

"You okay?"

I was anything but okay. She was still on my lap, and all I wanted was to pull her into my arms and lose myself in her. And I hated that I couldn't.

But I just gave a sharp nod and looked around for my phone that I'd lost sometime in the middle of kissing her.

"I'm on the pill," she said a little uncertainly. "I'm clean."

Fuck, fuck, fuck . . .

I forced myself to remember every reason why I couldn't do this with her and continued searching for my phone. Gritting my teeth when she scooped it up in the exact spot I'd been staring at.

I flashed a smile that felt feral and hurried to open the notes to give her a bullshit excuse.

I want to get to know you

My heart did that pained beating thing again, followed closely by the feeling of my stomach dropping straight to the fucking floor when rejection sliced across her face.

"Right," she said, struggling to recover and sending me a quick smile as she got off me and then the bed.

I sat up and dragged one of my hands through my hair. Gripping at the longer strands on top as I tried to bury that sinking feeling in my gut because there was no coming out of this unscathed for either of us.

But from that first night, I'd already been in far too deep with her to ever be able to walk away.

"Pizza?" she asked a little too brightly as she hurried from the room.

I stood to stop her and automatically glanced down at my phone when it vibrated. I tapped on the text from Leo, my feet stopping when a few keywords jumped out at me.

Leo: *Want to tell me why you're at the Forest Knoll mansion when you're supposed to be on a date?*

My stomach twisted as I tried to think of any reason that would pacify him, but the text that came through next had ice-cold hands curling around my lungs, squeezing the oxygen from them.

Leo: *I know you're here. Where are you?*

Fuck.

I stalked out of Hollis's room and down the halls and stairs. My chest pitching and my heart limping through weak beats as I thought of Leo anywhere near Hollis.

Of what she might say.

Of what he might do.

My hands were curled into fists by the time I made it into the kitchen, gaze immediately snapping to where he stood away from Hollis, narrowed stare shifting from me to her.

"There you are," Sarah said with a saddened smile. "Ari told us about what happened at Asterisk."

I didn't respond in any way, just let my fingers trail across Hollis's as I passed her and then Leo, knowing he would follow.

"Um, bye?" one of the girls said as I headed for the entryway.

Not more than a few seconds after I stepped outside, the front door shut, and Leo appeared beside me.

What the fuck are you doing here

"No, no. You don't get to ask me that. Same question, *you* answer," he demanded. When I just held his stare, he continued. Voice low and threatening. "You're here working. Tell me that now."

I slanted my head before shaking it.

"Adam, what the fuck? Have you lost your goddamn mind?"

My head shook as I looked down at my phone, but he pushed my hands away to stop me.

"No, you don't get to talk right now," he hissed. "Do you have any idea what you're doing—what you've *done*? This ruins everything—*she* ruins everything. You just took years of work and threw it away for what? A night?" He took a step away only to turn back around. "And you lied to me. We don't keep things from each other. We can't. The fact that you kept this from me?" He let that linger for a while before continuing. "Says a lot. Says dangerous things, Adam."

My jaw ached with the pressure I was putting on it, but he didn't release me from his furious glare.

"When I realized I was falling for Sarah, what did you say?" He gave me a meaningful look and answered for me. "You told me to put an end to it before it could make me lose sight of what we're doing. You told me falling for her would risk too much. And yet, I wasn't sleeping with Hollis fucking Donahue."

I shoved him back when he took a step closer, trying to get in my face.

Frustration built and burned in my throat, but I took another step back as I choked over it all. An irritated smile pulling at my mouth as I typed.

And now look how deep you've gotten
You're gonna be a dad
And Sarah has no idea who you are

"End it," he said gravely. "Sarah and Hollis are two completely different pieces to this game. One of them was a means to get to the end. The other is the end."

Wow
Does Sarah know you think of her as a pawn

"I will destroy you," he vowed in a low tone, those lethal eyes cutting back to me. "You know exactly what she means to me just as you know what I meant."

I nodded and gave him a disbelieving smirk.

"Adam," he snapped when I started for the door, but I shoved his reaching hand away and furiously tapped out commands.

I've left Sarah alone now it's your turn

Leave this alone

Leave Hollis alone

Don't go near her or say anything to her

Or I'll tell Sarah everything

"You don't get to make the demands here. Do not make me do this," he said in low warning, stopping me cold just before I reached the door.

I took in a shuddering breath only to release it before facing him. Holding his stare and refusing to type out what we were both thinking.

He couldn't do this without me.

Instead, I confessed it all. Knowing it would make everything so much worse just as I knew it needed to be done.

I've wanted this girl for years

New York

Sarah was asking about New York because I met Hollis there at one of the parties I went to

I had no idea who she was then

But I swear to God she ruined me for anyone else that night

To the point where I've doubted what we're doing

How we've gotten here

Because I couldn't be sure if I just wanted to be following her

A cold sort of dread settled over Leo's expression as he read. His dark stare slowly shifting to me as he asked, "And you didn't think to say anything until now?"

How was I supposed to
Like you said it would ruin everything

Questions and frustration flashed through his eyes before he finally spoke again, voice barely above a whisper. "How long have you been seeing her in California?"

Romantically
Last night

"God damnit," he mumbled before scraping his hand through his hair and stalking away from the house.

And I let him have that time of coming to terms with everything I was potentially doing just by wanting Hollis, knowing he needed it.

"I need to know something," he began when he came back, head shaking as if he couldn't believe he was even about to ask. "Is she worth it? Throwing away years, destroying everything we've gathered, losing our jobs? Is she worth it?"

• • •

She's worth everything

He gave a hard nod, looking at once disappointed and like he understood. "All right," he said and took the last steps toward the house. Just as he grabbed the handle of the door, he looked back at me. "Don't doubt how we've gotten here. You triple-check everything before you ever run it past me, and then I do the same. We're solid. This is it."

I nodded in thanks and followed him into the house, easily finding where Hollis was sitting at the table with the rest of the girls. Smile fake as hell and stare distant even when she looked my way.

And when I sat beside her, she shifted away from me.

Shit.

Twelve

HOLLIS

"I have a hairy vagina."

I looked up and then to the side, eyebrows raising in shock. "What?"

Stevie was turned in the chair at her backstage station at Raven, eyeliner in hand and narrowed eyes studying me. "You've barely said anything all day," she said softly, concern filling her voice. "The only time you seemed at all like yourself was when you were on stage, but even then, it was clear something was up. And you finished removing your makeup a few minutes ago." She used her eyeliner to point at the makeup remover still in my hand.

"Oh," I said lamely.

"You never even mentioned the fact that Russell and his friends were here, and you *always* mention them."

I blinked slowly as I thought through our show. My hands moving at the same sluggish pace as I put away the makeup remover and reached for my makeup so we could go to Ampersand.

I wasn't sure I'd even realized they'd been there.

"Hollis, what is going on?" she nearly begged.

"Nothing."

"Okay, bullshit," she whispered, offense coloring her tone. "What is with you not telling me things lately?"

"Because you wouldn't understand," I snapped and felt terrible when her eyes widened with hurt. But the filter had broken, and I couldn't stop now that I'd begun. "You've always mocked the 'New York Guy' and 'Ampersand Guy' dreams and the fact that I knew they were the same person."

"That isn't—"

"No, Stevie, you're all about Adam because he's hot and mysterious and dangerous, and you're the one who won't drop the 'soulmate' thing. But whenever I talk about what I actually feel for him, you start making a joke of it because you can't imagine people caring about other people in a romantic way. You can't handle the thought of someone wanting a relationship. You panic at the idea of love, which is why you've been ignoring Russell."

Her expression went void of emotion at the mention of him.

"And that's why I can't talk to you about what's happening," I went on. "Because you wouldn't care."

"I care about *you,*" she whispered before turning to the brightly lit mirror.

I dropped my head into my hand, guilt unfurling in my stomach.

I'd never snapped at Stevie or any of my friends. But a couple days with no word from Adam had me on edge and had my mind racing down roads I knew I shouldn't go. It had me aching because nothing had ever been like this. No one had ever been *him*. And despite what he'd said, with each day,

I was more sure that whatever was between us wasn't the same for him.

It wasn't consuming. It wasn't at the forefront of every thought and the fuel of every dream. It didn't make his heart race faster and force chills to rush over his skin. It didn't leave him feeling lost and wandering around until we were near each other again. Our kisses didn't make him feel like he was taking his first real breath in years.

A pained breath pushed from my lungs, and I sat back, twisting to look at Stevie just as she stood and grabbed her bag.

"Stevie, I'm—"

"I might struggle with the thought of relationships and love, but at least I care," she said coldly. "At least I'm paying attention to you. If you could say the same, you would know Russell was here tonight because we've been talking the last couple of nights. You would know that I'd told you on the way here that I was going home with him."

"Stevie," I called after her when she stormed off, then hurried to gather my stuff, ignoring the looks from the other girls still in varying stages of undress and preparing to go out for the night.

I burst out the back door of Raven just as Russell was shutting the passenger door behind her, an excited smile on his face when he saw me.

"Night, Hollis," he called out with a wave.

I slowed to a stop, my stomach twisting as I battled with the need to apologize to Stevie and to let her go so she could have this time she'd been avoiding. "Good night," I choked out. "Take care of my girl."

He gave a nod and slid into the driver's side of his car.

I let out a ragged sigh as I watched them pull away, then headed for my car, my mind a mess of ranting at Stevie and what was going on with Adam. Or, well, what *wasn't* going on with—

The hairs on the back of my neck lifted a split second before a large hand landed on my waist. Gripping me possessively and turning me in his hold as a scream caught in my throat.

"Miss me, baby?" Russell's friend asked.

The scream turned into an enraged scoff as I shoved against his chest. "For the last time, I am not your 'baby.' And what part of 'fuck off' don't you understand?"

He leered down at me as he continued trying to pull me closer, liquor practically seeping from his pores. "The part where you keep shaking that ass and those tits in my face night after night."

"You're disgusting," I seethed, shoving harder still and managing to break away for a second before he gripped my arm and jerked me back. "Let go."

"You play hard to get," he said, tightening his hold on my arm when I tried yanking it from his grasp, "but every time you're up on that stage, those fuck-me eyes are directed right at me."

"You're delusional and drunk and—*let go*," I yelled when he palmed my butt and pressed me against him.

"I've watched you on that stage long enough," he went on, and despite his intoxicated state, he effortlessly shoved me back against a car and blocked my leg when I tried to knee him, using his grip on my thigh to spread my legs. "Think it's time I get the front-row show of you sliding down my di—*fuck*."

He reared back, holding his face from where the tips of

my keys had slashed across his cheek. But I only made it a step away before stars burst across my vision.

I staggered to the side, blindly reaching for the back of the car we were near as I struggled to shake off the impact of his backhand.

"Shit. Shit, baby, I didn't mean to."

I swung at him again, keys still firmly secured between my fingers, and screamed, "Get the fuck away from me," when he blocked me.

"Hollis?"

"Hey, asshole!"

Relief surged through me when I caught sight of a few of the girls running toward us as another one yelled into the building for someone to call the cops.

"Fuck, *fuck*," he hissed, looking between them and me a few times before bolting across the parking lot.

"Oh my God, are you okay?" one of the girls asked as she reached me, glancing over her shoulder long enough to see another one of the girls running a little farther down the lot.

"Didn't you come out here with Stevie?" another asked. "She just left you with that creep?"

"No, no," I said quickly, my chest pitching with my uneven breaths. "I don't think she realized he was here."

"Oh, girl." She gently touched my cheek and then quickly took her hand away. "I don't want to mess anything up before the cops come, but you're bleeding."

My hand lifted to my face, but she pushed it back down.

"Just a little bit, from your lip," she whispered, trying to keep her voice calm and soothing.

"Asshole," one of the girls said as she came back from trying to chase him through the lot. "I don't see him anywhere and I didn't see a car leaving."

"Police are just a couple minutes away," someone said from the doorway. "You okay, Hollis? What do you need?"

"I want to go home," I whispered as tears pricked at the backs of my eyes.

I wanted Stevie.

And, as much as I hated it, I wanted Adam.

"You break a lot of hearts?" Mia asked from where she and Ariana were sitting in the living room when I finally got home that night, voice soft and teasing.

"Um . . ." I cleared my throat as I tried to think of the answer I always gave her, head bobbing lazily. "Me? Never."

I could hear how dull and lifeless I sounded, but I wasn't sure how to muster much else after going around and around with the cops after trying to dodge filing a report.

"So, this was a random attack?" one of the officers had asked.

"No, he's been coming on to me for a long time," I'd answered. "Touching me and getting bolder each time."

"So, you know him then," another had assumed.

I'd hesitated for a moment before saying, "Not exactly."

They'd looked at each other before the first had said, "All right then. What's his name?"

"I don't know."

"And how long have you known him?" he'd asked.

"Over a year," I'd responded hesitantly, realizing exactly how my answer would come across.

They'd shared another look before the second had taken over. "And you don't know his name?"

"Um . . . no. I mean, I think my roommate said his name was um . . . uh, Chris," I'd said, his name sounding more like a question than anything. "But I'm not sure, I don't know if that's—"

"And you said he's been coming onto you for a long time?" the second had asked, her brow lifting in understanding. "Have you been engaging in this?"

"What? No, of course not. It's always been unwelcome. I've always told him to stop. I've hit him the last couple of times."

"Did you report any of the times?" she'd asked.

"No . . ."

I was exhausted and angry and humiliated and just . . . done. I was done with tonight.

I avoided Mia and Ariana's gazes and shuffled off to my room so I could shower, grimacing when I finally saw myself in the mirror. There was a small trickle of dried blood coming out of the corner of my mouth, and my cheek was red in a very telling way.

"Fantastic," I choked out, my throat tightening with emotion. The tears I'd been fighting for the past hour finally breaking free once I was standing under the hot spray of the shower.

Tears for what happened. Tears for how I'd lashed out at Stevie. Tears for the mess Adam was turning me into.

And I hated that I was letting him.

I paused when I stepped back into my room to find Mia and Ariana waiting for me, faces set with concern.

Letting out a deep sigh, I went around the room to dress in my pajamas, a pathetic laugh crawling up my throat when Ariana said, "I never should've helped bring you and Adam together. I should've left it alone."

"*I* should've left it alone," I muttered, then turned to face them. "How can someone make me feel like this? Make me feel like I'm flying and then make me feel so insecure and, and, and just—*God*."

"You deserve so much better," Mia said. "Someone who makes you feel insecure? Someone who does *this*? That is never love, and it's a prison people get trapped in."

"We're not even in a relationship," I said miserably. "That's what's so stupid. I hate that he makes me feel like this. I hate that I want him so badly. That I care about him so much, and he just . . . doesn't."

"I'm sure that's so painful, but it's his loss," Mia tried to assure me.

I gestured to the bed with a frustrated laugh. "We've been together. We've had an entire night of the most mind-blowing sex. But now, it's like he remains totally unaffected. Everything just shuts off for him, and he stops us from kissing, and it sends me spiraling down this path of *why*."

I held up a hand to stop them before they could add anything. "The first time, he said it was because we'd rushed into it before and he wanted to get to know me this time, and I thought that was incredibly sweet." My head shook. "That isn't what's happening. It's like he realizes that he *doesn't* want to be kissing me, and it just—" A sob worked up my throat. "It hurts."

"Hollis," Mia whispered when tears slipped down my cheeks.

"Does he not find me attractive anymore? Was that night in New York only because we'd been drinking? Like, why is he even pretending with me if he doesn't want me? But then . . ." I added on quickly, "God, then he looks at me like I'm *everything* he wants, and it makes me think that I'm just making it all up. But then he hardly says anything to me through an entire dinner and doesn't talk to me for two days, and it's just . . . so confusing and messing with my heart, and I hate that he can do this to me. I was so much stronger and confident before he came back into my life."

I looked between Ariana and Mia when they didn't say anything, their expressions a mixture of sorrow and confusion.

"Wait, you haven't seen him since . . . dinner here on Monday?" Ariana asked slowly.

I lifted my hands, then let them fall to my thighs as I sank to the bed. "He said he'd push me away, and I told him I'd be okay with it. But I'm just . . . I don't know how to be okay with this."

Ariana's tongue darted out to wet her lips as she looked at Mia.

"Hollis," Mia began softly, "if it wasn't Adam, then who did this to you?"

My eyes widened when she gestured to her cheek. "Oh no. No, no. You guys thought—no one," I quickly rambled. "Just something that happened at work."

"Bullshit," Ariana said as Mia pled, "Hollis."

"I'm not doing this tonight," I said, voice wavering. "Please."

Mia was the first one to nod. "My door's always open to you. You know, as long as I'm here." When I gave her a grateful smile, she said, "And even if Adam wasn't the one to hurt you, he's still hurting you, Hollis. You deserve more."

She smiled gently at me as she left the room, leaving me with Ariana. Looking an odd mixture of enraged and guilty. "Was it Russell's friend?" she asked after a minute. When I didn't respond, she nodded slowly, then pushed from her spot against the wall. "I'm sorry for bringing you this pain with Adam."

"You didn't."

She huffed in disbelief as she left.

And I just sat there, weighed down from these days and the night until I finally got up and finished getting ready for bed. Movements slow as my mind raced and jumped between the thoughts plaguing me.

Not long after I climbed into bed, my door opened and a bottle of aspirin was set down on my nightstand.

"In case you're hurting," Ariana whispered as she crawled into bed behind me and curled up close.

"Thanks, Ari."

A soft laugh rumbled from her when the bed dipped as Mia climbed onto it as well.

"Room for one more?" she asked as she wiggled her way in between us.

"You guys are the best," I murmured, throat tight, and Mia squeezed my arm in response.

"Rusted motherfucking forks." Stevie's outraged voice sounded through the house just as my eyes slipped shut.

"You called Stevie?"

"She was already on her way," Ariana said unapologetically. "Someone from Raven must've told her."

"I'm going to run my crystal-covered Louboutins right through his dick," she snapped just before she stormed into the room. Never slowing as she dropped her purse and kicked off her shoes before pulling back the covers to crawl into the bed in front of me.

"My bed is going to break," I said halfheartedly and felt my eyes fill with tears all over again when she gently placed her hand on my stinging cheek. "I'm sorry for yelling at you."

"Already forgotten, babe," she said honestly as she rested her head on the edge of my pillow. "I'm sorry I wasn't there."

"Don't."

"I'd already talked to Russell about Chris," she went on, voice soft and wrenching with guilt she shouldn't be feeling. "He was so mad when he found out and had promised me Chris wouldn't be coming anymore—he wasn't there tonight. Not with them anyway. I wouldn't have left if I'd seen him."

I offered her a smile and grabbed her hand from my cheek, pulling it between us and gripping it tight. "You didn't have to come back. You needed a night with Russell."

"You're more important. Always."

I squeezed her hand tighter. "Love you."

She rolled her eyes playfully, ignoring when a tear slipped free. "Obviously, have you seen me?"

Ariana and Mia laughed softly behind me, but I just gave Stevie an understanding smile and let my eyes close again. I didn't need Stevie to say the words to know she cared. Her dropping everything to be here for me said it all.

The three of them being here said more than words could.

Thirteen

ADAM

You're gonna lose her.

That's the text I'd woken up to this morning from Ariana.

Considering how everything had gone down the other night at their house and the days that followed, I'd say that sounded about right. Then again, I wasn't sure I'd ever actually *had* Hollis.

I sat up and rubbed at my jaw, but the words wouldn't come.

They were there, I knew exactly what needed to be said to put an end to it all. But I couldn't make myself type them. Getting out of bed, I stalked out of my room and through the house, slamming my fist against the door to Leo and Sarah's room once I got there.

Muscles twitching restlessly as I waited.

When he answered, his eyes were narrowed in that way that Leo had of looking at people—all murderous intent that couldn't faze me. "We just got back a couple of hours ago. This better be the best news of my fucking life."

I just rolled my eyes and walked away, knowing he would follow.

Once we were in the kitchen, away from where Sarah could overhear, I handed him my phone so he could read the text.

He pinched the bridge of his nose and released a slow exhale, those dark eyes drifting my way. "You woke me up for this?"

I smacked his shoulder, then gestured to the phone.

With another rough sigh, he nodded as he handed it back. "All right, fine. You already know what I have to tell you, so I won't. You wouldn't be waking me up if you wanted that answer." He reached behind him, toward the room I'd just pulled him from. "I can't make you listen to me, all things considered. But you have to really think about what you're doing."

His voice was soft and grave when he continued. "After everything we just saw, after everything being watched, the likelihood of someone else finding out is high. You can't interrupt her phone service forever, Adam. She's going to realize something's going on, if she hasn't already. And if you decide to continue with her, she'll eventually say something on her phone about you." He lifted his hands as if to say *game over*.

I already knew all this.

I'd been going over it on repeat for the past two days.

Still . . .

I switched over to my notes and typed out what my thoughts always led back to.

Everything

. . .

Just as he had the other night, he looked disappointed and understanding. "Tell me you've come up with a story to unfuck us if this blows back on us."

I dipped my head as I typed.

My chest twisting the way it did every time a question or conversation with Hollis benefited me in ways she couldn't understand, all while I was genuinely just wanting to get to know her.

Unfortunately
I get information while talking to her
Information that we couldn't get otherwise

Leo grimaced and shifted away to look in the direction of his room. "It sucks, doesn't it?" he asked when he glanced my way again. "When they end up meaning something."

I scrubbed a hand over my face before quickly typing out pleas.

Send me back to Virginia
Take me off
Anything
I can't be the one who does this

"No." When I gave him a frustrated look, he repeated, "No. You know if I do any of that, you can't go anywhere near her.

And send you back to Virginia? Fuck, Adam, we weren't even there thirty-six hours, and you were a miserable bastard wanting to get back here. At least here, you're near her. That's the best I can give you."

Here
I'm hurting her
More and more each day I'm with her

A dark look stole across his face. "And what the fuck do you think I'm doing with Sarah?" he asked bitterly. "Either she's worth all that bullshit in the end, or she's not. Either way, I need you here, doing your fucking job." When I nodded, he pointed to my phone. "I need to know what you're going to do so we're on the same page. I can't have any more surprises."

I battled over what I knew was right and the needs pulsing through my veins before scrolling up on the notes to the top and tapping on the word *Everything*.

"All right," he said with a determined breath. "Do you know how you're going to play this with Ariana? With *Hollis?*"

I gave a sharp nod as I scrolled back to the bottom to respond.

Covered bases while we were gone in case

. . .

"Good." He jerked his head in the direction of my room. "Before you do anything, make sure Hollis's phone service is fully restored. We don't need her getting nervous about using it."

I didn't tell him that it was all part of my plan.

I just nodded as I left the kitchen and headed for my bathroom, leaving Hollis's phone exactly as it was—so all her calls and texts were rerouted to my system.

Once I had the shower on, I finally went back to Ariana's texts. Hoping like hell this would work—that I could somehow salvage this.

Me: *Yeah. Think that's what she wants.*

Me: *Besides, I already told you it's for the best.*

I'd just set my phone down when it vibrated with a text.

Ariana: *Okay, fuck that.*

Ariana: *And fuck you.*

Ariana: *Real talk, Adam, I regret ever helping bring the two of you back together. If I would've known you were gonna treat her like this, I wouldn't have.*

Ariana: *Love you, man. We're basically family. But you don't deserve her.*

I turned to lean against the counter before firing off responses, my chest tight with unease.

• • •

Me: *No shit. I've been telling you something along those lines this entire time.*

Me: *But I told her I'd push her away. I warned her that's what I do.*

Me: *Except I'm actually trying with her, and she's ignoring me.*

Ariana: *. . . what?*

Me: *She won't talk to me.*

A couple minutes passed before I eventually set my phone back down and started undressing. Just as I was about to step into the shower, another text came through, giving me the slightest bit of hope.

Ariana: *I'll leave for work early. Meet me at Asterisk in twenty.*

Me: *Asterisk? No. Fuck you.*

Ariana: *Love you too! See you then.*

A sharp exhale ripped from me as I tossed my phone on the counter and finally got in the shower. Hurrying through it and getting ready, all while that pressure on my chest grew.

As the words I'd said to her began taunting me.

Because it *would* be for the best if Hollis and I were nothing. But just as Leo said, a couple days across the country from her, and I'd been miserable. Anxious to get back to her. To try to fix the strain between us.

But in fixing the strain, in doing *anything,* I was lying to her. I was using her. I was hurting her more in the long run.

And that shit weighed heavily on my soul.

It made me feel like I was on the edge of losing my mind with how conflicted my thoughts and wants and needs were.

But before I knew it, I was stepping out of my car and making my way up to the coffee shop's doors like an addict needing their fix.

Because that's exactly what this was.

There was no staying away from Hollis no matter how much I tried—no matter how badly I knew I needed to. And anything that had to do with her, even if it was just information, had me drawn.

As soon as I stepped through the doors, Ariana said, "You're late," from where she was leaning against the counter, talking with their other roommate.

I dragged a hand through my hair, eyes shifting across the café. Searching.

"He was let go," Mia said, knowing exactly what I'd been doing. *Who* I'd been looking for.

When my attention pulled to her, her eyes were narrowed in a glare.

Ariana tapped her drink on the counter near Mia and muttered, "We're hearing him out first."

"I haven't said anything yet," she said defensively and slid a drink toward me. "No-whip mocha. Don't worry, it isn't poisoned or anything."

Comforting.

Ariana checked the watch on her wrist and sighed. "All right, I have to leave in about four minutes. So, you have less than that."

I pulled up my texts to Hollis and slid my phone over to them.

Texts apologizing for upsetting her before dinner and the

tension that had lingered between us. Asking if I could see her again. Sending her songs.

All sent over the past couple of days while she wasn't receiving a thing.

"Hollis said . . ." Mia began, then pressed her lips together, her curious stare shifting to Ariana.

"She wouldn't have made that up," Ariana murmured.

"She was devastated," Mia agreed.

I lifted a hand in question, but the girls looked back at my phone when Ariana began tapping on it while pulling out hers to set it beside mine.

I knocked on the counter to get their attention.

"I see you," Ariana said and tapped my arm placatingly, "but I'm trying to figure this out for you before I have to go."

"Hollis said she hadn't heard from you in days," Mia informed me, then shrugged when my eyebrows lifted.

"That's her number," Ariana murmured, confusion clouding her features. "I don't know, man, Mia said it—she's really struggling over the fact that you've been ignoring her."

Mia hummed in agreement as Ariana picked up her coffee and took a step away.

"But then again," she went on as she pocketed her phone, "I think she's been struggling ever since Sarah said you'd never lived in New York. So, what do I know?"

I stopped her from walking away and quickly swiped my finger across the screen.

When the hell was this

What else did she say

. . .

"When you stayed the night." She glanced at her watch. "I can't get into all that in thirty seconds. But she was wrong . . . right?"

Fuck.

I'd known about Sarah's text to Leo, but I hadn't known the context behind it. The tension between Hollis and me that night was starting to make more sense.

I just gave a rough nod as Ariana started for the door.

"I gotta go. Maybe go figure things out with Hollis," she suggested.

"You know, it might not be for me to say," Mia began before I could follow, her words coming out on a rush. Her eyes darting around, never settling on me as her discomfort pulsed from her. "And I've never been in a real relationship, so it isn't like I have room to give advice . . . but your silence isn't the only thing hurting Hollis."

My head slanted in an unsettling mixture of question and acceptance.

Because I'd already known I was hurting her and would continue to, but I wanted to hear it from Mia . . . I wanted to hear it from *Hollis* that my wanting her was worse than keeping myself from her.

She cleared her throat and set my coffee on the edge of the counter. "That still doesn't have poison in it, and Ariana paid for it. So, you know . . . there you go."

I stepped closer but didn't grab the coffee. Just waited for her to look at me. To explain.

"I'm not afraid of guys like you," she breathed, her eyes darting up to meet mine in a look so unlike anything I'd seen from her yet.

It was cold and hollow, all the life draining from her eyes as the seconds passed.

"If this really was some miscommunication, then go fix it," she whispered. "But anyone who makes a girl feel like that . . . anyone who can strip her confidence and mess with her emotions the way you have? Who can make her feel like *nothing*? Yeah, you don't deserve her."

My head shifted back, my brow furrowing at the depth of her words that only partly sounded like an accusation.

I dipped my head in a nod, then grabbed the coffee and stalked out of the shop and to my car. My fingers twitching against the steering wheel as I hit red light after red light on the way to Hollis.

Like even the traffic was telling me not to do this.

To turn around.

But then I was hitting my knuckles against the door. My body moving restlessly as I prepared to explain the entire thing again. As I thought of how to fix things between us without revealing things about my life that were better left secret.

A lifetime of pain and all those secrets I was trying to bury climbing to the surface and getting caught in my throat as I typed and deleted excuse after excuse because they all sounded like bullshit next to the truth.

I erased another poor excuse for an apology just as the door opened, everything falling away when she filled the frame.

And I saw fucking red.

Fourteen

HOLLIS

"Oh my God, Stevie," I muttered and pushed against her, struggling to wiggle out from beneath where she'd sprawled across me like a starfish. "Move."

Her breathing didn't so much as change when I finally managed to shove her away from me and get off the bed.

"I feel bad for Russell," I said around a yawn, wincing halfway through and gently touching my cheek.

That felt so much worse than it had the night before . . . damn it.

I hurried to my bathroom, groaning out a curse as I took in my cheek—that was still too red to be natural—and my swollen and bruising cheekbone. At least my lip had gone down even though it felt huge.

"Great," I said on a sigh before freshening up and then padding through the house to start the process of waking Stevie up with coffee.

But just as I was scooping out the coffee grounds, a knock sounded on the door. I glanced at the time on the microwave, then hurried to start the coffee before rushing for the door.

And came to a stop when I glanced out the peephole and saw him.

Head down and hand rubbing at the back of his neck agitatedly before he went back to typing on his phone. And just seeing him that way had my heart betraying me. Taking off in a dead sprint and forgetting about all the pain and confusion of the past days. Reaching for him and begging me to open the door. To remove the barrier between us.

So I did, my stomach dipping with excitement when he looked up at me.

And I had a feeling I would do it again . . . go through days of not hearing from him and days of unknown, for *this*.

For those dark eyes to sweep over me and devour me as if he'd been slowly dying without me. For this electricity between us, pulling tight and making my knees a little weak. To feel like I could breathe fully again.

And then he went still.

That dangerous energy bursting from him like a shockwave as he took a step toward me. Face set in a calm sort of rage as he reached out, the tips of his fingers barely grazing my cheek. His cold stare shifting to mine in demand.

"Um . . ." My tongue darted out to wet my lips, and I rocked back a couple steps.

He followed.

Those eyes saying and asking so many things as he grabbed the door and shut it behind him. Hand curling around my waist and pulling me close as he led me through the entryway and into the living room.

A soft inhale ripped down my throat when the couch touched the back of my knees just before he gently sat me down and followed so he was leaning over me. His hands pressed on either side of me.

Caging me in.

I was sure after last night, some part of me should have been afraid to be in this position. But this was Adam . . .

And all that darkness and wrath swirling around him was in response to something that had been done to me. That look in his eyes was a vow to protect me. To make it right. It was sorrow . . .

He didn't reach for his phone again.

His throat didn't work the way it sometimes did when he was clearly struggling with not being able to speak.

He just watched me. Waiting.

"Where have you been?"

His head slanted and he shifted his weight to one arm to brush his fingers across my cheek again. The touch so soft, I barely felt it. But I knew in it that he wouldn't talk about anything else first.

"It isn't a big deal," I finally said.

His chest pitched, his expression all disbelief.

"It's over. I took care of it. There's nothing else to say."

He watched me for a few more seconds before pushing from the couch and pulling his phone out of his pocket. Thumbs tapping furiously before he handed the phone to me.

Tell me where and who and exactly what happened

I looked the words over for a while before handing the phone back to him and shaking my head. "I'm not going to do that. Adam, I don't know all that much about your life . . . but if I tell you, I have no doubt you'll do something that I *can't* let you do."

. . .

And tell me why that is
Because of whoever this person is or some other reason

"I'm afraid of the lengths you'll go," I admitted. "I'm afraid of the repercussions of your actions."

Are you afraid of me

"No, but I'm wondering if maybe I should be." I watched the surprise flash across his face and gently added, "Because of the people you were so clearly at home with when I first met you. Because of the things you can do with a computer. Because of all the secrets you're surrounded in—like that Sarah's positive you never lived in New York, yet you took me to an apartment I was sure was yours."

His head dipped after a moment and he gripped at the back of his neck. All his movements clearly showing how agitated he was.

"Where have you been?" I asked again as I handed the phone back to him, a hint of my hurt weaving into the question.

"Ugh."

I glanced to the side in time to see Stevie staggering out of the hall leading to the den, rubbing at her face and coming to an abrupt halt when she saw Adam.

"Well, bless my ovaries," she whispered.

My eyes rolled. "Jesus."

"Yes, I would scream that . . . among other things."

"Stevie!"

She lifted her hands as if she'd done nothing wrong and padded off to the smell of coffee in the kitchen.

I looked up at Adam, an apology on my lips, but he was fighting a laugh. "I really have no excuse for her. She's uncontrollable."

The corner of his mouth lifted in a smirk as he tapped on his phone. But as soon as he handed it to me, he started walking away, toward the front of the house.

"Where are you going?" I asked as I stood to follow him.

He turned and gestured to the phone, the reassuring look on his face keeping me in place.

She's your best friend

Why don't you get some coffee and we'll talk

I left mine in the car

I couldn't help the dip of disappointment at the word *talk* even though I knew it was necessary. Knew that after the days of silence, talking was all we should be doing. Except, just reading that word had my mind racing back to the times he'd shut down mid-kiss.

Seeming not to notice that my mind and body and heart flew into a frenzied state at the simplest touch. Completely unaffected by what we'd just been doing. Easily slipping back to the calm and imposing man who'd filled my thoughts for so long.

"So, like, do you think if I just showed up with a minister one day, I could marry him before he realized what was happening?" Stevie asked, pulling me from my thoughts and forcing a stunned breath from my lungs.

I slowly looked in the direction of the kitchen and then started that way after another second, trying to figure out how we could possibly be friends.

"I can tell that you're trying to figure out why we're friends by your lack of response, but just remember that you love me," she called out from where she was prepping our coffees.

A scoff fell from my lips as I set Adam's phone on the breakfast bar and rounded into the kitchen. "Unfortunately," I muttered sarcastically as I walked up to her, bumping her hip and grabbing the creamer to put it away. But after a step, I paused and leaned toward her. "Thanks for coming back last night."

She looked over at me, eyebrows drawn close. "Where else would I have been?"

"With Russell."

She shrugged as if it hadn't been a big deal. "He understood. But he's definitely coming home with us tonight, not the other way around." Her voice dropped to a low murmur. "Not taking any chances with this asshole again."

Gratitude pulled at my mouth as I finally moved across the kitchen to put the creamer away. "And does Russell know about your obsession with a certain tall, very handsome, and terrifying man?" I asked, voice getting softer and softer when I turned and saw Adam making his way toward us.

"Oh, he is well aware." Stevie held up her mug toward Adam, continuing with the conversation as if he'd been there the entire time. "He knows there will be a wedding and some babies and a divorce."

Adam gestured to himself with the Asterisk to-go cup he was holding.

"Who else?" Stevie asked with a wicked smirk.

"Not happening," I countered as I grabbed my mug. "Russell's a saint to put up with you, by the way."

She gave another quick shrug, but I could see the panic creeping across her face at having so much of the conversation focused on Russell, so I headed toward Adam, blowing a kiss at her as I did.

"We're gonna go talk."

"Yeah, I bet you are," she mumbled wryly before taking a sip of her coffee. "Just make sure you're ready to go by five."

"I'm not the one who's always late," I reminded her.

She lifted her mug to the side. "We make it to the stage on time, do we not?"

"Love you," I called out as I slipped away with Adam right behind me.

I didn't say anything as we wove through the house, and he didn't ever offer me his phone even though he was tapping on it nearly the entire time we walked.

But when we made it into my room, he held it out to me, the tips of his fingers trailing across my wrist when I took it and sending a shiver up my spine.

And Adam just stood there, looking as calm and threatening as ever, as if I was the only one struggling to catch their breath from that brief touch.

With a shaky exhale, I spared him one last glance as I set my coffee on my dresser and then looked down at the phone.

Just so there's nothing between us

Ariana messaged me this morning and had me meet her at Asterisk

She and Mia weren't happy with me for numerous reasons

Mainly the way I've been ignoring you

Except I haven't

"You haven't been ignoring me," I said slowly, clarifying. Doubt clear in every word.

His head shifted slightly as he reached for the phone, quickly moving to the messages to show me a one-sided thread of texts to *me*. Texts that he'd begun sending a few hours after he'd left Monday night all the way through late yesterday morning.

"Wait, what?" I tapped on my name and then the Info icon, my eyebrows drawing close when I glossed over my number. "I don't understand, I haven't gotten *any* of these."

I gave him the phone, looking around my room until I realized I'd never taken my phone from my bag the night before.

Once I had it in my hand, I pulled up the messages, my movements slowing when I noticed the last message I'd received was from Mia on Monday evening. I'd gotten it just before she'd called to tell us about what happened with Adam and Tucker.

Adam stepped up beside me so I could see as he sent me a message with the word *hi*.

"I don't understand," I whispered again, my confusion deepening when it went through on his side but didn't come through on mine.

. . .

You forget to pay your bill

I glanced at the note before shaking my head, my eyebrows pulling together as I looked back to the screen of my own phone. Wondering how I hadn't noticed I wasn't getting any texts.

Then again, most of the people I spoke to on a regular basis lived in this house with me, and we'd all been coming and going between work and rehearsals since then.

"Okay, so you haven't been ignoring me?" At the shake of his head, a mumbled curse left me. "So, I've just been agonizing over you and snapping at people for absolutely no reason."

His troubled stare danced over my face before a slow smile tugged at his mouth.

You've been agonizing over me

My lips slowly parted as heat filled my cheeks. "That word might have been an exaggeration."

His smile widened, pure amusement and adoration. The sight of it doing amazing things to me in the brief moment it was there before it fell away. Leaving all that calm indifference and bringing me right back to the doubt I'd been wrapped up in these past days.

Adam shifted back a step as he typed, his fingers moving slow and his face twisting up in a mixture of uncertainty and frustration.

. . .

I'm sure it was

But apparently my silence isn't all that's hurting you

Your roommates think I don't deserve you because of the way I make you feel

Because I mess with your emotions and take away your confidence

Because I make you feel like nothing

Is that true

I stared at the screen long after I'd finished reading. My chest moving with quick, shallow breaths as embarrassment swept through me.

Strong fingers pressed under my chin, lifting my head to meet dark eyes, pleading with me to respond.

I tried to swallow, but my throat felt dry and tight. "I wouldn't say 'nothing.'"

His jaw shifted, his eyes flaring with question and anger.

"I don't know what you want me to say," I whispered, pushing his phone against his stomach and pulling away from him when he took it. "It's different—things are different. And that's fine. Just because we had . . . whatever we had in New York doesn't mean . . . well, it doesn't have to mean anything now."

Confusion settled over his features as he took a step in my direction.

"But this clearly means much more to me than it does you," I went on, matching each of his steps and faltering a little when his eyes widened in surprise. "And being the only one physically and emotionally invested in the other is—" A jagged breath ripped free when my back met the wall, and he closed the last of the distance between us.

"It's painful and devastating," I admitted on a breath.

He placed his hands on the wall on either side of my head, once again caging me in. His movements slow and his body twitching. His restlessness and the way he was working his jaw showing how badly he was struggling with not being able to verbalize his thoughts.

After a while, he lowered one of his hands to slide his finger across the screen of his phone.

I've told you what you mean to me
I crave you

My head bobbed quickly before shaking. "You say that, but you always look so composed while I'm struggling to tame the chaos you create inside me whenever you're around. And you steal my breath just by touching my hand, but there's no indication from you that you've even done anything. To the point where I sometimes wonder if I imagined it." I shut my eyes tightly when my voice hitched. When I opened them again, I kept my gaze on the sliver of space between us as I voiced every pain, laying it out before him. "Then when you kiss me, it's like you suddenly realize you don't *want* to be kissing me. And there's just nothing there from you afterward. Like you're not affected by me in any way. Like we weren't literally just on my bed, or you weren't making my knees weak."

His hand curled around my neck. The touch sending chills across my arms and filling my lungs in a way so pure, I knew no other man would ever be able to make me feel the way he always had.

My eyes lifted to his when he pressed his thumb to my jaw and tilted my head back just before his forehead dropped to mine.

Sorrow swirled from him as he held me for long moments before his lips brushed across my own. Stealing the breath he'd just given me and making me tremble.

My chest shuddered when he pulled away, but instead of the calm, unaffected expression I'd been fearing, his was all hesitation as he stared at his phone. Nearly a minute passing before he finally began tapping on the screen.

You're wrong

Fuck Hollis you're so wrong

If only you knew what you do to me

But I told you I wanted to keep you from me

And in that I try to refrain from a lot with you

From getting in too deep with you when I know I already am

My heart took off, but I quickly shook my head as I thought back over the past week combined with his words then. "Adam, I can't . . . I thought I could, but I can't handle that pit of uncertainty when you pull away—of not feeling like enough." When his expression fell, I gestured to him and cried out, "We can't be anything when you're already committed to your secrets and a life you want to keep me from."

You don't understand what being with me means anymore

. . .

"So, tell me," I softly pleaded.

His stare locked on me.

Pleading with all that pain and worry and fear and longing.

"Or don't," I finally said, trying to sound understanding when cold reluctance was slicing through my stomach. "That's fine, it's your life and you don't owe me anything. But I can't do this."

My mind was screaming to take back the words as soon as they slipped free. But I just stood there, unable to move or make my throat work as I waited for him to respond.

Long minutes passed before he scrubbed a hand agitatedly through his hair and grabbed my hand to lead me to my bed. Once I was sitting, he took a couple steps back and looked vacantly at his phone. His face drawn and haunted as if the screen were an executioner.

"Adam—"

His head slanted as if he were asking me not to say anything, and he finally began typing.

But the words he gave me weren't anything like I was expecting—then again, I wasn't sure what to expect.

I would destroy my life for you
Can't that be enough

From his grave expression, I knew his words weren't weightless declarations, but I was struggling to grasp the depth of them.

"What? Adam . . . what do you mean?"

He grabbed the phone and handed it back just as quickly.

You know I can't tell you

We both have things in our lives that are hidden Hollis

This needs to be mine

But you are everything to me

I would turn my back on everything for you

"What if I don't want to hide from you?" I whispered and watched panic sweep across his features and battle with what he clearly had no plan to tell me.

Sorrow wove through me, knotting in my throat and burning the backs of my eyes.

I stood from the bed, my chest shuddering when I handed him the phone. "I can't—" My words hitched and caught in my throat when he erased the distance between us.

Expression pleading and hands curling tenderly around my neck.

That war he'd been waging more evident than before as he struggled over his own words.

"Everyone has secrets, I know that," I whispered, my head shaking slowly. "But yours are already coming between us before we can begin. They're stopping you from getting too close to me—can't you see that's a problem? And at this point, I don't know if you're in a gang or the CIA because the things you say and the way you are could easily go either way."

The fact that he didn't so much as flinch had my stomach dropping.

"Oh my God, are you in the CIA?" I asked, my voice lowering to barely a breath.

When his head shifted the slightest bit in response, I felt the blood drain from my head at the alternative.

Oh God.

Then again, I'd already known, hadn't I? With the things I'd heard and seen at the party that night, I would've been naïve not to realize what kind of people were there. And even though Adam had stood apart from them all, he'd still fit in with them all too well.

I blinked quickly, bringing my focus back to where Adam had released one side of my neck to write to me.

Couldn't tell you if I was
Could I

"Which—the CIA?" I asked lamely. "Oh my God, Adam, who are you?"

Computers and codes Hollis
I've told you

"But that isn't who you really are," I said, my voice surprisingly calm.

The hand still cradling my neck shifted higher. Fingers weaving into my hair and thumb sweeping across my cheek before he pressed his forehead to mine. Eyes burning with an intensity I felt to my core. Lips brushing across mine in a kiss so soft that it stole the breath right from my lungs before he pulled away from me.

You already know who I am
What matters
That's what you know

I nodded, knowing the connection between us had always told me what I needed to know about Adam from that very first moment. But it wouldn't help us get through this.

"Tell me something real," I softly begged.

I don't know how to walk away from you

A shuddering breath tumbled past my lips at the confession that made my heart beat a little faster. But he and I both knew that wasn't what I meant.

Before I could repeat the question, he was handing me his phone again.

One of your guesses was correct
Sort of
I think you already knew that though

My head dipped in a nod after a moment of hesitation, and my tongue darted out to wet my lips. "You're in a gang."

Leaving the phone in my hand, he dragged his finger over the screen to type out the word 'was.'

"What, so you aren't anymore?" My brow knitted in confusion as I looked up at him. "How does that happen? Can you just . . . *leave*?" I asked, feeling incredibly naïve.

A ruthless smile flashed across his face as he gently took the phone from me.

Only one way out

Again

I think you already know because I got out a couple years before I met you

My lips parted to ask how I would know, but the question caught in my throat when he grabbed the back of his shirt and slowly took it off. Showing all hard planes and muscles that were so much more defined than they'd been six years ago. Newer tattoos mixed in with ones he'd had back—*oh*.

I wasn't sure when I'd moved, but I was directly in front of him, stare locked on the scar just below his left collarbone. My fingers hovered above it, my chest moving quickly as I studied the discolored skin there.

He was right. I should've known because I vaguely remembered him having this scar in New York. And even though I shouldn't, I had a horrible feeling I knew what it was from.

How he'd gotten out of that life.

I tried to form any number of questions, but then my stare shifted to one of the tattoos on his chest for a split second before snapping back there. And everything in me went so, so still.

My stomach dropped and ice-cold fingers gripped my spine as I stared at the old ink staining his chest. As I thought about the coincidences of us being here together. Across the country. Running into each other in a random diner. Of his best friend and roommate dating *my* roommate's sister.

All of it was *too* coincidental, and he'd come to Los Angeles just as I—

Oh God.

Adam took his phone and lifted it for me to read whatever he'd written. But it still took me a few seconds to pull my focus away from his chest, and then it went to his eyes instead.

To the worry there.

The *expectation*.

I stumbled back a step, and he moved with me. Gripping my upper arms gently and trying to calm the panic he'd clearly known this would cause.

"What the hell is that?" The demand came out on a weak breath, and I quickly shook my head. Pushing away from him when he tried to pull me closer. "Who are you?"

He lifted one of his hands as if wanting to explain before curling it into a fist, frustration ripping across his face as he sucked in deep breaths and looked to his phone again.

My gaze dropped to his chest again. To the tattoo there that I had no doubt had decorated his skin during our night in New York.

But it hadn't meant anything to me then.

It meant something now.

I turned and rushed from my room before he could stop

me, hurrying for my bathroom and locking myself in there because I wasn't sure where else to go when he was still in the house.

When my mind was running wild.

The doorknob turned almost as soon as I had it locked. A few seconds later, he softly knocked. Even the sound of it seemed to encompass his sorrow and worry.

But I just backed up to the wall and slid down to the floor as I struggled to sort my thoughts.

It probably should've bothered me more to find out about Adam's past—but again, I think I'd always known. And how could I judge him for his past?

Then again, I was sure I'd look past it even if it was still his present. I had then, and as complicated as each day with him was now, I couldn't stand the thought of not being with him.

But that tattoo changed everything.

Made me doubt everything Adam had ever said, all the way up to his current status as a gang member. Not that I knew much about gangs or gang activity, but I knew enough from being surrounded by politics.

From the politicians wanting to put criminals in jail to the ones getting caught doing illegal dealings with said infamous criminals. And the tattoo on Adam's chest marked him as a member of a notorious gang in New York.

And to top it all off, *my parents* . . .

I couldn't be sure if my meetings with Adam had been by chance or planned anymore because six years ago, just two weeks before I'd met Adam, I'd been introduced to the young mayor of a small town in New York.

I hadn't cared about him. I hadn't wanted anything to do with him.

But my parents had wanted it. Demanded it.

The night I'd met Adam, I'd stood up the mayor at an event that was supposed to kick off our relationship. I'd played my role eventually, dated him for a few years, if it could be called that. It was all arranged, and I'd managed not to see him for most of it by moving out here.

When he'd told me we should consider taking our relationship to the next step—*for the press*—I'd told him to save the money on a ring since I wasn't moving back to New York.

My parents had nearly gone into cardiac arrest.

I'd been hounded relentlessly by them until it came out a few weeks later—the morning after I first ran into Adam at Ampersand—that he'd been working with a gang in a drug trafficking ring.

The one on Adam's chest.

Fifteen

HOLLIS

I looked up when a phone was slid underneath the door, my chest hitching as I stared at it for far too long before standing from my spot against the wall to get it. Eyes locking on the door for a while before I walked over to sit on the edge of the tub.

My chest squeezed at the way he'd written out everything, clearly having taken his time since I'd shut him out.

For the first time in my life, I want someone to know me. I want you to know me. But that's so fucking complicated, and I warned you you didn't want to get mixed up with a guy like me, so I'm sorry for this. I'm sorry for hurting you—unknowingly and knowingly because I knew dragging you into my life would hurt you.

I don't know how to explain something that always felt out of my control but, Hollis, I need you to know I'm not that guy.

My life in New York was inevitable. From the moment I was born, the family I was born into, my life was laid out for me.

My entire family was wrapped up in it and sometimes, you don't have a choice.

But like I said, I got out.

There's a price to be paid for getting in and there's a higher one for getting out.

I paid it. It's done.

It was done before I met you.

However, that's still my family. The night we met? That was my brother's house—my brother's party.

I went to see him and ended up finding you. Simple as that.

But no matter what happens with us, I need you to know I never meant to make you feel like you were anything less than the girl who wreaks havoc on my heart. I just don't know how to let myself have you, and I don't know how to let you go.

But so we're clear, you're all I think about.

You've ruined days and months and years, Hollis. And I want to continue being ruined by you.

I pressed the phone to my chest, my heart beating fiercely beneath it as his words played out in my mind again and again. As they contradicted everything I'd just been worrying over.

With a sigh, I pushed from the tub and made my way over to the door. My movements slow but sure as I unlocked and opened it to find him leaning against the wall with his arms folded over his chest.

Looking just as dark and terrifying as ever.

And exactly as he'd said, he was wreaking havoc on my heart.

"You're not in the CIA too, are you?" I asked as I leaned against the doorframe.

His face twitched, looking wholly remorseful as he slanted his head in denial. Lifting his hands, he mimicked typing on a computer.

"Computers and codes," I murmured, nodding when he did. "Got it." Handing his phone back to him, I worried my bottom lip for a moment before straightening. "You said you don't know how to let yourself have me, but you don't know how to let me go . . ."

His hand slowly curled around the phone as he returned to his position. Arms folded and looking at once terrified and terrifying as he waited for me to continue.

"You need to choose one," I said firmly and then took a step into the hall, a step *away* from him. Fully expecting him to leave. Expecting to go days or even a week without seeing him again while he hid away, deciding which was more important—his secrets or me.

But he grabbed my hand to stop me not even a step later. Pulling me close so my back was pressed to his chest and his lips were skimming the shell of my ear as he brought his phone around me to see as he typed.

I might not be any good at this
But I know when I'm messing up something so damn good
And I won't let you slip away

"Then I think . . ." I released a shuddering breath. "I think I need you to kiss me."

The responding curl of his lips when he turned me was slow and sinful and did dangerous things to my body.

One hand slid around my waist while the other came up

to gently rest against my cheek. His eyes searching me as he leaned in, drawing out the moment and making wings take flight in my stomach.

And then he was pressing his mouth to mine. The kiss soft and gentle and stealing my breath when he parted my lips to tease my tongue. Giving me the sweetest hints of him and taking my heart in return.

My shock faded into a soft laugh when he lifted me into his arms and started walking us toward my room. Quietly shutting the door behind us and gently lowering me onto the center of my bed.

Every movement was slow and tender and so different from what I'd experienced with him before. And I craved it just as much.

Craved his calculated, powerful movements as he leaned over me and settled between my legs. His lips finding my neck and then moving down my chest as he drove me crazy.

Craved the way he paid careful attention to my body. His hands gripping and worshipping and learning all over again as he took his time removing my clothes.

The way he moved as if we had all the time in the world when he shifted off the bed to remove his own. Revealing every hardened muscle across his body and drawing my attention to where his thick length stood proud.

My body trembling and my breaths coming out shaky and shallow when he gripped the base of his length, slowly pumping himself as he climbed back onto the bed and between my legs.

Because this was different.

This wasn't some guy I was hooking up with to pass the time. And this was no longer a night between strangers with an inexplicable connection.

This was someone I'd fallen for in brief meetings. This was someone who'd started taking pieces of my heart with tortured glances and the way he spoke to me.

This was years of wondering and dreaming and waiting for this moment.

I just hadn't expected this moment to consume me so completely. To feel so overwhelming in the purest of ways.

Adam stilled, his face falling and one of his hands reaching out for my arm when he noticed the tremors rolling through my body. Question and worry tearing across his face as he searched my eyes.

My head shook as I slid my hand into his. "No, no, I'm fine. I'm perfect," I said, trying to assure him. "I've just never wanted someone so badly in my life."

Wonder and longing swirled through the pain in his dark eyes before he crushed his mouth to mine.

I sucked in a sharp breath at the sting of pain and then choked out a laugh when he sat back, his face scrunched up in regret and apology.

"I'm still fine," I promised through my whispered laughs and squeezed his hand when that earlier wrath came swirling back as his eyes drifted over my cheek.

He nodded subtly, a soft smile on his face as he leaned in to kiss me again. His lips all a gentle tease against my own before they drifted over my cheek to sweep across the bruising there.

By the time he made it back to my lips, his hand was drifting down my body and between my legs. Making feather-soft trails along my skin as he parted my thighs and inched closer and closer to where I was now aching for him, but keeping just out of reach until I was dizzy with need. The faint touches and restraint making it hard to breathe.

A breath tumbled free when he dipped a finger inside me, slow and teasing. My body trembled and a whimper climbed up my throat when he slid it back out to swirl it around my clit. "*Adam.*"

Dark, tortured eyes met mine when he added a second finger. Pumping them thoroughly inside me. Building me higher and higher until my heart was racing and the heat in my stomach was spreading through my body.

My head fell back onto the bed as that heat inside me grew until I was standing right on the ledge, waiting to fall. My body buzzing with anticipation as he kept me just out of reach for torturous seconds.

And then his mouth was on mine.

Taking everything I had to give and somehow filling me just the same. And just when I was about to beg him for that release, he pressed a deceptively soft kiss to the corner of my lips before crushing his mouth to mine again. Curling his fingers inside me and pressing his thumb to my clit.

And I fell.

Apart. Into that coveted abyss. Harder for him.

Trembling beneath him and clinging to everything he was giving me.

Reaching for him and guiding him to me, a moan raking up my throat when he removed his fingers and pressed his thick length against me. Savoring every moment and driving me crazy in the best way as he claimed me inch by inch.

The groan that vibrated in his chest causing chills to rise along my skin.

"Adam, please," I whispered once he was fully seated, my voice breathless as I moved my fingers through his beard and then wove my hands into his hair. Gripping tight and silently urging him to move.

To love me. Fuck me. Stay with me forever.

He swallowed the whimper that fell from my lips when he began moving. Slowly pulling out and pushing in, again and again, before he found a rhythm that had my eyes rolling back and my breaths quickening.

That white-hot knot forming in my belly all over again as his long, powerful thrusts took me to a place I wasn't sure I'd ever been.

Then again, it'd never been Adam *this way*.

"Oh God," I cried out when he sat back and pulled my hips off the bed, angling deeper and driving harder than before. His eyes devouring me in a way that was all carnal need and had my heart skipping for reasons that had nothing to do with exertion.

I reached back, pressing one of my hands to the headboard to help keep me in place as the energy swirling around us shifted. His hands raced over me, demanding and possessive. His hips snapped harsher and faster until I was swallowing back another moan as I shattered around him.

Floating in all that pleasure and need and crashing back into the safety of Adam as he barreled toward his own release. His broad muscles tensing and flexing as he lost all sense of rhythm until he came inside me. Stilling and gripping me tight for long seconds before he set me on the bed and curled over me.

His touch gentle when he pressed a hand to my cheek and pulled me into his arms to roll us to our sides.

Those dark eyes opened and locked on mine, fierce and curious and adoring.

I love you, I love you, I love you.

I pressed my lips together so the words wouldn't slip free.

My heart racing and my mind reeling over something so impossible.

Not long before, I'd been thinking the worst about him. There was still so much I didn't know—too many secrets between us to feel this way and yet . . . from that first night, I'd known he was different. Known we were different together.

No.

No, because that's insane, and I've clearly lost my mind. There's something about the way Adam fucks me that makes me loopy or something because I am undoubtedly in love with him.

Not!

Not! No.

Adam's brow furrowed and he did that thing he sometimes does like he wanted to talk—lips parting and throat working. And it tore at my heart when frustration ripped across his features before he shifted away from me to search the floor.

He dragged a hand through his hair when he handed me his phone, looking anxious as hell.

You're overthinking something

One of his brows ticked up when my lips parted to deny it because that's absolutely what I was doing.

"Adam, I just—"

He released a deep exhale as he shifted to his knees, worry and regret saturating his features as if he'd pushed me into doing something I didn't want to.

"I think I'm in love with you."

He went still and his face went utterly blank for long seconds before his stare shifted to me.

Cold.

Terrifying.

And filled with so much devastation and dread, it might've broken me if I hadn't just confessed words I'd never said before.

My tongue darted out to wet my lips and I tried to swallow even though my throat was so, so dry. "I know it sounds crazy and impossible for a million reasons, but nothing has ever felt like we have from that first night. And whenever you're gone, it feels . . . wrong. Everything without you has felt wrong since I first walked away from you."

Oh God, Hollis, shut up.

A minute must have passed before Adam ever moved, but it felt like an hour as I waited.

Holding my breath.

My chest slowly splintering and then cracking open wide when he shook his head. The movements slow as he gripped my hands, looking like whatever was going on in that guarded mind was destroying him. But just when he started leaning away from me, something broke in those dark eyes. And then he was pulling me closer and crushing his mouth to mine in a kiss that was all passion and pain and love.

A kiss that made every other a distant memory.

Stealing what was left of my heart and imprinting on my soul until I was ruined. Hopelessly and completely ruined and desperately in love with this beautifully afflicted man.

Sixteen

ADAM

Just as she'd asked, I hadn't told Hollis I was going to her show. But I'd wanted to see her. Wanted to see what she did—what could make someone so damn happy at the idea of going into work.

"I have to rinse off," she'd said when she'd realized what time it was, her green eyes brightening and a wide smile crossing her face. She'd darted from the bed and then raced back to press a lingering kiss to my lips. "I don't want to leave this, but I have to start getting ready."

Her body had practically vibrated as she'd wavered for a moment before pulling me into the bathroom and shower with her.

Never stopping as she'd bounced between rooms, practically dancing in her lithe movements. Nonstop smiles and laughing eyes as she'd hummed to herself. Dressing and gathering things in a large purse, all between calling out the time for Stevie while muttering to me that she would still be late.

She had been.

By the time we'd parted at the driveway, I was smiling in response to her because she was fucking contagious.

And I'd needed more of her.

So, I'd gone to the club she worked at—Raven. Not that it was my first time there, just my first time inside.

I'd about had to pick my jaw up off the floor when the lights had come up, and she and a bunch of other women were on stage in nothing but strings of jewels. Because even though I'd known what she did, I hadn't known what to expect.

And god damn . . .

But even as breathtaking as she'd been, I hadn't seen much of it. Of her.

My focus had been pulled to the tables up front. To the men yelling and howling like they'd never seen a woman before. Like they were expecting them to start stripping or leave the stage for lap dances.

For the first two dances, I'd thought of every single thing I could do to them. To shut them up. To make them reconsider ever wanting to come back. Reconsider objectifying women the way they were.

But this was Hollis's job—the one that made her so damn happy.

And the last thing I could do was get involved in that way.

So, I'd left and had just walked into a tension-filled house. One look at Leo, I knew he was ready to explode.

"You didn't fix her phone."

Grabbing my phone, I tapped out a message and tossed it at him.

I'm about to

I needed to keep it the way it was for a while longer

"You—" He cut a cold glare at me and tossed the phone back, pointing in the direction of my room. Once we were out of hearing distance of wherever Sarah must've been, he snapped, "You don't get to just decide that. And you damn sure don't get to make decisions without running them by me."

I rolled my eyes as I walked through my room, turning on my system and tapping my fingers against the hard surface of my desk as I waited for it to power up.

"I have to answer to people when things happen, Adam. That's difficult when I don't know what you're doing."

I grabbed my phone and typed out a quick message before going through the process of fixing everything.

I told you I'd covered my bases with Hollis while we were gone

Keeping her service disconnected when I went to her was part of that

I also never agreed to turn it back on

"You can be a dick sometimes," Leo said under his breath as he set my phone back on the desk. "Your battery is almost dead."

I gestured to the monitor, letting him know it was done, then searched for my charger.

"And was she suspicious at all?" he asked, still sounding anxious about it all.

. . .

Confused
More concerned with things between us
You need to calm down

When he lifted a brow, I waved off the warning there.

He knew it didn't scare me.

Look I need to talk to my friend
Not my boss
So talk to me or get the fuck out so I can work

He stared at the screen for a long moment before letting out a harsh breath and scrubbing a hand over his face. "Both, Adam. I'm always both—I can't drop one." When I just waited, he stepped back to lean against the wall, dipping his head. "Talk."

I hesitated for a moment, looking at where my phone was basically tied to the desk, then picked up a notepad and pen.

You ever consider telling Sarah who you are

His brows lifted and his eyes widened. "One day over there with her, and you're asking me this shit? What the fuck?"

I shook my head and tapped on the paper with the pen.

"Of course I do, but I can't. I won't."

. . .

Even now that she's pregnant
That you're starting a family with her

His jaw twitched and feathered as his narrowed stare shifted from the paper to me. "If I could, I would." The words were said slowly, all with that veiled warning.

Why don't you
You're always telling me you love her
That you actually want a life with her
How the hell are you supposed to do that if she doesn't know who you are
If when this is all over we're supposed to just disappear

"You know why," he bit out, pushing from the wall as I turned a page and continued writing, his voice lowering even more. "You know exactly why I can't, just as I know why you're pushing this now."

Or do you plan on disappearing from her and your kid

"Fuck you, Adam," he said softly. "Sarah's part of the job, I can't risk that. Hollis *is* the job, which means you will not tell her a goddamn thing."

A huff left me.

My gaze slanted his way for a moment, a smirk tugging at my mouth that was equal parts amusement and irritation.

. . .

I don't know who you're mistaking me for but you didn't grab me because you expected or wanted absolute obedience from me

"Adam—"

I slashed a hand through the air, telling him to stop.

Everything over these years has been mine
I'm the one who led us here
So I'm not going to be what fucks this up
I'm also not going to fuck up what's finally within my reach with her
And for the record
I think there's a chance Sarah would be understanding now
I doubt she'd give you a chance to explain later

Nearly a minute passed as he studied the words before he looked at me and said, "Never promised you an easy life." But I could see the doubt lining his face. The worry. All of which forcibly slipped away when Sarah could be heard coming down the hall.

I flipped the page, and he turned just before she came into the room, her head jerking back and eyes widening.

"What did I just walk into?" She gestured around with the pint of ice cream in her hand. "It's like a wall of tension in here."

I turned the notebook around to her, a smirk shaping my lips as I waited for her to read it.

. . .

Where do you put all that

She pointed at me with her spoon just after she took a bite. "You know what? I think you're just jealous."

I lifted my shirt, giving her an incredulous look as I did.

"Okay, showoff," she said with a roll of her eyes, then fell into Leo's arms.

"Do you have to tempt her with what's on the opposite side of the house?" he asked me.

I gestured to her as if to say she started it.

She sighed and patted his neck with her free hand. "That's a disgusting thought. Thanks for ruining first dessert."

Leo just smiled, not at all apologetic as he took the ice cream from her.

"So, what's the big work drama tonight?" When I just stared at her, waiting for her to realize this wasn't a conversation for other people, she pointed at me and said, "I told Hollis you give people this look. Ari and I told her you're a broody bastard, but she seems to think you're funny."

Leo choked over the bite of ice cream he'd just taken.

"I know," Sarah said in agreement. "I don't get it."

Leo waved a hand through the air as he struggled to speak. "Shit, babe. I don't think I've ever heard you say anything like that."

Sarah's neck flushed with heat. "Ari's the one who said it. I just agreed because it's true!"

His smile widened as he wrapped the hand holding the

pint tighter around Sarah's waist. "She called you a broody bastard."

"I—" Sarah's mouth parted and shut a few times as her embarrassment deepened. "Okay, but we all know it's true."

"Agreed," Leo said as he took another bite.

Have you met the guy holding you

Sarah did a little dance, nestling deeper against Leo as a smile spread across her face. "Perhaps."

I just rolled my eyes again, even as a smile of my own tugged at my mouth.

As much as I like being known as that

Let me be the asshole who tells you you can't be here for this

It isn't work drama

It's guy talk

Just as I turned the notepad around, my phone began repeatedly vibrating on the desk.

"I might be offended by that if the two of you weren't allowed in on girl talk." Sarah grabbed the pint from Leo and playfully stuck her tongue out as she turned to leave.

Once she was gone, I grabbed my phone just as it vibrated with another message from Ariana, and hurried to open her responses to my earlier text.

• • •

Me: *I don't know how Hollis's cheek slipped your mind this morning, but she isn't telling me who did it or what happened, so you're going to.*

Ariana: *Sorry, so many babies to help bring into the world!*

Ariana: *Also, I was busy making sure you weren't breaking her heart.*

Ariana: *But, yeah . . . right? I was fucking livid and devastated for her. She didn't really want to talk to us about it either, so I don't actually know what happened. I took a guess at who did it though and was right.*

Ariana: *IDK if you know who Russell is, he's Stevie's non-boyfriend. Super great guy. Has the world's worst friends apparently? They were frat brothers or something.*

Ariana: *One of them has been getting handsy with Hollis. She's kept it hush-hush to not upset Stevie, but it still came to light recently.*

Ariana: *So my guess is he started getting handsy with her again after her show. Hollis tried to stop it and he didn't like that. But again . . . IDK because she wouldn't tell us.*

My hand had been curling around the phone as I'd read her messages, but my head slanted as I read the last one again and again.

I dropped the notebook on my desk and tapped out a quick response. Thankfully, I didn't have to wait more than a few seconds before the three dots appeared, indicating she was typing.

Me: *This happened after her show?*

Ariana: *Yeah last night. Russell sometimes goes to the shows for*

Stevie and brings his friends with him. I guess his friends are really loud and obnoxious. Stevie and Hollis can't stand them.

A growl built in my chest as I remembered the men from the front tables. Unplugging my phone, I stood and started moving for the door, shoving Leo's hand away when he reached for me.

Me: *Appreciate it.*

Ariana: *Anytime. The show ends right about now. Go play hero ;)*

"I know exactly who you are," Leo said in a soft, lethal tone as he positioned himself in front of me. "So, I need to know what the hell this look is for."

Need to teach someone a lesson

"Yeah, you don't do that anymore." He pressed a hand to my chest, trying to get in my face to catch my eye. "And I know damn well just how much you like disregarding orders, but we haven't gotten to where we are by keeping things from each other. Everything's going to fall apart if we keep going down this road. So, talk to me."

Half of Hollis's face was bruised today

Think the guy who's been giving her trouble is at her job right now

I'm leaving

And if he's there I'm taking care of it

"Fuck." He roughed a hand through his hair and glanced behind him at the opened doorway. And I knew in an instant where his mind went.

It was all over his face.

If someone so much as touched Sarah, he'd do the same thing. There would be no stopping him—damn the job.

He gritted his teeth, already looking like he was regretting what he was about to ask. "Connected at all?"

I gave a hard shake of my head.

"Need you to be positive, Adam."

My hands were trembling when I lifted my phone to respond.

Just some asshole who wants what isn't his

"If there's a single cop, I will kill you." He gave me a hard look until I nodded, then stepped out of my way with the soft reminder, "Quietly."

No promises there.

The drive back seemed to take twice as long. My aggravation growing with each minute that crawled by. My mind racing, wondering why Hollis would also want to keep what was happening from her friends.

But then I was finally climbing out of my car, my feet

taking me in the direction of the loud voices I'd heard earlier. Laughing and making obscene jokes. Trying to one-up each other with all the things they could do with the women they'd just been watching.

I slowed as I came up to the last of the cars on the side of the building, then kept to the shadows as I entered the back lot. Moving closer to where four of them gathered together—another guy stood off to the side, head shaking as he looked at the building expectantly. At the door there.

None of them noticing when I stopped a couple cars away, leaning up against it and watching. Waiting.

Then again, I'd always preferred to remain unnoticed.

"Russ knows," one of the guys shouted, goading the man standing apart from them.

"That's enough," the guy muttered, shifting his stance as he kept his stare on the door.

"Does she do any of those dances for you?" the first continued, voice slightly slurred. "Or does she just show you what she can do with—"

"I said that's enough," the guy snapped, a southern drawl weaving through as he continued. "I'm surprised all of y'all haven't been kicked out yet. Bunch of disrespectful jackasses."

The four that were grouped together looked at each other before breaking into laughter as another began taunting, "Russell just thinks he's all high and fucking mighty now that—"

They all looked toward the door when it opened, and I followed their line of sight. My body tensing when I saw Hollis do the same as soon as she saw the men. Her expression fell, but she struggled to recover it and kept close to Stevie's side as they headed toward Russell.

"As always, your catcalls were so endearing, it's a wonder I didn't vomit right off the stage," Stevie said in a sugar-sweet voice when the four men began crowding closer. Flipping them off as she fell into Russell's arms to kiss him.

And I was already moving.

Stalking closer and stare locked on where one of the guys had placed himself directly next to Hollis. Grabbing at her hip and hand and arm, trying to pull her closer even when she jerked away.

Each grab for her fueling the rage pumping through my veins until I was shaking with it.

"I said *stop*," she hissed, ripping her arm away just as I slipped up beside them and slammed my hand into his chest. Using the momentum of his unsteady balance to send him back farther. Tripping over himself, away from her and closer to the cars.

I heard Stevie and Russell's confusion and outrage when they realized what was happening. I heard Hollis's shock when she noticed me. But my focus didn't falter as I followed him.

Each one of my deceptively calm steps for a few of his staggering ones.

Just as he started regaining his footing, I grabbed the side of his head and smashed it against the rear window of the car we were next to.

"*Adam*," Hollis cried out as other people started yelling.

Threats and disgruntled shouts that couldn't faze me as I studied the scabbing cuts on his cheek and then set my glare on glassy, furious eyes.

"The fuck you think you are?" he spat, struggling against my hold. "I'll fucking kill you."

A smile slowly crept across my face at the weightless threat.

Looking at someone . . . it wasn't hard to see what they were capable of. What they'd possibly already done. There was a shadow that lingered in their eyes. A chilling darkness that radiated from whatever was left of their soul.

From the way his eyes were widening with fear, he was all talk and would've never survived in the world I'd grown up.

"Adam, stop. You have to stop," Hollis begged as she came up beside me, gripping my arm and my back.

Her near-frantic plea pulled my attention to her for a moment until the man in my grasp said, "That's right, baby, call off your pit bull."

I pulled him away from the window and smashed my fist into his jaw before slamming the side of his face against the window again. Pressing him harder and harder against it as the yells behind us grew, and Hollis begged me to stop.

"Adam, oh God," she whispered. Her breaths coming fast and harsh as she reached between the guy and me, gripping at my arm in an attempt to make me stop. "Adam, Adam, *please*."

When she looked up at me, eyebrows drawn close and eyes filled with absolute fear, I looked pointedly at her cheek.

"I told you it was fine, that I took care of it."

My arm flexed beneath her as I pressed the guy's head harder to the window, earning curses from him.

Hollis's jaw trembled as her stare darted all around, her worry bleeding from her and crawling across my skin. "Russell," she began, her voice reducing to nothing as she mouthed, "is a cop."

Shit.

"You *have* to let this go," she softly begged. "Nothing happened, okay?"

I nodded after a moment and started releasing him just as Stevie said from close behind us, "One of those assholes called the cops, saying his friend was getting attacked."

Damn it.

Leo's going to kill me.

But all worries of what would happen when Leo found out faded to nothing when I locked onto Hollis. Face white as a ghost. Eyes filled with dread. Chest heaving.

"I'll show you attacked."

Shit. I pulled Hollis away just in time for Stevie to come in swinging with the heel end of a stiletto.

"Nope," Russell said, stopping her arm and turning her away from the guy pushing himself from the car, blood dripping from his temple. Releasing Stevie, Russell forcefully shoved the guy to sitting. "I'd stay there if I were you."

"*This* is attacking," Stevie said loudly, waving her shoe around before pointing it at me as she spoke to Hollis. "*This* is handling it, babe. Why the hell didn't you tell me?"

"I did," Hollis said, voice soft and hollow but still defensive.

"You said *Chris*," she argued. "I've been fantasizing about chopping his dick into little pieces ever since."

"I worry about you sometimes," Russell muttered from where he had an arm wrapped securely around Stevie's waist, then looked at Hollis. "But she's right. I hate that this has been happening to you because of me at all. Need you to tell me what all's been happening and with who. Also,"—his focus shifted to me—"who are you?"

"That's my future husband," Stevie said as if Russell should've known. "By the way, husband, that was incredibly hot. Talk about going caveman and getting me all kinds of bothered."

Russell's eyes rolled, the corner of his mouth twitching as if her blatant flirting did nothing but amuse him. "I've heard a lot about you." His expression fell when he looked back at Hollis. "What's been happening? Who else other than Chris and James?"

Hollis's head had been slowly shaking but jerked back. "Who is James?"

Stevie chucked her shoe at the guy on the ground. "This asswipe."

"She's assaulting someone under arrest!" one of the guys from earlier yelled from where they were waiting behind us. Arms crossed and looking ready to fight or flee.

Russell sighed and rubbed at his forehead. "I told him to stay there. He isn't under arrest." His voice lowered to a mumble. "I'm also not on duty. They never understand that."

"Because your friends are dipshits," Stevie bit out, glare set on the one sitting in front of us before everyone glanced to the side at the sound of approaching sirens. But I looked to Hollis, my heart thumping painfully when she went absolutely still beside me.

There was no running from this.

There was no running from her.

But depending on the outcome of the next few minutes, I might've just single-handedly destroyed everything Leo and I had done for the past seven years.

Seventeen

HOLLIS

"Babe, I'm the worst friend ever," Stevie said once the last person left from where she was tucked close to my side. "It's my fault it kept happening because Russell and I thought we'd taken care of it."

"Stevie, no."

"How did I not know what was happening in the first place? I mean, I didn't even know until it happened at the diner," she whispered, her eyes searching mine before darting to the ground.

She'd been alternating between beating herself up and raging in a totally Stevie way ever since the police officers had shown thirty-ish minutes before.

They'd talked with Russell's friends, who had quickly disappeared after their stories were negated by the rest of us. Other girls from Raven had started trickling out just as the first officer arrived and repeated what they'd seen the night before. Russell and Stevie offered what they knew and had seen tonight. And between all that, the attention had been on Adam and me.

Too much attention.

I avoided being noticed or having my name brought up for any reason, and that included interactions with law enforcement.

I knew from experience that the name *Donahue* being taken down, even for a report made by me, could quickly circulate from a department to a newspaper. Which is why I hadn't reported Chris—or, well, *James*—when he'd started going too far.

It's why I'd said numerous times I didn't want to file a report last night until the girls at the club had decided to file one for me, pulling me into it just the same.

It's one of the main reasons I'd never wanted to tell Stevie . . . because it would've gotten back to Russell, and as amazing as Russell was, he would've wanted to report it.

Like tonight.

My stomach had been in knots ever since Stevie announced Russell's friends had called the police. All I could think about were the details they had. How it would look in a report. Who would eventually get ahold of it. How long I had before my life in Los Angeles and at Raven was no longer solely *mine*.

But throughout it all, Adam had stayed.

He'd remained by my side, composed and calm and seemingly unfazed by the situation in that way only he could, helping soothe me. The only indication that he was struggling with what happened was the way his hand would flex against me whenever I'd recall my encounters with James.

"Russell feels terrible too for bringing all this to you," Stevie went on, pulling my focus away from where Adam was talking to Russell. "He warned those douchetwats against coming back to the club. But I think he's finally done with them, thank God."

"He shouldn't feel bad, and neither should you." My voice sounded numb even to my own ears. I tried to shake off the worry swirling in my chest and forced a smile. "Not that I'd mind if he ditched them."

"Frat brothers shouldn't always last forever," she teased. "Also, can we talk about how sexy my husband looked when he came in like a motherfucking caveman?"

A stunned breath burst from me. "Oh my God, Stevie. Russell can probably hear you."

Her eyes rolled. "I told you—he already knows."

"Unfortunately," Russell called out from where he and Adam stood a dozen feet away and smiled adoringly at Stevie.

"See?" she said offhandedly, but the way she was looking at him was anything but indifferent. She cleared her throat and looked at me, blinking away the obvious love she felt for Russell. "Anyway, you can't tell me that wasn't one of the hottest moments of your life."

"I . . . I wasn't even thinking about it," I said slowly, trying to figure out how that *had* been what she'd noticed.

"How? How do you not ogle him every second he's in your presence?"

"It's a struggle," I said dryly, even though when I glanced his way, that's exactly what I did.

Tall.

Imposing.

So handsome it was a wonder I wasn't constantly clinging to him the way Stevie wished she could.

A smirk shaped his lips as he accepted his phone back from Russell, his dark eyes never leaving mine, and Stevie whimpered beside me.

"I am so pregnant."

"Gross," I mumbled.

"Where did he even come from?" Before I could beg her to stop with her fantasies of him, she said, "It was just us, and suddenly he was there, shoving James back."

I blinked slowly as I thought through leaving Raven, a soft huff climbing up my throat. "I don't know. I wasn't expecting to see him tonight. I didn't think he even knew what time the show ended."

Stevie made a humming sound and then gasped. "Ooo, he's like a guardian. Like a dark and terrifying guardian."

"Oh Jesus."

"I bet he isn't human."

I exhaled loudly and walked away from her.

"I know what you're thinking, and the answer is *because you love me*," she said happily as she caught up to me, then placed a kiss on my cheek and skipped past me.

I stopped in front of Adam, trying like hell to sound as calm and collected as he looked. "You need to stop, you know, being *you* in front of her. She can't handle it. Sorry, Russell," I tossed on as an afterthought.

"Again, I'm already well aware of this," he said dully even though he looked anything but mad.

Adam's chest shook with a laugh, but he just nodded and slipped a hand around my waist, pulling me closer. Taking me in as if we had all the time in the world to study each other.

Making all that worry slowly ease away as my heart began racing at an unforgivable pace, beating out Adam's name.

"Swooning over here," Stevie said pointedly when he brushed the tips of his fingers across my bruised cheek.

"Stop making my roommate swoon," I whispered even as a smile pulled at my lips.

Amusement lit in his eyes as he looked her way, pointing between them before mimicking a baby belly.

"Um, yes, please," she said eagerly as I shoved at his shoulder, a laugh bubbling free.

"Don't encourage her, or I'm never letting her near you again."

"Oh, I don't think she needs any encouragement," Russell teased.

A huff burst from Adam, everything about him looking so much lighter than he had just minutes ago as he pulled me close again while lifting his phone.

Can I take you to my place

Butterflies took off, making me feel like I was flying right along with them. "Really?"

His head slanted subtly as he slid his thumb across the screen.

Only if you want to

"Of course I want to." I tried to fight the ridiculous smile tugging at my lips. "Just wasn't expecting this. Gosh, it's such a huge step. First olives, now this? I hope you don't try to make me listen to music next—I'm not sure I'm ready for that level of commitment yet." A soft laugh left me when he rolled his eyes, my lungs expanding fully when he pressed his forehead to mine.

Those dark eyes all old pains and adoration and love before he brushed his lips across my own.

"Swoon," I muttered, mimicking Stevie and earning a laugh from him.

"You ready?" Stevie asked when I relaxed against Adam's side, playfully pushing Russell away from where he'd been whispering in her ear, her smile wide and unrestrained. "He's going to follow us home."

"Actually . . . I'm going home with Adam tonight."

Her jaw dropped, eyes brightening with excitement as she pulled me away and lowered her voice though I had no doubt the guys could still hear her. "You let him take care of you. And tomorrow, I want every single detail—especially the dirty ones, like exactly what he's packing down there."

"*Stevie.*"

"I'm obviously sort of kidding," she said with a roll of her eyes as she grabbed Russell's hand and began towing him with her, calling over her shoulder as she did, "Don't be late to rehearsal."

When I turned back to Adam, instead of the amusement that had been lighting his expression the last handful of minutes, he looked reserved. All that dark warning bursting from him so thick and heavy, I nearly choked on it.

When I took a step toward him, he held out his phone.

Fuck Hollis

I'm sorry

You told me not to let you know if I was coming to a show

Not that I stayed

Some loud assholes had me a little too infuriated to stay

But then Ariana helped me piece together that one of them might've been the one who hurt you

You should've told me

"Damn it," I whispered, my eyelids closing tightly when he pulled me against him and lowered his forehead to mine. "I didn't want you getting involved. *I* didn't want to be involved."

His fingers trailed over my jaw before quickly skimming down my arm to grab the phone.

I see that now and I'm sorry

But tonight

I want you with me

I want to hold you

And maybe you'll tell me exactly why you looked like you were spiraling before you ever started giving your statement and during

My breath caught in my throat at his observations, and when I looked at him, he had a brow raised knowingly.

He gestured to the side and then began leading me that way. All that earlier worry exploding through me again as my mind raced with possibilities and new ones rose to the surface.

Because Adam knew I was keeping something from him. He was giving me the chance to tell him, and I wasn't ready.

I wasn't ready even though I'd just demanded all of his past and pain and secrets so they wouldn't ruin us.

Eighteen

HOLLIS

I trailed my fingers over Adam's bare chest the next morning, my breaths slow and even, though just waking up like this had my body doing all sorts of crazy, wonderful things.

One of his arms tightened around my waist at the contact, but his steady breathing never faltered.

We hadn't talked much after leaving Raven.

Actually, we'd hardly talked at all.

Once we'd gotten to the house, and he'd realized I wouldn't be offering any of the same secrets I'd just demanded of him, he'd led me inside and straight to his room, turning off lights as we went. Giving me a shirt to sleep in as he'd gotten ready for bed himself, all that dark energy rolling off him even after I'd climbed onto the bed and watched as he finally grabbed his phone and began tapping on it.

It scares me how much I want you

. . .

He'd kissed me deeply, passionately, as he'd climbed onto the bed and pressed me against the hard lines of his body. Leaving me dizzy and breathless when he'd pulled the covers over us and wrapped me in his arms.

I'd been sure I wouldn't have been able to fall asleep after something so incredible and promising, but the next thing I knew, I was waking up still secured against his chest.

With one last look at his handsome face, I eased out of his hold and off the bed, slipping into my jeans and opting to keep his shirt on as I headed for the bathroom to freshen up.

My face was looking worlds better than it had the morning before, but it was still too noticeable to go without makeup.

Once I felt better about my appearance, I went back through the room, grabbed my bag, and searched for something to write on. My lips tilting up as I got a small glimpse into Adam's life while I did.

Computers and codes.

He hadn't been lying.

One side of his room was nearly taken up with multiple monitors and towers. On the same desk, there were two laptops and a few opened notebooks. The pages filled with his scrawl in some kind of nerdy language I didn't understand. And just as he'd said, there were those rectangular, thick-framed glasses he'd been wearing when I'd first met him all those years ago, as if he'd just tossed them onto the desk without a care.

I ran my fingers over the frames, a small smile touching my face before I flipped through one of the notebooks to tear out a blank page, my face scrunching up when it made a louder noise than I'd been expecting.

I glanced over my shoulder, but when he hadn't so much as moved, I grabbed a pen and wrote a note mocking the one he'd left for me the other morning.

I'm not panicking or running.

I just have rehearsal.

See you tonight? Unless . . . oh my God, Adam, you're so clingy. Give a girl a second to breathe.

Literally, a second would do.

I folded the paper and quietly walked across his room to place it on the pillow and got overwhelmed in wanting to slip back into bed beside him. To forget everything else for a day.

To not have one of us slip away before or as the other was waking . . .

I forced away the impulse and went back to his desk to grab my bag. My eyebrows drawing close when I began flipping to the page the notebook had been on, and the pages fell open to one with large words covering it.

I don't know who you're mistaking me for but you didn't grab me because you expected or wanted absolute obedience from me

Everything over these years has been mine

I'm the one who led us here

So I'm not going to be what fucks this up

I'm also not going to fuck up what's finally within my reach with her

And for the record
I think there's a chance Sarah would be understanding now
I doubt she'd give you a chance to explain later

I glanced over my shoulder at where Adam lay, confusion and hesitation swirling as everything inside me shouted to shut the notebook even as I reached out and gently eased the page over to read what came after.

But the words filling the next page had a completely different tone. As if he'd begun talking to someone else.

I quickly flipped back a few pages until I found one that was blank, then started at the beginning.

You ever consider telling Sarah who you are
Even now that she's pregnant
That you're starting a family with her

Why don't you
You're always telling me you love her
That you actually want a life with her
How the hell are you supposed to do that if she doesn't know who you are
If when this is all over we're supposed to just disappear
Or do you plan on disappearing from her and your kid

Oh my God.

Leo.

He'd been talking to Leo.

What were they talking about, and what the hell did he mean they were supposed to disappear when this was all over.

When *what* was over? *Who are they?*

I jolted, a gasp ripping from me when my phone began vibrating in my bag, pulling me away from the spiral my mind had started going down.

I quickly flipped the notebook shut and hurried from the room, being careful to close the door softly behind me as I dug through my bag. The blood draining from my head when I saw "Mommy Dearest" splashed across the screen.

Oh God.

I faltered for a moment, then rushed down the hallway before answering the call. "Mom?"

"Goodness, Hollis, every time . . . is it that necessary for you to make me wait?"

"I'm sorry, I was just—"

"I was calling because your father and I were speaking to the previous governor of California while at the benefit a couple weeks ago."

"Mmhm." I hummed as I got turned around in the house and went back the other way, unable to focus on anything other than I truly didn't know Adam at all. Sarah was having a baby with someone she didn't know. And my mother was calling me after I'd filed a police report.

"Excuse me, did you just *hum* at me?"

"N-no," I said quickly. "I was—"

"Anyway, he has a son who is the newly-appointed mayor of Ojai."

That's great, I thought to myself as I struggled not to panic.

"He's quite the catch and is very driven by a career in politics, just like his father."

I stopped dead in the kitchen, no longer caring about finding the front door of the house now that I knew exactly why she was calling.

"Mother, I—"

"He's also been single for quite some time after having a long relationship, and he reached out to your father and me."

One of my hands lifted to my head, my eyes wide. "What do you mean he—no. Absolutely—"

"Well, as I said, your father and I ran into his father. We were on the topic of our children, and one thing led to another. You can thank me after you have dinner with him this weekend."

"I'm not having dinner with him," I said harshly and then lowered my voice. "I am not—"

"That's absurd, of course you are. Everything is already set for—"

"Mom, I'm seeing someone." The words poured from me on a rush before she could talk over me again.

"How dare you interrupt . . ." Silence filled the other end of the line for long seconds before she delicately cleared her throat. "Excuse me, I misheard you. What is that you said?"

"I'm seeing someone."

"Uh-huh. And is this *someone* from our social circles?" Just as I started answering *no,* she demanded, "Tell me his name."

"Adam."

"And he's a politician, an heir, a celebrity, a social media guru . . . give me something I can tell the tabloids, Hollis."

I swallowed thickly. My stare locked on the tile floor beneath me as her voice brought me back a decade and made everything else fade away. "He's just Adam."

The silence was so weighted even through the phone, I felt it pressing down on my chest.

"Then I believe, as I said, I misheard you. I'll send over the details of your date once we get off the phone. I truly think you'll enjoy this fellow, Hollis."

"Mother, I'm not—"

"Good, solid family. Promising career. Fantastic looks. And he's quite impressed with your successes as well."

"I don't care. I don't—"

"I know you'll do the right thing here." Her voice was firm and unkind, leaving no room for an argument. "There's a ring waiting for you if you play your cards right with this one, and I have no doubt you'll play your cards right. *Now,*" she said loudly before I could argue, "you've kept me far longer than necessary, and I'm running late for a luncheon. I'll get you those details."

"Bye," I whispered after she'd already ended the call.

Lowering the phone, I let out a shuddering breath and squeezed my eyes tightly shut as I tried to force away the feeling that so easily slipped back in whenever I had these kinds of conversations with her.

That incessant need to do whatever they asked. To gain their approval. To stay on their path.

But their path was a life of unhappiness, and I refused to go back down there ever again.

With another unsteady exhale, I opened my eyes and clicked on an app to order a car so I could get to rehearsal—so I could get far away from Adam while I tried to sort through what I'd read. Turning as I did so I could find my way out of the house and swallowing back a scream when I saw the man standing directly behind me.

"Oh God," I said breathlessly, staggering back a step. "God, sorry, you scared the shit out of me."

He tilted his head, his arms unfolding to hang at his

sides. Leaving his chest bare and displaying the tattoos there—none of which matched the symbol on Adam or even hinted that he belonged to a gang.

"You okay?" he asked softly, but something in it held a hint of warning. "You look a little . . . nervous."

"Yeah, um . . . yes." My head moved in a jumble of nods before I could gather myself enough to stop looking like someone who'd just stumbled upon things I shouldn't have. "Yes, sorry. I just need to get to rehearsal."

He tilted his head in assent, then slowly dragged his stare to the phone in my hands. "Everything okay with that call?"

"What?" I looked down at my hands on a delay. "Yes. Yeah, it was just my roommate making sure I was on my way."

"You have a habit of calling your roommate 'Mother?'"

"Do you have a habit of conning women into dating you and getting them pregnant when they know nothing about you?"

The retort was out before I could begin to filter myself, but then I was swallowing back apologies when his expression slipped into something absolutely terrifying.

He took a step closer, and my stare darted all around the kitchen, trying to figure out how to get to the door. How to leave.

But I was frozen in place.

"Now I need to know what Adam told you."

"I need you to let me leave before I tell your girlfriend what you're hiding from her."

A savage look crossed Leo's face, making him look so, so menacing and seizing my lungs. "That would be a mistake. Tell me what you know."

The only problem was I didn't know anything other than Adam and Leo were lying about who they were.

I sucked in a pained, shallow breath and forced myself to stand tall and hold his stare. "If you're trying to scare me, you can't."

The corner of his mouth twitched. "You should be."

Oh, I was, and he knew it. But I refused to back down to him.

When he didn't get the response he was waiting for, he began talking. Voice rough. Low. And unable to hide the absolute outrage or worry over what Adam might've told me.

"Think carefully about what you do with everything you now know. Run, we will find you. Speak, you'll only be destroying yourself." He took a step closer, piercing me with an icy glare. "Knowledge isn't power. It's a steep path to a grave."

Just as he began rocking backward, he was flung in that direction. His curse ricocheting through the kitchen when Adam followed through with a straight punch to his nose.

Hand gripping his throat and quickly leading him back until Leo smacked against the wall.

"The fuck did you tell her?" he bit out, shoving against Adam's chest. But Adam just pushed Leo harder against the wall as he pointed toward me with his other hand in obvious demand and question.

Adam glanced at me for a quick moment before his head snapped back in my direction. His eyes widening with confusion and worry as they searched my face. His moment of distraction giving Leo the chance to push Adam far enough away to get a hit in.

"What does she know?" Leo demanded.

But Adam just looked between us for a moment before his

stare stayed on me, his chest rising and falling harshly as horror fell across his expression. As if Leo's questions and the betrayal pooling from me had finally clicked.

"Adam."

He waved a hand through the air, the movement slow and looking weighted as he studied me.

Pleaded with me.

The hand he'd used to answer Leo curled into a fist and lifted close to his face as he sucked in a deep breath. His body vibrating and his chest now pitching wildly.

And I saw it.

That look that Adam sometimes got, like he was frustrated with not being able to speak. Only this time, it looked like Adam was about to break as he slowly moved toward me. His shoulders caving when I stepped to the side, taking me toward one of the entrances to the kitchen, in response.

"My driver's here," I said, my voice strained and shaky. "I'm leaving now, and I need you to let me."

His face creased with sorrow and fear as he took another step closer, but Leo grabbed his arm to stop him. That Adam let him spoke volumes.

I started past them, my heart lodging in my throat when Adam's plea slammed into me, drenching me in all his worry and pain and lies.

Choking me as I hurried from the kitchen and finally found my way outside and into the awaiting car. Wondering how everything had gone so wrong so quickly.

How I could've been blinded by him for so long.

Who exactly I'd been falling in love with.

Nineteen

ADAM

I waited until the door closed before shoving Leo away and stalking out of the kitchen. Chest pitching roughly. Muscles twitching. Jaw clenching.

"What does she know?" he demanded again.

I tossed a glare at him from over my shoulder and stormed into my room, going to where I'd dropped her note when I'd heard their voices.

Grabbing it from the bed, I handed it to him before looking around my room. Because she clearly hadn't known anything when she'd left it.

He read it, flipping it over to look at the back before looking at what she'd written again and dropping it to my bed.

"She got a call from Senator Donahue's wife."

My head snapped up, my eyebrows lifting at the news.

"That's what I walked into the kitchen hearing—the end of it. Then she told me it had been one of her roommates. Now she suddenly knows things about us?" He stared me down for a moment, trying to assess if her information had come from me. When I didn't so much as flinch, he said, "We need to know what was on that call."

I nodded and turned for my desk, dragging my fingers through my beard and trying to ignore the way it felt like my chest was ripping open. Like each breath felt like a struggle.

Like the longer I stayed there, the greater the chance I lost Hollis forever.

"Adam, you need to focus," Leo said when I hadn't made it more than a step, understanding weaving through his voice even though his words were clearly a command.

I gave a rough nod and erased the rest of the distance. Yanking back my chair and throwing myself into it as I booted up my system. Forcing myself to go through the motions when my blood was pounding Hollis's name in a punishing rhythm.

I entered my passwords on autopilot, my gaze dragging to the side as I reached for my glasses before shifting back to two of my monitors. Already going back to everything we had that was monitoring and recording Hollis so I could pull up what we'd caught of her call with her mom.

Just as I was about to play it, my stare snapped back to the side of my desk. To where my notebooks were laying haphazardly, the way they always were.

Except one of them was fully closed.

I slowly reached for it, turning my chair around and looking from Leo to where he'd dropped Hollis's note before quickly fanning through the pages. My stomach encasing in ice when halfway through, my messages to Leo and Sarah from last night began.

Fuck.

I folded it open so the notes were on display and flung it

at Leo, then pushed to my feet and stalked across the room to grab my phone.

"Shit, shit, *fuck*," he hissed before throwing the bound paper at the wall.

I finished the short message and turned my phone for him to see the screen.

You didn't get rid of them

What the hell were you thinking

"How was I supposed to know you were bringing her back here last night?" he asked, his voice a low growl.

My head shook furiously as I began typing again. Fingers tapping hard and showing every bit of my outrage.

No

No no no

You were still in here when I left

The last person gets rid of evidence

Always

What the fuck Leo

And you've been telling ME not to fuck this up

His head slowly shook as he handed my phone back, releasing it like just holding it incriminated him. Gripping his hair in his hands, he released a ragged exhale and looked up at the ceiling.

"I wasn't thinking," he admitted, sounding so damn

ashamed by the fact. "I wanted to get back to spending time with Sarah because we'd been gone."

Fucking careless

I tossed the phone at his chest and stormed past him, going to where he'd thrown the notebook. Dropping to a crouch and flipping back through it to find the one-sided conversation Hollis must have read.

Once I got there, I quickly skimmed the words, then stood and walked back to Leo, pointing at the pages as he handed my phone back to me.

She doesn't know details

Only that we aren't who we should be

He nodded when he glanced at the phone, then jerked his chin toward the monitors. "We need to know what happened on the call with the senator's wife. I heard Hollis say your name, but I don't know what it was about."

Just as I was reaching for the chair again, my phone vibrated with an email.

EMERGENCY MANDATORY MEETING IN THE LOS ANGELES OFFICES AT 0930.

A harsh breath left me as dread began unfurling through my body. With a knowing look at Leo, I gave him my phone to read and turned to get ready, grabbing my gun and badge from their hidden place in the closet as I went.

Twenty

HOLLIS

"We're going to stuff our faces with ice cream, curse stupid boys that are unreasonably hot, and maybe you'll tell me what happened," Stevie said casually as we walked into the house that night.

I held back a sigh, but the day had been unbearably long, and all I wanted was to climb into bed and obsess over what happened that morning in private.

I'd missed too many steps during rehearsal, banging into other girls and tripping over others until I'd landed flat on my butt and had been told to take five minutes to get my shit together.

I'd managed to. Barely.

But my mind had stayed on Adam throughout the rest of the day and our show, making it hard to focus. Making my smile not quite right. Making my chest constrict painfully and stealing breaths until I'd finally broken down when I'd sat at my station at the end of the show.

Struggling to breathe and feeling like I was on the verge of a panic attack because I didn't know who I'd been sleeping with. Who I'd been falling in love with.

And I hadn't had a minute alone to think about it all day.

"I can't . . . Stevie, I can't," I said for the umpteenth time today and tried to give her a placating smile when her expression fell. "I'm fine, really. It's just . . . complicated, and I need to go to sleep."

"I'm great at complicated," she urged gently. "I kinda think I wrote the book on it."

A soft huff left me, but my head shook. "I honestly just—my mom called," I blurted out. "She's mad that I'm seeing Adam and wants me to date someone else. And I'm just struggling with what my life was like before Raven and how my parents are and that they're still trying to control me. Okay?"

She studied me for a moment longer before nodding. "Okay, babe. I get it . . . Mommy Dearest is honestly the worst. I always need a nap after listening to one of her calls."

I reached out and gripped Stevie's arm gratefully, then whispered, "Eat all the ice cream for me," before heading upstairs.

My mind and heart being pulled in so many directions that it took me a second too long to realize I wasn't alone in my room.

I turned, a gasp ripping through me as I stumbled back into my dresser when I saw Adam standing there.

Tall.

Calm.

Wholly intimidating and fiercely handsome. And looking like he'd been breaking as badly as I had been.

He held up a notepad similar to the one I'd found that morning, eyes pleading with me.

. . .

I'm here to talk

"Of course you are," I said, my voice all a pained wheeze. "That's all you ever want to do, except everything you say is bullshit, and I'm done. I don't want any more of your lies."

He flipped the page as I spoke, his eyes never leaving me as he wrote.

"I want you to get out. I want you to stay away from—"

I'm in the FBI

"Holy shit."

My knees went weak, my legs threatening to give out from under me as I stared at the words that had the power to break every memory of us.

My gaze slowly dragged up to him when he reached into his pocket and pulled out what looked like a wallet, opening it to show me a badge and ID.

Tossing it over so I could inspect it, he went back to writing and then waited while I trailed my fingers along the hard ridges and grooves of the badge and studied the picture on the card. The name.

It was still his.

I finally looked up, my jaw trembling as I read the words there.

None of this is allowed
What I'm saying

What we're doing
But you and I met before I ever knew who you were
You consumed my thoughts long before I knew who you were
I won't lose you because of this

"How am I supposed to believe you, Adam?" I asked around the lump in my throat.

Pain and worry flashed across his face, but he still nodded as he flipped the page and quickly scrawled across it.

You've been our target for the last year

My body bent at the waist. Iron hands crushed my lungs at the words I knew but couldn't make sense of. "What?"

I think you should sit down before we continue

I roughly fell to my butt, and Adam hurried across the room, hand outstretched as if he might've been able to catch me.

He dropped to his knees in front of me, looking me over and cupping my face, dark eyes searching mine.

"I don't understand," I mumbled numbly. "I don't—why would I—why me? I haven't done anything. All I ever wanted was to live my life."

He gave me an apologetic look, then reached for the notepad again.

. . .

Can we talk now

I'll explain everything and answer every question you have

"Adam, I don't understand," I whispered as tears burned the backs of my eyes.

He leaned forward and pressed his forehead to mine, jolting when I shoved him back, finally pulling myself together enough to remember that he couldn't do that anymore.

That he was someone I no longer knew.

I didn't let myself linger on the shattered look in his eyes. I couldn't. I just pulled my knees up to my chest and choked back the building tears.

Nearly a minute passed before he pointed to the paper again.

"Sure, whatever. Let's talk," I said tightly, then jerked my chin toward the opposite side of my room. "My laptop's over there." He made a hesitant look that had my stomach dropping to the floor when it finally registered. "You hacked my laptop, didn't you?"

He dipped his head as he wrote.

Linked it to my system

And your phone

"Jesus," I breathed, then demanded, "Why? Tell me that. Tell me *why*."

He nodded and moved to sit beside me so I could see the page as he wrote. Looking hesitant and apologetic and wrecked as he held the pen above the paper for a moment.

I'll go back to the beginning

But first what's brought us here to the end is you

Your signature your name all over insider trading

Campaign donation bribes

Illegal government contracts

Hush money

"What—no," I stammered. "What are you talking about?"

He held up a hand, asking me to wait, then continued.

Right we've figured out it isn't actually you

But everything can be traced back to an account in your name

Everything has your signature on it or is linked to you in some way

You didn't see what I'm about to show you

He pulled out his phone and hurried to open the photos, pulling up screenshots of banking information and documents from when the account was opened.

With my signature.

"That's my . . ." My head shook fiercely. "Adam, that isn't me," I vowed. "I don't even know what bank that is. I only have my one checking and savings account. Well, there's—"

My lips pressed tightly together, and he gave me a disappointed look.

Where do you think all that money came from Hollis
Your trust fund
I already know about it
If I'm going to be honest with you I need you to do the same
Help me here

"I don't owe you anything."

He inhaled slowly. His head slanting to hide what my words were doing to him.

I'm doing everything to save you right now
So help me do that

He glanced my way, all that dark warning that radiated from him reaching out to me like a plea and comfort before he looked back at the papers.

"I've never touched that trust fund," I said when he started writing again. "You and I haven't talked about my parents because I want nothing to do with them, but they held that trust fund over my head as a way to get me to do what they wanted."

He stopped writing and looked at me, eyebrows drawn close and gently urging me to continue.

"I got access to it when I was twenty-five, which you probably already know," I said bitterly. "But by then, I'd already removed myself from my parents and their path for me as much as possible. I don't even know how much is in there, and I don't care. I don't want it."

He nodded after a moment and went back to writing.

"If it isn't me doing all that, then who is it?"

His stare shot back to me, eyes wide with surprise and a hint of unease. As if he was worried about what my reaction would be if I hadn't already figured it out.

Going to the very top of the page, he wrote two words, his eyes on me the entire time.

Your parents

A sharp laugh burst from me only to die when his apologetic stare didn't waver.

If I hadn't already, I was sure I would've fallen then. I felt dizzy. Numb.

I felt lost.

I stared at those words, unable to make sense of them—of any of this. "My parents are . . . terrible at parenting," I said, choking over the words. "But they aren't—they wouldn't—they wouldn't do anything illegal. They . . . no."

Adam brushed his fingers over mine. The touch all sympathy and sorrow and matching the pain emanating from him.

With a heaving breath, he continued what he'd been writing, but I couldn't focus on the words. My mind was a jumbled mess of chaos and doubt.

Because none of what he was saying made sense, and yet the more I thought of it . . . I couldn't be sure that it didn't.

But just as quickly, I'd fall back into that place where I didn't know how to believe anything Adam said anymore.

I didn't know if I could trust that he was actually FBI or Adam Ortiz or *anything* that I'd come to know.

I wasn't sure who I was sitting beside or who my parents were.

I wasn't sure who I was anymore.

How had my life turned upside down so quickly?

I flinched when he set the notepad on my legs, a trembling breath ripping from me as I was pulled from my thoughts.

"Oh," I muttered, thumbing through the few pages he'd written before going back to the beginning. My chest tight and my stomach clenching as if my body was already trying to prepare for what I was about to read.

Or rebelling against it.

Leo found me when I was twenty-two. I'd hit their radar because I'd been hacking multi-million-dollar companies. Not that they'd been able to trace me until I'd decided to do it when I was wasted one night.

He came up to me when I was out getting coffee and was calm about it. Put the handcuffs in front of me and told me I could either put them on myself, or I could decide to actually do something with my life.

Honestly, there were about two seconds where I thought about running. But I ended up sliding them back over to him and asked something like, 'And what's that?' He told me they needed someone like me at the Bureau, but he wasn't going to stick his neck out for some thug who'd rather commit cybercrime than prevent it. He was only interested in someone willing to protect and defend our country against any type of threat, no matter the cost.

I told him there was a brand on my chest that would prevent any of that shit from happening, and he said if that brand actually meant something to me, I wouldn't be talking to him. He also said I already knew it would get me killed one way or another. More likely in prison since he would be taking me in cuffs if I tried walking away.

I told him it didn't matter if it meant something to me or not, there's no escaping it. He said, 'Looks like you've made your choice then.' When he handed me the cuffs again, I just looked at them and asked what exactly he thought I could do for the Bureau. Once he laid it all out, I took a step away and said I hoped he had access to doctors because I would need at least one.

Told the crew I was out that night. Paid for it. Leo was waiting and rushed me to the hospital. While I was recovering, I told him about the crew's ties to a certain NY mayor you're well-acquainted with. But throughout that and during my time at Quantico, Leo kept coming back to me with different analysts, thinking I was giving them bullshit leads because they couldn't find anything.

Then again, I'd been the one helping Mayor Bianco launder his money, so I was good at covering it. So, I uncovered it. In doing that, it started leading us other places. Spider-webbing. Leo and I went back to NY and were following trails when I met you. I'd been hanging out with my brother a lot, trying to get any information while also trying not to raise flags with him and the crew.

I had no idea who you were.

You weren't on our radar at all.

If someone had told me your full name, it wouldn't have

even registered with me because I was so new to everything, I didn't even know your dad yet.

Then we started following leads with other politicians and billion-dollar-company execs and eventually came out here because of the governor. And right after we did, I looked to my side, and there you were.

Next morning, Mayor Bianco went down for covering up a drug ring. Except the gang I'd been part of had nothing to do with drugs other than using them. He'd *had no ties to drugs until then. And you suddenly decided you wanted to be a ghost . . . after you'd been dating him for years.*

That was when you first hit my radar for the wrong reasons.

We needed to stay in CA because too much was happening here, but we kept going back to the East coast, mainly NY. Trying to see if we missed something and coming up with nothing. But everything we were following. All these leads. They all had a pattern, and I knew they were connected. Some major scandal that knocked a politician out of office or had a CEO stepping down even though there was no evidence. So, I knew there had to be other damning evidence somewhere, and I just had this gut feeling whoever was blackmailing them had to be one group.

And then I found it . . .

So you know, after you left today, we got an email for an emergency meeting. Leo and I thought it was because you'd found out about us. But it was because an analyst noticed my pattern . . . the one that happens just before the "scandals" are leaked and chaos follows. It was for the mayor of Ojai.

That mayor is how I made the connection to you in the first place. To everyone.

McKay just became mayor about a year ago, even though he

wasn't set to win at all. And it was all surrounding a lot of opportune events. Two weeks before his fiancée went missing, his dad sent money to an offshore for who-the-fuck-knows-what, but it was a lot of money, and she's gone. We still haven't found her. And they didn't say a word about it, just went on with their lives.

His opponent, Stoll, dropped out the same day a million was deposited into his account. And then McKay's dad dropped out of the race to be reelected governor for "health reasons" even though his health is fine, as far as we can tell.

However, the exact same amount Gov. McKay sent to that offshore was wired two more times and ended up in an account. The same account that wired a million to Stoll before he dropped out. It was the first time that account had directly sent or received anything.

But once we had that account, we were able to go back years. Even with all the offshores they used, every single transaction in that account could be traced back to political figures who are still in office or who have met suspicious or scandalous ends to their careers. Including your Mayor Bianco.

And it's all in your name.

Your trust fund? Hollis, it's gone. It was emptied to start this account right after you turned eighteen.

We started following you, obviously. We had to. But I knew immediately something didn't make sense, so I started digging deeper.

Couldn't link it to all, but over half of the people who had their careers ripped away had been at a fundraiser or dinner party with your parents within a couple months of their downfall. We started thinking maybe it was a family thing, maybe you were working with them. Still, it didn't feel right, but I couldn't be sure if that was because of what I'd always felt for you or if it was instinct.

The more time I've spent with you, the more sure I am that it's just your parents. That you've had no part in any of this.

But Leo thinks I'm too wrapped up in you to see clearly because your parents came into town for a fundraiser a couple weeks ago. And remember we're watching everything going through your phone and computer, so we know your mom called you this morning, wanting you to have dinner with Mayor McKay.

"No, because—no," I said, struggling to speak when my throat felt so, so tight.

None of this was real.

It couldn't be.

I pointed to the bottom, my face twisting up with disgust and anger. "She wants me to marry him. I said *no*, which you should already know." I slammed the notebook onto his lap. "And Bianco was never my *anything*. I was forced to date him —I didn't feel like I had a choice. My parents had control over every part of my life, and as you apparently heard, they're still trying to."

Oh my God.

"Oh God," I breathed as what I read and what was expected of me collided together like a horrible scene I couldn't look away from. "Oh God, they want me to have dinner with McKay tomorrow night. For what—his fiancée—are they trying to get rid of me too?" I asked, my voice rising as my panic grew.

Adam's head shook quickly as he shifted toward me, reaching for me and trying to comfort me.

"Don't touch me," I snapped as I leaned away from him. Ignoring the agony that ripped across his face and tore through my soul, I pointed at the notebook and said, "Tell me what you meant. The pattern . . . I want to know. He's the pattern? Am I part of it?"

His head continued shaking as he gathered up the paper.

His writing messy and short as he hurried through the response.

When Bianco couldn't make it work with you I think your parents made it clear to him that he'd made a mistake

Now they've found someone here for you

Made sure he got in office

And they're telling you it has to work out

If it doesn't I have no doubt something similar will happen to McKay

However I think Gov. McKay stepped down for a reason but there was no scandal

Nothing

Which is weird

I also think whatever the bigger picture is now he's in on it with your parents

And I'm positive their next target is the current CA governor because money started going in and out of that account again about a week after he said he would run for senate next if only to oppose your dad.

"So, what . . . what does that have to do with me?"

What I've come up with

Even though Gov. McKay is currently working with them

your parents are in control of it all

They always have been

By getting you to marry his son your parents can more easily control that family

Your parents have done favors for them by keeping whatever the governor did out of the spotlight and taking care of things for his son

If things go bad for you

For them

The favors stop

My head bobbed slowly. "I don't know anything," I whispered, my voice twisting as the tears I'd fought burned and filled my eyes.

Adam reached for me, his fingers curling into a fist and falling to his lap before they could reach me.

"I can't help you. I do everything to avoid my parents. They only call when they're in the area. Or for something like *this*." I gestured to the paper before wiping at the tears slipping down my cheeks. "To demand I do something to help my dad's career. And if I don't do it correctly or if, God forbid, I refuse to marry someone I don't even like, I never hear the end of it until they get busy with their lives again." A soft cry climbed up my throat. "Adam, they don't even know what I do for a living. They still think I'm a dancer at the Los Angeles—"

I reared back and looked at him as I thought about the night we'd stayed up well into the next day, talking about everything.

"You already knew I danced ballet."

He gave a hesitant nod, looking so damn apologetic.

"What else—is there anything you *don't* know about me?"

His lips parted, his throat working as all that frustration tore across his face.

"Are you even mute?"

Everything about him went so cold and so still as he stared at me with those dark, tortured eyes.

"Don't look at me like that," I said through clenched teeth. "Everything with you feels like a lie. I don't know what has been real—if *any* of it has been real."

He swallowed thickly, his movements slow and calculated as he turned the page and brought the notebook up to write again.

I knew details about you

But I wanted to get to know you

The you I couldn't find out through a computer and following you

Or from what we knew of your life as your parents' daughter

You didn't know the truth about my job even though the extent of it has basically always been computers and codes

And I'm so damn sorry for that

But I couldn't tell you

I'm not supposed to be telling you now

<u>YOU</u> are the job Hollis

Doesn't mean it wasn't real

I've tried to be taken off this job because of you

Because I can't stand lying to you

I've struggled keeping any part of me from you

Emotionally

Physically

But I gave you every truth I could
I like classic rock
Pizza should only be eaten with olives
Falling asleep with you is something I'll never get enough of
And I've never wanted anyone the way I want you

My heart ached and reached for his, but I forced down the need and focused on all the pain as I glared at him. "Because you feel this connection too? Or because I'm the end of those leads you've been following all these years?"

The impact of my words might as well have been a physical blow from the way they affected him. Chest caving with a harsh breath as he looked at me with a devastating mixture of desperation and a plea for me to understand.

"You need to go now."

His lips parted and his free hand lifted, his fingers curling into a fist as if it was infuriating for him to not be able to speak, and it made my chest ache. Fear and frustration bleeding from him as he hurried to grab up the notebook and pen.

Hollis please

"No," I said thickly. When he started writing again, I grabbed his hand to stop him. "How can I believe *anything* you've said, Adam? For all I know, you just sold me that story to cover whatever horrible truth you're really hiding. How do I trust you after this?"

Sorrow billowed from him as he tilted the pen, pressing it

to the last words he'd written. Repeating them. Emphasizing them.

My heart whispered betrayals as I studied his dark eyes, but I forced my head to shake as I released him and sat back.

You trust me because everything inside you is telling you to
I can see it written all over your face

Just as he turned the notepad toward me, he made an irritated sound and sat up to reach into his pocket. Movements jerky and agitated as he pulled out his vibrating phone and tossed it on the floor.

But the second his stare met mine, it snapped back to his phone, and he hurried to scoop it up. Eyes darting over the screen, expression falling into something cold and unreadable as he absorbed whatever was there before he started putting his phone away again.

And then went still.

Body going tense as a wave of that dark energy burst from him and rushed through my room. Seconds passed as he knelt there, face set in a hardened, chilling mask before he scrambled to respond.

And then he was pushing the notepad out from between us and putting the phone in my hands, showing me the messages he'd just received from Leo.

Leo: *I keep going over this new theory you had today.*

Leo: *The Donahues have managed to maintain a squeaky-clean image throughout the senator's career even though they're at the head* *of this and the worst of them all. So pushing their daughter onto politicians with dirty backgrounds wouldn't make sense unless you're right.*

Leo: *They're offering their daughter as a way of showing they'll continue supporting the McKays. But in return, I think they're ensuring she has status again because, remember, they're all about their image.*

Leo: *So Adam . . . what happens to Hollis when it gets out that she's a burlesque dancer? Because that taints their image, and they won't allow for that.*

Adam: *Holy shit*

Adam: *I know what they're doing. On my way home.*

Twenty-One

ADAM

I stood, gathering up the notepad and pen and writing out a few words for Hollis. Body feeling tight and restless as I waited for her to finish reading the messages from Leo.

"What –" Her question died when she looked up, her eyes widening with shock and irritation as she read the paper.

We have to go
Now

"I'm not going anywhere with you."

My head shook fiercely as I tapped on the page with the pen before underlining the word *now*.

"I already told you to leave," she said, trying to sound firm even as her words dipped and shook with emotion.

Frustration built in my chest and caught in my throat

because we didn't have time for this. Not with what I'd just put together. Not if I was right.

Then again, I'd make time for her. Always.

I let the notebook and pen slip from my fingers as I reached for Hollis, curling my hands around her slender neck and tilting her head back as I brought my mouth down to hers.

The way she responded was instant and had my heart slamming around in my chest and my blood pounding.

Opening up for me and reaching for me, sliding the tips of her fingers through my beard before letting them fall to grip at my shirt, pulling me closer.

All unrestrained need for those seconds before she was shoving me away and stumbling back until she was pressed against her dresser. Chest pitching wildly as her wide eyes danced across my face and body, love and desire clashing with all that betrayal and hurt. The tears that filled them felt like a dulled knife dragging through me.

I pressed a hand to my chest meaningfully before doing the same to hers, hoping she understood.

I'd lied to her. I'd had to.

But she fucking knew me, and this thing between us wasn't the product of deceptions and my job. It was the truest thing in my life.

"You can't expect me to just believe you," she said, choking over a muffled cry. "You can't expect me to just forgive you."

I waved a hand through the air as I bent to grab the notebook and pen, the movement lazy and feeling like it took all my strength.

. . .

I don't

I'm hoping like hell you'll give me a chance to show you that we're real

But right now I think I know what's happening

What your parents are planning

What they've been planning

I need to go talk to Leo and I need you there because it directly involves you and things you know that we don't

Please come with me

She wavered, hesitation blooming from her as she thought. "What are you going to do to my parents?"

If I'm right

Stop them from hurting you

But just so you don't feel like I've used you for anything

Whether or not you come with me I'm already on the verge of connecting them to everything we've been working on for years

When I do I'm taking them down

She studied the page for a moment before tightly closing her eyelids as another tear leaked free, then turned to leave the room without a word.

I bent to pick up my phone from where she'd dropped it during the kiss before following after her. Walking in the wake of her hurt and confusion and wishing more than anything that I could take it all away.

But I was only going to make it worse with what I was about to reveal—*if* I was even right.

The more I thought it through on the way back to my house, the more it made sense. And I had a sinking feeling anything Hollis told us would only solidify it all.

By the time we were getting out of my car, Hollis hadn't said a word. I took one look at her rigid posture and thought of a handful of curses as I reached back into the car and grabbed the notebook.

Flipping it open and quickly scrawling across it as I caught up to her.

Don't worry about Leo
I'll take care of him later
We just need you to confirm and clarify things

My steps faltered when she just glanced at the page before sending a glare over her shoulder as she continued away from me.

I dragged my fingers through my beard and took a second to let it all consume me.

The guilt and sorrow and regret and pain . . .

Then pushed it down.

I needed to focus. I needed to do my job.

I needed to figure out their plan before they could put it into action.

Then I could fight for Hollis's heart.

Turning to the next page, I quickly prepared for Leo's fury and then let us into the house.

Just as I'd known he would be, he was waiting near the

entryway. Looking ready to murder someone . . . and that was before he noticed Hollis walking in behind me.

His brows lifted in surprise. “Hey,” he said uncertainly, stare slanting back to me in question before everything shifted with his realization. That look that could paralyze lesser men narrowing on me as he charged forward, voice a low hiss. “What the *fuck*, Adam? Tell me you didn’t. Tell me you aren’t that stupid.”

I just released a slow breath as I added a few words to the bottom of the page before turning it around so he could read.

Take a breath and stop looking at me like you’re going to kill me

You can threaten me later

We need to talk to her

She knows things we don’t

Put a shirt on

That look magnified. “Do you have any idea what you’ve done?”

“I don’t know why you’re mad,” Hollis murmured from where she stood just behind me. “I’m the one who just found out the FBI’s been targeting me and that my parents might be terrible people.”

Leo breathed a curse and glanced behind him, making sure we were still alone.

I looked at Hollis, taking in her pulled-back shoulders and the way her arms were wrapped around her waist. Chin lifted just enough to look like the picture of a stuck-up, rich girl, but I could feel her pain and discomfort radiating from her.

"Room," Leo demanded, word a low rumble. "Now."

I reached back for Hollis, but she shifted away from me, closer to the door.

And goddamn if it didn't have that dulled blade dragging through me all over again. Slow and brutal.

With a sigh, I slipped past Leo and headed for my room, letting them follow.

"What were you thinking?" he snapped as we wove through the halls. When I just shook my head, he grabbed my shoulder and brought me to a stop just outside my room. "This puts everything at risk—you knew it would."

I ground my jaw, my stare sliding past him to where Hollis lingered a handful of feet behind. Glare set on me.

Lifting the paper, I wrote all that mattered and slapped it against Leo's chest, letting him grab it before it could fall to the floor as I continued into my room and to my desk.

I did what I had to for her

Once I had everything on and pulled up on the appropriate monitors, I went to my third monitor and opened up the notes.

I still think my latest theory is correct. I think they're going after the current governor and that it's going to happen soon. But your text about what would happen if they found out about where Hollis works made me think of something because of what she told me tonight.

When I told her everything, she was worried that her

parents wanted her with McKay because she was part of the pattern—to make her disappear like his ex. Obviously, that hasn't been a thought for us, and I told her that wasn't it.

But what if it is?

"Seriously?" Hollis asked, sounding at once horrified and enraged and like she might faint.

I turned in the chair, already starting to stand, but Leo was there. Hand on her elbow and leading her toward my bed.

"You should sit," he said firmly as he helped her down.

That she even let him said exactly how difficult this all was for her. Not that I'd expected it to be easy.

When Leo moved back, her face was pale and her eyes were wide.

I moved closer to her, but her vacant eyes met me as she said, "I want to know why you think that. My parents—the pattern—why."

I studied her face for a moment longer before dipping my head and moving back to my desk.

Leo thought your parents wanted you with someone high profile so you'd maintain your status. But if they were worried about that, they'd always be trying to pull you back into the spotlight somehow. They wouldn't let you go years hidden from the public's eye, all while never really talking to you.

"You don't talk to your parents?" Leo asked, voice soft and curious but still holding an edge of his frustration.

"I thought you already knew that since you're apparently watching everything," she muttered bitterly.

"Jesus," he breathed. "You really did tell her everything, didn't you? And no,"—he turned to her—"we didn't know that considering we just got access to your phone and computer and, *surprise*, your mom called."

"Right," she gritted out. "I already told Adam they only call if they're nearby for an event or something, which isn't often, or if they want me to do something—like this date."

I tapped on the desk to get their attention, then let my fingers fly across the keys.

We need to know what you mean by that.
WHAT exactly do they have you do?

"The date with this Ojai guy," she said, annoyed at having to repeat herself.

"And what else?" Leo asked, matching her tone.

She made an exasperated sound, her shoulders caving a little as she thought. "I don't know. There hasn't been much of anything since I moved to L.A. But it was little things—I told you, they've always controlled my life. I went to the best private schools and dance studios. Had the best tutors and private instructors because I had to *be* the best. I had to be well-versed in the arts and know multiple languages so it would look good on my *dad*. Because anything could somehow help him in his career down the road. Dinners with diplomats or fundraisers—'you never know, Hollis.'"

Her expression faltered as she recalled her life. "When I got older, it was things like, 'This event will happen at this place and this time. Make sure you're there and seen doing something.' Or, 'There's a new charity forming. Make sure you're the first one to approach them and offer assistance as well as whatever money they need. We need our name to be the main backer.'" Resentment wove into her words when she mocked, "'No photo op, no trust fund. Let us down, no trust fund. Be anything less than perfect at a fundraiser, no trust fund. No Julliard, no trust fund. Fall on stage, no trust fund.'"

"I'm gathering you don't like your parents," Leo said dryly.

She huffed out a bitter laugh but didn't respond otherwise.

You told me they forced you to date Mayor Bianco.
How many times has that happened?

She exhaled slowly before looking over at the screen, then gestured to it before letting her hand flop to her lap. "Just that one time. Well, and then I guess now. Not that I'm going to. But Bianco was the same situation. I got a call, and they told me what was expected of me and with who . . . except that was the first time I hesitated with my parents on anything. It just seemed . . . well, I didn't want to date someone just because they told me I had to. And he really had no interest in me either. It was all very much a publicity thing for him.

"Because of our 'relationship', my parents weren't happy that the company I'd accepted a role in was in California, but they didn't say much about it because I had been told my entire life I needed to get that role. But when I broke it off with him, they were livid. Called anywhere from ten to fifteen times a day for weeks until it came out that he had been involved in that drug trafficking ring, and then they went back to not talking to me again until the next time they were in the area."

I studied her for a moment before looking at Leo as I let my fingers drift across the keys.

Yeah, except like I told you, it was laundering. Not drugs.

Which your parents would have known, yet they were calling you nonstop. Mad that you'd broken it off with him.

And now they want you with McKay. Your mom's demanding it.

And as Leo said, he also has a past that isn't so clean.

"What are you saying, Adam?" Leo asked, stepping close to my chair.

I worked my jaw, my head tilting as I hurried through what had become so clear when I'd read Leo's text earlier.

I think they wanted Hollis with Bianco because of his ties to the gang. An easy group to pin it on if something happened to her.

When that didn't work, they waited for the next best option, which is McKay. He already has one fiancée who went missing. Something happens to Hollis, people are going to look at him for both because, like you said, the Donahues have remained clean throughout all this. Somehow.

. . .

"They want her taken out," Leo said before I could type it.

I nodded and continued on.

Donahue has faded into the background the last few years.

This brings his name back. Makes him relevant.

"Fuck me." He released a harsh groan and gripped the back of my chair. "Sympathy votes?"

I started lifting a hand in a *maybe* gesture, then hurried to release the thoughts pouring into my mind.

No. No, think about it.

There has never been a slip with this main account except when Stoll was wired a million before he dropped out of the race against McKay. For years, every other transaction has gone through offshores. The account is under Hollis's name, and now her parents are demanding she gets with McKay?

They've been setting up Hollis and McKay since he was running.

Right around the time she disappears, it'll come out that Hollis was the reason McKay got into office. The heat will already be on him, he'll have no choice but to step down.

Senator Donahue will have the chance to play the grieving and ashamed father, giving him the opportunity to make claims against what Hollis did. Using it for campaign fuel down the road. All while showing his support for the man Hollis bribed if he runs again.

. . .

"You're wrong."

Leo and I turned to look at where Hollis was sitting on the edge of the bed. Tears streaming down her cheeks and phone in her hands.

Her chest and shoulders shook with a shuddering breath as her gaze dipped to her phone before lifting to me again. "I'm not saying your entire theory is wrong, even though I'd love if it were. But I do know . . . I know the last part is wrong, which makes me think the rest might be *right*."

A soft sob crawled up her throat as she held out her phone. Leo gently took it from her, movements slow and cautious as he stepped back to show me a news article from the Ojai campaign.

I glanced at the picture before looking back at Hollis when she said, "I wanted to know what these guys looked like, and there was a dual picture of McKay and Stoll from the campaign." She gestured to the phone. "That man's name isn't *Stoll*. That's my mom's cousin, Everett Cleary. He isn't even from California, so I don't know how he was able to run for mayor in the first place, let alone how he was winning."

"You're sure that's him?" Leo asked, but I was already back on my monitors, searching Everett Cleary and Stoll while pulling up the bank account that had received the million dollars.

"I'm positive," Hollis whispered.

Nothing.

There was nothing.

No account. No record of anyone with those names except for the files I'd saved to my system a year ago.

"Shit," Leo hissed when I leaned back, dragging my hands over my face. "Make sure you're secured. Now."

I nodded and hurried through checking my security, but everything was locked up tight.

"What's going on?" Hollis asked hesitantly.

I gestured to Leo as I started a search, seeing who else might've been looking into the people and events of this case.

"It looks like your parents have someone in their pocket," Leo finally answered, words pure reluctance. "Either on our end or in the CIA."

"What do you mean? How can you know?"

"People don't just disappear the way your mom's cousin has," he said, sounding more irritated by the second. "They still have files in our systems—something. But he's not a person at all anymore."

I don't see anything that shouldn't be there.

The only IDs that have searched anything relating to the case are people who are working it with us.

What's being said in this room doesn't leave this room.

Agreed?

Leo wavered for a moment before grunting out, "Agreed. We don't know who we can trust anymore."

If it's someone with us, the more we push our theory about the current CA governor, the less likely the Donahues and Gov. McKay will go through with whatever they'd planned with him.

So, let's make that our main focus in meetings.

The three of us will stop what they're planning on doing to Hollis.

"Three?" Hollis choked out as Leo said, "She can't be part of this."

She already is.

"Adam," Leo began, jaw clenching when I looked back, cutting him with a glare.

This involves her.

We can't shut her out from what's happening.

"It's always involved her," he said, tone all a soft warning. "It always involved her *this* way—we just didn't know it yet. She was never supposed to know what was happening."

I ignored the warning and looked at Hollis, but she was staring at my monitor. Face a strange mixture of devastation and disbelief and making me ache for her. But I forced myself to stay in the chair when all I wanted was to comfort her.

"If any of this is real, if my parents are actually doing these things, what would I need to do?" Her eyes drifted to me, glassy and red from crying, making the green look so much more vibrant.

Leo slanted a glare my way as if to say everything that happened from here on out was on me, then turned to look at her. "Nothing out of the ordinary. You need to go on with your life as normal as possible."

I leaned back and grabbed the keyboard, bringing it closer so I could watch her as I typed.

You need to go on that date with McKay.

Twenty-Two

HOLLIS

I pressed the towel to my face, letting the soft material and Adam's scent comfort me for a moment before I lowered it to pat my skin dry from washing away the dried tears and streaks of makeup. Immediately locking onto where dark eyes were watching me from the doorway of the bathroom. All those old pains mixing with new sorrows and regrets. Reaching out to me and gently caressing me with a thousand apologies.

The night had been longer and more devastating than the day, but as wrecked as I felt by it all, I wasn't sure there was anywhere else I wanted to be than right here. With that mystery of a man who'd stolen my heart all those years ago.

Leo had just left after the three of us had gone around and around on my knowledge of what was happening and my refusal to accept certain things—nearly all of them. Even though it'd all been right there in front of me, evidence nearly impossible to refute. And with my input, it'd only helped solidify what Adam and Leo had been doing all these years.

But even with what I knew of my parents, my feelings on them, it was hard to accept they could be capable of the things the guys had laid out in front of me. Made worse because I still accepted it more easily than I had the news about Adam.

Then again, I'd always known my parents weren't good people, even if I hadn't known the extent of their depravity.

I hadn't expected to fall in love with a lie.

Hanging the small towel back up, I turned to face where he waited for me and leaned a hip against the bathroom counter. "So, New York and two years ago . . . those were completely by chance." When he dipped his head in a nod, I asked, "But these last times haven't been, have they?"

His chest expanded with a slow inhale, and just before he pushed away from the doorframe, he shook his head, then gestured for me to follow him. Scooping up his phone from where one of us had left it on the bed, he quickly tapped on the screen and then handed it to me.

We knew your parents were in town for a fundraiser and needed to have access to conversations you might have with them following it

Leo wanted me to sneak into your house and do everything I needed to your phone and computer that way

But I had to see you

Talk to you

It'd been a fucking rough two years watching you from a distance

Even worse when things all started pointing to you

I told Leo it would be easier to get proof that it wasn't you if I was your friend

He didn't agree at first

So I knew you'd be at Ampersand and Asterisk those times I ran into you

But I kept fucking things up

Constantly lying to Leo and hurting you because I was so wrapped up in you and trying to protect you from the amount of betrayal you'd feel when you found out about me

Clearly did a great job of that

I looked into his hardened stare as my head and my heart said so many different things. "As upset as I am, I get it. I do. I mean, I kept who I was from you just because I wanted to live a life where I wasn't Hollis *Donahue*. I didn't want people to know me as the senator's daughter. I didn't want you to look at me and see money or some girl I'm not." I gestured to him with his phone. "You *literally* couldn't tell me about your life. But do you see why it makes me question everything about us? About what I thought we had?"

His head shook, the action fierce and adamant as he erased the little distance between us. Driving his hand into my hair and pulling me close as his forehead fell to mine. The small tremors moving through his body transferring to my own as he pressed his other hand to my chest.

Saying everything without saying a word.

Nothing had ever felt like us.

From that first night to this moment.

I gripped his shirt in my hand and pressed my head harder to his. "Adam, if you don't kiss me, I just—"

He crushed his mouth to mine, silencing my plea and making my heart falter before it took off in a wild sprint.

Nothing about the kiss or the way we were trying to get closer to each other was slow or gentle.

It was all fierce lips and mind-numbing bites. Demanding hands and possessive grips as we tore at each other's clothes.

This was pure desperation.

Passion.

Need.

An inexplicable draw that couldn't be sated.

I cried out when he pressed a finger inside me. And then another. Fucking me roughly and making my legs tremble as I struggled to finish with the button on his jeans. My eyes rolling back as a knot of white-hot need formed in my stomach.

He gripped my jaw with his other hand, bringing my mouth back to his. Demanding more and more of me until I was standing on the precipice of ecstasy.

"Adam!" His name ripped from my throat when he pressed his thumb to my clit, my knees nearly buckling as pleasure tore through my body.

He bit down on my bottom lip, dragging it between his teeth before capturing my mouth again. Drawing out my orgasm until I was a shaking mess. With one last, hard kiss, his hand drifted to my chest to lead me backward. A husky laugh bubbling from my lips when he suddenly gripped my thighs, lifting me and dropping me onto the bed. A wicked grin playing at the corner of his mouth as he finished undressing. His movements and stare predatory as he curled his hands around my thighs and pulled me closer until I was nearly hanging off the side of the bed.

And I was there.

Completely at his mercy.

Aching to get closer as he teased me with the tip of his hardened cock.

"Adam," I whispered, begged, as I struggled to move. His name morphing into a sharp whimper when he took me in one long thrust.

Pausing once he was fully seated to search my face, making sure I was okay.

"Move," I pleaded. "Oh God, please keep going."

That grin was back and doing cruel things to me as he slowly inched back out before taking me again. Each time harder than before until he found a punishing rhythm that had me right back on that cliff.

Ready to fall.

He lifted my hips higher, and I locked my legs around his back. The angle pushing him deeper and hitting that spot that had little bursts of pleasure racing through me with every thrust. Until my entire body was buzzing. Burning with the promise of what was waiting just out of my reach.

His hands slid up to my back and his body disappeared from mine, a whimper falling from my lips when he let me fall onto the bed. But before I could protest, he gripped my hip and rolled me onto my stomach. A gasp tearing up my throat when his teeth scraped along the sensitive skin of my lower back and then again on my shoulder blade and neck as he lifted my hips off the bed and pushed back inside me.

"Oh God," I moaned, my eyelids shutting at the feel of him this way.

I gripped at the comforter when each thrust brought me closer and closer to the edge, another gasp breaking free when he pulled me upright so I was on my knees with my back to him.

The change in position sending me into oblivion. Body

trembling and lips parting with a hushed moan as wave after wave moved through me. My orgasm never seeming to end as he drove in harder and deeper, fucking me savagely until he stilled behind me.

Muscles straining as he held me against him.

Chest pitching with his ragged breaths.

Forehead falling to rest against my shoulder.

I reached back to weave my hand into his hair, my heart clenching when he shifted his head to press a gentle kiss to my forearm.

"Nothing should feel like this," I said, voice breathless as I repeated words I'd said to him in New York.

He passed his mouth across my shoulder and gripped me tighter in response before removing his body from mine. A whimper tumbled from my lips at the loss and abruptly turned into a shocked laugh when he tugged me down onto the bed with him.

Never losing his hold on me as he pulled the comforter over us and settled against the pillows with me curled close. His dark eyes slowly drifting over my face as if he planned on staying in this moment forever, memorizing my face and the curves of my body.

And I wanted to.

I wanted to lie here and forget everything because I knew him, and I knew we were real despite what I'd said and despite what my head wanted me to think.

But I still had questions.

"Is there anything else I don't know about you?"

He leaned back enough to give me a look that said *of course.*

I rolled away to prop up on my elbows and clarified, "Anything else that will hurt me?"

His gaze slid to the side as he thought, his expression grave. After a moment, he looked back at me and gave a slow shake of his head.

"That doesn't inspire confidence."

The corner of his mouth twitched, but he just reached out to trail the tips of his fingers along my jaw before turning away. Looking at the nightstand and the floor beside the bed before crawling over me. Pausing to press a slow, lingering kiss to my lips and then dipping to nip just below my breasts, drawing a gasp from me.

A wolfish grin tugged at his lips as he stretched to the other side of the bed to look for his phone that had gotten lost sometime during, well . . . *us.*

Once he found it, he rolled over beside me so I could read while he typed.

There's plenty about my life you won't like

You have to remember what I was doing when Leo found me

I was born into it Hollis

There's a lot of shit I did that I'm ashamed of and that I would hate for you to know about

I can't imagine what you would think of me

But in its own way it could hurt you

There's other shit in my life that I don't talk about ever

Leo only knows because I was forced to tell the Bureau

And in its own fucked up way it could hurt you

But there's nothing that will hurt you like I have today

Understand

. . .

"Yeah," I whispered, wondering what all he'd done and what he'd experienced. But those were things I might never know, and considering what he'd been involved in, it was probably best. "Can I ask you something?"

He lifted his head, prompting me to go on.

"When you were telling me about the day Leo approached you, I was surprised by it. That you talked to him, that you let him explain why he wanted you, and even that you considered what he was offering you. I was even more surprised that in one conversation, you decided to turn your back on a gang that you were born into. Something people don't just walk away from."

Adam's dark eyes searched my face for a while before he glanced at his phone.

What's your question

"What made you take his offer?"

It's complicated

Just because I was born into it doesn't mean I ever belonged with them

Leo offered me a way out

I stared at the words, still unable to understand how he'd made a decision so easily. "Adam, you could've died."

He shrugged as a huff scraped up his throat.

. . .

I could've died anyway by staying in

I nodded in acknowledgment as my mind spun with everything I'd learned. "And they just let you come back after all that? Hang out with them and everything?"

At that, Adam's expression slipped. All those old pains flaring until I could feel them bleeding from him. Crawling along my skin and slipping into my veins.

"One of those things you don't talk about?" I asked when at least a minute had passed under the suffocating weight of his past.

His dark eyes snapped to me and widened as if he hadn't realized I was still waiting for a response. After another moment, he forced a smirk that was both an answer and gratitude.

Yeah
It's complicated
But to put it simply
My brother leads them now
He doesn't have a problem with me so the rest have to deal with it whether they like it or not

"Okay." I relaxed against the pillows again and leaned my head against his shoulder, absorbing as much of his pain as I could while he battled whatever demons put that look in his eyes. When he eventually rested his head on top of mine, I asked, "Are you a sweet or sour person?"

His shoulders shook with a laugh and he reached out to tease my hand with the tips of his fingers before responding.

Jesus Christ Hollis

You know

I think everything's going fine with us

And then you have to go and pull something like that

Give a guy some time before you force him into a lifelong commitment

"You're such a jerk," I said even as my lips stretched into a wide smile. "Okay, okay, wait. Do you already know what I like?"

The amusement that had replaced everything else dipped a little when he looked over at me, his head shaking faintly.

That first night

I learned more about you than some people will learn about each other in years

I learned everything that mattered

Over the last couple of years

I've learned everything about you that is public in one way or another

But I told you I don't know details

I don't know how you like your coffee or where you'd travel if you could

I don't know what your favorite time of year is or what it is about burlesque that made you leave your life behind

I'm still getting to know you

. . .

My heart.

It wasn't going to survive the way it was wildly slamming around in my chest.

"You really want to know all that?"

His eyes widened as if he was struggling to understand why I'd thought he *wouldn't* want to know those things.

Hollis

Yeah

My tongue darted out to wet my lips. "No one's ever . . ." My head shook and I rolled on my side to face him. "I'm so used to keeping everything on a superficial level because that's how it's always needed to be. My parents were very detached, to put it kindly. They wouldn't be able to answer a personal question about me if their lives depended on it."

Adam nodded, looking at once aggravated for me and like he understood my hurt.

"Stevie's the first person I've had in my life who's genuinely cared about me. She knows more about me than anyone, and she asks things sometimes that stun me because no one has ever asked them. Or just because it's still hard for me to wrap my head around the fact that someone wants to know. But it's still hard with her sometimes because she has her own issues with connecting."

I get it

Trust me I do

But I want to know everything there is about you

I want all those little things that make up you like your favorite flower and your favorite restaurant

But I want the rest too

Also

Sour

My eyebrows drew close at the ending that seemed totally offbeat with the rest of what he'd been saying. But after a second, I sucked in a quick breath and looked at him. "Gross."

He pressed a hand to his chest in feigned offense.

"Sour things are the *worst*. I can't handle them. My face does this really unattractive thing, and I can't—I just . . . no."

A wicked grin slowly tugged at his mouth.

"Absolutely not," I said, already seeing where this was going.

If it's anything like the face you make when you take a shot

Then I want to see it

A stunned laugh bubbled free. "What kind of face do I make when I take a shot?"

He dropped his head back as if he was trying to think, then shook it.

I can't explain it right

But it scrunched up in a way that finally shattered that rigid flawless mask you had on

Fucking beautiful
Adorable

"If I remember correctly, I choked on that shot. That isn't adorable." When he just lifted a brow in disagreement, I rolled my eyes then settled in beside him again, my tone softening when I said, "When I walked into Raven the first night, I couldn't look away from the girls on the stage. They looked so confident—demanding attention in a sexy yet beautiful way. All while looking like they *loved* what they were doing."

Adam shifted onto his side. His dark eyes studying me as if he was absorbing every word I said, truly wanting to understand me, prompting me to go on.

"It awakened something deep down inside me, and I knew I needed to be there, to be on that stage. I've never felt more alive or free while dancing than I do there."

His brows drew together for a while before he placed his phone on my stomach to type on it. Lifting it to show me once he was done.

I've said this before
But now that there aren't secrets between us
How do you feel like that when you have to hide it

I lifted a shoulder. "Hiding my life now is still living more freely than I was ever able to before. Is it not the same for you?" When all the emotion slipped away from his face, I lifted my hand, letting my fingers trail from his beard to his straining neck and then to his chest. "I didn't mean it in an accusing way," I assured him. "But does your brother know what you do now?"

Adam slanted his head just enough to give me an answer.

"Then you're still hiding—you have to." My eyes rolled as I conceded, "My earlier reaction and lingering reservations aside, I *know* you can't just advertise what you do. So, do you feel like you're freer now even though you're hiding?"

Lingering reservations

I grabbed the hand holding his phone and met his questioning and worried stare. "As much as I can understand why you had to do the things you did, it's going to take more than a few hours to get over the fact that I was your target. Doubts will creep in, making me wonder if you're hiding things from me or if you're asking questions because you genuinely want to know or you're trying to get information from me. I can't promise you those doubts won't make me question *us* again."

Remorse swirled in the dark depths of his eyes as he studied me, looking at once like he wanted to fix it and already knew he couldn't.

If I could go back to that first morning
I would stop you from leaving

A sad smile tugged at my lips. "I wouldn't have let you."

He dipped his head, his expression saying he was well aware of that.

. . .

Yes

To answer your question

I feel free in this job

Leo saved me

I owe him my life

"I'm glad he did." The corner of my mouth fell into a frown as the previous hours blasted through my mind again. "Seems I'm about to owe you mine." He began shaking his head, but I just asked, "You really believe this is my parents' plan? Getting me with McKay so they can have me taken out?"

Sorrow and anger swept over his features, and he reached out to brush his fingers along my cheek. As always, his movements seeming so deliberate and giving the illusion we had all the time in the world as butterflies took flight in my stomach.

With a sigh, he sat up and roughed a hand over his head before quickly tapping on the screen of his phone.

You will never owe me anything

Let's get that straight now

As for your parents

I'm pretty fucking positive

I've been studying this pattern for years

Following it to person after person all while knowing they weren't our big bust

But no one wanted to incriminate your parents because

everyone's afraid of them

It was easy enough to follow this latest pattern to the current governor

And we can see the other pattern leading to Mayor McKay

But we wouldn't have realized you were tied to the same one if you hadn't told us what you did

I sucked in a quick breath when it felt like my lungs began protesting the lack of oxygen, my head bobbing slowly as I read the words again and again before confirming, "And you want me to go on the date with him."

Adam grasped my chin and forced me to look at him, his eyebrows drawn low over his eyes and making him look so cold and dangerous at that moment.

But it wasn't fear that had my heart racing.

His throat worked, and that familiar frustration took over his features before he released me to type on his phone. Thumbs tapping furiously before he handed it to me.

The last thing I WANT is for you to go on a date with another man

Especially this one

I know I made the mistake in holding back with you in the beginning but I've watched Sarah fall for Leo and I know it's going to destroy her when she finds out the truth because of how deep they've gotten

And I swore I'd never do that to you

Then at the first chance that's exactly what I did because I couldn't help myself

But make no mistake Hollis

It has taken every effort not to stop you from going home

with someone these past years

Or to remain outwardly unfazed when Leo told me that you'd hooked up with someone

And that was before

It will take a goddamn miracle to keep me away if he so much as touches you now

No

I don't want you to go

But we need this

I slowly looked into Adam's fierce stare as my heart raced faster and harder.

"Okay." The word came out nothing more than a breath as I thought back to my confession the morning before.

"I think I'm in love with you."

Words I'd been sure I was crazy for thinking and feeling, but words that were true nonetheless.

And Adam had looked devastated.

He'd shaken his head and started leaning away from me as if he'd been about to leave.

But I got it now.

Because he always looked at me like I was everything to him, and now that the walls were gone between us, he wasn't holding back with the intensity of his feelings.

It wasn't that I'd scared him yesterday, it was that he hadn't wanted me to fall in love with him when I hadn't truly known him. He'd been worried about the fallout when I learned the truth.

He'd been worried about *tonight*.

But I sensed it in his words, I felt it in his touch, and I saw it in the way he looked at me.

Adam loved me too.

Twenty-Three

HOLLIS

"It's Saturday," I called out as I entered the house with Adam behind me the next morning, weaving through the entryway and living area, and smiling at where Ariana was leaning against the breakfast bar in nothing more than a sports bra and her women's-style boxer briefs.

"She's still asleep," she said as she reached to the side, making a grabby hand for the coffee she knew I'd have. "*Hey*," she said when she finally looked up and saw Adam behind me, then continued making grabby hands.

I took her drink out of the carrier Adam was holding but kept it just out of her reach. "You could've warned me this one"—I gestured to Adam with her coffee—"was in my room last night."

"Would you have gone upstairs?" she challenged, a smirk shaping her lips. "He said you were upset with him."

Adam glanced back at me knowingly when he stepped up to the breakfast bar to set the carrier and pastries down.

"Well, I'm not answering that," I finally said and watched as Adam's chest pitched with a laugh.

"Which is exactly why I didn't tell you." She pressed a kiss to my cheek and grabbed the coffee from my hand. "You're welcome, by the way."

"Thank you. I'm gonna go wake the monster."

"I got it," Ariana offered. "Just give me her coffee."

Once she was gone, Adam turned his phone so it was facing me.

She's right
You would've left me in there

"I absolutely would've," I agreed. "For a little while anyway. I mean, all I knew was that you were hiding something big from me—like who you were." I playfully rolled my eyes and huffed. "Can you imagine if it'd been something really bad? What if you were in the FBI and targeting me or something? You never would've been able to find me if that'd been the case."

A bright smile flashed across his face, dark eyes dancing as one of his large hands slid around my waist and pulled me in closer. His lips capturing mine in a kiss that was slow and gentle and had my heart going wild.

"You don't have to go," I whispered hopefully against his lips when he started pulling away. His reluctant sigh moving through me and trying to heal the remaining cracks from his betrayal.

Taking his time, he let his fingers drift over my jaw and down my neck before sliding them into my hair to crush his mouth to mine again. His lips fierce and demanding as his tongue did wicked, torturous things to me. Making me all kinds of weak until I was falling into him.

"Don't go," I breathed into the kiss, a soft laugh tumbling free when he lifted me into his arms and moved into the living room to set me on the back of the couch.

"Yes, please. Me next," Stevie mumbled groggily.

I broke away from the kiss, my horrified words bursting from my lungs. "Oh my God, Stevie!"

"I'm just saying." She shrugged, waving her coffee around and leaning heavily on Ariana. "You know . . . things."

I let my head fall to Adam's chest with a sigh. My stomach filling with fluttering wings when he tightened one of his arms around me, keeping me close as he slid his thumb across the screen of his phone.

Ask me not to go and I won't

But I have a lot of work to do

Need to try to figure out where your mom's cousin went and prep for McKay

Before I could respond, he hurried to add something else.

I could always be in your room when you get home tonight

A huff fell from my lips, amusement pulling at my chest when I looked into his eyes, getting lost in all that pain and adoration again. "I think I'd like that."

He nodded as if he planned to do exactly that before

claiming my mouth again, his lips all a soft tease against mine before he pulled away and set my feet on the floor.

"Hey, future ex," Stevie called out from where she was standing halfway in the pantry, eating cereal out of the box. "Should we figure out custody arrangements and child support now . . . or now? Think the whole house got pregnant somewhere in there."

"Jesus," I muttered, dropping my head into my hands and forcing back a laugh when Ariana choked on her coffee.

"For the kid," Stevie added on as an afterthought, then gestured toward us with the box when I looked at her again, shaking my head. "I get Hollis weekdays, weekends, and all holidays—no exceptions."

"Well, no one can say you have attachment issues," Ariana teased around clearing her throat from what she'd tried to inhale.

Adam just slanted a look that was pure amusement my way as his fingers teased my hip, then took a step back just as Stevie gasped and yelled, "Mia's here!"

"Why wouldn't I be?" Mia asked as she stopped in the space between the kitchen and living room.

"Uh . . ." Ariana huffed out a laugh.

"It was a joke," Mia said with a wink. "I know how to joke too. I go in later."

"Which means *we're all here,*" Stevie said as if that should mean something to the rest of us.

From the way Ariana stifled a laugh a few seconds later, I was wondering if it just didn't mean something to me. And then I realized I hadn't brought anything for Mia because she was never home on Saturday mornings.

I made an apologetic face as I glanced at the remaining coffee in the carrier. "Mia, I'm sorry, I wasn't expecting you to be here. But you're more than welcome to have my drink."

"Oh no," she said quickly. "I'll be drinking coffee all through my shift, I'm fine."

"Are you sure?"

"Absolutely." She sent me a gentle smile that turned wicked as she looked from Stevie to Ariana. "So, are we interrogating?"

Shit.

Ariana's laugh finally broke free when my expression fell, and Stevie shouted, "Yes!" far too enthusiastically.

"No," I said vehemently now that I finally realized what was happening. Because this couldn't happen. Not with Adam. "Absolutely not."

"Absolutely *yes*," Ariana argued.

I turned to look at her. "You already know him."

"House rules," she said with a shrug as Stevie gasped and said, "Don't even think about it. The three of you interrogated the hell out of Russell."

Adam squeezed my side and gave me a questioning look when I glanced back at him. "It's this thing we do if one of us is seeing someone."

"Nope," Stevie and Ariana said at the same time, considering both of them had strong aversions to dating.

"Or if we've slept with the same person more than a couple times."

Ariana pointed at me and then tapped her nose.

"They get interrogated by us. But,"—I added quickly before the three of them could start—"Ariana already knows Adam really well, and Stevie can't keep her mind out of her pants around him. So, no."

"So, yes," the three said excitedly.

"The faster we begin, the faster it ends . . . unless you can keep going," Stevie said with a sly wink.

"Stevie!"

She lifted the box of cereal and free hand in the air, looking at me like she didn't know what could be wrong. "I said literally not one thing."

Ariana made a face. "That isn't entirely true," she said to her and then looked at Adam. "It's chalkboard time."

"I'm so sorry in advance," I said when the girls started walking over to where the massive chalkboard hung on the wall, their voices and laughs pure excitement. "This can get very personal, and I've never had anyone be on the receiving end of it."

My hookups in the past years had all been more of a *hi, you're cute, where's the nearest dark room?*

Adam lifted a brow at that, seeming to like that he was the first for me.

With a nod, he slid his finger over the screen of his phone before giving it to me.

If they ask certain questions I'll have to lie

"I know, I'm sorry in advance—you don't have to do this," I hurried to add, melting a little when he curled his large hand around my neck and pressed his thumb to my jaw. Tipping my head back to press a slow kiss to my lips.

When he walked away, I pocketed his phone and released an uneasy sigh when Ariana came up to me and hooked her arm around my neck. "We'll be gentle," she said as she lifted her cup to her mouth. "Mia and I will. No promises about the other one."

"*The other one* is what I'm worried about."

A soft laugh left her as she released me. "You know it's all a joke."

"I'd prefer if she just stopped fighting what she feels for Russell."

Ariana's eyes widened as if there was no hope of that ever happening, then turned back around to face where Adam was standing beside the chalkboard and studying me.

"All right, here we go," Ariana said loudly. "I'm Ariana, and this is Mia and Stevie. You clearly know our Hollis, but we don't know you. So . . ."—she pointed at him with her cup—"your full name."

Adam looked at her as if she'd lost her mind, and she scoffed.

"That's how we open with everyone. We're not giving you any favors just because I already know you."

Adam rolled his eyes and then gave me a look that was so adoring, it seemed to freeze time for a few precious seconds. As if even my soul knew that look and this moment were ones I wanted to remember for the rest of my life.

Turning for the board, he grabbed a piece of chalk and wrote ***Adam Ortiz*** before facing my friends as if waiting for what they would toss at him next.

"What do you do for a living?" Stevie asked.

He turned back to the chalkboard, writing ***Information security analyst*** as flawlessly as he'd written his name, but I saw it. The slight twitch of his jaw as he wrote. The darkness in his eyes when they caught on me as he turned back around.

Nothing in his expression had changed, but it was there in his eyes. Telling me everything I needed to know.

He was sorry. He didn't want to be doing what he so clearly had to.

But this was necessary.

The next questions came from all three of the girls in rapid-fire and had me dropping my face into my palm as Adam's eyebrows rose.

"How tall are you?"

"Where are you from?"

"So, what exactly are you packing down there?"

"Okay, we're done!" I yelled over Stevie a while later, pushing Ariana away from where she was clinging to me, bent over laughing.

Mia just caught her in her arms as she softly laughed, and I went to save Adam.

"No," Stevie complained, "he still has so much more to answer."

"I'm pretty sure he answered more than anyone's ever had to." I pointed at her in warning. "You're in trouble."

She grinned wickedly, more than proud of herself.

Adam had answered everything from his favorite color —***black***—to his preferred way of dying—***what the fuck? In my sleep, I guess?***—to who had a better six-pack, him or Ariana. He did, obviously. Not that Ariana's toned stomach could be considered a six-pack, but they still made him prove it.

Throughout it all, I'd found myself laughing with the girls. But whenever things turned personal again, I'd worried for Adam and wished for it to end.

Like, why did Adam leave New York, and did his parents still live there?

And then Stevie had broken through it all with her question posed as a challenge. "Who's a better kisser, you or me? I'll be the judge."

"You aren't kissing my roommates," I said firmly as I took the chalk from Adam and placed it in the metal basket.

He gave me a look that said he hadn't planned on it before his expression shifted.

In an instant, he was staring at me with a passion and intensity I felt down to my core as he reached forward to place the tips of his fingers on my throat.

His mouth parted as if he was about to speak, a hint of that old pain flashing across his face before he added his other hand. The touch so soft and gentle and reverent even when he slid his hands around so he was cradling my neck, his thumb brushing across my bottom lip as he studied me.

After the sweetest eternity in his gaze, he moved one of his hands down my body, his touch firm and claiming and stealing my breath as he deftly removed his phone from my back pocket.

I like your laugh

I wish I could hear yours.

As soon as the thought entered my mind, I felt like the worst kind of person. Guilt twisted my stomach for wanting something so selfish, and I hurried to push the thought away.

"Best interrogation we've ever had," Ariana said as she

came up beside us and clapped his shoulder, thankfully taking the focus from my thoughts.

"Oh, I have to go!" Mia said before running through the house, toward the stairs.

"I have to agree," Stevie said as she plopped into one of the chairs at the kitchen table. "Best yet."

"And I found out new things about you," Ariana added. "Imagine that."

Adam rolled his eyes and gently pushed her away, only to tap on his phone and hold it out for her to read.

She scoffed. "What do you mean? I'm clothed."

Stevie barked out a loud laugh.

"That's an argument you won't win," I warned him, then gestured to the little Ariana *was* wearing. "I'm surprised you don't already know about this."

About her walking around in underwear

No

I don't know why I would

"It's how I first met her," I said, my tone all surprise. "It's how she's dressed ninety percent of the time."

"You just proved what I'm always saying—I'm *dressed,*" Ariana said as if that was that and then fell into her chair at the table.

"Underwear," Stevie and I said at the same time.

"Clothing," Ariana said with a shrug. "I don't see a problem."

. . .

She has a point

I looked at the words and then pointed at Adam. "Don't you start."

"Ha!" Ariana said. "He's on my side, isn't he?"

"Nope," I said even as Adam shrugged.

"Bye!" Mia yelled as she ran through the living room to the entryway.

The three of us called out *hi* or *bye*, so used to her rushing in and out without ever actually seeing her, and I reached for Adam's hand, knowing he had to go too. "I'm going to—"

Ariana held up a hand for me to stop, her head listed until the front door slammed shut. "We need to have a house meeting."

"But Mia just left," I said unnecessarily as Stevie shook her head wildly and added, "It's morning, and it's Saturday."

"Right, well, I need to have an answer before noon, and as for Mia . . ." Ariana's stare drifted from the living room to the table as she released a heavy sigh. "It can't wait until Monday night."

Stevie and I shared a look, her eyebrows raising when Ariana added, "I don't care if Adam's here for it."

"Um . . ." Stevie gave him a mischievous look. "No one wants you around more than me—"

"Wrong," I interjected dully.

"—but house meetings have always been *house* meetings."

"Like I said, I need to have an answer before noon," Ariana said, sounding hurried. "So, can we get over who's here and do this?"

I looked at Adam in question, but he just shifted his phone around for me to see.

. . .

I'm intrigued now

"In what way?" I asked softly, but my suspicion didn't faze him.

His expression remained playful and wholly contradicted the darkness permanently emanating from him as he tapped on his screen.

In seeing more of your life
In understanding you
In figuring out why you hate sour things

A soft laugh bubbled free as I pushed him away from me and headed for the table as Stevie dramatically gestured for us to take a seat.

Once Adam was sitting beside me, Ariana took a breath to begin, but Stevie cut her off.

"If you say you're moving out, I'm throwing this coffee in your face."

Ariana lifted a hand and huffed out a laugh. "You're so dramatic. I'm not moving out."

Stevie pointed at her with the coffee as if making sure Ariana knew the threat was real. Leaning closer and studying her as if she could see whatever Ariana was about to say. "You can't move one of your girlfriends in either."

"One of—" This time, Ariana's laugh was freer and filled with an adoring irritation she reserved for Stevie. "Okay, one, you've known me practically my entire life. When have I ever been tied down by a relationship? And two," she went on before Stevie could answer, "I was there when your dad laid down the rules: No boyfriends or girlfriends living in the house. However—"

"I knew it," Stevie said quickly.

"I don't know why I love her," Ariana said with a sigh, looking at me.

I matched her growing smirk. "Because our lives would be really boring without her."

"I can hear you," Stevie bit out.

"Anyway," Ariana went on, "Michelle in HR pulled me aside yesterday. I don't know if you guys remember her, but she's been here a few times and wanted to know if we still had a spare room."

"You slept with her. She can't move in," Stevie said with a shrug.

"Obviously." Ariana made a face. "But they're hiring this girl from up in Northern California. They're going to tell her about some places to live near the hospital, but Michelle thought our house would be a good option since this new girl will be on my shift and is our age—maybe a year younger."

"Oh, that'd be nice for both of you," I said as I leaned into Adam's side, all those butterflies going wild again at the easy way he pulled me closer. "Carpooling and stuff."

"I think she's shadowing me for the first couple weeks too," Ariana said, but her voice was soft as we looked at where Stevie was staring vacantly at the table.

"When's she moving?" she finally asked.

"She starts in a month—they're giving her extra time since she needs to move. So, before that."

Stevie nodded for a while, uncharacteristically silent and

solemn as she thought. “I’ve known you forever,” she said a minute later. “We knew Mia through Asterisk.” Nodding at me, she lifted a shoulder. “Hollis was a no-brainer. I met her and knew she would fit perfectly with us. But bringing someone in we’ve never even met? That’s hard.”

“We don’t have to do this,’” Ariana said easily, as if it didn’t bother her either way. “Or if you want, we can put her on a trial. Ask your dad to change the rental contract—she signs on for a certain amount of time, and if it doesn’t work out, it doesn’t work out.”

“He wouldn’t do that,” Stevie mumbled, then sighed heavily. “Yeah, okay. Tell Michelle the stranger danger can live here.”

“We don’t have to do this,” Ariana repeated firmly.

Stevie’s head bobbed as she lifted the cup to her lips. “I know,” she said before taking a drink. “If we don’t like her, I’ll make sure she knows she isn’t welcome.”

“There she is,” I said with a roll of my eyes, and Adam’s chest shifted with laughter.

“You’re welcome,” she snapped, slipping the sleeve off her cup and chucking it at me.

I curled my hand around it as if it were a prize, smiling when she glared.

“Now that that’s done . . .” Ariana began uncertainly, “have you guys noticed anything weird with Mia lately?”

My head jerked back as I looked at her again. “What?”

“She was fine just now,” Stevie said, confusion coating her words and making it sound like a question.

“Yeah, I know,” Ariana said with a shrug. “But I grabbed a smoothie from that one place she works at on my way home the other day—she wasn’t there. When she came home an hour later, she said she smelled like smoothies and needed to shower. When I asked, she said she'd been there all day. I can't count how many times that's happened in the last few months. I started going there more and more after it started happening, just to see if she'd be there."

"That'd be awfully coincidental for her to have been on a break each time," Stevie said slowly.

Ariana dipped her head in agreement. "And when I go to Asterisk, she's almost always there. It isn't like she isn't making rent or paying her portion of the bills. So, I don't get why she's saying she's working there when she isn't."

"Maybe she got a role, and she isn't ready to tell us about it," I said after we'd sat in contemplative silence for a minute.

"She has to know we'd want to know about that, right?" Stevie asked, and I just shrugged.

"She keeps to herself—Hollis might be right," Ariana said as she tapped her cup on the table.

"Do we ask her?" Stevie asked a while later.

Adam gripped my hip tighter, and I glanced at him in question. His expression remained impassive, but the slight shift of his head was enough for me to know whatever he knew about Mia wasn't something he could tell me. At least not then.

It also had me looking back to the girls and saying, "I don't think so."

"Agreed," Ariana said as she pushed away from the table. "I was just wondering if you guys noticed. Now I need to go make a call."

I held my hand out on top of Adam's lap, silently asking for his phone, my eyes on where Stevie was vacantly staring at the table as I did. "You gonna be okay with this?"

She slowly looked over at me, a delayed smile tugging at

her lips. "Like I said, if she doesn't work out, I'll make sure she knows she isn't welcome."

I playfully rolled my eyes even though I knew she would do exactly that, then glanced to the phone Adam had placed in my hands, note already ready and waiting for me to tap out a question.

Is Mia okay?

"Ugh," Stevie said dramatically as she stood from her chair. "Guess I'll call my dad and let him know."

"It might be great."

"It might be the worst thing that's ever happened to us," she countered.

I just let out a soft laugh as Adam's phone was placed into my palm again with his response.

As far as I know

We knew what we needed to about all of your roommates

Not everything

But enough

But she said something the other day that made me think I needed to look into her again

She just has her own secrets that I won't be sharing with you

She'll tell you if she's ever ready

My lips parted to protest, but I let out a sigh instead.

Everyone needed to have their secrets—Mia and Ariana still didn't know who I truly was. And as much as I hated it, I knew Adam couldn't tell me everything about his job, even if it had to do with the people in my life. That'd been one of the things we talked about the night before.

"Okay," I whispered as I handed the phone back to him just as mine began ringing from where I'd left it in my purse. I hurried from the table to get it, my stomach dropping when I saw "Mommy Dearest" across my screen.

Hearing from her two days in a row would normally be cause for alarm—hearing from her in the same week or even month would be. But with trying to get me to date Mayor McKay, I was actually more surprised that she'd lasted over twenty-four hours between calls.

"Adam, it's my mom," I said as I caught his stare from where he was slowly making his way over to me.

His easy expression immediately shifted into something calm and cool and oddly terrifying, and he made a gesture as if he wanted to hear the call.

I hurried to answer and put it on speaker as I said, "Mom?"

"Honestly, Hollis." She let out an irritated sound. "What in your life is so important that you have to wait until the last moment every time?"

"My phone was—"

"I'm very busy, Hollis. I don't have time to wait around for you to deem my calls worthy of answering."

"That wasn't—"

"I'm assuming you've had time to look over the details I sent for your date tonight?" she asked over me, the way she always did.

I pinched the bridge of my nose, my head shaking in

response for a moment before I said, "About tonight. I can't—"

"Yes, yes. It'll be lovely, I'm sure. Make sure you—"

"Mom, would you listen to me?" I snapped.

Silence filled the phone for long moments before she spoke, tone low and laced with warning. "How dare you speak to me that way. After everything I've done for you. The lengths your father and I have gone for you."

If she'd said those words to me just yesterday, I might've laughed.

But that was before.

As it was, my stomach was churning with acid and I had a jagged rock lodged in my throat.

I leaned into Adam when he placed a comforting hand on my waist and took a fortifying breath. Struggling to keep my voice steady when I said, "I've been trying to tell you that I can't go on the date tonight, and you aren't listening. You won't even let me get the words out."

Another few seconds passed before she echoed her words from the morning before. "I believe I misheard you."

"I can't—"

"If this is about that foolish idea of a relationship you mentioned yesterday, I thought I was plenty clear that will not be an issue. You are not seeing anyone. You will not be seeing anyone unless it is the man we've chosen for you. And whatever that issue's name was, he no longer exists for you. Am I understood, Hollis?"

"Yes, Mother," I whispered, my eyelids slipping shut when Adam's hold on me tightened in comfort and possession. "But I *cannot* go tonight."

"Hollis—"

"Monday," I yelled over her. "I can go Monday."

She let out a sigh that showed every ounce of her irritation. "I'll have to move the appointments I made for you at the salon and spa. Just one more thing I have to do for you."

"I don't need to go to—"

Her sharp, berating laugh sounded through the phone. "We can't have you looking anything less than perfect for this dinner. If that prostitute roommate of yours has rubbed off on you at all, it'll take a miracle and a team of professionals to make you look somewhat presentable."

"She isn't—"

"I have a few outfits being delivered to you today. Take pictures and send them to me so I can decide what you'll wear." When a stunned laugh left me, her tone turned cold. "I don't think you understand the importance of this, Hollis. However, your ungratefulness has been noted."

The call ended after that, and I just stood there. Shaking and shaking and shaking as I stared at the screen of my phone.

"Are you sure they're doing all these terrible things—that they want me dead? Are you sure they aren't just shitty parents?"

Adam turned me and wrapped me in his arms, responding with that simple act and forcing a pained cry from deep within me. Once my trembling body calmed, he gently gripped my shoulders and shifted me back just enough to search my face with his dark stare. His expression saying everything in those silent moments.

He was sorry. He wished he could give me the answer I wanted. He was going to keep me safe.

He wanted to unleash the wrath dancing across his skin for what they had planned for me.

I lifted onto my toes and pressed my mouth to his.

Curling my fingers into his beard and sighing when he parted my lips only to sweep his tongue across my own. The action so effortless and sensual as if we'd spent years perfecting it. Sending a different kind of tremor through my body and raising chills across my skin.

A groan rolled up my throat when the doorbell rang, and Adam's chest pitched with a laugh as he placed unhurried, open-mouthed kisses down my jaw, neck, and chest.

Always taking his time.

Always keeping me in the moment for a little while longer.

I loved it.

"Can we go somewhere?" I asked when he brought his mouth back to mine as he started walking me backward. "Somewhere we won't be interrupted every few minutes?"

He nodded, his expression playful as he pressed another quick kiss to my lips and released me. Staying close as we moved through the house but keeping out of view when I opened the door.

"Hollis Donahue?" the man standing beside a dressing rack asked.

And just like that, I was brought back to where I'd been when talking to my mom.

Stomach feeling like it was dropping and churning all at once. Breaths a little too shallow and feeling like I might cry and rage at the man in front of me even though he had nothing to do with this.

"That's me," I managed to say, head bobbing as I reached for the clipboard he handed me.

"Where would you like this?"

Adam pushed from the wall at the question, that dark energy bursting from him in alarm and suspicion.

"I've got it," I hurried to say, reaching for the rack and wheeling it into the house before the man could offer to bring it in again. When he opened his mouth, I channeled my mom and spoke over him. "I'm perfectly capable of handling a rack of clothes. Have a good day."

Once the door was shut and locked, I looked at Adam. "What do I do?"

He held out a hand, letting me know everything was okay, then reached for his phone.

He was probably no one

I think your parents are going to wait until after you're dating McKay

I just won't take any chances with you

I nodded quickly as my gaze shifted. Knowing I needed to suck it up and let Adam go back to his house. But I was struggling to choke back my plea for him to stay as I blankly stared at the covered outfits.

"Adam—" I looked up, swallowing back the question when I saw his phone waiting for me. A smile spreading across my face when I read the words there.

I wouldn't dream of leaving you right now

Besides

How much better will it feel knowing I'm the one who took the pictures you send to your mom

. . .

A soft laugh sounded in my chest as my stare lifted to his. Gratitude swirling through me as I studied that incredible contradiction of a man who had every piece of my heart.

Slipping my hand into his, I let him pull me closer and press his forehead to mine, feeling all those fluttering wings take flight again. "Thank you."

His head slanted against mine as if to say he didn't want my thanks.

"Thank you," I repeated as I gripped his shirt in my other hand. "I love you."

Those eyes pierced mine for immeasurable seconds, that connection between us flaring to life and filling the entryway with an intoxicating energy.

Lifting our joined hands, he trailed the tips of his fingers along my jaw and then over my lips. His chest rising and falling with a deep breath as if this moment and my words meant so much more to him because I knew him.

All of it telling me everything I needed to know, even though I knew long before he released me that he had no intention of saying it back.

Twenty-Four

ADAM

Irritation wove through me when a knock sounded on the door to my room late Monday night. I switched over my windows to hide what I was working on in case it was Sarah and turned up the music in the chance it was Leo's umpteenth attempt to talk.

He'd refused to let me tail Hollis and McKay tonight—saying I was too close to her to think clearly.

He wasn't wrong, not that I'd admit that.

But he'd fucking *lost* her within half an hour.

Thinking it'd be less suspicious if he went out to dinner with Sarah at the same restaurant where McKay and Hollis were supposed to meet. But apparently, McKay had different plans.

After a drink in the bar area, he'd led Hollis to an awaiting car and *left*.

If it weren't for social media blowing up over seeing them out together, I would've been gone. Found McKay and kept Hollis in my sight at all times.

But the idea of McKay moving on after the disappearance

of his fiancée was barely being overshadowed by the number of posts of women obsessing over him and hating any woman for catching his eye.

Regardless, it helped me know where Hollis was and that she was okay.

I was getting her a fucking tracker first thing tomorrow.

A heaving sigh left me when the door opened, and I rolled far enough away from my desk to turn around, my heart just about tearing out of my chest when I saw her standing there.

Shoulders back and head held high, but this wasn't the girl I'd first met all those years ago. This was all confidence mixed with that hesitation in a clashing combination so damn sexy that it took actual effort to stay in my chair.

She made a humming sound, her head tilting slightly. "Still like you in those glasses."

I liked her . . .

With each passing day, she became more consuming. More of a craving. More of a steady thrum in my veins.

And I would never get enough.

I lifted my chin in response and rolled back so I could switch back to everything I'd been working on. Still trying to track her mom's cousin, though I was getting closer. Finalizing the connection from her parents to everyone . . . from her parents to the account. Everything I could dig up on the McKays.

Pictures of McKay holding Hollis's hand and kissing her fucking cheek . . .

It was probably best I hadn't been the one to tail her.

"Right, I can't do that again," she muttered and cleared her throat. "Please don't make me. I felt sick every time he touched me."

Ice rushed through my veins as I pushed from the chair

and closed the distance between us with a couple steps. Pulling her into my arms and holding her close as she struggled to gather her strength.

My throat working as my apologies gathered and caught there.

I'm sorry. I'm sorry. I'm so fucking sorry.

She dropped her forehead to my chest, her hands gripping my shirt as she said, "I kept wondering what he'd done to his fiancée. What he knew about this, if anything. *When* it was supposed to happen. But even if there wasn't all of that, he isn't the person I want touching me."

I gripped her to me a little tighter, then led her to my desk and pulled her into my lap when I sat. Keeping one hand moving up and down her spine and using the other to pull up a note and tap on the keys.

I will gladly destroy him for touching you.

A small smile tugged at the corner of her mouth. "Stevie's right, you are a caveman."

I passed my lips across her temple as my fingers drifted over the keys.

For you? Always.

I'm sorry for tonight, Hollis. So damn sorry.

She rested her head against mine, a sigh heaving from her. "Don't make me meet with him again."

. . .

I won't make you do anything.

She nodded for a while before muttering, "Whatever they have planned, I think it's soon, Adam."

I went still.

A rage unlike anything I'd ever known building inside me and threatening to escape.

I forced my fingers to press the keys when all I wanted was to smash everything closest to me.

Explain.

"It was the things he said tonight," she said after a moment. "Again, I don't know if *he* knows what they're planning, but he said our parents had set this up, and he could see why—that it was smart. Then he started listing all my accomplishments, like they'd given him a list or something, and said they would look good next to his."

Reluctance crept from her, and she shifted to look at me. "He said they'd done polls, and married politicians with families were better received. He said he didn't have time to do the public dating and engagement, he wanted to move things along faster than that. Our parents already came up with a plan for it and everything."

Of course they did.

I worked my jaw as I waited for her to explain.

Knowing I needed this information even though I hated every moment of it.

"They want to play it like I was friends with his fiancée, and I've been there for him since her disappearance. That we grew close in our *grief* and started dating but kept it out of the public eye out of respect for her and her family. And in case she was to be found . . . *of course*," she added on with an eye roll, then struggled to meet my stare. "I think that's why he kept touching and kissing me tonight. So it would be more believable when he asks me to marry him next week."

I didn't move.

I was afraid of what I'd do if I did.

Like leave the house and murder a mayor.

"Say something," she pleaded.

I swallowed thickly and reached out for the keyboard.

Then we have until then to finalize everything and take them down.

She placed her hands on either side of my face and forced me to look at her, her green eyes filled with a mixture of fear and sadness and absolute trust that just about floored me.

After everything, I wouldn't have expected the last.

"Talk to me as the Adam holding me in his lap," she softly begged. "Not the Adam who belongs to the FBI."

I'm both, Hollis.

Always both.

But if you think your parents are capable of terrible things,

you don't want to know what I want to do to McKay just for thinking he can marry you.

Her head listed and her eyes widened. "Are you . . . Adam Ortiz, are you jealous?"

He was touching you.
He kissed you.
Absolutely.

She shifted around in my lap so she was straddling me, excitement pushing out the sadness and fear as she asked, "Of someone I have no interest in? Of a date I only went on to help you get information?"

I pointed to the last word I'd typed on the screen in response.

"But he isn't you."

Goddamn.

This girl.

I reached up to brush my fingers along her jaw, then pulled her closer to press my lips to hers for an unhurried kiss. All apologies and claims.

Because I was pretty fucking sure Hollis owned my heart. And I refused to let anyone else try to take her from me.

"I love you," she whispered as if in response to my claims before pressing another kiss to my lips. When she leaned back, her lazy smile was soft and beautiful and all hesitation.

That smile was going to be the death of me.

"I'm not sure if you know this, but I have a thing for guys

who have beards and wear band tees and glasses." Her laugh burst free when I stood from the chair with her in my arms. Her legs curling around my waist and that mouth pressing firmly to mine as I led her to the bed.

Drinking her in and wishing I could say so many things as I laid her out.

That she was beautiful.

That I wanted her in a way I'd never wanted anything.

That I'd fallen in love with her too.

Twenty-Five

HOLLIS

I woke to an empty bed.

The desk chair unoccupied, and the pillow and sheets beside me cool. I sat up, looking around and listening for any sounds of Adam before slipping out of bed and grabbing his discarded shirt off the floor. Once I was slipping into my pants, I padded off down the hall, my steps slowing when I heard Leo's low, unmistakable voice.

". . . right. With everything McKay said, they're pushing for it to happen soon. Get them engaged, then get rid of Hollis and maybe McKay too." He loosed a long sigh. "The question is when."

There was a pause as I crept closer to the kitchen and then the sound of something sliding.

"Obviously, we aren't waiting around for it to happen," Leo grumbled before the sliding sound happened again. "We'll need to have someone on Hollis twenty-four-seven from here on out. She can't be alone. Ever."

I leaned up against the archway of the entrance to the

kitchen in time to see Adam slide his phone across the island toward Leo.

Leo studied the screen for a while before shaking his head. "I don't know, Adam. You're too close."

Adam smacked his hand on the counter and then gestured angrily at Leo, communicating something Leo clearly understood because he responded with a withering glare.

"Yeah, okay," he conceded with a harsh breath before sending the phone back to Adam. "But you need to keep your cool. You can't lose sight of what we're doing and ruin everything if something like last night happens again. Got it?"

Adam shrugged and made a face that screamed *no promises*.

"Fucking hell." Leo scrubbed a hand over his face, letting it fall just in time to catch the phone sliding his way. "No. No, I'm not."

He let his head fall back, only to drag his hands over his face again and again before looking at Adam and asking, "She knows everything about you? Your past and all that?" When Adam began nodding, Leo tapped on the phone a few times and emphasized, "Does she know about *you*?"

Adam straightened and visibly stilled, the glare he was giving Leo a clear warning to stop talking.

Leo gave him a sympathetic look but pressed on. "Then she doesn't know everything, Adam. I know it's hard. I know that shit fucked with you in a way I'll never be able to understand. But if she means that much, she should know."

Adam reached across the island, snatching up the phone and flipping off Leo as he turned, then came to a standstill when he saw me there.

"Did you volunteer to be stuck with me?" I asked, a teasing lilt to my voice. When neither guy so much as moved,

I sucked in air through my teeth to hide the waver of nervousness. "I don't know about that . . . twenty-four-seven? That's a lot of fighting over pizza and possibly watching you eat sour things. Talk about commitment."

Adam cracked a smile at that and erased the space between us. Tossing his phone onto the counter and curling his hands around my neck to hold me close. Those tortured eyes studying me and saying so many things.

He was worrying over what I was thinking about what I'd heard.

He loved me.

He was worried *for* me.

"One of those things you don't talk about?" I whispered as I placed my hand on his bare chest, trying to sound understanding even though I was more curious than ever to know what it was. When he dipped his head, I reached up on my toes and pressed a swift kiss to his lips. "Okay then."

I curled into his side and glanced over at Leo, my expression falling when I got my first full look at him.

All dark circles under his bloodshot eyes.

"Are you okay?" I asked softly, hesitantly.

He speared me with a look. "I lost you last night because I made a bad call. Because of that and the way I scrambled to unfuck myself, my girlfriend thought I was breaking up with her. So, I came clean to her about everything. She left me and moved out. I already had a call from our director this morning, but we still don't know who we can trust, and so because of *all* of that, I'm withholding part of my job for the first time in my career. Lying to my superiors." A smile crossed his face, making him look feral as he sneered, "I'm fucking fantastic, Hollis, why would you ask?"

Adam slammed his hand onto the counter, but Leo just

hung his head as he gripped the edge of the island as if he needed it to stay standing.

"I'm sorry about Sarah," I said as I studied him. "Just give her time, she loves you."

He huffed out a bitter laugh, his head moving in slow shakes. "And that's the problem, isn't it?" He looked over at me, his eyes glassing over. "I never should've let it get that far. But I did, and I fell right with her. I let her move in . . . we're having a baby . . . and I kept lying to her."

He pushed from the counter and stalked out of the kitchen, leaving a wave of grief behind him.

"When did that happen?" I asked, turning in Adam's arms.

He lifted a hand to the side, then leaned over to grab his phone.

Apparently throughout the night

I didn't know until this morning

My eyes widened. "Seriously?"

I'd been livid and gutted by the betrayal when I'd found out about Adam. But if I'd been in Sarah's position, the neighbors probably would've been able to hear me screaming and throwing things.

Adam gave me a knowing look as he quickly tapped on the screen of his phone, his expression shifting into something more subdued before he handed it over to me.

I think you're right

I think she'll be back after she takes some time to think through it all

But I can't figure out why you're acting like you're just OKAY with what you heard

Why you're letting it go so easily

My tongue darted out to wet my lips as I read the words again and then slowly tapped the phone against my palm, trying to think of a way to explain the chaos running through my mind.

"I wouldn't say I'm *okay* with it," I began a little uncertainly. "Of course I want to know what you were talking about. And, to be honest, it kind of made my stomach drop for a moment because it brought back everything from the other night. But you told me there were things from your life that you don't talk about, and I heard what Leo said. Those things clearly hurt you, so what I heard isn't something for me to get upset over or demand to know."

He nodded as he gently took the phone from me long enough to write something, his brow furrowing as he did.

I know you're strong Hollis

Fuck I know that

You took everything I threw at you

Everything Leo added on

And accepted it

But you don't have to pretend that all the rest of this shit doesn't scare you

. . .

"What . . . what do you mean?" I asked as I gave him the phone. "I don't even know what happened to you."

His head moved in small, tight jerks as he typed.

You made a joke of what's happening and what we have to do to keep you safe

We already know you're strong

We already know you're brave

You don't have to pretend you aren't scared

Not with us

"Can I be honest?" My face scrunched up in hesitation when he gave me a look that said *please*. "My first thought when I realized what you guys were setting up was 'oh God, he's going to get so sick of me.'" Adam's chest pitched with a laugh, and I admitted, "That's what I was worrying over when I made that joke."

His eyes rolled, amusement tugging at his mouth.

We're talking about how to keep you from being killed

And you're worried I'm gonna get sick of you

Something that absolutely won't happen

I smacked at his stomach with his phone. "Okay, well, when you put it that way."

His grin broadened as he pulled me into his arms for a kiss that immediately had all worries slipping from my mind.

I wove my arms around his neck, a soft laugh skating up

my throat when he gripped my thighs and lifted me onto the island. Every powerful movement seeming so effortless as he claimed my lips and heart until I was dizzy with need.

"Bedroom," I breathed against his lips.

He pulled me closer, large hands curling tighter as if he was about to pull me into his arms just before he loosened his grip and broke away from the kiss. A sound building in his chest that was obviously frustration as he turned to look behind him and then locked those dark eyes on me. All carnal need and desire and indecision that eventually tipped.

He grabbed his phone, irritation bleeding from him as he hurried through a message.

It's Tuesday

I stared at the words for a while before looking into his heated stare, lips parting with confusion. "Do you not have sex on Tuesdays?"

Despite the tension so close to bursting between us, his eyes widened with surprise before his body shook with a laugh.

Just as I was about to demand to know what I was missing, I caught sight of the microwave behind him, the time there, and gasped as I realized what he already had. "I have rehearsal!" I pushed against his chest when he pointed at me, a playful scoff ripping free. "Why do you have to be such a stalker?"

He helped me from the counter, his eyes rolling even as the corner of his mouth lifted in amusement.

"So, does this mean you're coming with me?" I asked

when he grabbed my hand and began leading me back to his room, voice uncertain. "Are you really going to be with me all the time now?"

Using his free hand, he slid a finger across the screen to give me a single word.

Necessary

"Okay," I muttered and began worrying my bottom lip.

Adam released me once we were in his room but handed me his phone just a moment later.

I need to know what you're thinking

"I'm wondering how you're going to get into the rehearsals without revealing who you really are because they're closed to everyone else."

Let me worry about that

I'll make sure you're safe and you'll be able to keep dancing as long as Leo and I don't think you're in immediate danger

All you have to worry about is your roommates

Make sure they don't think anything is weird with how much we're together

We'll stay at the mansion sometimes so they don't think I kidnapped you

But we need to be here just as much because I need to be able to work

The words *immediate danger* stood out among everything else, making my heart race and my head feel light until Adam tipped up my chin so he could study my eyes. The look in his own saying he understood my fear. That it was okay.

I won't let anything happen to you

I glanced at the screen when he showed it to me, my head bobbing unsteadily for a moment before I sucked in a fortifying breath. And then another.

"Okay . . . appease roommates and house hop between both of us working." I gave a firm nod. "I can do that. That sounds like a normal relationship minus one of us being in the FBI and the other being set up by her parents—*not*," I said loudly. "We are not in a relationship."

A slow smile curled at his lips. The look all doubt and challenge and sending a tendril of heat through me.

"Are—" I shifted back a little to better look at him. "Are we?"

He lifted one of his shoulders and slanted his head, neither a confirmation nor a denial. That smirk and those eyes and the dark warning billowing from him somehow making a shrug look so casual and dangerous and unreasonably sexy.

And now I was wondering how bad it would be to miss a rehearsal . . . all because of a shrug.

. . .

We need to get you home and then to Raven

I hummed something that might've been an assent.

Or a refusal.

Either way, it had his smile widening as he rocked back, his eyes dipping over my body and stopping on my chest. Something raw and primal churning in his stare as he tugged on the shirt I was wearing before tapping out a quick message.

You should keep that on

I glanced down to see his shirt, my cheeks filling with heat before I sucked in a breath. "Oh! I was wondering last night, but we were talking about bad things, and then we got carried away." I waved a hand through the air to dismiss the ramble I'd started down and then pointed to the logo and name on the shirt. "I'm guessing it is, but is *Boston* a band too?"

Adam's expression went totally blank before he shook his head as if trying to make himself understand what I'd really asked. A second later, he began walking away, looking at me like I was an alien before his gaze dropped to his phone.

After a few steps, he tossed it toward me and then headed for his desk.

. . .

I'm going to pretend you didn't ask that
Get ready

"I'll take that as a *yes*?" I asked softly, a hesitant smile tugging at my mouth when he glanced at me over his shoulder from where he was leaning on his desk.

He looked back to the screens, head slowly shaking before music filled the room. Pushing from the desk, he pointed to the monitors.

"Boston," I said in understanding, trying to fight my growing smile. "Got it."

His eyes rolled, but his expression faded into pure adoration as he quickly crossed the room and scooped me into his arms, never slowing as he took long steps toward the bed.

"Staying?" I asked, already breathless when he followed me down onto the messed-up sheets.

He gave a single shake of his head as he reached for my pants. Easily ridding them with sure movements and capturing my mouth to swallow the whimper when he drifted his fingers up between my thighs.

All power.

All tease.

And he was mine.

He pushed the shirt I was wearing up and over my chest as he slowly moved down my body, a wicked grin crossing his face at the shiver that moved through me.

Weaving my fingers through his hair when he placed his lips low on my belly, I let my eyelids shut and gave over to everything only Adam could make me feel. "Late then."

Twenty-Six

ADAM

"Stevie, you better already be awake," Hollis called out when we eventually made it back to the Forest Knoll mansion. She turned toward me and made a face that was all kinds of adorable even through her frustration. "I don't know exactly how close you have to follow me, but I'm about to go get ready."

I nodded for her to go and slowly began following her, intent on waiting in the living room.

But we'd barely made it out of the entryway when someone yelled, "What in the *fuck*?"

"Well, she's definitely awake," Hollis murmured as she began hurrying toward the voice.

Just as we reached the edge of the living room, Stevie shouted, "Please tell me what the fuck I've been seeing and where you've been and what all this—" She stilled from where she'd been charging down the hallway, her eyes widening when she saw me. "Uh . . . hi, husband."

I waved.

She looked between Hollis and me for a moment before narrowing a glare on Hollis. "We need to talk."

"I know," Hollis said, all agreement as her earlier frustration came out. "What the hell is Tucker still doing at Asterisk?"

Stevie's head jerked back. "Wait, what?"

Hollis gestured to me, an apology ripping across her face because I'd told her not to do this. "He is such an asshole, Stevie. I thought your dad fired him."

"He did," Stevie responded, words slow and unsure.

"Well, Tucker was just there," Hollis argued. "Working. And he was a dick."

Even with the distraction of getting lost in Hollis's body for a while longer, we'd still managed to get out of my house in time to stop by Asterisk in case Hollis needed to wake Stevie up.

Something we'd regretted not long after setting foot in there . . .

Stevie blinked slowly, then shook her head. "Okay, I'll talk to my dad. But you and I need to talk. Like, *yesterday*."

"Okay, then let's talk. I have to get ready."

Stevie started walking back the way she'd come, only to stop and gesture to me with her phone. "Are you staying?"

"Yeah, he's, um . . ." Hollis gave a little nonchalant shrug and said, "He's gonna drive us to rehearsal."

Surprise flashed through Stevie's eyes before pity replaced it, but she didn't respond otherwise. Her hand dropped as she turned to leave, giving me the perfect view of her phone as she did.

A picture of Hollis and Mayor McKay from the night before.

Well—oh shit.

I turned at the familiar gasp that came from behind me, my jaw clenching when I saw Sarah's tear-streaked face.

"What are you doing here?"

I pointed to the couches, then hurried that way. Reaching out to guide her and letting my hand fall when she jerked away from me.

"What are you doing here?" she repeated, refusing to move. "Is Leo here?"

I gave a hard shake of my head and reached for my phone.

He doesn't even know where you are
He figured you went to your parents
Are you okay

"No, I'm not okay," she said, her voice twisting as new tears filled her eyes. "Why would you think I'd be okay?"

You're right
You're right I'm sorry
And I'm sorry for this but I have to do it
Sarah I need to know who you've told

She took a step back, looking at me as if I'd insulted her. "No one," she said firmly, her voice wavering with her pain. When I gestured around us to show the house she'd come to, she coughed out a sob. "I told Ari we got in a big fight and broke up. She had me come here for a couple days instead of our parents' because she's betting I'll change my mind—I think she thinks I'm being hormonal or something."

Sarah he's a wreck

He's been a wreck long before this

I hate to say this but you were only ever supposed to be a step closer to Hollis for us

He was never supposed to fall in love with you

But he did

Lying to you when he loved you has been killing him

But we've been working this for years and we're so close to ending it

Telling you could've ruined everything

But hurting you

Losing you

Sarah

I've never seen him like this

A sharp cry burst from her, and when I held my hand out that time, she didn't flinch away, she fell into my arms. Shoulders jerking and choking over sobs as she softly rambled, "How do I know if anything was real? I don't know who he is. I thought he was a geeky computer guy . . . like you. And now you guys are in the FBI with badges and guns and—*oh my God,* I'm having a baby with a stranger. I don't even know what his real name is. What if he has a family stashed away somewhere?"

My head shook as I leaned back and gently took my phone from her.

. . .

You know his name
You know the important things
You just didn't know his job or why we'd moved to California
You didn't know why your relationship started
But it became real for him fast Sarah
Believe that

"I don't know how," she cried, her water-filled eyes looking to me for help.

Maybe talk to Hollis later today

Her shoulders jerked with a shuddering breath. "She . . . she knows?"

She found notes between Leo and me a few days ago
I had to make a decision
She had a lot of the same questions and doubts you're having now

She pushed my hand away, her face lining with emotion as she tried to fight another round of sobs. "But the two of you just met. You haven't been together for a year—you aren't having a baby together."

I slanted my head as I typed.

. . .

No

But I met her six years ago and then bumped into her again a few years after that

I started falling for her before I ever knew who she was

She didn't become a target for us until about a year ago

And now I'm trying to prevent her parents from killing her

So we have our own struggles

"Leo said that," she said under her breath, her eyes darting around before meeting mine. "That's real? That's what's happening to her?" When I nodded, she loosed a harsh breath. "I can't imagine—that's terrible. Who does that to their child?"

Bad people

And they're doing a lot of shit to a lot of other people

We've been following it and working all those cases for a long time now

Bringing us to this

And because we couldn't risk everything we've worked for I almost lost the girl upstairs and you moved out

Be mad Sarah

Be devastated

Take time to think about everything you need to

But I need you to know that Leo loves you

That you and your baby are real for him

He could've easily let you walk out without fighting for you and I could be pretending you don't exist

But he would do anything to have you in his life

. . .

She nodded and looked away just as Hollis and Stevie came walking in.

I glanced that way in time to see Hollis's eyes go wide with worry and sorrow.

"Oh yeah," Stevie said, gesturing to Sarah. "I don't know what he did, but your best friend is a piece of shit if his pregnant girlfriend is here, looking like this."

I just nodded because there was nothing I could say.

"Yeah, uh . . . we should go," Hollis said hesitantly, stare bouncing between Sarah and me before locking on Sarah as she mouthed, *I'm so sorry*. As if she were the reason for all of Sarah's pain.

Grabbing Stevie, Hollis began dragging her toward the entryway, head lowered even though the rest of her was so stiff, showing all her discomfort.

Let me or someone know if you need anything

We'll be back here in a couple hours

Sarah barely spared a glance at my phone before looking away. "You think I want anything to do with you either?"

I worked my jaw, dipping my head as I began stepping away.

"Not saying I would throw away mozzarella sticks if you came back with them, though."

My lips twitched into a smile, and I just used my phone to wave as I jogged after the girls. Slipping out of the house and into my car just after them and in time for Hollis's warning look.

"So, Mommy and Daddy Dearest demanding our girl go

on a date with some stuffy whatever-he-is, I get," Stevie said with a disgusted huff. "Hollis giving in to their demands, I mean, I also sort of get. She's only human, and they are admittedly terrifying and impossible to say no to. But you allowing it without charging into the middle of their date and ripping his hand off for being all up on our girl? What the fuck is wrong with you?"

I just suppressed a sigh and cranked the engine, ignoring when Stevie leaned forward to rest her arm on my seat.

"Come on, hubby. We don't have all day, and I've got a studded pair of Jimmy Choos ready to go through this guy's dick."

Hollis snorted over a laugh as I slowly looked at where Stevie was waiting, her expression deadpan.

Jesus Christ.

If this assignment didn't kill me, keeping the girls alive and out of jail just might.

Your girlfriend is insane by the way

She threatened a guy's dick with a studded heel this morning

I showed my phone to Russell that night, earning a rough laugh from him from where we were waiting for the girls after the show—*inside*. I would let Hollis out of my sight to go backstage for her shows, but I wasn't leaving the building she was in.

Besides, as far as everyone who worked at Raven knew, Hollis's boss was *playing favorites* with me since I'd saved one of her girls from an asshole who didn't understand the word *no*.

In reality, some people just needed to be in on the truth.

"Ah, man," Russell began, stretching back in his chair and folding his arms over his chest. "Don't let Stevie see you calling her my girlfriend." His head moved in a faint shake. "She'll run away from me so fast, and she just started coming back to me."

I gave him a questioning look, prompting him to go on.

"I've never met anyone so afraid of commitment or even just the idea of *caring* about someone—forget about love. Should've seen the look on her face when 'I love you' slipped out of her mouth." His eyes darted around, making sure she wasn't about to come walking up on us. "Swear to God, you would've thought she'd killed a puppy, she was so horrified."

I thought over that for a second before tapping out something.

Then why doesn't all the shit that she's always saying to me bother you

I can tell she's joking

And Hollis can too for the most part

Still think it gets to Hollis every now and then

"Because I know she doesn't mean it," he said simply. "Because of the way she talks to me." He shifted a little to better face me, his expression all obvious adoration for the girl. "If Stevie doesn't know you or like you, *you'll know*. If you're one of the few people she likes, you'll know that too. Then you just have to get used to Stevie. Her crazy way of showing affection by being vulgar and brash as hell. If you're different for her . . ." He shrugged, the corner of his mouth slowly lifting. "*I* know."

Understood

"Her mom left," he said just as I started looking toward the backstage entrance. "When Stevie was young. Had a suitcase when she took her to school one day, and Stevie kept asking why. She said she was donating clothes, but that afternoon, she didn't pick Stevie up. No one ever heard from her again."

Damn.

Russell let out a huff when he caught sight of my expression. "Yeah. It fucked with her, obviously. But because of it, she doesn't trust or like people—especially women. She resents her mom *because* her dad is still holding out hope that she'll come back, almost twenty years later. And she's fucking terrified of her own feelings."

So you don't care when she plans marriages and kids and divorces to other guys

And you let her pretend you aren't together

I set my phone in front of him, a small smile crossing my face when he huffed in response.

"Yeah," he said as he slid the phone back toward me. "As crazy as it looks when you put it like that . . . yeah. I'll pretend with her for the rest of my life if that's what she needs."

I dipped my head in understanding and glanced toward the door again, my body going still when Russell's voice lowered as he asked, "The girls don't know you're FBI, do they?"

I stared at the door for a second longer before slowing looking to where he sat at my side, but Russell was staring straight ahead.

"What happened last week . . . I knew I had to make sure you didn't get dragged into it—that you didn't get charged with anything—because . . . well, because I would've done the same thing if I'd seen it happening." He lifted his shoulders. "And you seemed like a really good guy, but there was something about you that I couldn't shake. So, I looked you up."

He lifted one of his hands in a gesture that was at once apologetic and unapologetic before folding it over his chest again. "If the girls knew, I definitely would've heard it at some point from Stevie, and I'm guessing you would've said something when the officers were taking your information. And if you're keeping it from them, then I have a feeling you're around them for a reason." He looked over at me, brows drawn close. "Do I need to be worried about something?"

Fuck.

I loosed a deep breath and dragged a hand through my beard before leaning forward in the chair and grabbing my phone. Head shaking as I gave him the bare minimum of what was going on.

The more people who knew, the trickier this got, and Leo and I were already struggling with not knowing who to trust.

But Russell had already had enough time to tell people what he knew about me, and he'd kept it to himself.

"Jesus Christ," he breathed when I was done, looking from my phone to me a few times before sitting back. "You're serious?" When I nodded, he let out a stunned breath and went back to staring straight ahead with his arms folded over his chest.

Looking like he was digesting what I'd told him before eventually giving a firm nod. "All right, what do you need from me?" he asked.

To do what you've been doing
Keep Stevie occupied
And don't say a word about what you know

He nodded just as the door opened, revealing a hesitant smile that had me pausing from getting out of the chair.

Goddamn.

That girl and the things she did to my heart.

"Hope you enjoyed the show, baby daddy. Did every one of those dances for you," Stevie called out as they walked toward us, voice all wry amusement and earning an affectionate eye roll from Hollis.

I tapped on my phone, then held it out for Russell as I glanced at him.

You're the one who loves her

. . .

A wide grin stretched across his face. “Fuck, man. I do.”

I looked back to those mint green eyes wrapped up in all that hesitation, drawn to her like a siren from that very first night. My heart pounding out that familiar, unforgiving pace whenever she was around . . .

Knew exactly how he felt.

Twenty-Seven

HOLLIS

W*hat are you doing*

I jolted as if I'd been caught doing something wrong but immediately relaxed into Adam's body when he curled his arm around my waist and pulled me against his chest the next morning.

"I was just, um . . . looking at something."

He used the hand holding his phone to tip up my chin to study my eyes. His eyebrows drawn close together in doubt.

After a moment, he released my chin and then held out his phone, pointing to his question again.

"It's . . ." I let out a disappointed sigh and then pulled from his hold to reach up and grab one of my shoe boxes. Brushing my fingers over the box as something I refused to define swirled inside my chest before clutching it close to my stomach. "It's stupid," I muttered.

. . .

I doubt that

Not if it has you looking like this

I stared at the box for a moment longer before turning to face him. "I hated dancing growing up. I hated it because it was always forced on me, and it was always to be *the best*. But even when I was the best, I still wasn't enough for my parents." I lifted a hand before clutching the box again. "I told you I've never been freer than when I'm dancing at Raven, and it's true—I feel alive there. But soon after I started there, I realized something was missing from my life, and it's *this*. And I *hate* that I need this in my life just like I hate that I feel like I'm going through withdrawals because I haven't danced in over a week."

His dark eyes burned with emotion as he listened, looking like he was at once worried and confused and struggling to figure out how to fix it.

Ballet

My head moved in tight, shamed nods.

When do you dance ballet

"Nearly every morning I don't have rehearsal," I answered, surprised he didn't know since I'd learned more and more that he and Leo knew my entire schedule. "I go to Raven."

Understanding washed over his face as he tapped on the screen.

We didn't know what you were doing
We guessed you were getting in extra rehearsals

"Oh." The corner of my mouth twitched as that shame and need swirled through me. "Different kind of rehearsal, I guess." I turned to put the shoes back in my closet, but Adam grabbed them from me. "What are you doing?"

Adam tucked the box gently under his arm before bringing up his phone to write to me. As if he'd noticed how I'd held it—how precious it was—and was taking extra care with it.

Get ready
You need this
I'm taking you

My head slanted. "I don't . . . I don't dance for people anymore—not like this. Burlesque is different."

Hollis
The way you hold yourself
The way you walk
The way you move when we're together
It's all grace and seamless movements

You're always dancing with me

Oh.

My heart did this funny kind of hiccup before taking off faster than a hummingbird's wings as I looked from the screen to all that adoration clashing with the cold, dark intensity that always emanated from Adam.

"I—" I looked down when his phone began vibrating in my hands, my brow furrowing when I saw Leo was *calling* him. "Why—"

My bedroom door was flung open, and Stevie came stumbling in, hastily pulling what I assumed was Russell's shirt over her naked body.

"Jesus, Stevie!" But my reprimand and horror died when she looked up at me, eyes wide with dread—at the soft alarm when she said my name.

"Hollis . . ."

I started looking toward Adam and then over to my nightstand when my phone began ringing.

Adam's free hand slowly reached out to me, cautious and comforting as we all seemed to freeze at that moment before his phone began vibrating with another call from Leo.

"Here," I said, voice weak as I handed the phone back to him, his own alarm seeping through the room like a veil of lethal shadows when he saw what was on the screen.

He answered the call, lifting it to his ear and walking over to my desk to set my ballet shoes there as I backed up toward my nightstand. Gaze drifting between Adam's unreadable expression and where Stevie was slowly moving deeper into my room as her wide eyes darted over her phone. Each step feeling like it might shatter my rigid body.

"Mommy Dearest" lit up my screen, my stomach clenching tight and quickly turning into the feeling of being encased in fire.

I wasn't even sure what was happening, but I knew it was awful from the atmosphere in my room. From the way my mother immediately began calling me again as soon as the first call ended.

"Look," Stevie whispered as she came up beside me, handing me her phone that was opened to the news site's webpage.

Alter Ego or Naughty Princess?

Donahue's Scandalous Stage-and-Beau Swap Will Shock You!

Connecticut Senator Donahue's daughter has remained away from cameras ever since she first landed in sunny California. But Hollis Donahue recently made a huge splash when seen with Ojai Mayor and political hottie, Jordan McKay, at a private dinner that seemed anything **but** *political, if these pictures are any indication.*

But the very next morning, she was seen in a downtown Los Angeles coffee shop, snuggled up to this hunk of a man.

We'll take one of those with our morning coffee, please and thank you.

When asked about Hollis's love life and where she's been all this time, an anonymous source stayed pretty hush-hush about the beau. However, the details of her private life had our jaws dropping.

In trying to confirm, we reached out to her last known employer, Los Angeles Dance Company, who said Hollis Donahue 'left her role as prima ballerina years ago.'

So, where has she been all this time?

The truth of this political princess's stage time just might shock you.

My finger shook as I started scrolling down, revealing a picture of me with wildly curled hair, wearing nothing more than knee-high boots, high-waisted leather panties, and pasties.

"Shit."

I was being punished.

Whether it was for lying to my parents for years or for the snobbish, privileged socialite I'd let them mold me into growing up, I wasn't sure. But I was definitely being punished.

The entrance to our driveway had been flooded with the press within an hour of the story being published.

Raven's shows were canceled until the press stopped blocking the entrances there.

And my phone hadn't stopped ringing, alternating between my parents and Mayor McKay's assistant, wanting to try to get ahead of this before it could get worse. His people wanted me to say the picture was old and come out as a united front with the mayor. My parents were so irate they were on their way to California but were still calling me every few minutes in an attempt to coach me through this.

Don't go outside, Hollis.

If you happen to go near a window, be collected and polished and look like the epitome of a politician's wife, Hollis.

If you must speak, claim photo doctoring. That isn't you in the picture, am I understood, Hollis?

Deny everything, Hollis.

You spoiled, selfish brat. How could you try to ruin your father's career this way, Hollis?

I thought I made it clear you were not seeing anyone. I thought I made it clear that man no longer existed for you. And there you are, traipsing around in public with him like some common whore. Honestly, Hollis.

A shuddering breath ripped from me when my phone began vibrating again. I glanced over to it from where we were all gathered at the kitchen table, tears quickly filling my eyes and slipping down my cheeks when I saw "Daddy Dearest" on the screen.

Adam paused from where he was simultaneously working on two of our laptops and texting with Leo to pull my chair closer to him. Hands curling around my cheeks as his eyes searched mine. Worry and sorrow creasing his face for long seconds before he reached for my phone and shut it all the way off.

"No, I can't—" His mouth captured mine, pouring all his calm and strength into me with the softest passes across my lips until I was melting into him and sighing against the kiss when he effortlessly pulled me out of the chair and onto his lap. The action pure comfort and lifting a weight from my chest at once. "Thank you," I breathed against his lips before pressing another kiss there.

"That *bitch*," Stevie shouted, causing me to jerk away from Adam. She slammed her phone onto the table before pointing at it. "He's bragging about it."

Russell looked from the phone to us, his expression all confusion as he waited beside her.

"Who is?" I finally asked when Stevie just sat forward and continued scrolling through whatever she was looking at on her phone.

"Fucking Tucker," she hissed. "He posted how he sold the photo and the story. And that if anyone wants other information on you—that *fuck*." She smacked her hand on the table before going back to what she'd been reading. "If anyone wants other information on you, to slide into his DMs because you and he might as well be related since you live with his cousin. Which means, wink wink, he knows where you live."

A sharp breath fled from my lungs.

Stevie pointed behind her. "*He's* why they're all outside."

"Stevie," I whispered, my chest going tight all over again as Adam went utterly still against me.

She tapped on her phone a few times, then put the call she was making on speaker.

"Stevie, did you ever talk to your dad the other day?"

She gestured to the phone, eyes wide. "Babe, yeah. He said he was going to look into it because Tucker was definitely let go. I never heard back—*Dad*," she complained when he answered. "Are you seeing all this bullshit with Tucker?"

He loosed a long sigh. "What'd he do now?"

She made a sound that was a solid mixture of frustration and exasperation. "Sending to you now, hold on."

I looked at Adam when he tapped my hip, my brow furrowing when he nodded to the side. "You want me to get up?"

His head listed and he hurried to slide his phone closer. Switching from the texts with Leo to a note to write out a message for me.

. . .

I want to take you upstairs to get away from all this for a while

Let's go

I glanced back to Stevie and Russell as I warred over what to do. Part of me wanted to stay. To wait it out and be there to answer every call that came through, even though each one was only making me more worried and paranoid.

But I needed to get away, even if it was only to the comfort of my room.

So, I slid from his lap and waited while he closed out of everything he'd been working on before letting him wrap me up against his side and lead me through the house.

"What are we going to do?" I asked once he locked my door behind us. "You and Leo were worried about what my parents would do if this happened . . . and now it has, and they're on their way here."

He didn't say anything until he had me in bed and stripped down to my underwear and a shirt. The act and his touch comforting and affectionate as his dark eyes studied me. Once he was propped up against the headboard with the pillows behind him, he pulled me against his chest and wrapped his arms around me. Waiting until I leaned my head against his shoulder before he began tapping on the screen of his phone.

What happens now is you trust me

You trust Leo

And know you have nothing to be ashamed of

Just because it doesn't fit in your parents' idea of how your life should go doesn't mean anything

I mean

They're blackmailing people and doing all sorts of illegal things

They don't exactly have room to judge people

A stunned laugh bubbled free, a whisper of a smile pulling at my lips when he pressed a soft kiss to my temple.

Never be ashamed of choosing the life meant for you

I pressed my fingers to his neck, pulling him closer as gratitude swirled through me. "Thank you."

Gripping my hand in his, he lifted it to his lips to press a soft kiss there before lowering our joined hands to my stomach as he released an exhale and relaxed deeper into the pillows.

He didn't need to say anything for me to know that he wanted me to rest. To try to relax and put everything that was happening out of my mind for a little while.

There, in his arms, it felt like I could do anything.

But shutting my mind off wasn't easy.

Countless minutes later, I was still there, going over everything again and again and again.

The article. Tucker. My parents' calls.

My parents' *plan*.

Shifting a little in Adam's arms so my side was pressed to

his chest, I looked up into his dark, patient eyes and struggled over how to voice what I was thinking.

A soft huff left him, his head shaking slightly as he ran a knuckle down my cheek. All adoration and amusement as if he didn't know why I was hesitating over anything with him.

"You told me you were born into that life—that gang." His eyebrows lifted in surprise, clearly not having expected my mind to have led me there. "You said your brother is now the head of it. You've talked about him a few times, but you've never said anything about your parents."

Instant . . .

The way his expression turned cold with warning was instant. The way that energy clinging to him burst from him and filled the room. All those old pains clashing with a hatred so profound in his eyes that it stole my next breath.

"Oh," I whispered. I swallowed over the knot forming in my throat and dipped my head. "*They're* 'those things' you don't talk about."

He pressed his hands to the bed to help him sit up higher, causing me to shift away from him. From the heaviness pressing down around us and the way he dragged a hand through his hair and then over his face, I had a feeling he wanted me to get away from him. That he needed space.

But when I began moving to the other side of the bed, his hand shot out and he gripped my wrist, keeping me in place even though he never looked at me.

At least a minute must have passed before he released me.

"Adam, I'm sorry. I didn't know."

I swallowed uncomfortably when he lifted a hand, his expression pained as if he was begging me to stop.

But when he reached for his phone, his movements were all hesitation and regret.

Leo was right the other day
And I know you heard him
You should know

My head bobbed awkwardly, my stomach in knots when I'd already been on the verge of losing the contents of it all morning.

But instead of taking his phone back and typing right away, he just sat there staring at it for long moments as if just the thought of what he was about to reveal was crushing something inside him.

"I don't need to know," I tried to assure him. "Whatever it is, it's your haunting past. It's fine that I don't know."

His head moved in subtle disagreement before he began typing—keeping the screen from my view as he did. Fingers moving quickly at some parts before slowing and then stopping altogether at others. All while that darkness burned and bled from him.

When he handed it to me a while later, I carefully took the phone, my chest moving with small, shallow breaths as I studied his vacant stare before finally looking down.

My whole world narrowing in on the first two lines.

Twenty-Eight

HOLLIS

I wasn't born mute

And honestly I can't remember when I stopped talking

It didn't happen all at once

Just less and less until it got to the point where I literally started choking over anything I tried to say

Until I eventually couldn't say anything anymore

Couldn't figure out how

Like I completely lost the ability to even though I knew I physically could

But my first memory of my dad is him beating me for laughing

If I ever said a word or made any type of sound he'd hit and kick me until I stopped

When I got older he started coming after me with whatever was close by

For a long time I thought it was just him being an asshole

I thought I needed to protect my brother so I was always trying to get him to stay quiet too

But our dad loved my brother which was good

He was a good kid and he'd be a good guy now if he hadn't gotten caught up in that life

It was just me he hated

And my mom never tried to stop it

Just blamed me for it

Said if I'd shut the fuck up and stay out of my dad's way my life would be a whole lot easier

"Oh my God," I said, the words coming out a strained wheeze. I looked at Adam, but his haunted stare was pinned on a spot on the wall. His body unnaturally still as he waited for me to peek at his demons.

My heart squeezed and ached when I let my gaze drift over him once more, but I forced my stare back to the screen of the phone.

So I tried

Tried to remain invisible when I was near him

Tried like hell not to draw attention to myself

Kind of hard because I was a little shit since everyone knew who my dad was and I thought I was untouchable around school and on the streets

We'd come home high off whatever shit we'd pulled or just high and I'd forget that I was supposed to be a ghost until his fist was cracking against my jaw

Found out when I turned fourteen that he wasn't my dad by way of him giving me my first gun and telling me to kill my mom

Guess she'd cheated on him and he'd clearly known the entire time

I didn't shoot her

He did

He's also the one who shot me when I said I wanted out

I mean someone had to do it and he was the leader

But with him I was surprised I survived it

I expected him to empty the magazine in me after all the shit we'd been through

My brother ended up killing him not long after that because of everything he did to me and pinned it on a rival gang

Oh . . . oh my God.

I couldn't imagine the life Adam was talking about. I couldn't imagine growing up with parents so cruel or heartless. I couldn't imagine how damaging it was to have your voice taken from you a little at a time.

To have a gun put in your hand and told to pull the trigger on anyone, let alone your own mother.

Even with the situation with my parents, it was impossible to understand what I'd just read was *real*.

"Adam," I whispered and looked up at him, setting his phone down beside me as I shifted closer to him.

Before I could reach him, he leaned over and scooped up his phone, that dark warning practically shouting at me not to come any closer.

Don't

Don't say my name like that

Our lives were wildly different Hollis

We don't talk about our parents for different reasons

But it's just the same

They were shitty people
Well
ARE in your case

"But, Adam, what he did to you—" My lips pressed tightly together when he held up a hand, eyebrows drawn tight like it was a struggle just thinking about it.

I accepted my life a long time ago
My dad was a dick
I can't speak even though
Fuck
I wish I could talk to you
But it is what it is and they aren't things I focus on
They aren't things I WANT to focus on
Understood

"Yeah," I said softly, unable to get the jagged lump from my throat. Taking a deep breath, I met his stare. All those old pains hidden within them finally making sense, and they made me ache for him. "Thank you for telling me."

He gave a single dip of his head and held out his hand, the action at once a request and an apology. Wanting me closer and sorry for pushing me away.

Not that he had anything to be sorry for. I couldn't imagine how difficult it had been to tell me, to relive those nightmares again.

I slipped my hand into his, a sigh easing from me when he pulled me onto his lap and pressed his forehead to mine.

His touch gentle when he brushed the tips of his fingers across my cheeks and down my jaw.

"I know you don't like pity," I said as I met his dark stare. "But, Adam, I need you to know that I'm sorry. I'm sorry for everything he did and that no one tried to stop him. And even though I wouldn't change anything about the caring yet terrifying man you are, I wish I could take away what he did."

You think I'm terrifying

I glanced down at the phone he held in the small space between our bodies. My eyes rolling as a soft laugh crept up my throat. "Oh my God. Don't pretend you don't know how unbelievably scary you and Leo can be."

A wicked grin lit his face as his hands trailed down to my waist, all tease and possession.

That soft laugh turning into a sharp gasp of surprise when he lurched forward, pinning me to the bed and caging me in. My own smile unrestrained as I let my fingers drift through his beard and mouthed, *Terrifying*.

He dipped down to capture my mouth, a rumble of frustration vibrating in his chest when someone started pounding on my door.

"Babe," Stevie called out. "Babe, you need to open the door, like, right now."

Adam's expression shifted back to that fierce protectiveness it'd been all morning in an instant as he hurried off the bed and across the room. Flinging open the door just as I managed to sit up.

"Husband," she said in way of greeting as she walked

right past Adam, heading for me even as she pointed to the window. "Guessing you haven't looked outside. What in the fuck, that nasty Jordan McKay is here."

My stomach dropped. "What?"

Adam was at the window a second later. Looking out and then moving back to us when Stevie continued. "No, no. He's already downstairs."

"Stevie, *what*?"

She held up her hands. "Babe, he told me I had to let him inside, and I kind of panicked. He said your parents sent him," she yelled over me when I started complaining again, shrugging helplessly. "Am I allowed to say no to a mayor or a senator? Like, is that legal?"

Adam's eyes rolled and his head hung as he gripped the back of his neck.

"Yes, it's legal. You just say *no*."

Apology splashed across her face. "I don't know this. You never say no to them."

My mouth parted, but no words came out.

As true as it was, her words made me feel oddly pathetic at that moment. Trying to push the feeling aside, I asked, "Well, what does he want?"

A sneering laugh left her. "Right . . . yeah, he's a real fucking peach, Hollis." She turned to leave, stomping all the way to my door before whirling around and pointing at me as if I'd done something. "He asked if *I* was the prostitute and then sent me up here to *fetch* you. Russell stopped me from threatening certain appendages."

My shoulders sagged because even though it'd been a joke between us before, she truly looked offended now. "Stevie, I'm sorry. My parents must've said something to him, and they're hateful. You know that."

"Whatever," she huffed as she turned again, mumbling as she left. "I'll get into voodoo or something and make a doll."

She scares me sometimes

I blew out an exasperated breath, rolling my eyes when I read the words on Adam's phone. "She's harmless. You know she is." Looking up at him, I searched his hardened stare and asked, "Do I have to go down there?"

You don't have to do anything you don't want to

I didn't want to.

Anything that had to do with Jordan McKay, I wanted nothing to do with. That my parents had been the ones to send him made me want to get even farther from him.

But at the same time, I knew I didn't have a choice.

Leo and Adam could finish this job on their own, I was sure of it. But it would take a long time, and, as insane as it sounded, there was a possibility I wouldn't be alive at the end of it.

Helping them finished it faster.

Finished it *now*.

I released another sigh and got off the bed. "All right, let's go."

Once I was fully dressed again, we headed downstairs. Passing where Russell and Stevie were sitting in the den, bent close and talking to each other even as she pointed toward the front of the house for me, toward the sound of an irritated mayor.

As soon as he saw us, his eyes narrowed on Adam and then rolled.

"I have to go," he said, then ended the call he'd been on and furiously tapped his phone against his palm as he looked between us.

After what felt like minutes, he gestured to us, his smile and eyes bright even though everything bordered on vicious. "There's such a thing as *discretion*," he said, his voice a mocking whisper. "But we're already on top of it. Your people and mine have already spoken to the press—"

"I don't have people," I said before he could go on.

An aggravated laugh left him. "You do now." Waving his hand toward the entryway, he said, "I also spoke with the reporters waiting outside. The agreed-upon story is that it is an old photo of the two of you. As for the one of you stripping . . ."

Adam's hand tightened around mine just before I snapped, "I'm not a stripper."

"Are you sure about that?" McKay asked, looking wholly unconvinced. "As for that photo, it has been doctored. A complete fake. We'll go into more detail about that . . ."—he looked at his watch—"when we get to lunch with your parents. So, go get dressed."

"I am dressed."

"Yep," McKay said with a flustered sigh. "Yeah, you are. Then let's go, we're already running late. And *you*,"—he pointed at Adam—"you will not leave this house until there aren't any more cameras left outside, waiting to photograph something. And for the love of God, stay away from the windows." The last was said with a warning glare.

From the destructive energy bursting from Adam, I knew without needing to look at him that it didn't intimidate him.

Adam squeezed my hand tighter and pulled me back a few feet despite the complaints from McKay, and handed me his phone.

You don't have to go

"I do," I whispered as I passed it back to him. "For you, for what you've done, I do."

His throat worked and his eyebrows furrowed, showing all his pain and frustration. But this time . . . this time it meant so much more. This time, it absolutely crushed me.

Still, I knew that look in his eyes.

I knew he didn't care about his job as much as he cared about keeping me safe—and letting me go with McKay wasn't keeping me safe.

"I'll see you tonight," I promised.

Just as I started pulling away, he pulled me back in. Crushing his mouth to mine in a short but powerful kiss that was all passion and need and fear and love.

"I love you," I whispered against his lips, turning from his hold before he could do anything else that would make me want to change my mind.

McKay looked more irritated than furious even though his hardened stare was locked on Adam. "Was that necessary?" he asked in a low tone when I neared him.

I fell into step beside him, wanting to turn back with each step farther and farther from Adam. Wanting to avoid whatever was coming. Wanting to be in a world where it was Adam and me, and none of this was happening.

I glanced over my shoulder just as we were rounding the corner to the entryway, my heart reaching out to where Adam waited. All that dark, threatening energy that had called to me from that very first night promising comfort and protection as he watched me leave then.

Was it necessary?

"Absolutely."

Twenty-Nine

HOLLIS

"We're having lunch with my parents in a suite?" I asked when McKay ushered me into the large space, my heart racing and my body rebelling each step forward because I didn't trust him.

I didn't trust *this*—whatever waited for me in that room.

He barely took a second to look up from his phone, which he'd been glued to the entire drive to the hotel doing *damage control*, to give me a wide-eyed stare. "We need to show that we aren't worried about the article and photos. We don't need to look suspicious."

Right.

Because going to a hotel and then meeting up in a penthouse suite with my parents who'd just flown here wasn't at all suspicious.

McKay hissed a curse when his phone began ringing. "In there," he said, pointing to the adjoining room. "I need to take this."

I watched him head back out the way we'd come, then looked to the room that waited just beyond where I stood.

Wondering how I'd come to a point in my life where I was terrified of a *room*.

Terrified of my *parents*.

With an unsteady breath in, I started toward it, each step shakier and shakier until I stumbled into the large lounge area of the suite.

The *empty* lounge area.

Oh God.

I turned in a slow circle, looking at everything with a suspicious eye as if it might attack me at any moment, and jolting when a low murmur came from the far side of the room.

After a second to hesitate and wonder if I would come to regret it later, I walked that way. Holding my breath and trying to make my steps as quiet as possible until I reached the hallway leading to a room.

The voices still low but distinct enough to recognize my parents mixed in with someone else I didn't know. Distinct enough to make out the words they were saying.

The names . . .

Leo Vega and Adam Ortiz.

Oh God.

I pressed a hand over my mouth to quiet the stunned breath that burst from me and closed my eyelids tight. Focusing only on listening to what they were saying. Trying to commit it all to memory.

Because the guys had been right: My parents had someone in the FBI in their pocket, and I had a feeling he was the third voice I was hearing.

"The source who sold the story will be dealt with soon," the man said a few minutes after I'd started listening in, having inched closer to the cracked-open door at the end of the hall at some point. "It will all be done in a way that doesn't raise suspicion, and we'll plant false information and evidence of Photoshopping Hollis's photos, as well as others, so no one will give any credit to the story."

My eyes snapped open, and I hurried away from the hall when his voice grew louder and louder, bursting into the lounge area just as my father's acknowledgment filled the space I'd just been in.

Except I was so freaked out by everything I'd heard and by that landmine of a place that I kept running.

Right for the entrance to the suite and barreling into McKay.

"Shit," he hissed, scrambling to catch his phone and then grab my shoulders to keep me upright. Once he was sure I was standing on my own, he gave me an assessing once over and then looked to the open archway behind me. "Parents run you off that quickly?"

"No, I just—I have—bathroom," I stammered.

His eyebrows slowly lifted and then he looked back at his phone. "It's a good thing you're *you*, Ms. Donahue. Not sure you'd be worth all this otherwise." Before I could manage to form a response with everything jumbling up my mind, he pointed behind me. "Bathroom."

"Right," I whispered when he gave an expectant look.

Turning, I walked back into the lounge room with him right behind me and felt a sinking pit open up in my stomach when I saw my parents for the first time since all this began.

I felt sick and terrified and furious all at once. The combination clashing and fighting for dominance in my veins, feeling like burning tar.

I wasn't sure I'd ever truly hated anyone until that moment.

But I hated my parents.

With every ounce of my being, I hated them.

Anyone who could use and control and hurt people the way they had was the lowest of low. Anyone who could set up their own child to be killed? There was a special place in Hell for them.

And at that moment, I understood the look in Adam's eyes from earlier. That old pain I'd always wanted to fix mixed with a fury I hadn't been able to fathom.

I got it now.

"You foolish child," my mother began, stepping up to me and looking down at me the way she'd done my entire life. "Humiliating your father would be one thing—one *unacceptable* thing. But then you have to go and try to destroy everything we've worked for by getting tricked into a fake relationship with an FBI agent?"

McKay's phone clattered to the floor. His voice this side of horrified. "What?"

Well, shit.

Here we go.

My parents were demanding I stay with them in the hotel.

To *monitor* me. To make sure I didn't mess up any worse than I already had. So they could make sure I continued stepping into the spotlight at the right times so we could put this story to bed.

I didn't believe a second of it even though I was sure they would do all those things just to keep me with them.

But I'd managed to get away long enough to pack a bag despite their objections.

My father hadn't wanted me to go alone, sure I couldn't be trusted to come back. My mother had claimed I needed a new wardrobe anyway—*after all, you've been living with a prostitute, Hollis. I think that speaks for itself.* But they'd given reluctant agreements when I'd told them my roommates would expect me to come home to at least pack, and McKay had quickly confirmed Stevie's *dramatics*.

I hurried to finish writing everything out, then put the cap on the Sharpie and flipped back to the first page as I got out of the car and rushed up to the front door of the house.

Knocking loudly, I took a steadying breath, held up the stack of papers, and prayed this worked.

Leo threw open the door, looking just as angry as ever even though the space beneath his eyes was purple from lack of sleep.

He opened his mouth, but I quickly switched out the first paper and lifted the stack higher so he would look at it as I slipped into the house.

JUST SAY "HI."

I need to talk to both of you.

But YOU can't be there. You can't say a word during.

Do you understand?

"Hi," he mumbled slowly, uncertainly, and shut the door softly behind me.

"Is Adam here?" I asked as I pointed to the bottom of the paper again.

He lifted an eyebrow and gestured toward the hall leading to Adam's room, "Yeah, he's in his room."

I gave him an irritated look and once again pointed to the bottom of the paper. When I received a nod that was only slightly more confident, I slid the paper to the back, revealing the next.

Trust me.

His expression showed anything but that, but with another steadying breath, I started down the hall, staggering away when Leo reached for the back of the stack.

I tried swatting at him, but he just picked at the last two papers to see what I'd originally had up front.

I don't have long.

Get Leo and tell him to keep quiet and stop glaring at me.

I need to talk to the two of you.

He rolled his eyes and released the papers, ignoring the scowl I sent his way. When I walked into Adam's room, I faltered. Nearly forgot everything I'd learned and everything I needed to do.

All I wanted was to fall into Adam's arms, to get wrapped up in all that dark, comforting energy, and let him help me forget everything for a while.

But we didn't have time.

He pushed from his desk chair. Eyebrows drawn low as his stare darted from my face to the papers in my hand to where Leo followed close behind.

Gesturing to the paper, he lifted his chin in question and stepped closer, but I took a matching step away and slid that page around to the back, revealing the next.

Your entire house is bugged.

It has been for some time.

"I think we need to talk," I said, my voice shaky, though I wasn't sure why.

Maybe because my head and my heart were rebelling everything I was about to say, even if they were only a ploy. Maybe because I already knew he wouldn't be okay with what I was going to do.

Or maybe because the reality of what was happening with my parents was becoming clearer to me with each passing hour, and it felt like the weight of it was crushing me.

Sliding that paper to the back, I revealed the next and the next, giving Adam and Leo everything I truly needed to tell them while saying what was necessary for whoever was listening.

There was a man named Akron at the hotel with my parents today.

I'm pretty sure he's FBI.

From the look Adam and Leo gave each other, I knew I'd been right in my assumption.

. . .

They know I know everything about you and this job.

They know Leo told Sarah.

They have someone tailing her in case she says anything.

I looked at Leo in sorrow and sympathy when his fear and outrage burst from him, then continued flipping through the pages I'd written on as I spoke. "We were wrong—you were wrong. About my parents . . . everything you thought they were doing."

But I'm not supposed to know any of that. I overheard it all.

They "told" me Adam is FBI, and I pretended to be shocked and hurt.

They obviously would have known I was lying, but that's the game we're playing with each other.

"My parents aren't bad people," I said, hoping I sounded like I actually believed what I was saying. "They wouldn't do any of the things you've assumed they were."

My parents are demanding I stay with them, and I'm going to.

I need to in order to figure out what's going on.

Adam's eyes widened. His expression pure refusal as he slashed his hand through the air.

I hurried to the next page, giving him a pointed look as I

said, "They're afraid someone's out to get them, and they think they're next."

Adam, don't tell me "no."
I have to do this.
I AM doing this.

Adam just held my stare, refusing to budge until I continued on.

Saying words that hit too low and too close to home for us. Sorrow weaving through me and making my voice shake. "And I can't be with someone who once targeted me and is still targeting my family."

My brows pinched together in apology as I switched to the next page.

Akron is frustrated that "they" can't get into Adam's system.
So, that's one good thing.

"I can't believe that I ever let myself fall for you in the first place or that I was stupid enough to stay with you after everything I found out about you. But I won't let you manipulate me anymore."

Also, I know we hate him . . .
But Tucker's life is in immediate danger.

. . .

"So, we're done, Adam," I choked out as I flipped to the next page. Looking down, I saw it was the last, and I held it out farther so he would know I meant it.

His hardened jaw and cold eyes making my heart clench.

I'm sorry.

I love you.

I don't mean any of it.

"I don't want to see you again," I said shakily. "I don't want to hear from you. Leave my family alone."

I looked between them and then focused on Adam, my face twisting up with emotion as I mouthed, *I have to go*.

I turned and hurried from the room. My heart feeling like it was trying to tear in two—half of it wanting to stay with Adam and the other half feeling like I'd just made a crucial mistake even though none of it had been real.

But his expression had made it all seem so real.

Just before I reached the front door, all that dark warning surrounded me as he came up beside me. Slipping one hand around my waist and opening the door with the other, ushering me outside as Leo quickly trailed behind.

"Where's Sarah?" he demanded once we were in the driveway.

"I don't know, but she isn't at our house anymore." I looked back at him, hating that I'd been the one to give him the news. "Leo, I'm sorry."

He didn't say anything as he rushed to his car, but then Adam was pulling me to a stop and handing me his phone.

. . .

Don't do this
It isn't safe

"I already told you, I have to." When he started typing again, I placed my hand over his. "Adam, you know I do. For everything you and Leo have been doing, I have to."

He gave a hard shake of his head, and I pushed up on my toes. Sliding my hand around his neck and pressing my forehead to his.

"If I were anyone else, you'd agree with me."

Not when YOU are their target

"You told me to trust you, and I do. I trust you to do everything that needs to be done and to keep me safe."

He stepped back, looking wholly furious with me.

"Adam, I have to go. They have a tracker on my car. They'll know I'm still here if they look to see where I am."

His eyes widened and he looked from me to my car.

After another moment, he let out a harsh exhale and tapped quickly on his phone before giving it to me.

We can't use your phone
Even if Akron can't get into my system
The way I linked your computer and your phone is that everyone else working on this with us can see it
I gave them access to that part
So take my phone

Text my number whenever you need me and I'll be able to see it on my computer

"Okay," I said with a nod. "Okay. Adam—" Whatever I'd been about to say faded into nothing when he crushed his mouth to mine.

The kiss all passion and worry in its fierceness and at complete odds with the gentleness in which he curled his hands around my cheeks.

I gripped his wrists and started pulling back—knowing I had to leave then or I would get lost in the moment and him. Pressing one last kiss to his lips, I whispered, "I love you," and turned for my car. Only making it about a step before I was pulled back into his arms.

His dark eyes searched mine as his lips parted and throat worked, looking like he was in pain as he struggled over what he wanted to say.

And it made me ache for him.

"Adam . . ."

He dropped his head with a shuddering breath and stepped back, letting his arms fall heavily to his sides. The frustration and fear seeping from him weakening my resolve.

But I had to leave.

Reaching out, I caught his fingers in mine, getting his attention. "I already know," I said, trying to assure him before finally getting in the car and leaving.

I already knew he didn't want me to do this.

I already knew he was worried about me.

And I knew he loved me too.

Thirty

ADAM

Hollis was right . . .

I really hated this guy.

"Okay, but can we just establish that you're *not* going to kill me?" Tucker demanded, the question just another variation of others he'd asked at least twenty times since we'd pulled him from his apartment a few hours before.

Kicking and screaming that Michael Myers had come to kill him, no less.

I'd knocked him out—*accidentally*.

Honestly, it could be argued that I did it for his own good since he'd been thrashing and fighting us so violently—despite Leo trying to calm him and explain the situation—that Tucker had slipped and hit one of his counters.

He probably would've done worse to himself if my fist hadn't *accidentally* met his jaw when I'd been helping him up.

So, call me a hero.

Leo had already written me up and was waiting to submit it once we knew who we could trust again.

Whatever, it'd been worth it.

I slammed the hotel notepad on the bed beside where Tucker sat, then paced away, dragging my hands through my hair.

For the last time
I am not going to kill you
We just saved your life
You're welcome

"Saved—I am *bleeding*," Tucker shouted.

I dragged in a steeling breath, my eyes rolling before I turned to swipe the paper. Relief barreling through me and mixing with my frustration when Leo came back into the hotel room.

"How original," Tucker said with a huff when he saw what Leo was setting down on the desk. "Coffee and donuts for the cops."

Leo gave him a feral smile as he bit into a donut. "We're FBI, bud," he said as he held out the box to Tucker. When Tucker just stared at Leo like he was offering up grenades, Leo asked, "The fuck did donuts ever do to you?"

"Make me gain ten pounds?"

Leo shoved the rest of the donut in his mouth, never losing that lethal look.

"Okay, so how long until you kill me?" Tucker asked, looking at me.

Fucking hell.

I slanted an exasperated glare at Leo, letting him know this was what I'd been dealing with the entire time he'd been gone, then went back to what I'd originally been about to write to Tucker.

You're not bleeding anymore

You WERE bleeding because you tried to get away from us even as we told you we were trying to protect you

Because YOU slipped and fell

If I wanted to kill you

I wouldn't have cleaned the nearly nonexistent wound on your head

Tucker shrugged after he read the words. "For all I know, that's just to make me feel comfortable."

I gave Leo another look, letting him know exactly how I felt about the kid.

"I know," Leo murmured as he handed a cup of coffee to me. With a sigh, he handed another to Tucker and eventually set it on the desk when Tucker refused to take it. "Suit yourself, bud. Don't know what all you and your favorite person over here talked about while I was out, but like we tried to tell you when we were picking you up, we're doing this to keep you alive."

Tucker huffed, his expression and body language all disbelief. "Picking me up. You mean *kidnapping me in the middle of the night?*"

Leo just waited, making sure Tucker wasn't going to continue ranting before he asked, "You know that information you leaked about Hollis Donahue?"

Tucker looked at me, a proud smirk slipping across his face. "Did I blow your cover by sharing that picture?"

Leo snapped in front of me, getting Tucker's focus back on him. "What you did was piss a lot of people off—a lot of bad people. And if it weren't for the people you screwed over with that story you sold, those bad people would've been breaking into your apartment about . . ."—he looked at his watch—"almost thirty minutes ago to kill you. To plant things on your computer to discredit everything you said."

Tucker's expression didn't falter, but his face paled. "I call bullshit. How would you even know that?"

Leo gestured between the two of us. "FBI."

Tucker made a face that was as condescending as it was disbelieving. "Yeah, sorry. See . . . I watch a lot of TV, which means I know how this goes. And you two are just . . . no, you're not the real thing." He shrugged. "Murderers, definitely. The good guys, nope." He placed his hands behind him to lean back on the bed. "So, I guess I'll just—*oh my God, help me!*" he screamed. "Someone help! They're going to kill me!"

Leo slowly dropped his head back so he was staring at the ceiling, and I just looked over at him.

"Don't," he warned, already knowing what I was thinking. When I held out the pad of paper, he sighed. "I said don't."

Duct tape

A stunned laugh burst from him before he could control his features, and then he was glaring at me. "No." Looking back at Tucker, he spoke over him even as Tucker continued yelling for help. "You can scream all you want. There's no one close enough in the rooms to hear you. But if you don't believe us, I'm sure it'll be on the news soon enough."

Tucker quieted almost as soon as Leo turned on the TV. Leaning forward to stare at the screen suspiciously as he asked, "What will?"

"They can't kill you if we have you. But they can still plant things on your computer. They can get it out to news stations that the story you sold was fake."

"But it *wasn't,*" Tucker said, enunciating each word.

"It's about to be." Leo offered Tucker the coffee again and waited for him to take it before saying, "When it's all over the news, you'll see we did you a favor."

Tucker had fallen asleep not long after we'd turned the TV on, and I'd never been so thankful for silence.

Normally, silence bothered me. I liked having music on. I liked listening to people talk around me.

But with Tucker? Jesus Christ. I would've given anything to make that silence continue for as long as possible.

Leo had slipped back out not long after. Picking up my laptops and notepads and then heading out again to check on where he'd taken Sarah. By the time he'd finally come back with an early lunch, Tucker was awake and asking what my favorite way to kill people was.

"Oh good," he said sarcastically. "It's my time to die."

"Give it a rest," Leo muttered as he tossed a bag of food at Tucker. His smile wry when he walked over to where I'd stationed myself. "Going well here?"

I flipped him off, then looked at the TV when the name *Donahue* could barely be heard over the soft volume.

I hurried to turn it up and moved to the middle of the room with Leo, watching intently as the celebrity news anchor spoke.

". . . suspected Tucker Gipman was readying to blackmail members of political families, not just the Donahues. Documents found on his computer show prepared emails demanding a variety of things with doctored photos as leverage—including the one of Hollis Donahue dancing practically naked on a stage."

Photos and emails were brought to the screen, nearly all blurred out.

I turned to look at Tucker, and he looked equally horrified and like he might get sick.

"But Ojai Mayor, Jordan McKay, and Hollis Donahue aren't letting this near-scandal get in the way of their happiness. The two were seen cruising around yesterday afternoon and again this morning with *both* sets of their parents." The anchor gave a mischievous look. "We can only wonder what's in store for these two if they're getting cozy with, dare we say, the future in-laws."

I muted the TV when they began talking about something else and turned to face Tucker.

"No," he said slowly, his head slanting as if he were struggling to wrap his head around what he'd just seen and heard. "I didn't. No, I didn't!" The last was a hysterical shout. "That was my name they said! They're using my name."

Leo crouched down in front of him, his voice calm yet firm. "This is where we take care of you, and you trust us. All right, Tucker?" When Tucker began wildly shaking his head, Leo said, "We're going to start the process of getting you into witsec, all right?"

"Is that a cult?"

"Witness protection."

"Oh my God, I'm in a TV show," Tucker cried out, looking like this was the last kind of show he wanted to be in.

I glanced back at the workstation I'd created when my laptop chimed with a message and then hurried over there. My heart taking off when I saw it was a message from my own number.

Hollis: *I love you.*

Jesus Christ, if she only knew how much I loved her.

I sank into the seat and hurried to respond.

Me: *Michael Myers is safe.*

Hollis: *What . . . ?*

Hollis: *OH! Oh good. Thank God. I've been worrying even though he's such a dick.*

Hollis: *Thank you.*

Me: *Of course.*

Me: *Akron called Leo. Said now's our time to act since your parents are in L.A.*

Me: *Said you and your parents are staying at The Mayhourne. Need to confirm that's where you are.*

Hollis: *No, we're staying at the Waldorf Astoria. Akron knows that. That's where I saw him.*

Me: *. . . all right.*

. . .

I tapped my hand on the desk to get Leo's attention and then nodded toward the laptops so he would read what she'd been saying.

"Got it," he muttered, dipping his head even though he looked more unsure with each new thing that was thrown at us.

Hollis: *Please be careful.*

Me: *Me? No, don't worry about me. Keep yourself safe until I can.*

Me: *Tell me your room number. Leo and I will make sure we're close by as soon as we finish up with Michael Myers.*

I waited, watching the screen as a minute came and went. And then another and another.

My heart slowing to that dull, pained beat I'd grown so accustomed to throughout my life when her response didn't come.

Grabbing one of my notebooks, I flipped to a blank page and scrawled out a message.

We need to finish things with Tucker
And we need to get to the Waldorf
Now

Leo nodded. "Agreed." Looking over at where Tucker was sitting on the edge of the bed in shock, he asked, "You ready to become someone else?"

Tucker glanced our way, mouth and eyes wide with horror. "*What*? Like, change my face?"

Jesus.

Leo held out a hand to me. "Don't."

This was going to be a long day.

Thirty-One

HOLLIS

"Who are you talking to?"

I placed Adam's phone face down in my lap and looked over at Jordan McKay, my heart racing for all the wrong reasons as I wondered if there was a way he somehow already knew before I lied, "My roommate."

He made a face between bewilderment and disgust. "Think about what you just said. You're twenty-six and have a roommate."

You're thirty-two and have a missing fiancée.

I swallowed back the words before they could slip free, but from the way his eyes narrowed, I had a feeling they were written all over my face anyway.

"What do you want?" I asked instead.

He studied me for a moment longer before taking a step back. "Come with me. I have something to show you."

I hesitated for a moment, not wanting to go anywhere with him even though I was sure it wasn't him I needed to be afraid of. At least, not at the moment.

Tapping on the screen a few times, I slipped the phone

into my pocket and stood to follow. Keeping my eyes and ears alert as I entered the lounge area of the suite, my steps faltering when I found two people I didn't know looking at me expectantly.

Smiles bright and unsettling.

"Hello," I said, voice a little uncertain as I finally forced myself to take another step closer.

"Lunch should be here soon," McKay informed me, glancing at his watch before walking quickly back over to me so he could usher me closer to one of the couches. "Until then, these are for you to look over and choose from."

"Ms. Donahue," the awaiting man said before lifting the top of the large box he had resting on the table.

My eyes widened with dread at the ten large diamond rings waiting for me.

Oh no.

"And *this*," McKay went on, gesturing to the woman chatting on her phone over in the corner, "will be our wedding planner. She's here so we can get started right away. I want to get as much done as we can in the two hours I have before I need to leave."

I swallowed thickly before looking up at him when he stood from the couch, already pulling out his phone. "And if I don't want to marry you?"

McKay gave me a look that bordered on sinister. "Pick out a ring, Ms. Donahue."

A cold pit opened up in my chest at the demand, making it hard to breathe. Making it hard to do anything at all.

Just minutes before, I'd been thinking Jordan McKay wasn't the one I needed to be afraid of. But that look was a stark reminder that I needed to be afraid of them all.

I slowly looked back at the man waiting for me to choose

one of the rings, his smile much more forced than it had been just a minute before. "These are all very beautiful," I managed to choke out.

His eyes darted over to where McKay had gone, then back to me. "Thank you, Ms. Donahue. I kept you in mind when picking them out, but if there's something else you'd prefer, we're always happy to accommodate. A different cut, color, size . . . a gun." The last was said as a whisper and had my jaw dropping.

"I'm sorry?"

"A gem." He offered me a knowing smile. "Colored diamonds are very fashionable right now, but I've had quite a lot of demand for precious gems to be the main stone."

"I think . . ." I waited until I heard McKay's voice near the doorway, well over a dozen feet away. "I think I'm fine without the gem."

The jeweler's head dipped in the faintest nod before he gestured to the rings sitting between us. "Shall we?"

"He's watching?" I asked, the question coming out so low I wasn't sure the man heard me until he held up one of the rings for me and responded with, "Of course."

I pretended to look at the ring before setting it down and picking up another. Unable to see anything as I tried to listen to McKay's conversation. As dread crawled through my veins.

"Such a difficult decision, I know," the jeweler said as he handed me the sixth . . . or was it the seventh? A moment later, he clicked his tongue. "I see you keep going back and forth between these two." When I made some sort of acknowledging sound, he said, "I think you might be able to better see which one gives you that *feeling* if you tried them both on."

I put one of them on, looking to the side without ever moving my head when McKay's voice disappeared.

"I've been told you need a ring," the jeweler said, brow raised as he helped me take the ring off and slip another on. "Whether or not it's the one you decide on, you need one by tonight, no exceptions."

"Oh."

His expression morphed into forced excitement when he looked beside me. "There it is." He gestured to me. "That's the look I always hope to see when someone's picking out their wedding set. Dress shops get 'say yes to the dress' moments. I get *this*."

McKay sat next to me just as the jeweler finished speaking, his perfect smile in place. "Well, if she loves it, I do."

The jeweler laughed, then lifted a finger. "I have just the band to finish the set for when the two of you tie the knot."

McKay twisted his neck to whisper in my ear. "Lunch is waiting in the other room, and your parents just got back from the spa. They want to talk with you."

"What do we think?" the jeweler asked.

I lifted my hand, forcing a smile even though I still couldn't focus on what was right in front of me. "I love it," I managed to say, voice thick with my fear and unease.

Because if Adam was right, the closer I came to being Jordan McKay's fiancée, the closer we got to where my parents' plan began.

"Great," the jeweler said, his excitement nearly sounding genuine.

"Why don't you go talk with your parents, and I'll join you in there in a minute?" McKay suggested.

I think I nodded as I stood to leave. I wasn't really sure of anything as I tried to focus on just doing one thing at a time. Making it through each hour.

"Whoa, wait a second," McKay said, laughing with the jeweler as he grabbed my left hand to stop me. He slid the band off my finger as he winked at me, leaving the engagement ring in place. "We're not married just yet."

A frantic-sounding laugh tumbled past my lips because we were never getting married. Not only would I refuse to marry him. But my parents' plan wouldn't let us get that far.

"Right, sorry," I said as I turned and hurried away, forcing another smile when the wedding planner popped up beside me and grabbed my hand to look at the ring.

"Well, isn't that just gorgeous," she said, inspecting it every which way. "Good pickings, good pickings. You ready to get down to business?"

"Um, I think I have to speak with my parents first?"

A scoffing laugh burst from her. "Baby girl, I know." She pressed a hand to her chest and gave me a belittling look. "Why do you think they cut their spa appointment short?"

"I don't . . . I don't know." The words came out slow and all sorts of confused because I wasn't sure my parents had ever cut a spa appointment short before.

"And here she is," the wedding planner announced as we walked into the front room of the suite. "Now officially engaged."

"What?" I turned, looking at her and then to the open archway.

She waved her left hand at me. "Baby girl, you have the bling. Let's keep up."

"Honestly, Hollis," my mother said, already sounding exhausted with me. "Mindy, please. I can't deal with her today."

Mindy looked at my mom as if she totally understood and then turned me so I was fully facing her. "I'll be taking care of everything wedding, but first things first, we gotta make sure people know you're getting married."

"To a mayor," my father said slowly. "Not some FBI trash trying to frame us for something we've had no part in."

"Mmhm," Mindy said, pointing at my dad. "Exactly that. Thankfully, everything about alter-ego-Hollis is already going away, and everything Jordan-plus-Hollis is in the spotlight. Yay! Clap, clap, clap."

My eyes widened with amazement that this woman had actually said the words *clap, clap, clap*. I couldn't wait to tell Stevie.

"So, tonight, you're going to have dinner with only your parents since you've already been seen with Jordan today. When you're out, make sure your left hand is always visible, but not in an exaggerated way. Wear your hair down so you have to tuck it behind your ear. Keep your glass on the left side of your plate so you have to pick it up with your left hand. Understand? Great. Moving on to tomorrow."

"What's tomorrow?"

She gave a short, haughty laugh as she looked at my parents again before focusing on me. "What part of 'taking care of everything wedding' do you not understand?"

"Exactly why I struggle to deal with her," my mother said dramatically. "What should take one minute always drags to half-hour conversations where I have to repeat myself no less than fifteen times."

Don't call her out. Don't call her out.

She already wants to kill you . . . literally.

"Anyway," Mindy went on. "Tomorrow, you'll leave the hotel in the morning by yourself because after the flashes you give them tonight, they're going to be waiting for more. Wanting to confirm that was an engagement ring and not just something paired with whatever glamorous outfit you wear this evening. So, wear something grungy." Her head tilted as she scrutinized my leggings and shirt. "Something like this. Go get a coffee or something. And *wear that ring, baby girl.*"

"Yeah, I figured that part."

"Well, who knows with you, Hollis," my mother whispered before releasing a drawn-out sigh. "The getaway, Mindy."

"Ooo, yes. Now we're getting somewhere," Mindy said, eyes lighting with excitement. "Jordan will meet you back here after your morning *look at my ring* to take you for a romantic getaway. During that time—"

"Our people will confirm to the press that we're engaged," McKay finished for her as he walked into the room.

"That," Mindy said, pointing at him.

"So, we're just engaged?" I asked him. "There's no getting down on one knee? No asking? No giving me the option to say 'no?'"

"Hollis," my dad snapped, but I didn't look away from McKay. From that charming smile that faltered just enough to make him look truly evil.

He studied me for a long while before he gave a short, simple answer. "No."

Thirty-Two

HOLLIS

I'm so sorry. McKay walked in when I was texting you.

I was already typing which penthouse suite we were in when a responding text came through from Adam that night.

Adam: *Don't worry about it. We already figured out where you are. We're directly beneath you.*

Me: *You are?*

Adam: *Can't keep you safe if I'm not near you.*

A smile tugged at my lips. My breaths coming easier just knowing he was close by.

But when the next text came through from him, everything about me fell.

My smile. My shoulders. My heart.

. . .

Adam: *How was dinner?*

I flopped onto the pillows and looked over at the engagement ring where it rested on the nightstand, that same pit opening up inside me that had been there ever since the jeweler had revealed what had been waiting for me to choose from.

There hadn't been a need to turn on the news tonight. My mother had come in when I'd been getting ready for bed to let me know everything was going just as *we'd* hoped.

Pictures from our dinner were already popping up on various news stations with the exact question they'd been hoping for: *Could it mean what we think?*

And Adam had clearly seen it.

Me: *It wasn't pizza . . .*

Adam: *With olives?*

Me: *Is there any other way?*

Adam: *If you're a monster, maybe.*

A breath of a laugh crept free, and I would've given anything at that moment to look over and see his dark eyes. All that old pain dancing with his amusement. Anything to be pressed close to him, to have that physical connection as we talked.

My eyes widened, and I sat up. Quickly looking from the floor to the door of my bedroom and then back again.

Without another thought, I jumped from my bed and

hurried over to the wardrobe. Barely taking the time to pull out a large hoodie and step into my sandals as I rushed to my door, slowing only to keep my steps quiet as I moved through the suite.

I wasn't worried about either of my parents checking on me throughout the night. My mother had already told me to go to sleep since there was so much happening tomorrow, and we'd already seen so much of each other today. But I also didn't want to give them a reason to come out here.

Cracking the main door to the suite open, I checked one last time to make sure I had Adam's phone and my key to get back in, then slipped out into the hall. Pulling my hood over my head as I walked to the elevators, I grabbed Adam's phone to message him.

Me: *I've been wondering something ever since I found that conversation between you and Leo.*

Me: *When all this is over, are you planning on disappearing from me?*

I'd just stepped onto his floor when his message came through.

Adam: *When all this is over, I'm never letting you out of my sight.*

Me: *Good.*

The corner of my mouth lifted as I locked his phone and went over to the suite directly beneath ours and knocked. Staggering away when Leo opened the door just enough to show his large frame and—

"Oh my God, what are you—*what the fuck?*"

"Hollis?" he snapped, lowering his gun and grabbing my arm to haul me inside. "Why are you dressed like that?"

I pushed back my hood and huffed. "Because there are cameras in the hotel, you grumpy asshole."

He just rolled his eyes and stepped away from me, gesturing to the side just as Adam came in from another room.

Eyes wide when he saw me standing there.

"I really have a thing for you in those glasses," I whispered, earning a heart-stopping smile as he stalked across the room and pulled me close. Forehead pressed to mine and that charged energy wrapping me up so completely.

Grabbing my left hand, he glanced down at it long enough to see that it was bare before crushing his mouth to mine. The kiss nothing less than a claim as he lifted me into his arms.

"Wait, wait, wait," I said when he started taking me back the way he'd come, barely managing to pull away from the kiss that already had my heart racing.

I grabbed his phone out of the pocket of my hoodie and handed it over to Leo, pointing at it when he took it. "I put a password on it just in case anyone got a hold of it. It's Adam's birthday."

Leo lifted a brow as he held up the phone. "You guys are at birthday levels now?"

"Well, we interrogated him." I looked over at Adam, a smirk shaping my lips when he dug his fingers into my thighs in a way that was all need. "But I've been recording everything," I said, keeping my focus on him even though I was talking to both of them. "Once you gave me the phone, I knew I had to do something. So, I've recorded every conversation that's happened around me since. They're all on your phone."

Adam's expression shifted to surprise and awe before his attention snapped to Leo as he clumsily set my feet on the floor.

"Hollis, thank you," Leo said, genuine gratitude weaving through the words. "I'll start going through them now."

Adam looked at me again, all that awe mixing with adoration and love as he pressed a gentle kiss to my lips.

"Did you want to go listen to the recordings?" I asked, noticing his torn look.

His eyes bored into mine and his head shifted just enough for me to know that he was where he wanted to be.

"Good," I said on a breath. "Because if I don't get some time alone with you soon . . ."

A wicked grin lit his face as he pulled me close so I was pressed to every hard plane of his body. Feeling the way his muscles twitched and stretched as he walked me backward into the room he'd come from, stopping to lock the door behind us. Never once taking his eyes off mine as he pulled the hoodie from my body and let it fall to the floor.

One of his large hands trailing over my jaw and down my throat as he pressed his forehead to mine. My eyelids fluttering shut when he dipped the other between my legs. A plea for him to touch me on the tip of my tongue when he teased the edge of my sleep shorts. But then his hand was splayed across my chest and he was walking me backward again. Pushing me onto the bed and following me down.

I gripped his shirt and pulled him closer. Stealing a lingering, frantic kiss and letting the feel of his body on mine and the connection that always swirled between us try to take some of the stress I'd been living under away.

Make it so what was happening with my parents and McKay wasn't real.

At least during these stolen moments with Adam.

He pressed another slow kiss to my lips before his dark eyes met mine, the look there telling me he could feel everything I was trying to hide . . . trying to forget. And it was crushing him.

To watch me go through this.

To let me.

To see what it was doing to me.

He drifted his fingers over my cheekbone before securing his hand in my hair, then pressed his head to mine. The pain there unmistakable.

"I need you," I whispered as I gripped him tighter, brushing my mouth across his. "I need this."

If he sensed the desperation and fear pouring from me, he didn't give any indication, just captured my lips. Slowing our kisses and movements as the moment shifted into something so powerful and overwhelming.

Something I was terrified I would never experience with Adam again.

My eyes burned and my throat tightened at the thought, but Adam just passed his lips across my forehead and cheeks and throat, trying to heal my grief as he sat back. Trailing his fingers up my stomach and taking my shirt as he went.

Heat pooled low in my stomach as he moved down my body. Taking his time to learn and worship my body. Branding me with searing kisses and gentle touches until the rest of the world no longer existed.

There was only him.

Only us.

And this connection that could survive anything.

By the time he'd finished removing my clothes and was kneeling back on the bed from removing his own, I was already wound tighter than I'd ever been. One touch, and I was sure I would fall over the edge.

A whimper broke free when he dipped down and dragged his teeth across the inside of my thigh. Closer and closer until he placed a slow, open-mouthed kiss against my sex.

"Oh my God," I breathed as pleasure barreled through me, my lips opened with a silent moan from the force of my orgasm.

A shiver ripped down my spine when he nipped teasingly at my clit before quickly moving up my body. Looking at me with unconditional love and possession in a way that had my blood pounding out his name.

He curled over me, caging me in and passing feather-soft kisses across my jaw as he settled between my thighs. My back arching when he dipped a finger inside me. Teasing me before he pushed his thick length into me, a stuttered breath forcing from my lungs at the feel of him.

At the promise of each deliberate action as he pulled out before sliding back in just as slowly. Each inch making me tremble.

At the claim when he began moving. His hips rolling to fill me again and again as he found a steady rhythm that set my world on fire.

I pressed my hand to his chest, my heart going wild when he placed his hand over mine, pushing my fingers in harder. The vow clear . . .

He was just as much mine as I was his.

His dark eyes swirling with pure devotion and love when I whispered, "I love you."

Releasing my hand, he gripped the comforter on either side of me. His pace quickening as our vows and claims seemed to shift everything. Because I would do anything to spend the rest of my life having these moments with Adam, and I knew he felt the same.

The realization clashed with what we were facing and created a need unlike anything we'd ever shared before. Until I was clinging to him, and he was taking each of my breaths and offering his own as he pushed me over the edge again, that passion building and building between us even after he found his release deep inside me.

His dark eyes bored into mine. All love and pain and frustration, looking like he wished he could say so many things.

One thing.

"I know," I whispered before pressing another slow kiss to his lips.

He dropped his forehead to my shoulder and released a shuddering breath, then swept his mouth across the skin there before rolling to my side. Keeping his arm wrapped tightly around my waist until our bodies stopped trembling from the aftershocks, and I was left more exhausted and relaxed than I'd been in days. Knowing it was more than the sex.

It was being here with Adam.

Feeling safe in his arms.

Grabbing up my left hand when I sighed contentedly, he played with my bare ring finger before weaving his fingers through mine and letting our hands fall to my stomach.

"Just so you know," I began, voice soft and full of understanding, "he never asked. I never said 'yes.' They're all just expecting it to *be*." When Adam nodded, I twisted around to better look at him, propping up on my elbow. "I'm scared. I know you can feel that."

That energy clinging to him turned lethal in an instant, promising harm to anyone who would try to hurt me.

His jaw worked and he gave a slow dip of his head.

"If you're right . . ." My stare drifted to the side and unfocused as I thought over every conversation I'd overheard the past two days. "Adam, if you're right, then this will happen soon. And they're pushing for things to move fast. McKay's supposed to pick me up tomorrow to take me on a *romantic getaway*." When I felt him go still beside me, I looked at Adam and hurried to assure him, "Trust me, there will be nothing 'romantic' about it. He's an ass, and I'm nothing more than an opportunity for him. But with that and with them wanting it to be all over the news that we are engaged, I'm just . . . scared."

I shrugged. There was no other way to put it because I'd been absolutely terrified.

"Every time I walk into another room up there, I'm worried about what's waiting for me. With this getaway they have planned, I'm worried I'm not supposed to make it back from it."

Adam wove a hand into my hair, forcing me to look at him as he studied me.

Sorrow and apology and fury written on every line of his face before he leaned over to grab a hotel notepad and pen from the nightstand.

Don't go back

And I'll keep you here with me

Safe
Or go back
And I'll still keep you safe
Either way
We're so fucking close to finishing this
With the recordings you just handed over to Leo
I have no doubt we're even closer

I pressed my head to his shoulder for a moment, releasing a deep sigh before placing a kiss there and then meeting his tortured stare. "I need to help you finish this. I have to go back."

He nodded. The movement slow and delayed as if he'd been hoping for a different answer.

Right now

I looked at the question in his eyes, then shook my head as I shifted to my knees and moved one of my legs over him so I was straddling him.

"You know, you have a way of slowing everything down. Of making it feel like we have all the time in the world even when we don't." Trailing my fingers up his chest, I pressed in harder on the way down and watched the way his eyes flared in response. "So, why don't you slow everything down," I said, lightly challenging him. "Give us more time."

He let the paper and pen fall off the side of the bed as he rolled, reversing our positions. Those dark eyes searing me with all that passion and love and doing exactly what I'd asked him to—slowing time.

Making it feel like we had all the time in the world.

Every touch savored. Every kiss lingered.

So that when I slipped back into my bed hours later, I could still smell him on my skin. Taste him on my tongue. Feel his hands where he'd worshipped and loved me—branded me as his.

Thirty-Three

HOLLIS

I kept my head down the way I'd been instructed as I walked back to the hotel the next morning.

Give the illusion you don't want to be seen, but make sure you are *seen, Hollis.*

I'd been seen. My photo had just been taken again as I hurried onto the curb from the street. Clutching my coffee with my left hand even though I wasn't sure I'd ever purposefully used my left hand this much in my life.

Pulling Adam's phone from my jacket pocket, I tried not to frown when I saw the screen was blank since there were still eyes on me. Just swiped into the phone and went to the messages, glossing over the ones I'd sent throughout the morning.

Me: *It's disconcerting waking up in a bed that isn't completely disheveled after our night last night.*

Me: *Good morning, by the way.*

Me: *I'm making my walk of horror to the coffee shop down the* *street in a few minutes. Any song suggestions to take my mind off what's happening?*

Me: *. . . did I wear you out that badly?*

I locked the phone once I was in the hotel without sending another message, my gaze darting everywhere as I headed to the bank of elevators. Looking for some sign from him or Leo . . . anything.

Not that I expected Adam to be sitting at the workstation he'd created in the hotel room at every minute of the day, but he and Leo had brought his entire setup over here so he could work the way he needed to.

I'd also expected *something* in the three hours since I'd sent the first message. Especially considering the last thing he'd said to me before I'd left last night was they'd be watching for any word from me.

Then again, *what should I listen to* wasn't exactly a cry for help.

I stepped onto the elevator and put my key into the slot, my finger hovering over the button for his floor before I pressed the one to mine with a sigh.

Soon.

This will all be over soon.

No sooner had I stepped into our suite than I wished I'd taken longer at the coffee shop.

Maybe sat and stayed a while. Found a book to read.

Joined a church.

Anything.

"Goodness, there you are," my mother hissed, stomping over to me. Already dressed for the day in a pantsuit and heels. "That should have taken ten—fifteen minutes tops.

What was that . . . two hours?"

My eyebrows lifted in surprise. "Are you being—"

"We didn't tell you to go out for a morning stroll along Rodeo Drive, Hollis," she went on. "This isn't supposed to be obnoxious flaunting. It's supposed to be *flashes*. Teases."

"I was only gone for—"

"I've had enough." She turned, pressing her fingers delicately to her head. "I need a drink."

"Half an hour," I murmured lamely when she quickly walked from the room.

Just as I began turning to go to my side of the suite, she came clicking back in, voice dripping with bitter sarcasm. "If it isn't too much of a burden on your busy day, could you please prepare for your upcoming getaway with the mayor? And do something . . ."—she gestured to me—"take a shower or something. You look homeless."

"I . . . what?"

She sighed, her entire body folding with the action. "You're already running hours late, Hollis. For the love of God, *move*."

I stood there another few seconds, unable to comprehend the level of frustration and loathing that poured from her. And when I did finally leave for my room, it was simply because I knew I had to keep going. I had to keep up the pretenses with them for as long as possible until Adam and Leo could finish what they'd begun.

It didn't hit me until I was getting out of the shower that I hadn't once had that incessant need to do whatever they'd demanded of me. That I hadn't had that churning in my gut whenever I'd done something against them, worried they'd find out. And for a moment, I wondered when I stopped wanting to please them.

Then again, learning your parents wanted to kill you had that effect.

"Hollis? Hollis," my mother said as she came charging into the room a while later. One look at me, and she immediately turned into a ball of exasperation. "Honestly, what am I going to do with you?"

I lifted my arms out to the sides before going back to packing my bag for the getaway. "You told me to—"

"Have you done anything since we spoke?" She looked at the thin watch hanging from her wrist, then looked back to where I stood at the edge of my bed. "Have you even showered?"

A breath of a laugh left me considering I had—I'd even styled my hair and done my makeup. I just needed to pick out what to wear, which should have been obvious considering I was standing there in a robe. "Thanks, Mom."

She lifted a finger. "Sass is not appreciated, nor is it welcome in this conversation."

I dropped the shirt into my bag. "Well—"

"After what I've seen of your wardrobe, I didn't trust you to have something appropriate to be photographed in for today." She waved a hand through the air. "You know, being seen with the mayor for the first time, officially engaged. So, I had Mindy pick something up for you. She should be delivering it any minute, and the mayor will be following not long after. Don't even think about wearing something else. We have all worked very hard to bring you to this point."

Yeah, I bet you have.

"Did you hear me?"

"Yes, I—"

"Then respond when you are spoken to," she said irritably. "I have to go. Your father and I have a brunch we'll now be running late for because, once again, you've kept me longer than necessary."

"Have fun," I mumbled as I picked up a jacket to pack.

She stopped and looked back at me, expression all shock, as if she couldn't understand why I would say that to her. After a bit, she took another step toward my door and gestured to me. "Try to do something with your face. You look ill."

If I looked ill, it was because my parents were leaving. Which meant they would be gone when McKay picked me up.

It was the perfect setup for me to *disappear* if you thought about it.

No one with us when he came to get me. The last people to see us together were all the photographers who would be waiting to snap our picture.

And my parents knew exactly what I would be wearing.

Once I heard the suite's main door shut, I hurried to grab Adam's phone and sent off a message even though he still hadn't responded to me.

Me: *My parents just left for brunch.*

Me: *I don't know if I'm just being paranoid now or if I'm starting to catch on to what they're doing. But it seems convenient that they won't be here when McKay comes to get me.*

Me: *Looking at it on a screen, I feel paranoid now.*

Me: *God, Adam, I feel like an idiot because what if I'm wrong? But I'm shaking.*

. . .

I jolted so badly when there was a knock on the suite's door that I dropped his phone. Picking it back up, I kept it tight in my hand and hurried through the suite to find Mindy waiting with a garment bag.

"Baby girl, wait until you see." She stopped walking halfway through the door and held a hand to her chest. "Just wait. It's to die for."

Shit.

My bag was by the door. I was dressed in the *to die for* outfit that I absolutely hated because it made me look like my mom. And I hadn't stopped pacing since Mindy left nearly half an hour before.

Adam still hadn't responded, and I was beginning to worry that something was actually wrong. With each minute that passed, that worry grew. With each minute, I wondered how much longer I would have to wait until McKay finally showed . . . and prayed he wouldn't.

When a knock sounded, a soft cry crept up my throat.

Because I wasn't ready.

Even though I'd told myself about a thousand times that I was wrong—that it wasn't happening this weekend or maybe at all—there was this twisting, knotting sensation in my stomach that told me to run.

To get far, far away.

Because I trusted Adam. He'd been following these patterns. He knew my parents better than I did.

And I'd *heard* their conversations. I'd heard their cryptic plans. Nothing had ever been said outright, but everything hinted that Adam was right.

"My bag—hi," I said awkwardly when I opened the door to one of the hotel workers instead of McKay. "Um, I . . . I'm sorry, I thought you were . . . *hi*."

"Hi," she said on a soft laugh and then held the tray she was carrying a little closer to me. "Coffee?"

"Oh, no. No, I'm fine. Thank you." I gestured into the room. "I'm actually going to be leaving soon."

"No. *Coffee?*"

My brows drew close as suspicion unfurled inside me. "No, thank you."

She glanced around before leaning close to whisper, "A man had this sent to you. He said if you declined it, to tell you Boston is always a good band to fall back on."

It took me half a second, and then I was lurching forward, a gasp ripping through me as I hurried to accept the tray she was offering. "Thank you," I whispered around the knot of unexpected emotion in my throat. "I really appreciate this."

"Thought you might need the pick-me-up," she said happily. "Anything else I can do for you today, Ms. Donahue?"

"No, this is more than enough. Thank you again." Once she was leaving and the door was shut behind her, I hurried through the front room to one of the small side tables there.

Setting it down a little too roughly and moving the creamer and empty mug, my heart sinking a little more when I got to the small carafe of coffee and still didn't see any sign from Adam.

I glanced at the carafe before placing it back on the tray, confusion creeping through my veins and mixing with that earlier suspicion as I pulled out Adam's phone again.

Just as I was about to unlock it, I saw a folded paper

hidden within the sugars and knocked the entire container over in my attempt to get to it.

Take a breath, Hollis.

I've got you.

Coffee? Or is that . . .

Jesus, that's taking this too fast, isn't it?

A shocked laugh tumbled free as relief barreled through me. Pressing my hand to the floor, I whispered, "Thank you," then forced myself to do exactly that.

Breathe.

I trusted him to be right in all his assumptions of what was to come. I needed to trust him to have control of the situation.

Once I was nearly done with my first cup, I topped it off with more coffee and creamer, then headed over to where I'd stored my bag to pull out my phone so I could update Stevie before I was forced to leave.

"Babe," she said in way of answering, sounding ten shades of pissed off. "I gotta tell you, I don't exactly understand how you're *mother fucking* engaged to the douche of Ojai when you just told me you weren't actually with him."

"Stop watching the news," I said, repeating the same thing I'd told her when I'd called her the day before.

"Um, *hello*, my girl's on there. I'm gonna watch it."

"But it's all lies."

She snorted. "By the way, you looked super sexy in an I-just-threw-this-on kind of way this morning."

Surprise stopped me from taking my next sip of coffee. "That's already on the news?"

"Babe."

"Right." My eyes rolled when I remembered my conversation with my mom. "Well, Mommy Dearest said I looked homeless. So, there's that."

A sharp laugh left Stevie, making my smile widen as I pressed the mug to my lips. "Okay, so spill. What's going on, and what does my husband say about all of this?"

I hesitated for a while, wishing I could explain it but knowing I needed to wait until it was over. "I told you, he understands. But right now, the press needs to think McKay and I are engaged. He's even picking me up to take me on a 'romantic getaway' in a few minutes."

Stevie made a gagging sound.

"I know. I don't know where we're going, but I'm pretty sure he'll be doing business the entire time, and I'll be talking to Adam."

"So, like, are you going to marry him but have Adam on the side?"

"Stevie!"

"Legit question," she said in offense.

"Absolutely not. It's just for show, and it'll end soon enough. But it has to be this way for now. Okay?"

"Um. No." She made another snorting sound. "I think this is the craziest thing you've ever done for Daddy and Mommy Dearest, but I'm here for you."

"Thank you," I whispered because there was truly nothing else to say. "I just wanted to let you know about the getaway. I might not be able to update you during, but I'll come home and give you all the juicy details when it's over."

"You better," she said, all seriousness. "I'm likely to have Russell send a search party if you don't come back soon."

"Speaking of . . . how *is* Russell?"

"Who?"

"Mmhm." I rolled my eyes and then stilled when it felt like the entire room continued spinning afterward. "Hey, Stevie, I need to go. Love you."

"I mean, who wouldn't?" she asked, feigning vanity even though there was a hint of worry in her voice. "Miss you, Hollis."

"Same."

I stood to put my phone back in the bag and had to steady myself when it felt like the floor was tilting beneath me.

What the hell?

I made it over to my bag and got my phone put away with mostly no issues, but I took every step carefully. Making sure the floor wasn't going to come up to meet my face the next time I tried to take a step.

I thought back over everything I'd ingested in the last day. Smelled the coffee before scrutinizing the handwriting on the note for probably far too long even though I *knew* it belonged to Adam. Drank two cups of water just in case. And then freaked out over the possibility of being pregnant because I *so* couldn't be pregnant, and I'd much rather have that panic attack with Stevie than with—

When the hell had I gotten in here?

I looked around at the couch opposite me in the lounge room, then over to McKay, who was looking at me like I might be an alien.

"You."

His eyebrows shot up. "Me?"

"No." My head shook. "Hi. When did you get here?"

"Jesus Christ." He pinched the bridge of his nose before dropping to a crouch in front of me. "You've already caused a lot of headaches, but I thought we'd revealed all the skeletons in your closet. If you do drugs too, that's something I need to know."

I jerked away from him. "What? No. I—I just don't feel right. Am I pregnant?"

His face paled as he hissed a curse. "Are you?"

"I don't know," I said, the words coming out too slow when I felt frantic. "I don't know what pregnant feels like, but my body is heavy. I'm heavy. My arms—" I lifted them and let them slam back to the couch. "I'm heavy. Flu? Yeah, it's the flu. Right?"

He grabbed my face, searching my eyes. "Ms. Donahue, tell me right now. Are you on drugs?"

"Fuck you, *Mayor* McKay."

He hissed out another curse as he stood, helping me with him. "Can you walk? Let me see you walk."

I rolled my eyes, my entire head moving with them, and then stumbled forward when the world decided to roll too.

"That's a clear *no*."

"No, I can," I insisted, pushing him aside to prove that I could, in fact, walk. After taking a few steps, I staggered to a stop when everything went black for a moment, then lifted my weighted arms to the sides when I was sure I wasn't going to lose consciousness. "See?"

He hesitated, coming around to study me, but now there were two of him. Maybe four. "Okay, we have to do this getaway. So, let's just make it outside and to the car. I'll stop somewhere along the way to get you fluids—something. I'll have a doctor come to the house to see you."

Suspicion moved through me as I struggled to focus on him. "Why? I don't . . . I don't trust you."

Oh God. I didn't trust him, and I didn't trust my parents.

This was it.

This is it.

Panic flooded me, but I couldn't do anything to save myself. My body was too heavy, and everything was going in and out.

"I care about you as a human being, Ms. Donahue," McKay said, his words sounding like he was underwater. "Come on, let's go."

"I don't wanna go," I said, the words slurring together as he steered me out of the lounge room. "I don't wanna die."

"What the hell? Okay, I'm taking you to the hospital now—"

I staggered back and tripped over McKay when the main door of the suite was thrown open.

No.

Kicked open.

"What the hell is the meaning of this?" McKay yelled as he caught and steadied me before hissing a string of curses when four people dressed head-to-toe in black came storming into the suite, rifles aimed at us. "Run," he snapped, pushing me back toward the lounge. "*Run.*"

But I couldn't move.

I wasn't sure if whatever was wrong with my body had me locked in place or if it was that the moment we'd been fearing had finally come. But there I was, staring in horror as the intruders blurred, morphing into sixteen people and sixteen rifles before slamming back into their original four.

"Hollis, *run.*"

I looked back at McKay when he grabbed me around the

waist and began dragging me backward, my body slow to react as horror trudged through me like tar when one of the people came at us from the side.

"McKay," I choked out, gripping at his arm to get his attention. "McKay, right there—*no*!" The word tore from my throat when McKay was ripped away from me.

I stumbled that way, the world tilting and tilting as I struggled to right myself.

As I struggled to think of a way through this.

To just *think*.

Adam . . .

Adam, I love you.

Adam, I'm sorry.

A sob burst from my chest as I rose to my full height and found myself a few feet from the end of a rifle just before the world darkened for the length of time it took my heart to pump out two pained beats.

"Oh God," I cried, my entire body trembling with the force of my sobs. "Adam, I'm sorry."

The air knocked from my chest a split second before my back hit the floor.

A cry sounded from somewhere nearby, and I thought it might have been mine, but I couldn't be sure.

I forced my arms to move.

To reach for my chest . . . for the pain there.

When my hands came back covered in red, a soundless cry heaved from me. The world blurring and fading in and out around me.

I tried to reach for Adam's phone.

To send one last message.

But I was so heavy, and it was such a struggle to keep my eyes open.

I coughed out a sob when the same masked face and rifle appeared above me. Before the fear of wondering if he would shoot me again could slip into my veins, he took off his mask.

Revealing four blurred heads that drifted back into one long enough for me to see the familiar face looking down at me.

My lips parted.

Betrayal and shock burned on my tongue.

Before I could utter Leo's name, everything went black.

Thirty-Four

ADAM

"Update?"

I lifted my head enough to send a warning look Leo's way.

He just rolled his eyes and rested a shoulder against the doorjamb. "She'll be fine."

I went back to trailing my fingers through Hollis's hair where we had her set up in my bed. Head on my lap so I could study her breaths and watch the color of her cheeks.

At least, that's what I'd told Leo.

We both knew I just needed her close to me after everything that had gone down.

"She'll be fine," he repeated, this time softer as he pushed away to leave, stopping to point at me. "By the way, we ordered pizza. Got one with olives for the two of you."

I dipped my head in thanks, then looked back at Hollis just as she woke with a horrified gasp. Grabbing at her chest and looking at her hands, expecting them to be covered in blood.

I grabbed them up in mine in an attempt to comfort her,

looking into her wide, terrified eyes as she looked from me to the room and then back again.

"Am I—I'm—Adam, I . . ." She scrambled to sitting and then pressed her hands to her chest again, looking down at it to make sure she was feeling everything the way it should be.

I grabbed up both of her hands in one of mine again, then handed her my phone that already had everything written out on it.

"Adam," she said again, making my name sound like a question. "Oh my God, Leo shot me." She held my phone out in front of her, then looked that way, jolting back and smacking her head against the headboard when she saw Leo standing there. "Adam, he tried to kill me!"

Leo pointed at her. "*Didn't.*"

"You *shot* me," she screamed, her voice pure terror.

"I just bought you pizza," he snapped back, all offense.

I slashed my hand through the air, telling him to stop, then curled my hands around her cheeks, forcing her to look at me.

Feeling the way she was shivering so damn bad. Her breaths coming too fast and too sharp.

I lowered one of my hands to press it to her chest, then inhaled deeply. Begging her to do the same and waiting until she wasn't in danger of passing out again before I urged her to read the phone.

Everything that happened today wasn't what it seemed.

Take a breath.

Remember, I've got you.

Leo and I will explain everything.

. . .

When she just sat there, staring at the phone, I grabbed the notepad and pen off the nightstand and hurried to write a message on it before throwing it at Leo.

He stepped forward to read it, rolling his eyes as he stepped back again.

I fucking told you not to be in here when she woke

"We were able to intercept an agreement between your parents and a group of former black-ops soldiers," Leo said, not bothering to wait for Hollis to be ready. "Unfortunately, Adam was right in his assumptions that you were a target. We can't totally confirm they were going to pin it on Mayor McKay yet, but they wanted him unharmed, unaware, and unable to prevent it."

"Did you drug me?" Hollis asked, looking over at me. Not seeming to care at all that we'd confirmed her parents had, in fact, paid a group of mercenaries to kill her.

When I nodded, a stunned breath burst from her.

"*Why?*"

"Because your parents wanted video evidence that the job was completed," Leo informed her. "It needed to look real."

I held up my hand, asking for him to stop, then took my phone from her. Letting her watch as I typed.

I'm sorry

You have no idea how sorry I am

But if we had told you

You would have been expecting it and wouldn't have reacted the way we needed you to

There was a sedative in the coffee

If you hadn't drunk it

That wouldn't have gone as well as it did

It wouldn't have looked like you actually died

Your parents would have just taken another hit out on you because now you know they'd ordered one

They would need to shut you up

Hollis nodded, but the betrayal lingered on her face as embarrassment swirled in her eyes.

I tapped her leg and gave her a questioning look.

"You knew . . ." Her stare briefly danced around the room. "You knew you were going to have to do all that when I was here last night?"

I quickly shook my head as I responded.

No

I stumbled across the agreement about two or three hours after you left

"I left near one in the morning," she said doubtfully, but I just gave her a knowing look.

Hollis

Do you realize the severity of the situation you've been in

That I've let you go into

I've been working nonstop to get you out of it
I haven't been sleeping more than twenty minutes at a time

"Oh," she whispered, then rubbed at her chest. Eyebrows drawing tight before she glanced down. "Ow . . ."

"Right, so you did get shot," Leo murmured as if being told those words weren't a big deal.

"What?" she asked, choking over the word as she scrambled to look down my shirt I'd changed her into.

I sent Leo a glare as he clarified, "With the equivalent of a paintball."

I lifted the rifle from where it rested on the bed beside me and fired one right at his chest, causing Hollis to jump into my side as she looked all around before her gaze caught on the fairly realistic paint now decorating Leo's shirt.

He returned my glare and asked, "Are you happy now?"

I shrugged.

"Those were airsoft rifles," Leo explained. "That was a blood-red pellet I hit you with."

Hollis started pointing at Leo and then pressed her hand to her chest again, her head slowly shaking. "Wait, but . . . *no*. I felt it. I *fell* because of it. You're just standing there."

"Well, that didn't tickle," Leo said. "I was also a little closer to you than Adam and I are right now, which explains why he's all sunshine and rainbows. Don't," he quickly added when I began lifting the rifle again.

When I just tossed it onto the floor, he looked back at Hollis. "You were also very obviously about to fall on your own from the sedative. I shot you before that could happen because I was the one wearing the camera."

"What cam—" Hollis's entire body sagged as realization hit her. "For my parents."

"Live feed," Leo confirmed.

She nodded after a moment, tears filling her eyes. When I grabbed her hand in mine, she asked, "Did it work? Did they believe it?"

Leo's stare shifted to me, all question on if he should continue or not.

Keeping her hand in mine, I reached for my phone and slid my finger across the screen.

You want to do this later

"No, I want to know," she said firmly, even as her jaw trembled. "I want to be done with it—with them."

I studied her profile for a second longer before nodding for Leo to continue.

"The other half of the money was wired to the group of mercenaries before we were even able to make it back here. So, yes. They did. Your parents were taken into custody about three minutes after that. Akron's questioning them—"

"No," Hollis said, nearly choking over the word in her attempt to get it out. "No. Don't you remember what I told you?" She glanced between the two of us, looking equally frantic and like she was wondering if she'd had everything wrong. "Didn't you listen to the recordings? He came back—he was there. You can't trust him."

Leo just waited, never once trying to stop her.

"Or—oh my God." She tried pulling from me, so I let her go because I had a feeling I knew where this was about to go.

"Are you . . . you're working . . ." The betrayal that darkened her eyes when she looked at me turned to crushing grief and then doubt just as quickly. "Adam, you wouldn't. I *know* you can't be working with him—with *all* of them."

I held out my hand in offering and response. When she took it, I placed my phone between us to write to her.

You already know me
EVERYTHING about me
If you trust me
Trust what we're telling you now
Don't let it put doubt in your mind

She released a heavy sigh and nodded. "I'm sorry, I just . . ."

"It's a lot," Leo said when she didn't continue. "You're also still coming off the sedation. The offer to do this later still stands at any time during this."

Her head shook, the movement slow and wide. "Tell me why Akron is the one questioning my parents."

"Because he's the right person for it," Leo said simply before explaining, "When you came to us and mentioned Akron, that was a huge shock to us because we would've never suspected him—not that we knew who it was that was helping your parents. Then, as we were on our way to grab Tucker, I got a message from him that was marked urgent. He wanted us to grab a civilian and take him to a safe location. There was an address and a deadline. It was Tucker's address."

Hollis inhaled softly. "Did he know you were going there?"

Leo shrugged. "He couldn't have. After you told us our place was bugged, we only talked using paper and searched our cars for tracking devices. But," he went on, "after we got Tucker somewhere else, I went back and waited. At the deadline, a team went in and stormed the place."

"So, what does that mean?" Hollis asked.

"Well, we weren't sure what to do with Akron," Leo said, sounding exhausted. "But when we were finishing up with some other things yesterday, he called to tell us where you were and that he'd set up this suite for us. When I asked what happened to The Maybourne, he said Mayor McKay had been sneaking off there instead of going back to his house. Akron hoped we would catch something we could use to make McKay talk if we hung around there. But we didn't think we had a reason to be there."

"And that's my fault because I said we weren't there," Hollis assumed.

Leo lifted his hands before folding them over his chest, stalling and sending me a glare when they slid across the paint there.

I hurried to put my phone back in Hollis's hands.

Not your fault

We didn't think we could trust Akron anymore

We wouldn't have done anything he said anyway

"It isn't anyone's fault. It just *is*," Leo went on. "We'll still get McKay—he and his dad are already detained and being questioned about his fiancée, among other things. As for Akron, he's the one who helped us the most by giving us keywords in the recordings. Not that he knew you were recording, but he figured you were still in contact with us. But that's how Adam intercepted the agreement—Akron didn't know when everything was going down, only *who* your parents had hired, and he kept saying their name in those recordings."

"Why didn't he just tell you all those things himself?"

"Because he's apparently been pretending to help your parents for over a year now. The message and call we got from him that contained real information . . . those could've cost him his life."

Hollis leaned deeper into me, face creasing as she thought. "And you believe him?" she asked, suspicion creeping into those mint green eyes. "After everything he said and did, you're just going to believe him now?"

Leo glanced at me before giving her a knowing look. "You believe us." He gave a slight shrug. "There are parts of what we do that people can't know. There are parts that *we* can't know until it's all over. It's the way things are."

Nearly a minute passed before she nodded. "So, what happens now?"

"Well, you were out for a long time—"

"Wait, how long?"

Leo hesitated and looked at me when I made a face that was all regret and apprehension. "We didn't know how much of the coffee you would drink, so it was heavily dosed—but you would've been fine if you drank the entire carafe," he hurried to assure her.

Hollis turned in my arms and sat back, looking horrified and pissed. "I nearly drank the entire thing!"

Well, fuck.

"That explains a lot."

"Adam," Hollis yelled, my name pure demand as she ignored Leo.

11 hours

"*Eleven—*" Her mouth dropped open as she looked between the two of us. "I hate you both."

I needed you to fake die

"If that isn't the most romantic thing you've ever said to me," she muttered, voice all dry sarcasm.

"The good news in all this is there is no longer a contract for your life," Leo said as if he were bringing us back to the bright side. "Your parents actually think you're dead, and they're going away for a long time, so you don't have to worry about them."

I slowly looked over at him, wishing like hell I hadn't tossed the airsoft rifle off the side of the bed.

"Right," Hollis said on an unsteady breath.

"Too soon," Leo said apologetically. "However, everything your parents did and tried to do is starting to come to light. Some of it is already on the news, and more will continue to be released." He waved a hand in my direction. "Adam and some of the people he had working on it were able to confirm that everything with your name wasn't actually done by you. And you're officially no longer a person of interest in this case."

Her chest caved with her next exhale, but she didn't respond. Just sat there staring.

"Food should be here soon," he said as he took a step back. "Sarah has already contacted Ari. Your roommates are all invited to stay here for the next few days, and then you can go home once we're sure there won't be any lingering press waiting to photograph you."

"Thank you," she whispered. "Wait, is Sarah here?"

A slow smile crossed Leo's face. "Yeah. And I would like a night with my girlfriend now that all this has been put to bed. Just as I know the two of you need to talk. So, I'll let you know when food is here. Otherwise . . ."—he turned, waving as he did—"leave me alone."

Once the door shut, I pulled her closer to my side, giving her time to come to terms with everything.

"You drugged me," she said a while later, the accusation coming out all disbelief.

A short huff burst from me as I dragged my finger across the phone.

I'd do it again if it saved your life in the end

"And Leo shot—" She hurried to pull down the shirt enough so I could see the welt and broken skin on her chest. "Did you see this?"

I had.

I'd already punched Leo for standing too close to her when he'd done it. And then I'd waited with that rifle, knowing Hollis would eventually want the satisfaction of seeing him get shot too.

I double-tapped the screen to highlight the words *saved your life in the end.*

She let out a heavy exhale, but her expression fell into something close to mourning and gratitude. "Thank you," she breathed and dropped her forehead to mine. "Thank you for saving me. I was sure . . ." Her head shook quickly as her eyes filled with tears again.

When the first cry heaved from her chest, I shifted her so she was laying against me. My eyelids shutting as the impact of her grief and desperation and exhaustion slammed into me.

I'm sorry.

I'm so damn sorry.

I held her close, absorbing the tremors wracking her body as she cried. Waiting until her tears dried and her breaths evened out. Sure she'd fallen asleep again until Leo came in with a box of pizza, and Hollis muttered, "Thank you," without ever lifting her head.

Leo offered her a small smile when he set the box on the end of the bed. Then caught my eye when he straightened to leave, apology creasing the corners of his eyes.

I just nodded and waited for him to leave before I loosened my hold on Hollis to start a slow trail up and down her back.

"Olives?"

I wrote out *yes* on her back and watched as she sighed.

"Sharing a box with you? That's . . ."—she inhaled deeply and held it for a moment before letting it out on a rush as she continued—"just such a big commitment."

The corner of my mouth twitched in amusement before falling.

I reached for my phone, hesitating with my thumb over

the screen because I knew I should wait. Give her time. Let her have a few days or weeks to get past everything that had just happened in her life.

But I never had been able to control myself with Hollis.

What if I want that commitment

What if I want you

She looked up at me, eyes wide and lips slowly parting. "Do you mean that?"

Told you I wasn't letting you out of my sight

God damn

I curled one of my hands around her cheek when that hesitant smile I'd missed so much touched her lips. The sight of it still having the same impact it first had all those years before.

"What does that mean exactly?" she asked. "Like, you still have to be my shadow?" Her smile widened when I rolled my eyes but faltered soon after. "And distance? You said you were based in Virginia."

I dipped my head, reaching for my phone again as she continued.

"Adam, I love it here."

. . .

Leo and I have been operating out of the Los Angeles field office for the past couple of years

He and I were talking about putting in requests to transfer here permanently

But I figured I should talk to you first

Excitement lit her expression as she pushed to her knees. "What, you thought I wouldn't want that?"

I drugged you

A stunned laugh burst from her as she pushed against my stomach. "Yes, and I'm not going to trust anything either of you gives me for a long time—including that pizza."

I looked at her, exaggerating offense.

It's pizza

"You drugged me," she said, enunciating each word.

You're oddly okay with this

"Yeah, well . . . my boyfriend is in the FBI." She rolled her eyes, feigning indifference. "Apparently, it comes with the job."

A wicked smirk tugged at my lips as I tapped on the screen. Repeating a question I'd asked what felt like a lifetime ago.

We're dating

A smile crossed her face, making her look so fucking beautiful. "Yeah," she said simply. "Someone should probably tell Stevie."

My chest shook with a laugh as I grabbed her up in my arms and crushed my mouth to hers.

Forgetting the pizza. Forgetting the stress of the past week.

Forgetting everything but her.

Thirty-Five

ADAM

A soft giggle sounded from Hollis the next morning, and I glanced over at where she was pulling another one of my shirts on.

"Can you hear them?" she asked, looking over her shoulder with an adoring expression.

I gave her an amused look because it was impossible to miss Stevie's voice now that her roommates were here.

Slipping up behind her when she went back to dressing, I wrapped one of my arms around her waist to pull her closer and pressed my lips to her neck. Then brought my phone around in front of her with my other hand so she could see the screen.

Before we go out there
There's something I've been wondering
Why did you say Adam I'm sorry

. . .

She turned in my hold, her eyebrows drawn close together. "What?"

When we came into the room yesterday
Before Leo shot you
You said Adam I'm sorry

She blinked slowly as if trying to remember, and then her eyes widened. "Wait, were you in there?"

I gave her a disbelieving look.

She couldn't honestly think I would've let all that happen without being there to make sure she was okay.

Hollis
I told you I had you

Her full lips slowly parted in shock. "But I thought . . . you were really there?"

After the way we heard him talking to you on the recordings
I can't tell you how fast I volunteered to be the one who made sure McKay couldn't prevent it
They said not to harm him
They didn't say anything about leaving him conscious

. . .

When her eyes widened with surprise and question, I hurried to assure her.

He's obviously fine

"Adam," she whispered, all shock with a hint of awe.

He tried to marry you

A soft laugh bubbled free, wholly scandalized and completely adorable.

Scrolling back up to the top, I pointed to my original question and waited as that earlier confusion filled her expression again as if she were struggling to remember the moment at all.

"I don't . . . I don't know," she finally said. "I don't remember saying that." She gave me an apologetic look before her gaze fell to the side. "I remember thinking I couldn't move because my body was too heavy. And everything was so blurry that it made it look like there were so many of you."

Her forehead furrowed as her head slowly shook. With a faint shrug, she said, "I'm sorry."

Just as I started waving off her apology, she gasped.

"Oh!" She blinked a few times, her stare slightly vacant as she struggled to grasp what she was remembering. "I was thinking about you and how I should've let you talk me out of it. I was wishing I had." Her head shook a little and her eyes slid to mine. "I don't think I realized I was saying anything out loud."

Guilt and regret sped through me and gathered in my chest until each breath felt harder than the last.

It'd been painful seeing that fear in her yesterday. To watch the girl who owned me, heart and soul, hit the floor the way she had. But I'd been hoping the sedative would've had her too out of it to realize what was happening when we'd come in.

Knowing she'd thought she was at death's door, and hearing that her last thoughts were of *me*? The guy who put that fear in her?

It was fucking excruciating.

I'm so damn sorry Hollis
    If I could take it all away
    I would
    If it could've ended any other way
    I would've taken it

She stepped closer so she was pressed to me, her head tilted back and her eyes nothing but understanding. "I love you," she said as if nothing else mattered.

My throat worked as I struggled over things I wanted to tell her.

"I already know," she whispered when I clenched my jaw tight, soothing the tips of her fingers over it and then playing with my beard the way she liked to.

"Babe, what the fuck?" Stevie snapped before the door bounced off the wall.

I gripped Hollis a little tighter, refusing to let this time with her end just yet. And for a second longer, she let me hold her.

Letting us linger.

With an affectionate sigh, she tilted her head to look past me just as Stevie slammed into my side to squeeze between us.

Hollis choked over a laugh. "I missed you—are you crying?" She grabbed Stevie's shoulders and held her back a little to study her, looking from her to me in outright shock.

Stevie's entire body shook with her shuddering breath before she rambled, "I can't believe you didn't tell me. You've been keeping everything from me lately, and now I have to find out from the stupid news that your asshole parents—and *you*." She turned, glaring at me through her tears. "I have a special pair of Manolos for you, you lying bastard! We are officially *divorced*. The kids are mine. Hollis is mine. You can fuck right off. I should've known there was something up with you when you let her get engaged to that—oh my God." She whirled back around to face Hollis. "Are you still engaged?"

I held up my phone for Hollis to read.

Did she say kids

As in multiple

She stifled a laugh and then looked at Stevie. "Technically, I never agreed to marry him," she said, her voice gentle and calm even though the corner of her mouth kept tugging up in the beginnings of a smile. "I told you, it was all because of my parents, and it was. They were demanding it, and I just needed to go along with it until all that was over. And it is now."

"You mean them putting a hit on you?" Stevie asked, the question all outrage. "*That* part? Because, what the fuck, you just decided not to mention that Asshole One and Two wanted you dead?"

That smile slipped, revealing a whisper of Hollis's pain. "Stevie, I couldn't. I wasn't even supposed to know that—I wasn't supposed to know any of it. A lot of things could've been ruined when Adam told me."

Long seconds passed before Stevie sagged. "Just don't do that to me again, okay?" she asked softly as she grabbed one of Hollis's hands. "I can't lose you."

Hollis gave a shaky nod and murmured, "Yeah, okay."

"Well, my dad is a mess over this," Stevie said as she released a heavy breath and started walking toward the door as if she couldn't get away fast enough. "Literally. He feels like he failed you because you're one of his girls. He said he hates that you have to be tied to 'those scumbags' in any way, so he wants to adopt you."

A stunned laugh burst from Hollis. "I'm twenty-six."

"Yeah, and?"

"And nothing." Hollis looked at me, fighting a smile even as amusement danced in those eyes. "Hey, Stevie," she called out when Stevie grabbed the door handle. "I love you too."

Stevie rolled her eyes. "I never said that."

"Sure you did." When the door shut, Hollis stepped back into my arms, eyes bright and that smile doing wicked things to my heart. "If I heard correctly, I no longer have to fight for you."

. . .

Damn

I was just starting to enjoy it too

A huff burst free when she pushed me away, but I just pulled her with me.

What do you say we go out there

We'll have breakfast

Your friends will make sure you're okay

And after a few days

We'll start getting you back to that life you felt free in

"I like that plan," she said, voice soft. "But what about you?" When I gave her a questioning look, she explained, "All of that was about me. What can we do for *you*? I don't even know what all you have to do now that this case you've been working on for so many years is over."

I shrugged as my thumbs hurried across the screen of my phone.

There are things Leo and I will need to be available for when it comes to your parents' case

Most of it gets handed off to other people

So other than that

I'll move on to the next thing

And the next

You know

Computers and codes

But right now I just want this time with you before I have to get everything settled in Virginia

Her mouth twitched, just a ghost of a smile. "And you're sure you want to do that . . . transfer to L.A.?" When I started typing, she hurried to add, "I know what I said last night, but I can't expect you to do that just because I like it here. I've moved before, I can easily move to Virginia."

I studied her eyes, knowing damn well the last thing she wanted was to leave this place or the people in her life. But she was trying so hard to look like it wouldn't bother her for the roles to be reversed.

I trailed my fingers down her forearm in gratitude.

I'm sure of you

Heat bloomed in her cheeks, but her tone still held a hint of admonishment. "Adam, but this is your job. I don't want you to resent me later because of this."

My head shook as I looked at my phone, hurrying through my response.

Leo's my superior but the work we do goes hand in hand
So where one of us goes the other has to follow
Even before he knew about my history with you
He wanted to transfer here because of Sarah
I clearly have my own reasons for wanting to be here
There was something about you in New York

When you left the next morning

I wondered at least a hundred times why I didn't try to stop you

I should have

I'd do anything to go back and start my life with you then

Because it was like you said

Nothing should've felt like that

Nothing's ever felt like us

So even if Leo had no reason to stay here

I'd fight for it because I'm not losing you again

Her blush darkened. Her eyes flaring with surprise and want.

Handing my phone back to me, she said, "Keep talking like that, and I'm going to be fighting Stevie off you again by the end of breakfast."

My chest pitched with amusement as I wrapped my arms around her and pressed my mouth to hers, silencing her laugh that had just started pouring free. The kiss all soft teases mixed with my claim that I was keeping her forever.

"I love you," she breathed against the kiss.

God damn.

My eyes opened, studying the soft lines of her face as all that pain and anger built and was overwhelmed with frustration and sorrow because they were there. Gathered in my throat and choking me.

Mocking me for trying.

Words I didn't know how to say to her because I *only* wanted to speak them to her.

But there she was. All grace and understanding when she opened her eyes and looked at me. Smile nearly bringing me to my knees as she playfully dragged her fingers through my beard and lifted up on her toes to press another kiss to my lips.

"I already know." Dropping back to her feet, she slid her hand into mine as she took a step away, that smile turning mischievous. "Come on. Let's see how long it takes Stevie to claim you as hers again."

I offered her a smile as I let her lead me to the door, all while my stare lingered on her. My vow continuing to stay lodged in my throat. Taunting me in time with the wild beating of my heart.

I love you.

I love you.

I love you.

Epilogue

HOLLIS

"I got it!" I yelled as I ran down the stairs to answer the door, ignoring Stevie when she snapped, "Could you maybe *not* break your legs before tonight? He'll still be standing there if you *walk* to the door."

But I couldn't wait.

After spending a few more days in the hotel, mostly just with Stevie and Ariana since Mia had been slammed with work and Adam and Leo had been in constant meetings, the guys had deemed it safe for me to go home and resume life as normal. And then flown back to Virginia just hours later.

That'd been over two weeks ago.

But they were finally coming back today, and a day had never felt so long.

I skipped around Ariana, narrowly avoiding colliding with her when she came out from around the kitchen. "Sorry!" I called out, never slowing as I continued racing that way.

"Didn't know you were so excited," she said from behind me.

A dry laugh bubbled free as I hurried through the entryway, already reaching for the locks on the door before I ever came to a complete stop. My smile wide and expectant as I threw the door open, my chest caving as all the oxygen rushed from my lungs and disappointment stormed through me.

"Who are—you are not . . . sorry," I said lamely as I glanced between the two people standing there, looking completely dazed, no sign of Adam behind them. "How can I help you?"

"Are we at the right place because this . . ." The girl gave a little shake of her head, her eyes wide. "Is there another Forest Knoll Drive? Because this is a mansion." The last word was said on a whisper as if she was afraid of saying it too loud.

A stunned laugh left me. "Uh . . . right. Sorry, was there something I could help you with?"

The girl sort of shook herself out, the action somehow adorable and bubbly even though it was small. "Oh my gosh, so sorry. I'm Kinsley."

"Okay," I said slowly. "I'm Hollis. How can I help—"

"Kinsley, hi," Ariana said, pushing me out of the way. "I'm Ariana."

Kinsley's expression fell when Ariana filled the doorway. Even though she hurried to recover, her shock remained evident.

"Don't mind this one, she's waiting for someone else," Ariana explained, then gestured inside. "Come on in."

Kinsley made an uncomfortable sound. "Um, this is . . . this is my boyfriend."

Ariana's head slanted. "I was told you were coming alone. Sorry, we can't have partners living with us."

"Oh, you're the new roommate," I said, catching on way

too late even though I was sure Ariana had mentioned her name a few times this week. "Of course you are. Forgive me."

Kinsley sent me a smile and then glanced at the guy behind her. "He isn't moving in, he just drove down to help move everything. But, um . . ." She looked from Ariana to me, her expression completely helpless. With a determined breath, she nodded. "Yeah, okay."

I smacked Ariana's arm and whispered, "It's because you're not wearing any clothes."

Ariana held her arms out to the sides. "I am *covered.*" She looked back at Kinsley. "I'm—you know what? Whatever." With a glare directed at me, she hissed, "If I have to wear clothes the entire time she lives here . . ."

I let my gaze drift to where Kinsley was standing, no doubt still within hearing distance of Ariana's hushed words. Offering her an apologetic look, I started pushing Ariana away from the door and kept my voice low. "She'll get used to you soon enough, but she doesn't know you, and her boyfriend's with her. Is it so bad to have a shirt on while he's here?"

"That's like telling Stevie to stop hitting on Adam."

"I literally do that all the time," I argued as she stormed away. Biting back a sigh, I walked back to where Kinsley and her boyfriend were whispering on the porch.

"We make really great first impressions here, I know," I tried to joke, giving them an assuring smile when they looked at me. "But despite what you just saw of Ariana, she's the fun one and she's also the mom of the house. She makes sure all the bills are paid and she cooks for us. She's arguably the responsible one. She just doesn't love clothes."

Kinsley quickly shook her head. "No, I shouldn't have said anything. I think it just shocked me."

I waved off her worries, though her boyfriend still looked less than thrilled about the whole thing. "Don't worry about it—people talk to her about it all the time. I promise she'll be over it and making jokes about something by the time she's back out here." I gestured to the empty space around them. "Where's all your stuff?"

"Oh, it's still in the cars," she said, that earlier bubbliness easily slipping out in everything she said. "We were kind of hoping to rest first." She made an adorable face, scrunching up her nose. "And also maybe see if we were even at the right place."

"Right, the house is kind of staggering at first." I winked and gestured for them to come in. "You get used to it though. Just think of it like an apartment complex where we share all the common areas."

A soft laugh left Kinsley that was wholly unconvinced. "Get used to this?"

"You will," I assured her. "You'll meet Stevie, she's upstairs. Her dad owns this house—he's one of those mega-rich guys but is honestly the sweetest man ever. And he lets all of us, including Stevie, rent out the rooms for about what an apartment would be."

"Which is why we thought we were in the wrong place," Kinsley said, expression teasing.

"I'm going to bash that bitch's nose in," Stevie screamed from upstairs.

I pointed toward the ceiling, faltering for a moment when I noticed Kinsley's boyfriend's frustration. "That would be Stevie."

"She sounds . . ." Kinsley's head bobbed. "She sounds nice."

I choked over a laugh. "Yeah, uh . . . Stevie has never

claimed to be 'nice,' and she probably wouldn't want to be labeled that way. But if she likes you, she's absolutely the girl you want in your corner."

"Fuck me," Ariana said, drawing out the words as she came jogging down the hall. When I glanced over my shoulder, she was rolling her eyes. "Watch her when you go to work tonight. Jenny posted an old picture of her and Russell, saying she misses the old times or something."

"She's goading Stevie, you know she is," I said, and Ariana just raised her brows in agreement before looking at the other people in the room.

"So, welcome to L.A." Ariana clapped her hands together and tried to fight the smile tugging at her lips. "Sorry for the shitshow as soon as you showed up. Our house can be a little dramatic at times, but we're a lot of fun too, I promise. So, what would you like to do first? I can make us lunch or help you get unpacked." She gestured back the way she'd come. "You want to see your room?"

Kinsley stood there, looking a little overwhelmed for a moment. Just when her boyfriend leaned in to say something to her, she said, "I'd love to see my room if that's okay."

He stilled, looking at her in a way that was all silent conversations and pleading and frustration before stepping back with a huff. "I, uh . . . guess I'll start bringing things in."

Kinsley's lips parted, but he stalked out of the house before she could stop him.

"I'm sorry," Kinsley said softly, gesturing in the direction he'd gone when the door shut. "He isn't normally like this. He's just been angry ever since I got the job here. He doesn't want me to move, even though I've begged him to come with me. It isn't the distance, even though he hates the idea of it. It's that he thinks L.A. will change me."

"And then you had to go and welcome them in your underwear," I murmured to Ariana, the words all an affectionate tease.

Ariana groaned obnoxiously. "For the last time—"

"This definitely won't be the last time."

She slid a mock-glare my way just as the front door opened again.

My gaze drifted past her and where Kinsley was watching us, that adorable energy being overshadowed by her worries and exhaustion, but everything stopped before my heart took off at an unforgiving pace when I saw the man walking into the living room.

Tall. Broad. Absolutely terrifying and doing dangerous things to me with all that chaos and warning billowing from him.

His name left me on a breath as I took off across the room, forgetting everyone else there as I barreled into him. Crushing my mouth to his and giggling against the kiss when he effortlessly lifted me into his arms.

"I missed you," I whispered when he began leading us in the direction of the stairs.

Those dark eyes pierced mine. All agreement and excitement and love.

I wiggled out of his arms before he could hit the stairs but wrapped my hand in his and kept close to his side, needing to feel him to know he was truly back.

"Are you all moved in?" When he shook his head, I slanted mine. "Did you come straight here?"

He gave me a look that was all adoration and amusement as he slipped his phone free.

. . .

You honestly think I would've gone anywhere else first

A smile tugged at my lips, and he reached forward. Tracing the corner of it with the tips of his fingers and stopping us halfway up the stairs so he could study me the way he sometimes did.

Like we had all the time.

You have no idea what that smile does to me

Heat rose to my cheeks as I leaned harder against him, my heart beating wildly in my chest. "I might have an idea. Hey!" I said once we hit the landing, dancing away from him so I could face him. "Will you come to my show tonight?"

His expression turned contemplative as he wrapped one of his arms around my waist, keeping my body pressed to his as he slid his thumb across the screen.

I thought you didn't want to know if I was coming to your shows

"Tonight's different."

We did special, one-night shows a few times a month. Sometimes they were for a holiday or a cause, sometimes they were whatever we wanted them to be. I'd made a request that everyone had readily agreed to, and I wasn't sure I'd ever been more excited for a show.

Then again, this was for Adam.

Our outfits were incredible: Barely-there bottoms with varying tops of leather and denim and torn-up band shirts. Hair would be teased to the high heavens, and makeup would be eighties perfection. The music was all his favorites.

Is that right

I hummed my assent, then pressed up on my toes to kiss him. A shocked laugh tumbling free when he lifted me again to carry me into my room. Only stopping to shut and lock the door before he was stalking over to the bed and dropping onto it with me still in his arms.

My laugh filled the room as we bounced a little, but he just tightened his hold around me for a second longer before pushing up to sit against the headboard with me on his lap. Dark eyes devouring me in a way that made me feel like he'd never seen anything more beautiful.

I missed you

"So much," I agreed, a small smile teasing my lips as I kept one hand on his chest to feel the pounding of his heart while the other played with his scruffy beard.

When he turned the phone back around, making sure I couldn't see it, I raised an eyebrow in question but didn't say anything even after he finally held it out to me. Stare locked on mine and conveying the depth and importance of whatever he'd said.

I took it with both hands, my heart faltering a little as anticipation swirled between us.

I need to know what you see when you think of the rest of your life

Before you I didn't see much

After you all that changed

But it was complicated

You kept slipping away from me like a wraith

And then you were there

In my reach

And I couldn't have you

When all that finally changed all I saw for my future was you

Just you

You and I have had very different lives but they've both had their hardships

I figured if anyone understood my want to never get married or have kids it would be you

But political move or not McKay wanted to marry you

I saw that ring on your finger

And I realized that just having you wouldn't be enough

So I need to know what you see

Because when I think of the rest of my life I see me putting a ring on your finger

I see us having kids

I see me getting to spend my life with you as my wife

. . .

"Adam . . ." My tongue darted out to wet my lips as I looked up at him, my head moving in a mess of nods and shakes as I stumbled over the words. "I want—yes—everything. I want everything with you."

His mouth twitched into a smile as he took the phone from me.

Shit
I don't know now
'Everything' is a big commitment

I pushed against his chest as a laugh tumbled free, but he caught my hands in his and pulled me closer. Capturing my mouth with his and letting the phone fall between us as his hands moved to cradle my neck. His thumbs pressing to my jaw and guiding the kiss for a moment longer before his forehead fell to mine.

His entire body tense and trembling as he held me there.

Just as I grabbed one of his arms and started moving back to see what was wrong, he spoke, freezing me in place.

"I love you." Soft as a whisper, yet powerful. The words scraping from his throat like gravel and easily more beautiful than any other sound in the world.

My vision blurred and my chest shook as his words seemed to rock my entire soul.

I love you.

I love you.

I love you.

The first tears slipped down my cheeks as I tipped my head forward to taste the remnants of his claim, lingering in the impact of the moment a little longer. The gift he'd given me.

"Thank you," I said, the words nothing more than a breath. "Thank you for trusting me with something so significant."

His head slowly shook as if he didn't understand my thanks, a small smile pulling at his lips. All adoration and love mixing with that old pain that still burned in his eyes, heavy and weary but lighter than I'd ever seen.

Pressing my fingers to his jaw, I leaned in, letting my responding claim wash over his lips before I pressed my mouth to his. "Nothing has ever felt like that."

The End

Look for more *Secrets in L.A.* novels from Molly McAdams!
Love (coming Winter 2021)
Fame (coming soon)

Coming Winter 2021 . . .

When Kinsley was offered her dream job at a Los Angeles hospital over six hundred miles away, she didn't hesitate to take it. Add on a great place to live with four other girls her age?

Yes, please.

But she wasn't expecting this.

Because her new roommate's slow smirks and mesmerizing laughs are making her fall in ways she shouldn't. Her soft touches and earth-shattering kisses have Kinsley questioning everything she thought she knew.

And did she mention she has a boyfriend back home?

Acknowledgments

Cory—As always, thank you for being my constant support. Everything I do is possible because of you. I love you!

Molly and Amy—A massive thank you for the never-ending support and encouragement. Your friendships mean the world to me. I don't know what I would do without the two of you.

Molly's Monsters—Y'all are literally the best group on Facebook. Thank you for all your support, encouragement, and the amazing uplifting spirit y'all have created in there.

Letitia & Shannon—Thank you, thank you, thank you for making this book what it is! From the cover to the edits . . . you're such rock stars!

Leon—Oh my goodness, thank you! I know you laughed and thought I was joking every time I said I wanted to write a book based off you, but I appreciate you letting me take up hours of your time so I could create Adam's incredibly amazing character.

About the Author

Molly grew up in California but now lives in the oh-so-amazing state of Texas with her husband, daughter, and fur baby. When she's not diving into the world of her characters, some of her hobbies include hiking, snowboarding, traveling, and long walks on the beach . . . which roughly translates to being a homebody and dishing out movie quotes with her hubby. She has a weakness for crude-humored movies and loves curling up in a fluffy blanket during a thunderstorm . . . or under one in a bathtub if there are tornados. That way she can pretend they aren't really happening.

Printed in Great Britain
by Amazon

60772086R00265